THE SE NS

RESOLVE

Brigitte Morse-Starkenburg

© Copyright 2021
Brigitte Morse-Starkenburg

The right of (Author) to be identified as the author of this
work has been asserted by (him / her) in accordance with the
Copyright, Designs and Patents Act 1988.

Cover Art: ©Miquel Gonzalez Lumigo-film

All Rights Reserved

No reproduction, copy or transmission of this publication
may be made without written permission. No paragraph of
this publication may be reproduced, copied or transmitted
save with the written permission or in accordance with the
provisions of the Copyright Act 1956 (as amended).

PROLOGUE

The room was dark. Pitch black. The boy, no older than eleven, shuffled tentatively around it, arms stretched out, stopping occasionally and taking a deep sniff. He tilted his head one way and then the other, listening intently, using all of his senses to understand his surroundings. Random noises sounded around the room and decoy scents were scattered everywhere. It was not an easy task the youngster had to complete. A man stood and observed through the one way glass, his arms folded and a stern look on his face. He checked his watch and shook his head, disappointed and disapproving at the same time.

"You have two minutes left to complete the task. You know the consequences if you fail," the man warned through the speaker, his voice betraying his annoyance.

The boy froze for a second, but then started flailing his arms around the room, frantically searching for what he needed. His legs moved with purpose now, but in doing so he stumbled over the obstacles placed randomly around the room. Panic started to set in. If only he knew how close he was to succeeding, he would have regained his calm and do just that.

"Markus, Sir, I...I can't do it!" the boy choked out, tears trickling down his cheeks. "Please don't do this to me. Please, Markus! Save him for me! Please!" The boy fell to his knees in utter despair, sobbing his heart out.

"You still have thirty seconds. Stop crying and focus, boy. Focus!" Markus urged, but to no avail. The buzzer went. Time had run out. Markus entered the room and quietly grabbed the rodent out of its predicament. He signalled for someone to take it away. It would be taken to someone to look after, but Zack was not to know. He must believe his failure cost the little guinea pig its life.

"Had it not been for your pathetic crying, you could have saved the poor critter. You were nearly there," Markus accused, without an ounce of sympathy. He firmly believed this was a lesson Zack had to learn, for his own sake. In the future Markus saw for him, there was no place for panic and crying. He needed to toughen up. His wife wasn't all too happy about his approach, but he'd pulled rank, much to her exasperation. He couldn't do it too often, he knew that. But in this case he felt justified. He couldn't stop Laura from consoling the heartbroken little boy, though. She had insisted, and he knew better than to cross her twice.

From that day on Zack had sneaked into the dark room at every available opportunity, to try and perfect his skills. He was determined to prove to Markus he wasn't a failure. He wanted to make Markus proud of him more than anything else in the world. And only, when he was satisfied he could rely on his senses never to let him down again, he permitted himself to spend time with his friends and sister outside school hours. When Zack put his mind to something, he would do his damned best to achieve it. Whatever the price.

CHAPTER 1
Zaphire

I wanted to be sick. My heart pulsated in my throat. My head felt like it was going to explode. People looked at each other, fear in their eyes. Right there, on my phone my own face stared back at me, next to Eliza's and a blurry image of Rick and Ned. A big headline plastered all over: DANGEROUS SECRET COMMUNITY TRYING TO TAKE OVER THE WORLD. And more: DISCOVERY OF A NEW HUMAN SUB-SPECIES: THE SENSORIANS. A whole article about us. I spotted Daniel's name. He was responsible for our exposure.

Markus glanced up from his phone, showing but a moment of despair before taking control.

"Listen carefully everyone. Don't panic. We have a contingency plan for this. We have to act as fast as we can, but stay calm. Our compound is now in lockdown. No one is to leave or enter it, without my express permission. We will brief everyone on our evacuation plan, but it will take a few weeks to complete. Be patient, be sensible, and we will get through this."

***

I had the most horrific, chaotic and stressful two weeks of my life following those fateful headlines. The full length article about the Sensorians revealed our location. Pictures of Eliza, Ned and Rick were plastered all over the internet. The source wasn't a reputable paper, but one that people read and believed under the old adage of 'where there's smoke there's fire.' Daniel not only divulged stories about our gift, but also about Rick's world vision and the violent rescue mission, somehow making it sound like all Sensorians were trying to take over the world.

Photos showing his injuries, together with the witness accounts of the shootings that happened during the rescue mission, caught the public's attention. A few other Dullards' testimonies that were at the scene corroborated Daniel's story, and made it quite a convincing tale.

I was on my own. All my friends were in isolation whilst this was going on. Markus and Laura were unapproachable as they were too busy organising the whole operation. I had no one to turn to, but Saleem. Eventually, I couldn't bottle my feelings up anymore and poured my heart out to him. He reacted predictably practical.

"Look, Zaphy. I know this is something we've been scared of all our lives; our worst nightmare, but now we have to face it. We simply have to make it disappear, and disappear ourselves too."

I sighed. I couldn't wait till Sam got out of isolation. I needed to vent and rant. I didn't want to hear solutions.

Saleem was right though, but it was proving difficult. We had reporters hanging around outside our compound and they were stubborn. We ignored them to start with, but after a week Markus succumbed. He made a non-Sensorian associate give a statement, dispelling all the rumours and calling them ridiculous and downright fantasy. He insisted that we were just a normal firm, trying to make a living, working hard behind the scenes on worldwide projects, many of them involving good causes. Markus tried to convince some of the reporters on the quiet that we couldn't do our job with all this publicity, and that people would suffer as some beneficiaries want to remain anonymous. He told them that some of them already threatened to pull their funding if we attract too much attention. He hoped by involving some of the reporters this way, they might work with him to disperse the press, but it wasn't having much impact. There was too much interest and the reporters were too scared of missing out on a big story.

In the meantime, we all prepared to leave for our new compound. We aimed to do so surreptitiously, without the reporters noticing. We had to travel light, only carrying briefcases and handbags, hoping we could retrieve our belongings at a later date. We left individually or in two's, only a few of us, each day.

"Zaphy, it's your turn to leave tomorrow. Sam will be out of isolation today, and I'd like you to take her to Saleem so he can explain to the both of you what you need to do," Markus instructed.

"Markus, I know the plans inside out. I can explain it to Sam. We don't need to bother Saleem with this," I protested, in a vain attempt to regain a little control over my own life. Being a trainee again as part of my punishment was harder than I thought. Markus just looked at me, not even willing to discuss it, so I traipsed out to collect Sam. At least we could complain to each other now she was out. It might make it a little easier to bear.

Saleem was a fine trainer, but ever so slightly smug to have been appointed my superior, and therefore unbearable at times. He treated me as if I were a novice, and insisted on going over every basic detail on all the cases I was working on. Not that there were many as we were more occupied with the move and keeping out of the reporters' way. However, Markus had decided that we should try to get on with our work, as best we could. It wasn't very effective, as we weren't able to go out in the field and infiltrate. For the moment it was just paperwork, and scouring the internet for followers of Rick who we might have missed, and of course keeping an eye out for Rick and his accomplices. Saleem informed me again and again which trigger words to look out for, what body signs to be aware of on CCTV, and insisting on double checking my findings. It was tiresome and he caught me eye rolling several times, and always felt the need to reprimand me. *Ugh.*

We heard nothing on the whereabouts of Rick, Angelique and Jean-Pierre, but our team had managed to round up quite a few of the other Sensorians involved in Rick's organisation. We were able to put the screws on some of the influential politicians, lawyers and police officials that had been at Rick's meeting, threatening them with exposure and other dirt we had managed to find on them. Our work had been made difficult, but the leadership was working flat out, often throughout the night, to get to grips with the whole situation. Our cells were overflowing, and having to move all the prisoners, made it a logistical nightmare. Zack was none the wiser, as none of the people in isolation were made aware of the situation we were in. I was dying to tell Zack, but was told in no uncertain terms to stay away from him.

Markus was horribly grumpy, probably because he missed Zack and Brody's input, but he was damned if he would admit to that. I heard him mutter under his breath on several occasions, cursing Zack for his 'stupidity'.

"Sam!" I shouted a little too exuberantly across the corridors when I spotted her being led to her room. Her glum face brightened instantly upon hearing me. I scurried past some people to get to her quickly and threw my arms around her stiffening body. She'd just come out of isolation and had to adjust to physical contact again, as being deprived of that, even for a short amount of time, always seemed to affect us more than ordinary people. Not surprising really, as we felt everything with more intensity, so the shock to go from deprivation to a full on hug was difficult to cope with for us.

"Soz, Sam," I whispered gently, slowly releasing my arms from her body. She smiled and beckoned me to come into her room. The guard checked her over quickly, asked if she was okay and left, but not before sending a warning stare signalling for me to take it easy.

"Tell me all, Zaph. Something's going on. I can feel it," Sam spurred me on.

"It'll have to wait. Saleem needs to inform you. I'm not allowed. You know he's our trainer?"

"Can you not tell me anyway? I won't let on I know," she pleaded, but she backed off when she saw my sceptic look. As if she was going to be able to cloak from Saleem!

"Okay then," she huffed. "What's Saleem like?"

"Alright, I s'ppose. He just loves being in charge a little too much and is making the most of it," I griped.

"How are you feeling? Are you up for seeing him now?"

"No, I need to freshen up and relax a little before I can face other people." Sam was mature enough to know what her limits were. I let her get on with it and chilled on her sofa for a bit, waiting for her to let me know when she was ready. I ordered in some lunch too, knowing she would love a change from the dreary, eat what you're given, lunches in isolation. I knew her favourite was poached eggs with smashed avocado and chilli and surprised her with it. After about an hour she appeared, minutes before the knock on the door with our food. Perfectly timed.

"I'm ready now," she said with a satisfied look

on her face, after finishing her plateful.

"Sure?" I looked her over, scanning for signs to tell me otherwise, but she appeared quite relaxed and in control. She nodded to reassure me and off we went to find Saleem.

Saleem also made sure Sam was ready to accept the shocking news he had to tell her. He observed her closely for a while, before starting. She knew nothing about our exposure and our imminent move, and could be vulnerable to having an emotional meltdown at the moment. I have to say that Saleem did a brilliant job, keeping it factual but sensitive to her emotions, and though I loath to admit it, I think I may have actually learned something! He carried on calmly explaining she needed to pack her essentials and that we would be leaving tomorrow, first thing. We had employed a whole lot of film extras for days on end to make a constant stream of people entering and exiting the building at certain times, so we could mingle and make our getaway safely.

He advised wearing hats, or a hoody and sunglasses, just in case a picture was taken, making it difficult to identify us.

Sam looked a bit lost when we walked back to her room, her face vacant and her gait listless.

"Shall I stay with you tonight?" I offered. "On the sofa," I quickly clarified, giving her a cheeky wink. That made her smile and shook her out of her apathy. She happily agreed.

***

We managed to move everyone in just over a month, prisoners and all. It was a pretty neat operation and we were confident we shook the press off our trail. There were less and less stories appearing in the media and we were quietly confident that after about three months in our new accommodation, we had the situation under control. We relaxed too soon. Little stories and rumours were starting to pop up again, and after some investigation we found out the source of them; Daniel. Again.

Markus was getting frustrated. Little progress had been made with tracking down Rick, and now that pesky Daniel had started to ruffle feathers again. It needed to stop. And it needed to stop now.

CHAPTER 2
Zack

Someone approached my cell. It wasn't routine so I was instantly intrigued, not having much happening in my life at the moment. The most exciting thing that occurred was about three months ago: I was marched out of my cell, put in a van, driven for four or five hours and then planted back into the drab cell I inhabited now. No words were exchanged, no explanation. Nothing. But I guessed we had had to relocate as our premises must have been compromised. I managed to keep my frustration at bay and didn't question it, though it had been fucking difficult.

His scent hit me before he'd even opened the door. I jumped straight to my feet, legs slightly apart, head bent in submission. Markus. I hadn't seen him for what must have been about four months, and I wasn't sure what to expect from this unanticipated visit. He stood tall and imposing, hands behind his back, inspecting me. It had been a while since I'd been this close to someone and being scrutinised at that. *Fuck.* It was painful in more ways than one.

"Sit down. We need to talk," he said matter of factly.

"Yes Sir," I croaked, coughing slightly at having to use my voice, and sat myself down. He remained standing as there was only one chair in the room, causing me to have to look up to him in an awkward position. I'm sure he'd fucking done that on purpose. I wondered what this was all about. My time in isolation was not nearly finished, so this was highly irregular. I hoped it wasn't bad news, suddenly becoming worried.

"We need to change the terms of your punishment. The situation is untenable at the moment and we need everyone to be able to work," he paused for a moment, maybe to gather his own thoughts as to how to proceed. My heart started to beat faster. Might I get let out early? That would be fucking awesome and totally unexpected.

"Don't get too excited," he warned sensing my

rising heartbeat. "You are not off the hook, but we have no option but to cease your period of isolation, as the community needs you. However, we have managed to get hold off a state of the art anklet tracker, which will record every move and sound you make. We have also installed CCTV in your room, which is where you will have to spend your free time. You will have no privacy. Your handler will be Vivian. You will be at her service 24/7, until we deem you trustworthy again."

"Yes Sir," was all I could utter. I wasn't sure how it would impact me, but for now I was happy to be leaving this fucking hellhole of a cell.

"Stand up and follow me," Markus ordered whilst he led me to Vivian's office. "He's all yours," he muttered as he opened the door and ushered me in.

Archie fitted my anklet tracker that Tristan had provided, under the watchful eye of Vivian, and he explained how the software worked. I started to realise how much of an invasion of my privacy this anklet and camera surveillance was. I wouldn't even be able to take a fucking piss or fart without someone knowing about it, let alone any other things you wouldn't want an audience for. Still, it was better than the mind-numbingly boring days in isolation.

"Sorry mate," Archie muttered, "But good to see you. We really need you. We're all flat out and have been during the last four months, whilst you've been sitting on your arse, doing shit-all," he quasi-joked.

"Not by fucking choice," I retorted grumpily, not in the mood for jokes yet. My senses were getting overwhelmed and I needed a break soon.

"Vivian..." I started, only to be interrupted sternly.

"You will address me as Ma'am."

I swallowed and sighed, but her frown warned I better not show my annoyance any more than that.

"Of course, Ma'am. My apologies. May I please have some downtime, Ma'am? I'm feeling exhausted and over stimulated."

I knew she wouldn't say no. In our community everyone knew that after isolation our senses were easily over stimulated, like Eliza had learned the hard way before. We had a right to withdraw. Everyone respected that, so she nodded and escorted me to my new room. It was next to Zaphy's, as I spotted her name on the door, but I couldn't sense her. She must be out working.

"Let me know when you're ready for an update. Just speak. I can hear you any time. And see you everywhere," she reminded me a little too eagerly. I bet she fucking enjoyed this. "Be available on your phone at all times. If you don't answer, I'll be sending people to check you out straight away," she warned menacingly. I was left under no illusion I was a free man.

After a long and relaxing bath and something to eat, only narrowly remembering to cover up when I left the bathroom *(fucking CCTV),* I felt a lot better and more in control. I wasn't going to let Vivian know that yet.

The room was quite cozy, with a sofa and lots of soft cushions, but it had hardly any of my possessions. Someone, probably Zaphire had put some of my clothes in the cupboard, but that was essentially it. To be honest, I didn't own a lot, apart from a battered old acoustic guitar, a couple of books and a photo or two, but I was attached to them. I would like them here.

I was just about to sink into the comfortable sofa, put my feet up and watch some tv, when a soft knock on my door sounded. I opened the door, knowing who was behind it already.

"Hey," her soft voice entered the room. "Can I come in?" she smiled, looking at my blank face, betraying I still felt a little overwhelmed.

"Of course, Phaedra, of course." I motioned her inside quickly, feeling sheepish at my sluggish reactions. I had to instantly fight the urge to grab and kiss her, knowing it wouldn't end well, as it would be too much at the moment. I needed her comfort though, so I let her give me a big hug. I pulled her next to me on the sofa.

"I've missed you," she whispered in my ear.

"I've missed you too, Phae."

She leaned over to whisper some more, but I stopped her, suddenly remembering my anklet and the camera.

"It records fucking everything. We have no privacy," I said regretfully.

At that I received a message on my phone from Vivian. -*'If you're well enough to snuggle up with Phaedra, you can damn well report for work. Now.'*-

I looked at Phae, showed her the message and rolled my eyes.

"See what I mean? Best go and report to Vivian now," I groaned.

My phone pinged again. -*'That's Ma'am to you.'*-

"For fuck's sake," I grumbled under my breath.

Another ping. -*'I can hear that.'*-

This was going to be fucking hard. Phaedra got her phone out too and texted something. -*'See you later. Msg me when u can xxx'*- I smiled at her and nodded but yet another ping rang out from my phone. It was Archie.

-*'We've hacked into your phone too. Nothing is private, mate. Sorry.'*-

CHAPTER 3

Zaphire

"I can't believe it's been four months of working our arses off! Bloody Daniel. I'm fed up with staying in, day in - day out, keeping our heads down," I moaned at Sam, whilst looking through documents online. She just ignored me, used to my usual gripes. We had virtually stopped doing our ordinary work, and were fully concentrated on keeping the lid on any more information that kept leaking out.

Adequate as the compound was, it was by no means perfect. I really missed our Room of Tranquillity. Although there was talk of creating a new one, it had been put on the back burner. Everyone was working hard on the case, and there was simply no time for anything else. The rooms were nice enough, and the top floor apartments were super flash, and the envy of everyone who hadn't been lucky enough to score one of them. They were mainly for families, but a few lucky bachelors got their hands on the smaller ones, including Phaedra. I was quite pissed off, and freakishly jealous as I wasn't that fortunate, and was stuck in a small en-suite room. At least Sam, Ned and Brody got the same deal as me.

"How are you feeling about Eliza?" Sam tentatively asked, whilst walking back to our rooms after a long day's work. She clearly wasn't sure if I was ready to talk about it. I welcomed it though. My heart was growing softer about Eliza's betrayal. They do say that time is a great healer, and I experienced it to be true. I had truly believed she was going to be 'The One' for me, and though, before her, I was known to be a bit of a player, I hadn't been interested in anyone else since.

"I miss her. Though, I doubt I could ever be in a relationship with her again. I don't think I can ever fully trust her," I sighed. I was grieving the demise of our short relationship, and I had gone from fierce anger to just melancholic sadness.

"Fancy a drink?" I opened the door to my

room, looking forward to a good chat, but jolted when a familiar scent entered my nostrils.

"Zack!" I shouted out loud, but no reply came. *Shit.* I must have just missed him! I didn't know he was out already, the lucky bastard. I wondered if Eli was out too. I decided to follow Zack's scent and track him down, leaving Sam in my room looking slightly bemused. I quickly realised he was heading to Vivian's office and when I arrived I hovered by the door, not sure what to do.

Unfortunately, all the offices were soundproofed, which was obviously needed within our community, to keep things private, but also a pain. Especially if you were nosey, like me! The blinds were pulled down too, so there was literally no way for me to find out what was going on. I just had to wait for him to come out. *For crying out loud.* I wasn't going to do that. I dithered for a few moments more, before I knocked and brazenly opened the door.

I was met by two pairs of eyes boring into me. One set showing surprise and utter joy, the other set showed nothing but annoyance and anger. Before the angry one could speak, I jumped into my brother's arms with shrieks of excitement. How I had missed his strong arms around me, making me feel safe and loved. Our embrace wasn't allowed to last long. Vivian slapped the table.

"Zaphire! Please get out of this room. Now! We're busy. Zack will see you when he has finished here," she scowled. Zack nodded, urging me to obey immediately, but his eyes twinkled mischievously.

I skulked out, but felt a whole lot better for seeing him. I couldn't wait to talk to him later and I skipped back to my room, but not before texting the gang to come and welcome Zack back in my room. I knew it couldn't be too much of a party, because he would be suffering from the effects of having been in isolation, but everyone was over the moon for him to be out, and keen to see him. I quickly ran over to see Markus and asked if Eli was up for early release too, but his answer was a firm 'no'. At least I wouldn't have to deal with her just yet.

I heard Zack approach after about an hour and went to greet him. One look at him warned me to take it easy. He looked emotionally exhausted.

"Hey, Zack. The guys are here to see you," I said softly. His eyes lit up, but he shrugged his shoulders in defeat.

"I have to go to my room. I can only spend my free time there."

Ned squeezed his head past mine.

"Bro, are you up to visitors? We won't stay long. Just want to say hi," he suggested, trying to contain his own exuberance to see Zack again.

"Yeah mate! Come over to mine. So fucking good to see you all! Just mind there's CCTV..." He rolled his eyes with disapproval but I could sense his endorphins hiking, ecstatic to see us all again. Even though he was generally an arrogant pain in the arse, I was so happy to have him back.

CHAPTER 4

Zack

I had to kick everyone out after about an hour. As good as it was to see them all, my head started to spin. I still had to do my exercises for today and I was looking forward to doing it on my own. An hour pounding away on the treadmill was perfect to clear my head and calm my senses. Afterwards, I managed to get to my room without interruption and flopped onto my bed ready to go to sleep. My phone pinged. Phaedra. *Fuck.* I'd completely forgotten to text her. I decided to give her a quick ring.

"Do you want to come over for a bit?" I dived straight in. She jumped on that and she was lying next to me within ten minutes. "You know we are under full observation," I reminded her, as it was easy to forget. Though, I had already worked out that the place we could possibly get physical, was the shower. I didn't care that I'd just had one! No camera, and the splashing of the water would cover the sound; perfect. It didn't take her long to work that one out either...

Utterly exhausted and satisfied we clambered back into bed. She didn't leave to go to her own place, and I woke up spooning her sexy warm body. How I had missed this. A fleeting thought of Eliza entered my mind, but I was quick to dispel it. Phaedra was good for me.

Vivian expected me to report to her office at 9am. I checked the time, as I forgot to put the alarm on, and I'd left my phone on silent after my meeting with Vivian. Five missed messages, a knock on the door, and the realisation I only had twelve minutes to get to Vivian, woke me up instantly. Samuel walked into my room without waiting for my invite.

"You didn't respond to your messages. Ma'am has ordered me to escort you to her office," he informed curtly. There was no love lost between us. He revelled in the knowledge that my responsibilities as trainer and mission leader had been taken away from me, and therefore had no authority over him. What he forgot was that I would most likely earn them back at some point. He would not want to make an enemy out of me. He felt his career was stuck being a guard, which was by no means a bad job and received respect in our community, but he always felt he was too good for it. Hence, Samuel wasn't much liked by his fellow guards, and it made for a bitter personality.

I threw on some clothes, brushed my teeth as I assumed time for breakfast was out of the question, kissed Phae, who looked dishevelled but also realised she was late for work, and nodded at Samuel. "Ready. Let's go."

***

"I need you to get Daniel to understand he needs to back off. We haven't really had much success in forcing him to change his story, as he's protected by his publicity. We've tried digging dirt up, but he's clean as a whistle. We can't make it up because he's too much under the spotlight. We can't even lock him up, as again, people would wonder what happened to him. After four months you would have thought the story would have died away, but it has sparked the imagination of the people and it's stubbornly staying on social media," Vivian explained.

"Couldn't Markus have used his authority to 'persuade' him?" I asked bemused.

"Markus doesn't want to risk it. So far he's managed to keep his face out of the media and he plans to keep it that way."

"So what do you want me to do?" I asked, realising Markus clearly didn't see it as a problem to have my face exposed.

"Lean on him, threaten him, use your natural authority or beg him, if you must. He needs to understand the damage he's causing to our community. I'm not sure what's driving him to do this, so find out, and use it to change his mind. But it must all be done under cover. He doesn't know you or Brody. We checked. He knows your name, but he never saw you. We checked the video footage that you sent to Eliza, and you don't feature on it. Your face is safe. You and Brody need to get close to him, find out as much as possible about what drives him, and then make your move."

"Yes Ma'am. That may work. But I know another approach that most definitely would work; get Eliza to talk to him. He has a soft spot for her, even though she betrayed him. I think he loved, or possibly still loves her."

Vivian looked at me icily.

"Nice try. But out of the question. Mankuzay will remain in isolation for the full term if not longer, and that's the end of it."

"It has a better chance of success, Ma'am," I tried again, in vain and frustration. She just looked at me, shaking her head.

Preparations started immediately to get this mission on its way. Brody had already been briefed and the meeting was in full swing, but I had to put a stop to the proceedings. I wasn't ready. I was still suffering from the after effects of having had my senses deprived for four months. That wasn't going to fix itself in two days. I needed to take it easy. But no one listened to me, as I wasn't in charge of the operation. I needed to ask for Vivian's fucking permission to take a break. I wasn't used to working like this. It was a fucking pain. Finally, I got my permission and went to my room, my head nearly exploding. I needed darkness and quiet. I closed the curtains and dropped on my bed. I hated feeling this fucking weak.

I woke up refreshed, but it was 15.45! I jumped up, felt dizzy and sat back down. I hadn't eaten all day. I texted Vivian to ask if I could get myself some food, before returning to her office. I got a text back instantly.

-'*Yes. Make it quick.*'-

I took that. Went to the canteen, got myself a

tuna baguette and arrived at her office still eating, to the dismay of my colleagues as the already rank room, now smelled of tuna too. It didn't make for a good mix. I chomped through my baguette as quickly as I could, all the while listening to the plan that was being presented to Vivian and Markus by Tristan. Zaphy was nowhere to be seen, so clearly not part of this mission.

"Zack and Brody, or Arthur and Neil as they will be called for this mission...," a little sniggering ensued, but was silenced by a flick of the chin by Markus. I did detect a tiny lift in the corner of his mouth, giving away he rather enjoyed the choice of names too. "...will go to one of Daniel's gatherings. It won't be hard to find out where they take place, as he's still making quite a song and dance about it, and the media hasn't lost interest yet," Tristan continued. Brody piped up.

"I've already found a location, which we will hopefully be able to attend. It's not too far away from here, but it's happening Friday evening.

That's in two days time."

He glanced over to me to see how I felt about the time frame. It was too soon and I was about to voice my opinion, when Vivian butted in just ahead of me.

"I'll make sure Zack is ready. Start arranging a vehicle and a plan of action."

Brody caught my eye again, to check I was okay with this. He knew I wasn't, but there wasn't much he could do about it. Vivian had been perfectly clear in her order, and Markus seemed happy with it too. They were quite desperate to put an end to all this, so they could go back to concentrating on the Rick problem. I requested to see Markus privately, which was promptly denied as the leaders all made their way into his office for an urgent meeting, leaving me, Ned, Brody and some new recruits behind. Laura closed the blinds, so we couldn't even see their facial expressions.

"This is frustrating as hell," grumbled Ned.

"Fuck this," I added

"Welcome to our world bro," sighed Brody,

equally annoyed.

"Something's up. There must be news about Rick or the two French gits. The leadership feels tense, and are way too keen to push this mission on Daniel through," Ned suggested. I agreed. It felt a bit off.

We buried our heads in our task and sorted all the arrangements and made a plan of action. Vivian should be pleased about that, at least. The meeting in Markus' room was still in full swing. I really wanted to be in there. It felt wrong not being involved. Vivian texted me with instructions for this evening, probably part of her plan to get me well-rested and ready for our mission in two days time.

"Guys, that's me done for today. Been fucking ordered to my room with no company," I complained to my two mates, who shrugged their shoulders and rolled their eyes. "For fuck's sake. I guess I'll have room service again."

"See you tomorrow, Zack. Get rested and

don't let it get to you. It'll all be back to normal soon." Ned offered, trying to lift my mood.

I fucking well hoped so, but I got the feeling Markus liked the complete control he had over me, and now being able to use me for their missions. I wasn't all that sure I was going to have my freedom and my position in the community back any time soon. I trudged back to my room, disappointedly texting Phae that I couldn't see her tonight. *Fuck it.*

CHAPTER 5

Eliza

"Who are you loyal to, Miss Mankuzay?" It never sounded like a question, more a command.

"The Sensorian community, Sir."

"Who do you answer to?" Michael barked again.

"You Sir, and Mr and Mrs Mackenzie, of course," I quickly added. Michael insisted I only referred to Markus and Laura by their surname, as a mark of respect.

"Who do you take orders from?"

"You and the rest of the leadership, Sir."

"Who is in the leadership, Eliza?"

"Mr and Mrs Mackenzie, Ms Johnson, Mr van der Veldt and you, Sir," I answered dutifully.

"Anyone else you take orders from?"

"No, Sir. Not without prior arrangement."

"Will you ever make a work or mission related decision by yourself?"

"No, Sir. Never again."

"Who do you check with?"

"You Sir, or any other member of the leadership, if necessary."

"What will be the consequence of breaking that rule?"

"Indefinite isolation, Sir."

"Too right it will," Michael confirmed sternly.

Every single morning for nearly four months, the same line of questioning occurred. I felt like a robot answering them, devoid of feelings. I tried to rebel in the first session after being told what the expected answers were. I told him the only person I answered to, was myself. But, like Zack, Michael was unforgiving. He just got up and left. I received a glass of water for lunch, a glass of milk for dinner, my TV didn't work, I had no books yet and exercise was cancelled. My cooperation returned the following day. I knew when I was fighting a losing battle. My pride gave way to practical-ism. Isolation was hard enough to deal with, without being deprived of privileges.

This question and answer farce and practising my remote Vision Hacking, were the only forms of interaction I had every day. The rest of the day was filled with reading, a strict exercise routine and an hour of television in the evening. Time moved at a snail's pace and I couldn't believe it had only been four months. Just over half way through, if I was lucky to get out after six months. It felt like an endless nightmare, a lifetime of loneliness and boredom. I missed listening to music, having my senses stimulated with food, smells, touch and feelings, laughter and banter and just a general sense of purpose. Everything felt dull and monotonous.

Rob Saunders was another person I was granted to take orders from. Every day, he came in just after Michael left. My senses, deprived of an ample supply of male or female scents, relished it. I could imagine how Stockholm syndrome happened; every time I saw him I thought I fell a little bit more in love with him. I knew it wasn't real. Just my senses playing games. It still made me feel guilty though, remembering Zaphire's beautiful eyes and smile, her lips softly kissing mine. I bitterly regretted how our relationship ended, but I hadn't completely given up hope of reconciliation. There was time.

When Rob entered, I remembered to cloak so he wouldn't find out about my embarrassing fake feelings. Funny it didn't happen with Michael though...

Rob practised VH with me, and it was the best half hour of every day. We didn't get to talk much as it was all task related, but it was better than nothing. Rob was fairly strict, but I knew he felt sorry for me, and unlike Michael, he occasionally forgot to be purely businesslike and I savoured those moments. A little too much, probably.

"Tell me what I see." Rob had his back turned to me and had something in his hands. I jumped into his eyes. It took me hardly any effort whatsoever. I was getting good at this.

"You're looking at a book. It's got paintings in it. You're looking at a Gauguin."

"Good. Keep with my eyes, don't break the link. What painting am I looking at now?"

"Easy; the boring Mona Lisa. Never understood the hype about that painting," I sniggered.

"Keep on task. I don't need to hear your opinions," he rebuked half-heartedly. He was no natural disciplinarian, but he knew he had to at least keep up the appearance, as all sessions were recorded.

"Practise hacking in and out for a bit, in quick succession. I want you to tell me what I look at every other page starting from now."

That was more difficult. I had to really concentrate but still wasn't completely successful, and missed a couple of pages. He was satisfied enough though with my progress.

"We'll keep practising that. I also want you to

start hacking different people around you, swapping from one to another. I know you don't have much opportunity here in isolation, but I may ask Michael's permission to allow another person in, at one of our sessions. Don't get excited as it will probably be him. I can't see him allowing you the pleasure of different company."

I nodded, agreeing that I couldn't see him allowing that either. I still felt excited to be able to practise my skills on two different people. Something to look forward to. These little things kept me going. I was determined to get through this ordeal, without losing the plot. I kept fighting my own feelings of dissent and sometimes downright hatred of the leadership. My brain knew I had given them little choice. They had to make an example of me and Zack, to quell any thoughts of insubordination by the other community members. They needed to see that the leadership wouldn't stand for it. They felt they had to show their strength through harsh punishment. That was Markus' style and had kept his community safe for years. So they were unlikely to veer from that now, when there was a threat as big as Rick, Jean-Pierre and Angelique still out there.

I kept telling myself I simply had to endure it.

CHAPTER 6

Zack

"I can't believe they actually let us go to this thing on our own!" Brody exclaimed in slight disbelief. He had only been assigned highly supervised junior tasks up until today.

"We're hardly on our own, bro," I reminded him, pointing disapprovingly at the device around my ankle. Brody shook his head in annoyance.

"Mate, I'm sorry man. It must be such a bloody pain," he groaned.

"As long as we remember it's there, and don't say anything to upset the powers that be, we'll be fine." I tried making it sound as if I didn't care too much about my predicament. I didn't want Brody to feel sorry for me. I should still be in isolation, so this was a hundred times better. My phone pinged. I didn't even bother checking the message properly, as it was bound to be Vivian issuing some kind of warning.

It was about an hour's drive to the location of Daniel's gathering and we settled into a comfortable silence, listening to the radio. We managed to get away from our compound unnoticed. Not that anyone had found out our new location yet, but we were told to always be on the lookout for potential reporters lurking around, as the whole community was still on edge. It would be an absolute nightmare, if we had to relocate again. I enjoyed the drive, but we arrived at our destination sooner than I would have liked. It was relaxing in the car, giving my senses the rest they needed. Though Vivian did her best to get me rested and ready for this mission, I was still not feeling in complete control. I wouldn't have let anyone in my state go and do a mission like this, but I suppose she was under pressure from the rest of the leadership and according to them, time was of the essence.

"Brodes, I have to ask you to keep an eye on me. If you see signs I'm not coping you have to jump in. I don't want a sensory overload situation ruining this mission." I hated admitting to my weaknesses, but I felt it was the right thing to do. Brody understood not to make a big deal of it, and just nodded. I knew I could rely on him one hundred percent.

We got out of the car and leisurely walked up to the insalubrious looking venue where the gathering was taking place. There was a cold nip in the air, not quite freezing yet, but the stiff wind was icy cold. Not surprising as it was winter, but having been cooped up indoors for the last four months, I hadn't noticed the change of seasons. Slightly distracted as I pondered the fact it was nearly Christmas, I was rudely brought back to the here and now, when I spotted Kas out of the corner of my eye. My heart took a fucking dive.

"What the hell is that Dullard doing here," growled Brody when he clocked him too.

We sped up, caught up, and followed him at a close distance, but he hadn't noticed us yet. I grabbed him just before entering the building and pulled him aside into a dark and dodgy looking alleyway, right next to the venue. Brody and I squared up to him.

"Don't even think about going in there. You know the deal. Go the fuck home. Now!" I threatened. The colour in Kasper's face drained away, making him look ill.

"How...how..d..did you know I was going to be here?" he stammered, looking scared shitless. I didn't correct his misconception.

"We know everything, Kas. Get the fuck away from here and never go and see Daniel again. Next time, your sorry arse will land in prison." I hissed quietly in his ear, not to draw too much attention to our kerfuffle. I let go of his coat, stepped aside and waited for him to scuttle off. I took a deep breath to compose myself.

"The fucking guy is unbelievable. Eliza would be distraught if he managed to get himself arrested for what we have lined up for him," I sighed. The threat we gave him before, that we'd fabricate a crime that would mean prison time, and being on the sex offenders list, must burn in Kas' mind right now. It was necessary at the time to keep him quiet about us, and it had worked up to now. It might just save him from doing something stupid.

"What Daniel is doing is so fucking dangerous. It gives people who know about us, but always felt alone in that knowledge, an ally. This has got to stop. Let's get in there Zack, and take back control." Brody turned resolutely around and made his way towards the door. I followed, gearing myself up for another challenge. We took our fake ID's out to match ourselves to the guest list that a burly man was overseeing. He nodded us in.

We sat ourselves down in the back of the little hall, together with about seventy other people, seemingly from all ages and backgrounds. Daniel's story had a wide appeal. He came on stage to a raucous applause and sat himself down on a stool, microphone placed in front of him. He cleared his throat and welcomed us all.

The screen behind him lit up, pictures of Rick,

Eliza, Ned, Angelique and Irena flashed past and then settled together as a backdrop to his talk. Noticeably Jean-Pierre was missing. Maybe he had been clever enough to erase his pictures from the public domain.

"These people you can see behind me are called Sensorians and are part of a secret community living among us ordinary people. They are special, they have the gift of extraordinary powerful and heightened senses, which could benefit us all. Unfortunately, part of the community is hell-bent on keeping their existence a secret, resulting in a violent power struggle that I fell victim to. I will tell you my story and urge everyone to spread the word, and force these people to use their powers for the good of all people, rather than destroying each other with in-fighting and violence."

Daniel took a breath and a sip of his beer and encouraged everyone to do the same with a hearty "Cheers!" In his head the guy had good intentions. I just didn't think he realised the damage he was causing.

"I think we have a chance to convince him peacefully," I whispered to Brody, who nodded in agreement.

The rest of the talk was uncomfortable watching; confronting us with Sonia's death and the violent treatment of Daniel himself, Zaphire and all the others. He admitted he got some of the stories from witness accounts as he was brought to hospital, but people didn't seem to care. They lapped it up, with gasps of shock and disgust interspersed with jeers and applause.

Once he wrapped it up, and finished personal conversations with some of the audience, we hung behind, out of direct sight pretending to drink some beers. We waited for everyone to leave and steeled ourselves for our confrontation with him. It wasn't ideal, as Daniel was making signals he was about to leave, but the man on the door was still around. He could cause us trouble. In fact, he was coming over to us.

"Drink up, fellas. We're about to close," he ordered in a rather unforgiving voice. We nodded, hoping he would just leave us, but he insisted on making sure we got up and left. This wasn't going to plan. There was no way out, we just had to leave and wait for Daniel to appear outside. We couldn't have witnesses to our conversation. It would just have to wait a little longer.

CHAPTER 7
Zaphire

Zack had texted me to say they had arrived at the hall where Daniel was holding his gathering. He asked me to make sure people didn't try and contact them for a while. He would let us know when they were done. I was stinking jealous of Zack and Brody, having been given the mission to persuade Daniel to give up his crusade against us. Sam, Ned and I grumbled about it, but we knew there was no option for us to go. Well at least not for Ned and me, because Daniel would recognise us instantly. Still, I decided to confront Markus and ask him when we would be allowed more involvement. I knew I was risking a bollocking, but occasionally he surprised me with a left-field decision.

I walked up confidently and was about to knock on his office door, when I heard Laura approach and something about her made me lower my hand and turn towards her.

"I know that look on your face, Zaphy. You are about to annoy Markus with some request or the other, aren't you?" A little smile played across her lips and her eyes twinkled, but she led me away from the door and I knew I shouldn't fight it. "Come with me. We have to talk."

She had forgiven me pretty quickly for my blatant abuse of her goodwill before, when I secretly went to find Eliza, leading to my fateful capture. She was and has always been fiercely protective over our community, especially over me and Zack. She had been furious and extremely disappointed that I had put myself, and the whole community in danger, but she was also ever so forgiving and understanding. You just had to let her decide when that would happen, and not push it, which was exactly what I did, and after about two weeks she stopped her icy treatment of me and let me apologise.

"What was it you wanted to ask Markus?" she asked straight out.

"I want to be more involved. I have learnt from my mistakes, I won't ever be reckless enough again to do things behind the leadership's back. I don't want to put myself and our community in that position again. And we; Ned, Sam and I, have knowledge and expertise that is being wasted at the moment. I know as well as you do that the community is struggling at the moment. We need to use everyone we can, to fight this," I blurted out.

Laura sat still, observing me for a moment, weighing up her words. The scent of stress slowly penetrated my nostrils. She exhaled loudly.

"We know you do, sweetheart and the leadership is aware we need all the people power we can get, but it's been hard for Markus. I don't think you understand how much anguish you caused when you were captured. The powerlessness we all felt, well, it really broke Markus' heart. He lost it, Zaphire. He lost control, and he hasn't forgiven himself for that yet. And in a way, he hasn't forgiven you for causing it. He doesn't want to be placed in that position again, and therefore is extremely reluctant to let you do anything remotely risky again. He also doesn't want to upset you further by giving your friends more useful tasks, so unfortunately they will be suffering the same treatment as you. It took a lot of convincing to let Zack and Brody do the mission, but he knew it was the best thing to do. In the end, he capitulated to our insistence. You have to give him time, baby. Don't confront him about it. Not yet. It would be better if it came from him."

I sighed and nodded, but felt empty.

"How am I ever going to convince him that I'll be fine? That I'll be careful and that I'll never do anything off my own back again? I feel so useless at the moment!" I pleaded, my voice sounding a little too desperate, even to my own ears. But I couldn't help it. I needed to be more active, more involved, I just had to.

"Hang in there girl. It won't be forever. Trust me."

Laura hugged me and kissed my forehead before she left, leaving me to my misery. I was bloody stuck with it for a little while longer it seemed. Frustration started to bubble up inside me again. I made my way to the gym, texting Sam, asking her to meet me there. I needed to punch it out. A good sparring match was in order and Sam was a willing opponent. My frustrations did abate, but I knew I was fighting a losing battle. I was scared something would snap inside me if the situation didn't change soon. Change was indeed on the cards, but not quite how I expected.

CHAPTER 8

Zack

"Hey, Daniel," I started, extending my hand out to introduce myself when he finally appeared from the hall.

"I'm Arthur, and this is Neil," pointing at Brody, who also offered his hand. "We just watched your talk, man. It was amazing." Daniel's lips formed a shy smile, clearly stoked to be complimented. "We think we may be able to help you with some more information. Is there somewhere we could go for a talk, a bit warmer than here, and a bit more private?" I pushed. Daniel looked a bit doubtful and bemused, but his trusting nature won.

"Er..., yeah. There's a place near here which has private booths. We could grab a drink there, if you like?"

In the five minute walk, I did my best to put him at ease. Brody was useless at small talk, so it was up to me to keep the conversation flowing. Daniel was nothing but genuine, his sensory output rendering him an open book to me. I sincerely hoped we didn't need to do anything drastic tonight. Our back up plan wasn't pretty.

"Are you from round here?" I asked, breaking a short silence.

"Born 'n bred. What about you? Did you travel here?"

"Yep," I laughed. "Does our Southern accent give us away?"

"Yours does. Haven't heard you speak much, mate. Neil, wasn't it?"

Brody nodded.

"He's the strong but silent type. Girls love it," I nudged Daniel playfully in an attempt to bond. It worked. He laughed heartily.

We soon arrived at the slightly dilapidated cafe Daniel was heading for. Some letters were missing of the signage, but it was meant to read The Bull's Eye. It still held a cosy charm and the warmth invited us in quickly. It was busy, but there were a few booths available, so I sent 'Neil' to get us some drinks, whilst Daniel and I slipped ourselves onto the comfy round bench sofa. I made Daniel go in the middle, making sure there was space on the other side for Brody to sit, making an easy escape route impossible. I was talking rugby now. Thank fuck I'd done my homework, as conversation flowed easily and I could literally feel Daniel relax and drop his guard totally. By the time Brody came back with our drinks, non-alcoholic beer for us as drinking on a mission was strictly forbidden, I had Daniel right where I wanted. Unsuspecting and relaxed. I changed position slightly, sitting up a bit straighter, but leaning towards and facing him as much as I could at this angle.

"Right, Daniel. We need to talk," getting straight to the point. His face gave away slight surprise at my serious tone. "We said we had some information for you, but it's actually a message. A message from Markus; our leader."

I waited a moment to let this bombshell sink in. His eyebrows shot up, and the distinct odour of stress and fear combined rose up in the air. His eyes flicked around looking for a way out, but he knew he had no chance.

"I should've seen this coming," he grumbled, scolding himself.

"Look, we're not here to do you any harm. We just need you to listen," I tried to reassure him before carrying on. "Markus asks that you stop these meetings, stop keeping our story in the media. You've had your moment, you've had your say. But your actions are hurting us, and stopping us from doing our duty. We want the same thing as you. Rick's ideals are not ours. We only try and do good, but we can't do that right now as we need to stay hidden. You have opened us up to persecution for our abilities and that is the last thing we want. We just want to do our job, the reason for our existence," I pleaded passionately, but firmly.

Daniel looked at me, then Brody. Indecision

written all over him.

"I get where you're coming from, really, I do. But, I feel people need to know about the existence of Sensorians. They need to be made aware of your potential, but also the threat you could pose. I really believed in Rick. I still do to a certain extent, but I think Jean-Pierre and Angelique took over. They seemed far more violent than Rick. I can't believe he would have authorised killing Sonia like that."

"I wouldn't be too fucking sure. You saw what he fucking did to Ned? He could have died," I threw at him, my blood starting to boil by the thought of it. I needed to keep calm. "Look, I know what you want, but think about it. Isn't it for the greater good to let us do our job? We are peaceful, keep ourselves to ourselves and help your society. What more do you want?" I fixed my eyes on his and waited for him to lower his gaze, which he did, eventually. "Daniel," I said as kindly as I could. "You seem like a decent bloke. Eliza said as much too. You know what the right thing to do is."

"Eliza? How is she?" he asked with genuine concern. He still had a soft spot for her. I think I even picked up signs of love. I felt a pang of guilt coursing through my body. We needed to convince him in a peaceful way. He had gone through a lot already, and I didn't want to add any more to that.

"She's fine," I lied. "Though a bit miffed she can't leave the compound, thanks to the photos you plastered all over social media," I accused for effect, with limited success. He looked a little embarrassed, but still no sign of him giving in. I decided to give it one more try, approach it slightly differently. I noticed Brody was getting impatient. His body language told me he was ready to put the screws on. He wasn't going to like my next proposal.

"How about I ask Markus if you could come to our new compound, and see how we live and work?"

Brody's eyebrows nearly hit the ceiling. He hadn't expected that and was far from happy about it. But he knew better than to challenge me in front of Daniel.

Daniel was also taken by surprise. He was struggling to make up his mind and trying to work out if I had ulterior motives.

"Would that be safe for me?" he dared to ask.

"Safe, yes. But there would be conditions attached, and if you were to break those..., well, that would be a different story."

"Er...I don't know...Arthur, I just..., I need to think about it, man."

He shrugged his shoulders in hesitation. I forgot he knew me by the name of Arthur and an involuntary smile broke through my stern facade. It made him instantly relax a little, as he misinterpreted that smile completely. I glanced at Brody, who couldn't wait to finish this conversation off rapidly. Time to put the pressure on. My whole body changed from appearing laid back and calm, to assertive, almost aggressive. I leant forward, my face only inches away from his.

"As I see it, Daniel, realistically, do you think we're going to fucking let you walk out of here, without having been given your word that you'll back off? Look, I'm doing my best to come to a peaceful agreement, with some sort of positive outcome for you too, but make no mistake; we will get what we want out of you, one way or another."

Daniel's mouth first closed and then opened readying for his retort. Resolve written all over his face, but moving slightly away from me, creating a safer distance between us.

"This is exactly what I mean. You lot think you have the right to do this to people! This is the danger I'm talking about! I literally have to do what you say, or else! That's not how it should work!"

"We did ask you politely first. I pleaded with you to make the right decision, by your own volition. We have not asked anything unreasonably, just to fucking respect our way of life and leave us in peace," I reminded him forcefully, moving closer to him again, but keeping my voice low, not rising to his outburst.

"But if you're not willing to do so, we'll have to force you to make the right decision," Brody finally piped up, unable to contain his impatience with the situation. We sat silently for a few moments, letting things sink in and calm down.

"Maybe, if you did decide to come to our compound and talk to the people whose life you're ruining by exposing us, you would change your mind willingly. You might understand us a bit more. All you've heard is Rick's version so far," I offered once more, hoping to hell that Markus would agree to it, if Daniel accepted.

"Fine. I don't have a lot of choice, so I'll give it a go," he said, finally giving in.

I was on the phone to Markus already. I didn't have to explain because the leadership had been listening in to the whole conversation of course.

"Glad you remembered you have to run these things by us first, though you haven't left us much choice either," Markus started off sarcastically.

"It's dangerous. You must make sure you blindfold and disorient him, so he won't be able to give away the location of our new compound. Nevertheless, it gives us an option for a peaceful resolution, so we should try it. He won't be able to deceive us. If he promises us to back off, we'll know if he intends to do so or not. If not, we'll have to think again. Bring him in, Zack."

CHAPTER 9

Zaphire

My phone pinged. A message from Zack, saying they were on their way back. With Daniel! *What the hell!* I stormed over to warn Ned. This guy had alerted Rick about Ned, starting off the whole chain of events leading to Ned's beating. I'm sure Ned wouldn't be receiving him with open arms.

To my surprise, Ned seemed fairly chilled when he heard the news.

"Daniel only did what he thought best. He had no idea I would end up like I did. I don't think many of the Dullards really knew what they were letting themselves in for."

Okay. Ned taught me something there. He clearly was very good at empathising with people and seeing it from their perspective. Maybe I should try and put that into practise myself one day...

"You're way too good," I whispered to him

lovingly, but couldn't help but tease him a bit too. "Goody-two-shoes Ned; cross him and you'll be punished by his understanding!" I mocked, putting on my best film voice-over. He punched me, good-naturedly, but it still hurt my arm. He'd been working out to get back in top form, and it was doing the job!

"Let's go and find Sam. Have some fun, before tomorrow's chores descend on us. Zack and Brody won't be home till much later anyway, so we don't have to face Daniel yet," Ned suggested.

We decided to watch a film and chill together. I was nearly dropping off to sleep, when a feeling of dread enveloped my whole being. I sat up startled, checking both Ned and Sam, but only now did they prick up, reacting to me emitting signals of stress.

"What is it, Zaph?" Sam asked.

"Can't you feel it? It's weird, something's happened. I can sense it. But I don't know what!" I felt panic rising in my chest. Ned told me to breathe. Sam left, saying she would check out the compound.

"It's Zack. I know, it's Zack!" I shouted. I had only felt this sensation once before, and it was when Zack was fourteen years old, and he managed to get hit by a car and nearly died on the spot. Thankfully an off-duty paramedic was in the right place, at the right time and managed to give life saving first aid, until the ambulance arrived.

"There's something wrong with him! We need to warn Markus!"

I desperately tried ringing Zack, but he didn't answer. Then I tried Brody. Nothing. I ran towards the door but Ned grabbed my arm.

"They have him tracked, remember. They would know if there was a problem," Ned urged.

"I need to find out! I need to see Markus now!" I wrestled out of Ned's hold and rushed to Markus' office. Ned right behind me.

He wasn't in.

"Vivian. We need to find Vivian." I raced across the corridors, the feeling of doom still gripping hold of me. We got to her apartment and I banged on her door, to be met by a grumpy looking Vivian. I rudely shoved her aside whilst I barged into her room, looking for her computer to see evidence Zack was okay.

"What the...," Vivian started angrily, but Ned had it in hand. He apologised and explained quickly, whilst chasing after me and stopping me from rushing around like a mad woman in Vivian's room.

"Sit down, Zaph," he gently said, but damn well making sure I did sit down. He held me by both arms and shoved me on the sofa.

Vivian checked the data and listened to the incoming sounds from Zack's anklet. Nothing. It was moving in our direction, and a radio sounded in the background.

"Nothing unusual there, Zaphire. They should be home in about forty five minutes. They had a quick stop about five minutes ago, but that was it. Probably needed the toilet or something. Go back to your room and make yourself a nice bath to relax." Vivian said, not unkindly. I wasn't convinced. The strange feeling hadn't abated.

"Can you please phone him. He won't ignore your call. Please?" I begged.

"Okay then. If it makes you feel better."

She rang, I felt sick. The phone was picked up immediately, but few seconds elapsed until we heard Brody's voice.

"Zack's driving," he answered curtly.

"Put it on speaker," Vivian ordered. It took a few moments, but then I heard Zack's voice. *Thank God.*

"Can't talk, Ma'am. Concentrating," was his gruff reply, clearly pissed off with being checked up on.

"Just checking your ETA," Vivian asked.

Another rather long pause, but he answered.

"About an hour. Is that all, Ma'am?" obviously wanting to get off the phone as soon as possible.

"Yes, I'll let you go," she answered quickly. "Satisfied?" Checking me over.

I nodded, but something felt off. I felt better knowing he was alive and well, but I was still not convinced everything was hunky-dory. The pauses were a little too long, and Zack's voice definitely sounded strained. Moreover, the feeling of dread in the pit of my stomach was still there, festering away.

Ned nudged me to go, apologising on my behalf once again, whilst we left Vivian in peace. He took me to my room. Sam ran me a bath and offered to stay over, which I gladly accepted. I was determined to stay up and wait for Zack to arrive though. I needed to see him to make sure he was fine, before I could even think about going to sleep.

CHAPTER 10

Zack

"Fuck! What's going on behind us, Brodes?" I urged him to check it out, whilst I adjusted my mirrors in an attempt to get rid of the glare of the dazzling full beam headlights of two vehicles that were behind me. Next thing I knew, I had one vehicle right up my arse, and the other overtaking quite dramatically. "What the fuck!" It cut in, right in front of us, and slowed down.

The other vehicle was by my side, leaving me no option to slow down too. They forced me to go in the upcoming lay-by.

"Vivian, Markus! Something's fucking up!" I shouted, knowing they could hear everything going on through my anklet. "Brody, ring them!" I was forced to stop and before we could do anything, they had smashed both our windows. They forced their way into our car, snatching Brody's phone out of his hand. Daniel screamed, but his voice got cut short by a deafening bang. A sick feeling spread across my body, but then I felt a sharp pain in my head and everything went black.

"Wake the fuck up!"

Someone slapped my face. I must have passed out. I groggily lifted my hand to the source of the burning pain in my head. It felt warm and wet and smelt rusty. Blood. *Fuck.* I tried to assess the situation around me, but I was by no means sharp. I felt dizzy and everything seemed to move slowly. I spotted Brody. I sensed he was scared, but unharmed.

"Zack! Listen." I heard a voice urgently screaming in my ear. It was familiar. It took me seconds to realise it was fucking Rick. "Can you hear me? Nod if you can," he ordered and I complied, no will to resist. "No one is coming to your rescue. We've been interfering with your tracking device from the moment we were behind your car, so don't be tempted to stall. All they can hear is a radio station, and you'll be on the move any minute now. Move to the back seat. Irena will drive, Jean-Pierre has got a gun trained on Brody and er..., Daniel is indisposed."

It didn't make much sense to me, as my head was still spinning, but I knew the threat and I clambered to the back seat to sit between Rick and Jean-Pierre, the other accomplice.

"Where's Daniel?" I managed to croak.

"We're leaving him behind," Rick said, avoiding a straight answer.

"Is he okay?" I dared to ask, but one look at Brody warned me not to hope too much, his head hanging down and shoulders slumped.

"He's dead," Jean-Pierre barked in his heavily accented English, to the dismay of Rick. He'd rather have kept that fact from me. I wanted to fucking puke. Probably a combination of the shock and concussion that I undoubtedly had sustained. I couldn't keep it in. I stuck my head between my knees and let the contents of my stomach splatter on the floor. Jean-Pierre cursed and opened the windows in the back, with the front ones already letting in air as they were smashed to bits.

"No more questions," Rick decided resolutely. "We've been keeping tabs on Daniel since the beginning. He was becoming dangerous. A loose cannon. And it didn't seem to blow over. We're better off with him dead. We just needed to wait for you to approach him, so we could make contact with you. We knew you would eventually. My men will make it look like an unfortunate accident."

What the fuck was this man on? He had become totally ruthless. I hoped he had some use for us, otherwise I feared the worse. I guess he had, otherwise we would be alongside Daniel, part of the unfortunate accident.

"People are after us, well, mainly me at the moment, thanks to bloody Daniel. They've taken Alice...."

"What the fuck!" I couldn't help but shout, but it earned me a slap.

"Let me speak!" he roared impatiently. "We're not sure what or who we're dealing with, but we suspect they're American. Don't know whether it's the mob or the government."

"They want me and Eliza in exchange for Alice's freedom. I've tried to persuade them to keep Eliza out of it. That I have no contact with her and no influence, but they won't take no for an answer. I can't let Alice be the victim of this. Keeping her away from us Sensorians is all I have ever tried to do. She doesn't deserve this!"

He sounded and smelled desperate and sincere, as far as I could make out amongst the stench of my sick mixed with the general odour of stress and fear. I knew he had chosen to give up Alice and Eliza when he left them years ago in the hope they could lead normal lives, away from the Sensorians. But why this fucking drastic move? There was an edge in his tone of voice I couldn't quite place. Something felt off.

"Permission to speak, Sir?" I dared ask quietly. He snorted, but nodded his head curtly. "Why did you not just send a message to Markus. He might not want to help you, but he would help Alice. Why all this?"

"Because it's urgent. It's dangerous and I can't be discovered and captured by either the kidnappers or Markus before we have done the deal. The only reason we have some leverage, is because they don't know where I am. They won't hurt Alice, as long as they don't have me and Eliza. We have been off-grid from the moment they left us the message. It was risky enough communicating with them, trying to make a deal, without giving away our location. Contacting Markus might have done that, but also Eliza's whereabouts. It had to be this way."

"Did you have to kill Daniel?" I challenged, risking another slap. But Rick glanced over at Jean-Pierre, not all together happy.

"I accept Jean-Pierre's point of view on this one. It's a compromise I made with him. He doesn't pussy-foot around when there's something he perceives as a threat."

He paused for a moment, but when I drew a breath to ask my next question, his glare stopped me in my tracks. Then the ringtone of my mobile broke the silence. Vivian's name flashed up. It sat in between the two front seats and Irena told Brody to pick it up, but to not even think about ratting them out.

"Just act normal," she hissed.

Vivian insisted on hearing my voice, so I spoke gruffly, trying to get her off the phone as quickly as I could. I didn't want Jean-Pierre to suddenly perceive us as a threat. When I hung up, Rick continued.

"We need you to persuade Markus to help free Alice, even if it does mean having Eliza involved. We cannot capitulate to this organisation, whoever they are. If you can't persuade him, you'll have to do it without his knowledge. We have no other option."

"I can't do anything behind the leadership's back. If they have so much as an inkling of something dodgy going on, my arse will be back in fucking isolation before you know it," I sighed, rubbing my temples hard.

"Well, you better make damn sure he agrees to

help me then."

He pushed a burner phone into my hand. Irena stopped the car and with a 'I'll contact you', they all left the car as quickly as they had entered it. The car that had followed us all the way picked them up, and continued to follow us at close distance. I assumed they wanted to keep scrambling my anklet signal.

"Try and phone Markus," I urged Brody. But he shook his head.

"I think they disabled the phones. There's no signal now," he groaned.

"Fuck. We just have to drive back to the compound fast then," I just about managed to growl.

CHAPTER 11

Zaphire

I heard a car pull up outside our building. I knew it had to be Zack. I shoved a hat on my barely dry hair and threw on some joggers and a jumper, and raced to the lobby, Sam right on my heels. I was expecting three people to walk up as Daniel was meant to be there, and was momentarily confused to see only two of them, but that unsettled feeling was soon replaced by shock. I ran up to Zack. Seeing blood smeared across the side of his face and his eyes full of urgency and stress made me feel sick. He *had* been in danger! I knew it! I'd been right all along.

"Zack! What the hell happened? Are you okay?" I screamed a little too loudly in his ear as I hugged him, causing him to shrink away from me.

"I'm fine. Don't worry," he whispered calmly. I felt he was stressed as hell, but he managed to cover it well. On the outside he looked in control.

"We need to see the leadership. They're all

coming to Markus' office. Come with," he ordered.

The whole leadership was silent. Each of them trying to digest what Zack had just told us. I felt numb. Alice was in danger and it seemed Rick was always involved and always a step ahead of us! How did he even know about the tracking anklet Zack had to wear? Who was blackmailing Rick? It was all very confusing. After what seemed like forever, I could hear Markus take a tiny breath, signalling he was about to speak.

"We need time to look into this before we make a decision," he started, his eyes fixed on Zack, who was bursting to say something, fighting himself not to interrupt. "I'm not going to jump into this by releasing Eliza immediately, and throwing her into the deep end. We need to find out if Rick's telling the truth. It could all be an elaborate plan designed to take back Eliza and undermine us further. Rick and Jean-Pierre are dangerous. Let's not forget what they did to Daniel."

Zack couldn't contain himself any longer. My brother oozed urgency. I tried to convey to him to stay calm, but he wasn't receptive.

"Sir, time is something we have only limited amounts of. We need to act now, before Alice gets hurt! What if they run out of patience! Alice means nothing to them. She's just a pawn, and if it doesn't work, they might get rid of her!" he interrupted, his voice strained and high pitched.

"If the organisation that's behind this is serious in their demands, they'll wait. But we cannot take whatever Rick says at face value. For all we know, Alice isn't even involved, or he's using her for his own purposes," Markus insisted.

"But Zack felt Rick was sincere and seemed worried when he spoke of Alice. Can we never trust our senses again?" I questioned. In our normal missions we relied so heavily on our senses to get information and deal with people, it was hard to function if we couldn't do that. This is what Dullards must feel like all the time, never really knowing when someone speaks the truth. It was confrontational to say the least. I didn't like it at all.

"Not where Rick and his allies are concerned. They can deceive us, and we must operate as if they are. We can't risk it. We also need to assess what we're willing to sacrifice to rescue Alice. She's not a Sensorian," Markus decided resolutely. "Zack, you are going to have to stall Rick and his demands, whilst the leadership works out a plan. Clean yourself up and go to bed. I'll speak to you tomorrow morning at 8am. Everyone but the leadership needs to leave now, and get some sleep. We'll update everyone tomorrow." Markus dismissed us with a little wave of his hand, ushering us out the door. We knew we weren't welcome anymore so we all left, feeling massively annoyed.

"Ugh, it's so frustrating, being put on the sidelines," I couldn't help but grumble. Zack pointed at his anklet, reminding me everything I said would be for all to hear, successfully preventing me from really having a go at anyone!

I didn't hold back once in my room though.

Zack had to retreat to his own room to clean up and go to bed as ordered, whilst Sam, Ned and Brody piled into my room to have a good old moan and bitch.

"Poor Alice, I can't believe Markus isn't more perturbed by this! She could be hurt by his slow action taking," I protested, but Sam disagreed.

"I don't know. I don't trust Rick. I can see why Markus isn't going in guns blazing. I think it's wise to suss it out first. They did kill Daniel!" she shuddered.

"Yeah, but Markus might even consider doing nothing, if he feels it will put us at risk too much! I can't believe he would abandon Alice!"

"I'm sure he'll help. Markus just wants to investigate properly, before taking any rash action. But, if Rick's right, we are in deep shit. I don't fancy being blackmailed by this mob or American intelligence," Brody chipped in.

"Do you think Markus will let Eliza out early? He said he wouldn't, but he might have to?" I asked, suddenly realising I might have to deal with her for real. My body started to warm up, my heart pounding. A combination of trepidation and, bizarrely, excitement. I didn't understand my body's reactions sometimes. I noticed the others' reaction to my senses too. Why did I not cloak! So embarrassing. I stared darkly at them, warning them not to make a glib joke. I wasn't in the mood. Unfortunately, my dark stares were nowhere as effective as Zack's.

"Look who's getting excited, hah! Have you forgiven her yet, or are you going to be stubborn!" Brody teased.

"I think her heart has melted already, but her brain is trying to keep up appearances," snorted Sam.

"Shut up! Seriously, he might let her out in preparation, if they feel it is necessary for her to make the swap. She can't be thrown into the outside world without acclimatising. She was rubbish last time, thinking she could do it all!" I remembered Eliza's meltdown in the club, totally engineered by Zack, all to well. My body reacted

.91

involuntarily again, but this time I was prepared and cloaked. *Damn Eliza!*

"You're right. It's more than likely they are going to prepare her for action, just in case. I'm sure we'll hear all about it tomorrow. Let's watch a film. Anyone fancy watching *Tenet* again? I need to work this film out!"

We all groaned at Ned's suggestion, but none of us had the energy to come up with a different suggestion. Sam wasn't interested.

"I'm off to bed, early start and all that. I'm finally starting my course tomorrow to be accepted into the technical team again."

Sam had been part of the team that got rid of the explosive device that Rick had strapped to Eliza's leg when their meeting had gone sour, as Rick found out Eliza was with Markus. But, after the last messed up mission, Sam was punished, like me, to go back to basics. So, to her dismay, she had to do the whole training again.

"Okay babes, good luck!" we all shouted in unison as she left, leaving us to get settled into being mind-fucked by *Tenet* again.

CHAPTER 12

Eliza

"So, here we are," Markus started off. This was totally unexpected. I didn't quite know what to make of his presence here, in my cell. It was early, I hadn't even got dressed yet. He looked serious, but beyond that I couldn't read his mood, apart from the slightly deepened crease between his eyes, telling me he was worried about something. "We have a problem, Eliza. A problem we might need your help with." My senses stood on edge. This was not good news, as there would be no way he would be asking me this, if he could have avoided it.

"What is it? Is it Rick? My mum? Is it...,"

"Did I give you permission to speak?" he growled in a low threatening voice. I opened my mouth to say sorry, but that would have contravened the command too. So I quickly closed it and shook my head demurely. I bloody hated it, but I had no choice. I wanted to know what was going on, so the quicker I complied, the better. "We don't quite know the situation yet, and I don't want to worry you before we have all the details. However, if we do need you, it might be fairly soon. So, as a precaution we need to release you early from isolation to give you time to acclimatise."

My heart made a little leap. That was unexpected! I couldn't help but feel happy, even though the situation that caused my early release might be dire. Markus looked me over and sighed.

"It's not going to be easy, Miss Mankuzay. We have a system in place where you will be tracked by an electronic anklet 24/7, until we feel we can fully trust you again. Zack has been out a little while under the same system."

Would he give me permission to speak at all? I was bursting with questions. Was I going to be treated like some sort of criminal under house arrest? What was going on? I needed to know! But he was making signs of getting up, leaving me in the dark about everything.

"Michael will be your handler and will explain everything later. Get ready to be collected," Markus ordered as he stood up to leave the cell.

Bloody hell. I was going out of my mind not knowing what the pressing issue was, and scared at the same time. Someone must be in danger. Or Rick was rearing his ugly head again. I hoped it wasn't my mum. Maybe it was something completely different. The shower I took in a bid to calm down did nothing. I felt like a ball of tightly wound up wire, which needed releasing before it would explode. I couldn't account for my actions if it did, but there was nothing I could do. I just had to wait to be collected by Michael, who Markus had called my *handler.* What was that all about! My emotions were working overtime, having had nothing much to think about these last few months.

I was going to see Zaphire soon, and Zack, as I understood he had been released early too. I hoped Zaphire would at least speak to me. It had been killing me, going into isolation without having resolved our issues. I hadn't even spoken to her. She hated me. My stomach started to tighten and my breathing became shallow, but my moment of self-pity was rudely interrupted by Michael striding into the room. I hastily stood up, feet slightly apart and hands behind my back, looking at the floor. It was a movement I performed almost instinctively now, after months of the same routine.

"Raise your right foot onto the chair," he ordered, looking quite grim. I obliged quickly and before I knew it, the device was clasped around my ankle. It was rather hard and clunky and didn't feel great. It certainly didn't account for the sensitivity of our skin! I mean, I disliked the feel of a label in my underpants, and never could you please me with a nice watch or clunky bracelet as a present. I hated the feel of anything scratchy or metal on my skin. This was going to take some getting used to.

I followed Michael out of my cell, my home for over four months. Excitement replaced my depressed feelings. I thought we were heading for his office, but the stairs we took led to an area that looked like living quarters. I hadn't explored the surroundings of our new place yet, as I'd only seen the exercise yard and gym, which was right next to the cells. He opened the door to a small but cozy looking room and ushered me in.

"This is where you'll live for the foreseeable future. As you can see, it has CCTV and I'll have to make you aware that I'll be monitoring your every move. Your phone is tapped, the anklet has a tracking device and sound. Do not assume you have your freedom back. You need to be in your room for your free time, and other than that you're under my orders. You will need to socialise to acclimatise, but we'll take it slow to start with. You will be given a little more freedom, once I'm sure you can cope, but I reiterate that everything you do will be monitored. Do you have any questions?"

I thought he'd never ask.

"I have so many I don't know where to start, Sir. What is the emergency? Why do you need me? Why did we have to move to a different compound? What happened?" I wanted to ask every single question all at once, but I knew I probably wouldn't get any answers, if I did. I had to be patient. Zack was always very hot on that!

"We had to move compound because our location was compromised. Daniel informed the press. The rest of your questions will be answered in due course. For now, all you need to concentrate on, is being able to function again. Get your senses under control, so there's no risk of melt-downs," Michael answered rather unhelpfully. Daniel betrayed us? I needed to find out more about that, but I had so many more questions.

"How long do I need to wear this contraption for, Sir?" The look he gave me warned me I wasn't going to like the answer.

"As Markus already stated before; until we feel we can fully trust you, without a time limit. This arrangement is also not a guarantee that you won't be returned into isolation. If it turns out we can manage this mission without your involvement, you will sit out the remaining time back in your cell."

Ouch. Suddenly my excitement of being out took a little bit of a dive. What if they never fully trusted me? Surely they can't make me live like this forever, can they? It seemed the world went a little darker with that thought. Michael noticed, and offered me something to eat, to stop the downward spiral. It worked. I forced myself to focus on the prospect of meeting my friends, hopefully sooner rather than later, and a spark of positivity brightened my mood.

CHAPTER 13

Zack

We all left Markus' office after having been told in no uncertain terms to sit tight. Our tasks for the next few days were distributed amongst us. My main task was to stall, whilst the leadership risk assessed the situation and investigated whether the claims that Rick and Jean-Pierre had made, were true. They were going to dig deep, contact everyone we had liaisons with in society and those with links to the criminal underworld.

Rick had already contacted me on the phone he had given me, assuming I had kept that phone's existence from the leadership, which I hadn't. They knew everything, and I had reported it dutifully. I had no intention of messing up my relative freedom this quickly. I was worried for Alice, as I did feel Rick had spoken the truth, or at least what he believed to be the truth, though I did also feel something else was going on. It may have been Jean-Pierre's feelings I'd picked up on. It was hard to tell. And as Markus had pointed out, Rick is a master at cloaking so we couldn't really take his word for it. But still, if it was true, we did need to respond and get Alice out. I decided to text Rick with my first stalling message.

-*'Eliza is being prepared for action. I don't know when she'll be ready, but the first step is in place.'*-

I got one straight back.

-*'Good. But hurry. They're on our backs. I'm worried.'*-

-*'You need to deal with them your end. If they want Eliza, they'll have to wait.'*-

I didn't really know what else to say, but it sounded reasonable enough. Rick would just have to use all of his charisma to deliver that message, if they were even being pressurised. I couldn't think what other benefit Rick could get out of this, but I also couldn't be sure that his fucked-up brain wouldn't have concocted some sort of scenario where Eliza, Alice and him could be together again or something. Who knew?

Five days had passed, and we were no nearer to any action. Feelings of frustration escalated. The leadership hadn't been forthcoming with much, and Vivian was getting on my fucking nerves with her constant orders and requests that meant nothing but control. Rick's messages were getting more irate by the day, almost desperate and there was nothing I could do. I felt completely fucking useless. On top of everything, I hadn't been allowed to see Eliza yet. She'd seen everyone else, apart from me and Zaphire. Apparently she was doing well. I didn't believe that for a moment. I knew Eliza better than anyone, and I bet I could see through her little charade of pretending that everything was fine. I needed to see her to check. I didn't want her vulnerable when the time came for her to get into action.

"For fuck's sake. I need to see Markus," I exploded rather unexpectedly, making poor Phaedra nearly jump out of her skin. I threw the quilt off me, accidentally exposing her naked body.

We had become a little blasé about the constant surveillance, and often forgot it was there, or simply didn't give a fuck. I had been warned several times for our indecent behaviour, but frankly, I was beyond caring. Phaedra was a little more discreet and quickly restored her cover, giving me a searing look, something between scolding and plain sexy. I momentarily got distracted, as she looked so damned hot. But, my frustration took over pretty quickly again. I grabbed some trousers and a T-shirt and stomped over to Markus' office, the red mist descending.

"Enter," was the curt reply behind the door. I marched in and stood in front of Markus' desk, waiting for him to acknowledge me. My being there can't have been a surprise to him, as he'd more than likely been notified by Vivian of my imminent arrival. Time was ticking away, giving me the opportunity to calm down somewhat, and think of exactly what I was going to say. I tried to use the anger management strategies I had learned, and it was working. I needed to think about the consequences of an outburst, and breathe. Focus on my breathing. My heart rate went down, and the red mist fell away. Though after about ten minutes of standing there like a fucking lemon, I felt my frustration rise again. More breathing. Finally, he looked up and gave me permission to speak.

"I can't stall any longer. Rick is freaking out and threatening all sorts. He warned he hasn't got full control over Jean-Pierre, and he fears he might do something stupid. We need a decision. Are we going to get Alice out or not?" I crossed my arms defiantly, but with one look at Markus' face I dropped them beside my body, trying to come across less confrontational.

"Calm down. We're doing the best we can. We can't act on the word of Rick alone and we haven't found any evidence of him being approached by anyone. There is no chatter on the streets at all, and we have everyone working on it."

"But the fact is that Alice has gone missing! And the only lead we have is Rick's word. Even if it is all a ruse, it will lead us to her if we give him what he demands. We have to do something!"

Markus slammed the table and stared at me hard.

"But not if it means endangering any of us! The last mission cost us too much, and I *do not* want a repeat of that. We have to proceed with caution. That's the end of it. You may leave."

Fuck that. I turned around and strode out of the office, leaving the stench of my frustration, as I couldn't cloak anymore. We couldn't sit here and do nothing! Alice might be in danger and she deserves to be looked after by us. My feet took me where I knew I wouldn't be allowed for long. Damned anklet. I bet Eliza didn't even know about her mum. The next thing I had to do, I had to do fast. No time to dither.

I burst into her room. She was alone. *Good.* I strode towards her whilst kicking my shoes off, her face in complete shock, her lips slightly parted. I put a finger on her mouth and pushed her towards the shower room, took my shirt off, and dropped my trousers, forgetting I'd gone commando this morning. I was hit by her exquisite scent, her pulse was high, her face flushed. *Don't even think about it, Mackenzie!*

"Undress. Get in the shower. Quick," I ordered. Eliza's face betrayed bewilderment, lust, but more dangerously, refusal. Her scent turned sour, putrid; indicative of high stress levels.

"You can't...," she started, but I practically manhandled her into the bathroom, ripping her clothes off. She lifted her hand to slap me, but I was quick and caught her arm.

"Shh, we don't have long...," I whispered whilst I put the shower on full, with the noise of the fan, helping to cover up my words for anyone listening. I shoved her under the shower, bra and knickers still on, quickly getting drenched and see through. So fucking sexy. *Focus, you animal!* I scolded myself. I pointed at our anklets to explain my actions. "This is the only place we can talk, freely," I explained, to remedy Eliza's furious glare.

CHAPTER 14

Eliza

"Whoa, whoa, whoa! What the hell are you doing Zack!" I finally managed to squeak out, totally drenched by the shower and feeling outraged, angry, embarrassed, curious and, bloody hell; horny! My heart raced, the butterflies in my stomach stirred. Zack shook his head, droplets flying everywhere, and to me it looked like it happened in slow motion, like a bloody shower gel advert. Oh, shoot. I needed him. I wanted his lips all over me. My skin tingled all over. His body, *Christ*!

His voice called me back to reality.

"Listen carefully, we don't have long. Did they tell you about Alice?" he asked, talking fast. I shook my head. "Thought as much. She's missing, and I need your help to find her. Markus is taking too long. Are you up to it?" He grabbed my face and looked straight through me, deep inside my soul. A feeling of dread engulfed me. I needed air. Mum. What the hell happened to her? "Answer me, Eliza. Are you up to it? Are you in control of your senses?" he repeated urgently.

"Yes, yes. I'm coping. As much as I can be," I whispered back. He looked me over for a second, but seemed satisfied. "What...," but he put a finger on my mouth.

"I'll send you a note. Make sure you hide it. Quick, kiss me...," he muttered, before planting his lips firmly on mine and seconds before the door swung open. The kiss only lasted a few moments, but my heart was on fire, my skin tingled and all I could feel was Zack's tongue tasting mine and exploring my mouth. Mine darted into his mouth and we were enthralled in each other's taste. Every single sense I had stood on edge. The feeling was overwhelming. No words could describe it. Nothing else mattered. Well, until two seething faces glared at us. Vivian and Michael roughly hauled us out of the shower.

"Put your clothes on!" Michael barked at the

both of us, kicking Zack's arse towards his pile of discarded jeans and shirt. I could see through Vivian's eyes exactly what this looked like, and hoped we convinced them, that it was just that; out of control urges. Zack had been quite clever. Naughty, crazy, but clever.

"Unbelievable," Michael muttered whilst pacing up and down my room. "I just cannot get my head around you lot. There's always trouble everywhere you two go. What the hell were you thinking!"

I wasn't sure if I was meant to answer that, but tried anyway.

"I wasn't really thinking. He just turned up and I couldn't help myself, Sir. I'm so sorry," I laid it on thick, playing the innocent hapless teenager. "I mean, I only just got out...,"

"You can stop the excuses, Mankuzay. I don't want to hear them," he interrupted roughly. "You can write me an essay on inappropriate behaviour and its consequences. You don't get to see anyone else today, and you're to stay in your room. Just a little reminder of what life will be like in isolation, if you pull a stunt like that again. You're lucky that Zack was the main instigator, and you could be seen as the victim here, but I didn't sense a lot of resistance on your part." He sat down on my sofa, after he'd thrown a pen and paper on my desk, tutting and sighing.

Writing an essay I could do. Easily. Wrapping my head around what just happened? Less so. What happened to my mum? My stomach revolted, just thinking of the danger she might be in. How could I keep my distress covered? Why did Zack feel the need to burst into my room like that and tell me? Why had the Sensorians not done anything yet? They must have known for nearly a week now, since I had been out of isolation for that long already. Why had no one told me? I know I was emotionally fragile when I came out of isolation, but still. I had a right to know. She's my mum! I felt my anger rise, but I had to play it cool.

They suspected nothing. They didn't know I knew, and it had to stay that way, at least until I knew more. Until I had the note from Zack, if he ever managed to send it. I hope he wasn't punished too severely.

I didn't want to think about my feelings for Zack at the moment, the sexual attraction clearly still very much alive. To distract myself, I dived back into my essay, but my tummy started to rumble. However, I wasn't expecting any food until I'd finished this. A furtive look at Michael confirmed my suspicions. He looked grim, and not in the mood for any requests.

CHAPTER 15

Zack

Vivian marched me straight to Markus' office. She was furious with me. I'm not sure if it was because I had disregarded the rules in going to see Eliza, or whether it was that in her eyes I assaulted Eliza. I knew it probably looked like that on the CCTV. I think I was lucky that they saw, and must have felt and smelt, that Eliza was quite into me too, or else I'd be in deep shit. But it's better they thought that, than knowing the real reason I went to see her. Though the little voice inside me left me with no doubt that I'd absolutely loved the encounter. Which was a good thing; because that's the sentiment I wanted them to pick up. My sexual arousal, over my frustration and secrecy. I wasn't looking forward to the next few hours, though. It wasn't going to be pleasant.

Markus had just finished watching the footage and was listening to Vivian's account of what she and Michael had seen in the shower. His eyes went dark, and were closely observing me. I prepared myself and started to shield. I would need it.

"So, what do you have to say for yourself, Zack?" He paused, but before I had opened my mouth, he continued. "Actually, scrap that. There is nothing you can say that would explain this behaviour. You were frustrated and angry with me, so you decided to go and assault Eliza. Makes perfect sense," he sneered sarcastically. "Where did we fail in your upbringing, to make you think it's okay to barge into a girl's room and force her to undress? How do you expect us to deal with this Zack? Do I report you to the police? I'm sure Eliza will have your back and won't make a complaint, but is that right? Even if she did enjoy it, as I get the feeling she did by how entangled Vivian and Michael found you two, it does not excuse your actions," he yelled exasperated.

I bowed my head. I had nothing to say. Of course it was wrong, if that was what I'd intended to do. But it had been a cover for my real purpose;

to inform Eliza and start a plan to find Alice. I had to forget about that for a minute, and play the contrite perpetrator of a rather sordid assault.

"What am I going to tell Laura? You should be deeply ashamed of the pain and disappointment you're going to cause her," he sighed. "Speak of the devil, she's here. In fact you can tell her yourself. Take responsibility for your actions."

Laura just looked at me. Michael must have informed her already. She didn't need to say anything. She despised my actions, that much was clear. Her face expected something from me, repentance, regret anything. I needed to perform. I regretted something, the pain I was causing her, so I focussed on that, hoping the signals I emitted, would convince her. I didn't dare look up to her face.

"Laura, Ma'am, I'm so sorry. I..., I don't know what happened to me,"

"Look your mother in the eye, son," Markus bellowed. I quickly lifted my face but kept my eyes slightly downcast, not wanting to challenge her, or look cocky and defiant. *He didn't call me his son, or Laura my mother often. Shame it had to be in these circumstances.*

"It was unforgiveable and I need to ask for Eliza's forgiveness. I must have scared her when I burst into her room like that. I know what I did was wrong, trust me. I feel disgusted with myself."

"So you should, Zack. I know it's hard to have complete control over our urges, being a Sensorian, but that's exactly what you need to gain. You're twenty years old now. You're a man and must always be in control. You can never lose it like that again!" She took a deep breath. "What to do with you? I'm going to leave it to Markus. I can't look at you at the moment." She swooped out of the room, emotions running high, with a tear trickling down her cheek. I was such an arsehole.

"If I had my way, I would parade you naked through our compound and have everyone shout 'shame on you', like bloody *Cercei*," Markus growled. I couldn't help but smile inwardly at his

Game of Thrones reference, but I imagined he could and would do it, if that was allowed. He loved a bit of public shaming and humiliation as punishment. I shuddered and kept wiscly silent, not wanting to give him the push he needed to actually try and put it into effect. "I could really have done without this Zack. You're not a child anymore, and this is taking time away from getting to grips with our mission to find and free Alice. You can go into the isolation cell for the rest of the day, standing, facing the wall. You'll apologise to Eliza later, when I can be bothered, and have time to deal with you. Vivian, take him."

Fuck it. Should have expected that. I must make my apology count later, and somehow slip a note to Eliza. It was going to be fucking difficult, but I had to do it one way or another. I didn't want to waste any more time. I somehow needed to let Rick know the deal was going to be on, with or without Markus' backing.

Hours later, I was still stood there, facing the

wall. I had no idea of the time, but I hadn't eaten at all and my stomach was growling like a bear. I also needed a wee desperately, as I hadn't even done that, having jumped out my bed in a hurry to see Markus this morning. My legs ached, my back ached. Everything ached. How much fucking longer did I have to wait?

Quite a lot longer as it turned out. Vivian came to collect me at 7pm. She only scowled at me. Her anger towards me hadn't abated one bit.

"Right, you idiot. Time to show your repentance to Eliza," she barked, barely looking at me. I had never seen her this angry and upset before. She didn't resort to name calling, ever. I really had hit a raw nerve with her. Maybe she had some gruesome history with men.

"May I please use the bathroom before we go and see Eliza, and have a drink, Ma'am?" I asked tentatively, expecting a rebuke. But she nodded.

"We'll go past your room where you can freshen up," she agreed, slightly less harsh in tone.

That was better than I'd hoped for. I could possibly grab a piece of paper and write a note for Eliza. I would have to enlist help from someone who was allowed to see her. I would never be able to get my plan, if you could call it that, across on a scrappy note. I would ask Ned or Zaphire, though I knew I could get them in trouble again. What a fucking mess. Why didn't Markus just get a move on with it. It was almost like he'd lost his nerve. But I couldn't let it drag on any longer. Something had to be done. I would just have to take the fall for it again. Life seemed to have that in store for me forever, as if it was my destiny to go against the leadership.

I dashed into my bathroom. Thank fuck I had gone commando, only narrowly making it to the loo. *Hell. That felt good.* I glugged down a glass of water and stuffed some tissue in my trouser pocket, in case I couldn't find any paper. Damn, I couldn't see a pen anywhere.

"Ma'am, would I be allowed to formulate a proper apology on paper?" I thought I'd ask, but to no avail. She just looked at me scornfully.

"Let's go," she simply said.

CHAPTER 16

Eliza

Zack stood in front of mc looking very sheepish and a little dishevelled. His short hair a mess, and his face strained and tired looking. I heard his stomach growl loudly, and he was still wearing the black cargo trousers and white T-shirt from this morning. Knowing what was underneath those made me blush instantly. Of course he (and probably Vivian and Michael) picked up the vibe straight away when my eyes lingered just a little too long over his crotch. *Damn it girl. Get it together. Ugh.* His eyes lit up momentarily as he narrowed them, his jaw tensing. He was cloaking hard. Then he snapped back into his remorseful pose.

"I overstepped the mark this morning and I apologise. I beg for your forgiveness, Eliza and hope that I didn't scare you too much or push you into doing something you didn't want to do. If I did, please make a formal complaint, and I will bear the consequences. I deserve that," he said in barely more than a whisper. *Wow*. I was impressed. He'd managed to conjure up a remorseful scent and all the senses he put out dripped with repentance.

"I accept your apology, Zack. Though, it took me by surprise, and you really did cross a boundary. I was a little too keen to go along with it, so it would be harsh to completely blame you for the situation we ended up in," I offered.

"That's where you're wrong, Eliza. I'm completely to blame, whether you...," he paused a second or two, licking his lips, "...ended up enjoying it, does not excuse my behaviour. I truly am sorry. It should never have happened," he stated more firmly and with a steady voice. I looked at Michael, who gave a little nod.

"Thank you, Zack. I won't be making a formal complaint," I reassured him, I think to the regret of Vivian, whose face looked grim, and not in a forgiving mood at all. Michael seemed relieved.

"The leadership has decided that you're not to see each other again for the foreseeable future, unless under strict supervision of either myself or Vivian. I'm sure you understand."

Both Zack and I nodded our heads and mumbled 'Yes Sir', and Zack offered me his hand.

"Thank you for being so understanding, Eliza," he said whilst he pressed a piece of tissue paper into my hand. His eyes bored into mine, just that second longer than necessary. My heart started to beat a little faster. I felt the shape of the tissue; it wasn't just crumpled up. It was the distinct shape of the letter 'V'. I knew what I had to do instantly. Vision Hack his eyes. I jumped in them immediately, as I'd learned to do so proficiently over the last couple of months. I had a strong connection, but so far I'd only been able to stretch it for a couple of minutes, if I were lucky. I needed to concentrate hard. I couldn't use my own eyes to see. As soon as I did that, I would lose the vision. I felt my way to the table and managed to sit down, a little awkwardly on the corner of a chair. I put my head in my hands, and tried to look unapproachable. Zack hurried back to his room, I could see they were walking fast. Vivian was talking to him, face stern. I think she gave him an order of some sort. I don't know if Zack answered, but I could see a short nod. In his room, he searched for something, opening a desk draw and rummaging through it. He got a pen. I knew what he wanted to do, I had to stay with him, block everything else out. *See Zaph 2pm tom...* I lost the connection. *Damn it.* But I understood. I somehow had to arrange to see Zaphy tomorrow afternoon. Hopefully he could get a message to her.

I had to be patient. Difficult under the circumstances, but as Michael hadn't been forthcoming with any information about my mum, it was the only way forward at the moment. I didn't want to let on that I knew anything, just in case Zack managed to magic a plan to help or find my mum. Luckily, in isolation, patience was a skill I had honed to perfection.

"Are you okay?"

I vaguely became aware of Michael's concern,

as he repeated his question again.

"Yes, Sir. Thank you," I hesitated for a moment, but I really wanted to confront Michael once again, to see if I could get any information out of him. "What's going on, Sir. Why do you need me? It's been nearly a week and I'm still in the dark as to what's happening. I think I deserve to know a bit more now, don't I? I've proven that I know my limits. I have demonstrated that I have strategies in place to prevent a sensory overload from happening. I'm ready for action."

Michael took a long deep breath in and out. That didn't sound promising, as expected.

"So you keep saying. I'll decide when you're ready *(I heard that before. Zack used to inflict this on me all the time)* and besides that, there is nothing for you to do at the moment. We are not ready to have the mission live yet, and it may never happen, so you don't need to know anything yet. Just concentrate on acclimatising. Tomorrow, you'll need to mingle more. We'll see how it goes."

He did not look in the mood to discuss it any

further. I couldn't believe they kept the fact that my mum was missing from me. My body started to tremble slightly, my head pounding. The familiar feeling of anger rose. I needed to visualise the sea and the waves. I didn't want to jeopardise any freedom I was going to be given tomorrow, by having an argument or by giving off the wrong signals.

CHAPTER 17
Zack

I didn't argue with Vivian's order to stay in my room until the next morning 8am, with no access to food. I needed to get that note written, and didn't want to waste any time protesting my fate. Annoyingly, I had no way of knowing whether Eli got my message or not. I hoped she'd understood my sign, and that she'd mastered her VH skills well enough to have lasted the three or four minutes or so that it took for me to get back to my room, and write that note.

I paid the price for it now, though. I hadn't eaten anything all day and no amount of drinking water or milk got rid of my hunger pangs. This was ridiculous. I think I was fourteen when I last got sent to bed without food. That time over some backchat to Laura. *'If you behave like an out-of-control child, you get treated like one'* were Vivian's parting words when she left my room earlier, still fuming.

.127

"For fuck's sake. What a bitch," I muttered on opening the cupboard door where I kept my stash of snacks and cereal. Vivian had fucking cleared them out. -'*Language!*'- A text admonished me. She clearly felt I wasn't punished enough. I still asked permission to have Phaedra over, but unsurprisingly that was denied. I didn't even know why the fuck I asked.

Word had got out about the incident, as was clear from the fuming texts I received from Zaphire. Actually from all the girls, even ones I barely knew. And very telling, no words of support from Brody and Ned. They must think I'm such a dick. Phae phoned, and even the usually quite laid back woman gave me an earful and was understandably upset. She knew about my feelings for Eliza, but she didn't understand the idiotic actions I had undertaken. I tried to explain the situation as best I could, without revealing the real reason I'd 'assaulted' Eliza, but that proved impossible. I mean, what could I fucking say, really.

Annoyingly, everyone accepted a bit too easily that I'd done this. That didn't sit well with me, but there was nothing I could do about it right now. Fuck it. I just had to ride this one out, until I could explain it properly. That, and my growling stomach made for a shitty night's sleep.

***

I woke up feeling a little groggy and headachy. It was 7.30am. Half an hour to go till I could go and get some breakfast. I decided to take a shower to kill the time and keep my mind off food. It wasn't very successful. I could almost see the eggs and bacon sitting on a plate. I needed something to eat. Now. I strode back into my room, flung my towel onto the radiator and reached for a pair of boxers in the drawer. I didn't care about the camera much; almost everyone had seen me in the buff anyway. Then a familiar scent hit me. Frank. I turned around and he stood right by the wall, a CCTV dead spot, a slight smirk on his face thanks to my bare arse. He put a finger to his lips and pointed to the TV, gesturing for me to switch it on. How bizarre. But I followed his instructions, whilst hastily putting my boxers on. Frank was nervous. Very unlike him, but his sensory output gave him away. He couldn't cloak the little tremor in his fingers, his eyes flitting ever so slightly from left to right, scanning the area and the distinct odour of stress started penetrating my nose. What the fuck was going on?

Frank put something on the floor, which looked like it could be some sort of jammer. As soon as he activated it, he started talking.

"Sit and watch TV; don't look at me," he ordered and I complied immediately, my hunger temporarily forgotten. "What did you tell Eliza when you went to see her yesterday?" he asked. I felt his eyes burning into the back of my head.

"Nothing, Sir," I turned my head slightly to avoid the CCTV picking up my mouth moving. "I just wanted her and...,"

"Don't give me that bullshit," he interrupted harshly. "I don't know why everyone thinks you're stupid enough to let your impulses rule you like that. You haven't fooled me. You went in there for a reason, and it was nothing to do with sex." Frank was adamant. "You can speak freely. I have interfered with the signal and rerouted it to only pick up the sound of your TV."

"How do I know I can trust you? This could be a trap," I whispered, barely audible. Frank got his phone out and tapped in a message. We waited in silence.

"I have ordered Zaphire to go to Vivian and report to me exactly what you're up to, and what she can hear. Wait for my signal and then talk to me," he paused, holding his finger up, waiting for the reply. "Now."

"What the fuck is this about, Frank? Does Markus know you're here?" I asked, still facing slightly away from the CCTV, but still making it look like I was watching the news. Frank received another message and showed it to me. I had to focus into it, but it read -*'Zack watching TV, can hear the TV'*- Then another message -*'why?'*- Typical Zaphy. Frank put his phone away, leaving her in the dark as to what his motivations were.

"No, Markus doesn't know. He's too busy figuring out what Rick is up to, and dealing with all the mess created by all the people connected to Rick. We still have cells full of them. What are you planning, Zack. Tell me. Now," he insisted. I kept silent, not wanting to get into trouble by admitting I'd gone behind the leadership's back again. Frank noticed my hesitation and added; "I might be able to help. I think we should take action and not wait any longer. We should approach Rick and arrange a meeting." My eyes shot up at him, but he quickly motioned for me to stare back at the TV again. I decided to fess up.

"I told Eliza her mum was missing. I needed to see what state she was in, and whether she was up for action if I needed her to be. I haven't quite formulated a plan, as it's damned hard with these fucking devices Eliza and I are wearing, but I'll think of something. I can't sit and wait any longer. Markus has dithered for too long." It felt good telling someone I didn't go to see Eliza out of frustration with Markus and to satisfy my urges. Frank nodded.

"I thought as much and I happen to agree, but Markus won't listen at the moment. I'm still not even sure if he wants to risk any more Sensorian lives to help Alice. Michael and Vivian are too busy making sure you two stay on the straight and narrow, they won't challenge him. Laura won't go against Markus, and my voice alone isn't being heard. I think it's dangerous waiting any longer. Even if it's some ploy that Rick has fabricated, we would find out and just deal with it."

"So, what are you saying? Do you want me to work with you?" I questioned, finding it quite hard to believe, but all his sensory output seemed genuine.

"Yes, that's exactly what I want to do. I need a small team, beside you and Eliza. We need an IT expert and a couple of bodies, so it'll probably be

Archie, Sam, Ned, Brodie and Tristan."

"What, no Zaphire?" I asked a little shocked. "She'll hate that, when she finds out."

"I'm not sure she's emotionally up to working with Eliza. We can't have volatile behaviour."

"It could be a risk, not to involve her. Look what happened last time. She's stubborn enough to go out on her own again," I warned. "It might be better to have her in our team, where we can monitor her."

"You might be right. She might do more damage trying to uncover what we're working on than if she's actually involved. I hadn't thought of it that way. What have you arranged so far with Eliza, in the shower?" he added, giving me a little wink. I didn't rise to the innuendo.

"Not much. When I apologised to her yesterday, I tried to give her a message to see Zaphire today at 2pm. I was going to get Zaphy to give her a letter. I don't know if Eli got the message as I had to give it to her using her VH. Not sure how successful it was."

"Get that letter to Zaphire. I'll make sure Eliza gets to see Zaphire today. You go and get something to eat. Your stomach is shouting out for food," Frank grabbed his jammer, slipped it in his pocket, but didn't move. "I got in here this morning as I got Sam to distract Vivian for a moment, to get past the CCTV on the door. I need to arrange another 'disturbance' and wait for the all clear. You just go ahead."

I nodded subtly and I threw on the rest of my clothes to head to the canteen. I was warned to abort if Eliza happened to be there as I wasn't allowed to go near her. Vivian obviously kept a close eye on me. I hoped I hadn't raised her suspicions.

CHAPTER 18
Eliza

A little knock preceded Laura entering my
room. I just about stopped myself from jumping up
into position, like I had done every morning when
Michael had entered my cell. It's funny how these
things get ingrained. I stood up anyway out of
respect for Laura, but she motioned for me to sit
back down, as she pulled up a chair.

"I'm here to apologise once more for Zack's
behaviour, yesterday." I started saying something,
but her eyes forced me to keep my mouth shut.
"Let me finish Eliza. I know you feel you're partly
to blame, as you think you weren't forceful enough
to stop him. You may even feel you'd wanted it to
happen, but it still doesn't excuse his behaviour. It
was wrong on so many levels. I feel embarrassed. I
clearly haven't taught him well enough about
respecting women's boundaries. He used his
authority, his charm, his knowledge of your
attraction to him to get what he wanted. It's wrong,

and I shall have words with him and warn him that if that was ever to occur again, even if no one puts in a complaint, he will not be welcome in our family again. And that would be final."

I believed her. Her face was grim and determined, but also full of pain for the implications that decision would have. It also showed compassion for me. I didn't deserve that. After the initial shock of Zack's rude entrance, all I wanted was for it to carry on. Instead, Zack wasn't there for that at all. He just wanted to deliver a message. He didn't deserve Laura's wrath, but then, I couldn't say anything. That would probably just make things worse. Poor Zack would just have to sit through another painful lecture.

"You look like you are quite in control of your senses today," she stated. Her manner had changed from super intense to quite light-hearted and I let out a little sigh, releasing some of the tension I felt. "I'll put in a word with Michael to give you some freedom today to explore and socialise," she added kindly. As she looked to be in a compassionate mood, I thought I'd try my luck and test the waters with a request. See what she'd say, when confronted. I put my biggest puppy eyes on for this one.

"Would I be able to see my mum soon? I really miss her, and she'll be dying to see me too." I observed Laura closely. She fidgeted the tiniest amount, her eyes moved slightly to the side and up, all within a fraction of a second, but a clear tell. She took her time and I knew she was going to spin the truth.

"We'll organise it soon. Just give yourself a little more time to adjust. You should be ready soon, but leave it to Michael to decide. Don't nag him about it, he'll just make you wait longer," she answered eventually, knowing she'd given herself away. I could tell she picked up my vibes showing I knew she had bent the truth, but she decided to ignore it, smile and leave me to it.

Laura had kept her word as despite Michael still being annoyed at me and my role in yesterday's shenanigans, he still gave me some free time at lunch to see my friends, bar Zack of course. I felt super excited walking through our new compound without a minder. I tried to forget about my anklet tracker, and pretended I was free. My stomach somersaulted a little and I had the urge to do something crazy. I burst out into a run and skipped like a child. For the first time in ages I felt like I could breathe freely and almost felt carefree. It was brief. An image of my mum, captured, hurt and bound, sprung into my consciousness. I gasped. I knew it wasn't real, it was my imagination running riot, but it brought my mood down like a sinking stone.

"Hey, crazy girl. What's with the glum face?" Brody interrupted my downward spiral. They would have all been made to vow not to speak to me about my mum's predicament, but I could still use her as my excuse for my miserable mood.

"Michael still won't let me contact my mum," I complained sulkily, immediately noticing Brody tense up slightly.

"Let's get some lunch. All of us will be there. Well, apart from Zack." He looked at me sideways, testing the waters. He looked angry and I decided I had to do something about Zack's public lynching. His friends should know the truth.

My heart skipped a beat and my stomach dropped at the same time. Zaphire. She sat at the table cuddling one of her legs, looking slightly reluctant. But she was there. She shot me a look, but gazed into the distance almost immediately. But she didn't leave.

I still loved her, desired her. My whole being wanted to run to her and sink into her arms. I longed for her fingers to trace my lips and eyes as she used to enjoy doing so much. My body gave an involuntary shiver. I missed her. We had enjoyed so little time together. Very intense, but there was still so much more to explore and find out about each other. If only she would give me another chance.

"Hey," I said weakly. She nodded. At least she acknowledged me. She wasn't going to like what I had to say about Zack. My defending his actions will just rub salt in the wounds. But I had to. I couldn't let his buddies, nor his sister believe he assaulted me. I had to say something. Ned and Sam high-fived me.

"They let you out!" Sam squealed enthusiastically, earning a derisive glance from Zaphy, which she promptly ignored. "I'll grab you some food, sweetie! Sit, sit," she carried on, pulling a chair out right next to her. And next to Zaph. My legs felt like jelly as I shuffled over and slid into the chair. Sam shoved a ham and cheese toastie in front of me in quick time.

"Just gonna grab some juice," I mumbled, postponing the inevitable grilling. They were all dying to hear what exactly happened with Zack. I sauntered back to my seat with my bumble berry juice, grabbed a piece of paper from my bag, and started writing, motioning them to keep casual conversation going.

Don't react to what I'm writing. Zack came into my room to tell me my mother is missing. He *checked me over to see if I was ready for action. He didn't assault me, it was a ruse. It took me by surprise, but I wasn't hurt or violated against my will. You can't tell <u>anyone</u> that I know about my mum! Pretend to still be cross with Zack.*

The others were brilliant. Apart from a slight rise in heartbeats, they managed to cloak pretty well, keeping the conversation going about some TV programme they'd all been watching. For Michael's sake I signalled to Sam to ask me about Zack. It would be very suspicious if no one mentioned anything. Sam happily obliged.

"Spill the beans about Zack. What the hell possessed him to barge into your room like that?" she asked quasi indignant. I let out an exaggerated sigh.

"I don't know what made him do that, but it wasn't as bad as all that...,"

"What. He didn't rip your clothes off and push you into the shower?" Zaphire cut in sharply.

"Well, he sort of did that," I paused to think how to play it, Zaphy's eyes boring into mine. "But,

I didn't complain too much," I winked at them, a little smile playing around my mouth. Zaphire's mood took a dive, as expected. Eyes rolling, she jumped off her seat and left.

"I've heard enough," she muttered. This wasn't the reunion I'd hoped for.

"Still, he shouldn't have done it. He must have been in a bad mood, cross with Markus or Vivian or something. It's just out of order," Brody added, keeping the pretence going.

"Well, we're all a bit out of sorts with Daniel's d...," Sam stopped mid-word, slapping her hand in front of her mouth, eyes wide open. The others drew in sharp breaths. The ambience went dark and, the stench of stress penetrated my nose instantly. My phone started ringing.

"What about Daniel?" I urged, ignoring my phone.

"I, uhm, I can't...," Sam stuttered.

"Pick up your phone, Eliza," Ned ordered, as it kept on ringing and ringing. I begrudgingly answered.

"Come back, now." Michael's voice sounded stern, not to be messed with. I got up and obeyed immediately. More secrets that were kept from me. I needed to know what had happened to Daniel. By the looks on my friend's faces, it didn't spell any good.

"What happened to Daniel?" I confronted Michael when I walked into his office. "And please don't try and fob me off, Sir. I need to know," I pleaded.

"Sit down, Eliza," he said not unkindly. I obliged. "Remember I told you we had to move compounds, because Daniel exposed us in the press?" Yes I did remember that. How could I not? The news had devastated me. I couldn't understand why Daniel had betrayed our kind. "Something happened when Zack and Brody were on a mission to persuade Daniel to stop spreading the word about us. Jean-Pierre and Rick tracked them, intercepted them, and got rid of Daniel,"

"Got rid off? As in, killed?" I gasped,

suddenly struggling to breathe.

"I'm afraid so," Michael confirmed.

My heart sank. Darkness filled my being. My heart burst. Tears forced themselves out of my eyes, the floodgates were opened. I sobbed, uncontrollably.

CHAPTER 19

Zaphire

I felt betrayed once more by Eliza. She had seemed to enjoy my brother's attentions rather too much. Why did I care so much? I grumpily kicked the door open of my room and sank into the sofa. I had another half hour before I had to report to Markus for my next, probably super boring, task. Life had hardly been exhilarating but it should be. Alice is missing; everyone is intel gathering about Rick's story. And me? I was stuck here, dealing with some of the prisoners' paperwork. We were slowly getting through them. The threat of long term isolation was enough for most prisoners to agree to our terms. They had to give us full access to their homes and technology to install spyware. Their right of privacy had to be waived and they had to fully submit to us, in the hope that controlling and monitoring their actions would prevent them from organising another rebellion. It wasn't foolproof, but we couldn't just keep them here. The fate of Lois was still in the balance. She'd been invited to Rick's meeting by Angelique, and had intended to go, without the leadership's knowledge. Markus wanted her exccuted, to serve as an example and make our community's three rules credible. Not everyone was in favour.

Ping. My phone disturbed my musings. It was Zack. My dickhead of a brother.

-'*Come to my room asap'*- The cheek of him. Who did he think he was?

-'*Fuck off'*- I typed back. I wasn't in the mood for him today.

-'*Now'*- What the hell. I threw my phone on the table, trying to ignore it. It kept pinging.

-'*Don't ignore me'*-

-'*I'm your brother and your superior. Come. Now.'*-

-'*Don't fucking ignore me sis'*-

-'*get your arse over to my room. NOW'*-

Brother? Superior? He was technically correct as, though he lost his status as mission trainer and coach, I was classed as merely a trainee at the moment. But what century was he living in to expect me to obey him because he's my brother! How I would have loved to have just carried on ignoring him. I really wanted to, but I'd have to see him at some point and I couldn't bear the thought of dealing with his anger. I caved in.

-'*on way dickhead*'-

"What do you want?" I grumpily stood by his door, barely in the room. He paced up and down, pounding the floor.

"Lose the fucking attitude," he growled, staring me down. "I don't need this from you."

"Well, what do you expect?" I challenged. I wasn't in a forgiving or amenable mood. "Aren't you meant to be more in control of your anger?" I taunted.

"I expect some respect as your brother, and maybe even some support!" His voice cracked slightly. I hadn't foreseen that. He was actually getting a little emotional. My resolve to be angry with him softened slightly.

"Oh, Zack. How do you get yourself into these stupid situations all the time?" I asked, but was looking for a piece of paper. Zack noticed and stood by the table, blocking the CCTV, looking at the drawer. I moved over and grabbed a pen and paper.

"I don't know, Zaphy. I just..." he exhaled deeply and just shook his head.

I positioned myself behind Zack so the CCTV couldn't pick me up, and wrote a quick note to tell Zack I knew he'd told Eliza about her mum. His head snapped up on reading it, surprise shone in his eyes. He clearly hadn't expected that. His eyes betrayed confusion too. I knew he was trying to work out my mood. My vibes had been properly narky, though a little less so now. *Ugh.* Zack's anklet was so bloody annoying. We couldn't have a real conversation. And my signals weren't very clear, mixed up with jealousy about Eli's and Zack's encounter, and bitterness about feeling constantly betrayed by the both of them. I knew it hadn't been real, but still, I suspected there was more to it. I knew they had feelings for each other, whatever they said. But worst of all, why was I that bothered? I didn't want a relationship with her anymore. Or did I? I needed to see Eliza and I wanted to turn around and find her now, but I narrowly remembered Zack had actually summoned me.

"So, what was so urgent? Why did I need to see you?" I said a little less hostile.

"I need you to help me check these files. Frank gave me this job and he said I should ask you to help so we get it done as quickly as possible," he clearly lied. Thank God the equipment didn't pick up vibes and scents! I noticed there was some sort of letter on top.

"What am I looking for in the files?" I played along.

"Oh, it's all explained in the note on top. Could you do them straight away. Frank wants them asap." His phone pinged. "Fuck, its Vivian. Sorry, Ma'am," he added quickly before she texted again, pointing out his bad language. "She says you can't stay in my room, any longer. She's still punishing me," he sighed.

"Okay, I'll go through them and get them back to you when I'm done," I offered, my curiosity to see what Zack had written taking over. I wanted to get away from the forever watching eyes and listening ears as soon as possible. I don't know how Zack coped with being under continuous surveillance. It would kill me. I got out of his room like a shot, leaving Zack to his lone misery. I practically ran into my room, my desire to see Eliza temporarily forgotten, and read Zack's note. My heart started racing, excitement levels shooting up. Bloody hell, it looked like they were planning on going behind Markus' back. With Frank involved it might actually have a chance to succeed! I sure as hell hoped so. I had to give the note to Eliza, explaining who was involved; Frank, Zack, Archie, Sam, Ned, Brody, and me, and what the first steps were going to be. Not an awful lot, but the intent was to go and arrange a meet with Rick and start the ball rolling on getting access to

Alice.

Eliza was meant to meet me around 2 pm, so I had to text an excuse to Markus' telling him I'd be a bit late. I would tell him I was in the middle of a file, and would come as soon as I'd finished it. I often took files to my room, so it wouldn't raise any suspicions. It shifted my focus back to Eliza. We desperately needed to talk. By the way she looked at me in the canteen, she would be more than willing to do so. I knew she still hoped for a way to work things out. A little itch inside me told me I was starting to feel that way too. My heart wanted to. I knew that much.

CHAPTER 20

Eliza

Michael had let me rejoin my friends, after I'd calmed down a bit. It felt good being able to sit, chat and eat with them. It distracted me from the low mood that had set upon me, ever since Michael told me about Daniel's fate. His death had affected me badly. I couldn't believe he was shot in cold blood. My hatred for Jean-Pierre boiled inside me, and for my father, who should have stopped it. It made me feel physically sick.

My friends tried to keep things light, knowing I'd just been told about Daniel. They also all knew about the anklet, so they did their best to stay away from controversial topics, instead focussing on teasing Brody about his crush on Eve. They'd been out on a couple of dates, and Brody was falling for her fast and deep. She was a year younger and they'd met at the gym, as Eve also was well into boxing. I'd only seen her a few times, but I remember her strong physique, with long dark blonde hair, worn in a high ponytail every time.

"Have you met her in the ring, yet?" I asked

"She'd have him. He can't concentrate on anything when she's around!" Sam jibed.

"I'm not letting that happen. I don't want to mess up her pretty face," he snapped back under a chorus of jeers.

"He's scared!" Ned carried on. Brody's face turned rather red. Not sure whether it was annoyance or embarrassment.

"Shut up! She's just there!" he hissed, nodding his head towards the entrance of the canteen, where, indeed, Eve strolled in, clearly looking to find Brody.

My phone pinged. I groaned. Michael had summoned me, again. It was 13:45pm. I needed to try and see Zaphire. I hoped Michael didn't have plans for me, so I could wangle a visit to her room. I wondered how she would react. She didn't seem that enamoured to see me in the canteen, and had left in a huff. I wanted to see what happened with

Brody and Eve but I reluctantly said my goodbyes and hurried over to Michael's office.

I was about to knock to go in, but I picked up Frank's scent and hesitated. I didn't want to barge in. Michael could react a little terse sometimes and I didn't want to put him in a bad mood, scuppering my chances to see Zaphire. He called me in though, probably having sensed me outside his door. I kept forgetting how little you get away with around Sensorians, nothing much is secret unless you really put an effort in with cloaking. I still often forgot to cloak or shield, not having grown up in the Sensorian community.

"Hi, Eliza. Nice to see you again. How are you?" Frank greeted.

"I'm fine, thank you," I answered politely. There was an odd scent in the air, which I couldn't quite put my finger on. Frank shuffled a little awkwardly.

"Did you need me to do something, Sir? Your text message?" I reminded Michael as to why I was actually in his office.

"Ah, yes. Well, that'll have to wait for a bit. Frank wanted to do a test with you. I think it's a bit soon, but he seems to think the sooner the better," Michael started, but then Frank took over.

"We're all aware of your, uhm, precarious relationship with Zaphire. I think it's important to get to the bottom of it, so we can resume normal working relations without awkwardness. That would prevent mistakes by people who are being ruled by their feelings, and perhaps could make the wrong decisions because of it." Frank drew a breath, of which Michael took advantage and butted in.

"I didn't think it was that necessary, as the likelihood of you working with Zaphire on this mission is slim, taking into account Zaphire is only a trainee at the moment, and therefore very unlikely to participate." I felt his tense vibes radiate off him. He didn't agree with Frank at all. "Also, I think you've had a difficult day, so I was a little worried it might all be too much."

"However, I've managed to persuade Michael of its importance, and if anything, it will help you focus on the task in hand, rather than any emotional problems. We, as Sensorians, work much better with issues resolved, which Michael knows, and has therefore agreed," Frank concluded.

I surreptitiously checked my phone for the time. This wasn't helping me get to Zaphire as per Zack's request, but I couldn't do much about it.

"Have you got anywhere else to be?" Michael remarked sharply, hinting at my checking the time.

"No, sorry. What do you want me to do Frank? I mean, Sir?" I hastily answered.

"To come with me. I've set up a meeting with Zaphire."

Ah. Damn. How could Zaphire give me a message under Frank's prying eyes? This was going to be even more tricky than it already was. But at least I got to see her.

"Er..., okay. But what am I to say to her?" This was going to be so awkward, and I wasn't sure how receptive Zaphy would be with this intervention. But Frank looked determined and optimistic.

"We'll solve this like adults. By talking it over."

"What, with you there?" I couldn't manage to hide my horror. I couldn't think of anything worse than talking to Zaphire about our feelings, with Frank physically in the room. That was never going to work, surely. Frank tried to suppress a smile, not very successfully, seemingly enjoying my discomfort about the idea a little too much.

"Yes, Miss Mankuzay. With me there. Let's go now. I've let Zaphire know we're on our way."

"Yes Sir," I mumbled, trundling behind him whilst he swooped out of Michael's office.

Zaphire opened her door less reluctantly than I expected. Her face was a bit of an enigma. In fact, did I spot a little excitement in the twinkle of her eye? Why would she be eager to have this conversation in Frank's presence, or even have the conversation at all? I didn't get the impression she was that keen to make up with me earlier today. I hoped she would find an opportunity to give me Zack's note. But to my horror she produced a letter, right in front of Frank and shoved it in my hand. Sweat broke out all over my body. *What the hell was she doing!* She mouthed and signalled for me to read it, but pointed at my anklet to remind me to be quiet.

Relief washed over me as I read, I understood now. Frank was part of it all too! My senses went into overdrive. Did this mean we were actually going to attempt to rescue my mum, without Markus' knowledge? With Frank's involvement it would all be far more feasible. I wanted to ask a hundred questions, but the anklet prevented me from uttering a word. At least there were no cameras in here, because my face would give everything away!

"Let's sit down," Frank started. We still had to go ahead with this talk, knowing Michael would be listening in to see how it went. Both Zaphire and I hesitated, not quite knowing where to position ourselves. Frank exhaled loudly, frowning.

"You here, and you there, Zaphire. Face each other. I'm going to be the referee. To make sure both of you will get your say. Make a start Eliza."

I took a big breath in, to steady myself and decided to just tell the truth. How I felt and what I wanted. Now, was as good a time as any. If anything, I could try and move on, if it all went tits up for me.

CHAPTER 21

Zack

I couldn't really concentrate on the task that Vivian had given me. Minutes earlier Laura had stopped by, and given me another earful. She even threatened me with expulsion from the family, if I ever behaved disrespectfully towards a woman again.

"Take a good long hard look at yourself and your behaviour, son. Right now, I can't stand the sight of you," she reiterated. My 'assault' on Eliza really had pissed her off. All I could do was accept her wrath, and look remorseful. I think I pulled it off. Eventually she left with a big sigh, slamming the door behind her.

I hoped Frank or Zaphire could give me some sort of message soon to say I should get in contact with Rick. I'd given Frank the burner phone number, but it would be hard to use, as I still had to show Vivian any incoming and outgoing texts. If I did receive a text on that phone, I'd have to make up some fake messages and delete the real ones. That way there was something to show, if they spotted me using it.

"Stop staring into space, Zack. You've got work to do," a stern voice sounded. Vivian took her task as my handler very seriously, and she didn't give me a chance to forget I wasn't a free man, constantly being on my fucking case.

"Yes Ma'am," I grumbled, trying to make sense of what I was actually meant to do with the papers in front of me and the files on screen. Fuck it. This work did not come naturally to me. Some people absolutely loved the paper detective work; delving into people's lives to work out their weaknesses and flaws. Figuring out how they could be used or manipulated in our fights against injustice. It was obviously totally against the law, but it worked and I didn't care less that we infringed on those people's right to privacy. We knew that they were a danger or guilty of horrendous crimes. We just needed to prove it, and we never shied away from slightly dodgy practices.

In this case, however, it was case files on the supporters of Rick. My job was to find ways to persuade them to never participate in such organisations again. We also needed to prevent them from revealing the truth about the Sensorians. We needed dirt on them. It was morally tricky to justify, as being a supporter of Rick was not a criminal offence. Manipulating them was purely for our own benefit, protecting our way of life and safety, not general society. But it was our most important task; protecting our Sensorian Community. Our number one rule.

In an ideal world it would be amazing to be able to live as free people, being respected for what we can do. But we all know reality wouldn't reflect that ideal. There will always be sections of the population that will fear us, or want to make use of us. Our secrecy is paramount to our happiness and survival. Rick's claims of supremacy won't have helped our case at all, making people feel fearful of us. If there was ever to be a future of us being able to live a free life, it certainly will have been put back quite some years by his assertions.

"Mr Mackenzie! Work!" Vivian's sharp voice penetrated my ears rather painfully. I shook my head a little to rid myself from the ringing, and focussed on the screen in front of me.

Finally, at about 5:30 Vivian gave me a break. On the way to my room, I texted Zaph. I asked if she was free, and wanted to meet up. I thought it would be wise not to annoy her with a straight out order. I hopped into the loo before she came over and almost immediately my burner phone pinged. I fished it out of my pocket, expecting another plea from Rick to make arrangements, but it was Frank. He must have monitored me, waiting for me to step into the bathroom, the only place without CCTV.

-*'Try and contact Rick asap and arrange a meet. Keep me updated'*-

Excellent. It must mean he has some sort of plan to actually get to this meet, without Markus' or the rest of the leadership team's knowledge. I quickly deleted the messages after sending a thumbs up emoji.

I sensed Zaphire was near. Her distinctive scent gave her approach away, and true to my feeling, a knock on my door sounded. As usual, the door opened without waiting for me to answer. Zaphire rushed in and plonked herself down on my sofa. She looked excited, far more animated and full of life than the few times I'd seen her since I was out.

"Zaph, who's the lucky girl or guy?" I teased, being rewarded with a scowl, but then a little cheeky grin broke through too.

"Wouldn't you like to know?" She patted next to her, indicating for me to sit down. "Eliza and I had a good talk, thanks to Frank. I dunno. It felt nice. I don't think I can ever fully trust her again, but I felt so happy being with her," she confided shrugging her shoulders.

"Yes, she does tend to have that effect on me too," I said without thinking, instantly wishing I could swallow back the words. I ignored her dark look and painful spikes of jealousy, and changed the subject.

"Heard anything from Markus about Alice?" I asked, having to keep the deception going, as if we were waiting for a decision from the leadership. Zaphire shifted a little, lent forward a touch and pushed a note in my hand.

"No nothing," she sighed. "The information he's given us is very difficult to verify. I don't think Markus is going to take action, unless Rick can give us anything more concrete to work with."

"Hmm, I don't think Rick can give anything else unless we agree to a meet. This is going fucking nowhere," I laid on my frustration thick.

"Sam sort of let slip about Daniel this morning. Eliza was hauled back to Michael's office and apparently looked distraught when she returned later. He must have told her," Zaphy said changing the subject. I shuddered and bile rose to my throat, thinking back to the moment we heard the shot, and then the realisation of what happened. The callousness of Jean-Pierre was extremely worrying. I worried for Eliza's emotional stability as well. I'd rather we could have hidden Daniel's death from her till after the mission.

"Fuck. This whole thing is so messed up," I sighed.

I wanted to read Zaphy's note, but was reluctant to go to the bathroom so soon after my last visit. Didn't want to raise suspicions, or them thinking I had the shits! I just had to wait a bit longer. Instead we just chatted and watched some *Brooklyn 99*, until the inevitable ping on my phone informed me that Vivian wanted me to do my exercise before dinner. *Whatever*. It gave me a chance to use the bathroom to get changed and check the note. It just confirmed what I'd already guessed. Frank had agreed to let Zaphire be part of the mission. He must have deemed Zaphire and Eliza's relationship situation to be stable enough to have them work with each other. I also sent Rick a request to set up a meet as soon as he made contact with Alice's captors, and to let them know Eliza was in. All we could do now, was wait.

After the gym, I invited Phaedra over for dinner. We needed to talk. I thought Zaphire had told her what the deal was with my attack on Eliza, as Phae agreed to come instantly. I hoped it didn't raise any eyebrows, as I didn't need more scrutiny. I didn't want anyone to question the assault, but if all my friends forgave me this quickly, especially the girls, it would look suspicious and questions might be asked. Frank worked it out pretty quickly, so it wouldn't take much for others to start asking questions. I used Rick's phone to ask her to be careful, and to pretend to be angry with me.

-*'I won't have to pretend too much'*-

Ah, okay. Maybe she wasn't going to be as forgiving as I'd hoped!

CHAPTER 22

Eliza

Zaphy had rushed off to see Zack, leaving me with Frank. I was exhausted and drained, but I could see Frank still had further questions. It had taken us all afternoon to come to some sort of agreement between Zaphy and me. I had made it clear that I wanted to build up our relationship, that I saw a future for us. I told her I still loved and craved her and that I missed her terribly. I laid all my feelings out in the open. I was scared she was going to trample all over them, but it turned out I didn't need to fear. She struggled. She was still feeling hurt and angry, and blamed me fully for the breakdown of our relationship. I apologised and told her I understood her feelings, but that I hadn't intended to hurt her. I'd believed that keeping her out of the loop would protect her. She still couldn't see it that way. I didn't know what else to say. She admitted she still had feelings for me too, but that she needed time, and that she didn't know if she could ever get over my, in her eyes, betrayal. We decided to take things slowly, and see how it would work out. To find out if there was a chance we could be together again. Her signals were confused and tinged with a dark aura. I wasn't holding out much hope.

Frank was mostly interested in whether we thought we could work together professionally. I immediately confirmed I could, but Zaphire needed assurances that I wouldn't be able to do anything behind her back ever again. I promised that I wouldn't. Frank reminded Zaphy that I was not a free woman, and all of my actions were going to be monitored, if not by Michael then by himself. Zaphire seemed to accept that. And that's how it was left. A feeling of impending doom washed over me as she left. I shook off a shiver and swallowed hard, trying to keep it together. I tried to focus on the positive. She hadn't rejected me completely. Zaphy had seemed quite relieved and happy when she left.

"How do you feel that went?" Frank asked,

looking me over carefully.

"Could've gone worse?" I offered, slightly cautious.

"Did you get any vibes of cloaking or was she being truthful?"

"No, I think she was open. I could feel her reticence of working with me. I know she doesn't fully trust me."

"Are you?" he enquired, his face as serious as it gets.

"Am I what?" I asked, staring Frank straight back in the eyes. "Am I to be trusted?"

"Yes. Answer me; can we trust you?"

"Yes, Sir." I didn't flinch. I didn't blink, or look away. I didn't cloak. I desperately needed him to believe me.

Frank asked Michael whether I could be excused for the rest of the day, what was left of it. He told him I needed to rest. Michael agreed, but asked Frank if they could have a word. I sensed a bit of tension. I wondered if Michael had picked up on something. I wish I could Vision Hack with sound. How awesome would that be! I would quite like to hear what they had to say. I had been practising my lip reading skills, but they were still far from perfect. If it was important, Frank surely would let us know.

For now, I needed sleep and darkness. My limit was reached, my emotions drained and my senses were shot. I couldn't deal with anything else.

CHAPTER 23

Zack

"Ouch! Agh! What the fuck!" I rubbed my cheek hard, trying to get rid of the sting Phaedra's slap left. She stared fiercely into my eyes. "That's assault, you know," I winked, daring to joke a little.

"That's what it felt like for me, when I heard what you did to Eliza," she bitched. If she did know what had really happened, she was bloody hiding it well. "I know you have feelings for her, but to just...," she took a deep breath and wiped a tear crossly from her eye. "What the hell were you thinking!" she hissed fiercely. "We could have talked about it," she sniffled a little more demurely. "I would've understood."

Despite the text message, I had no idea if she was acting, or whether I had falsely presumed someone had told her the real story. I had to react, for her sake, but also for the sake of my handler.

"I'm so sorry I hurt your feelings, Phaedra. I deeply apologise for my behaviour. I lost control over my urges and it's unforgiveable. I promise it won't happen again. This has been a true wake-up call, trust me," I grovelled.

She moved towards me, her eyes still cold and furious. I inched away from her a little, not sure what to expect. Then she grabbed hold of me and pulled me into her embrace. I happily obliged, feeling her warmth and passion burn, both physically and mentally. She placed her lips to my ear and whispered, almost inaudible; "I know. This is how I would've reacted, had I not." She lightly kissed my ear, a little smile playing across her lips. My level-headed, relaxed Phaedra was back.

She went to freshen up, whilst I laid out the dinner that had just arrived. I had managed to send Rick a message a bit earlier, but hadn't heard back. It was a waiting game now. I decided to make the most of my time with Phaedra, though it would be rather awkward to keep up the slightly icy atmosphere for the observers. We just ate, trying to avoid the Eliza subject to start with, but it did come up anyway in the end. She squirmed a little before bringing up the inevitable.

"I think you're still not done with Eliza," she sighed. "How do you feel about her, now? Do you think you're ever going to get over her?" Phaedra's eyes inquisitive and open. It wasn't an accusation. She was ever the pragmatist.

"I don't know." I paused a moment to give myself time to formulate what I wanted to say. "You know I love being with you. I care so much for you. And we are so good together. But, I don't think I'm over her. I'm sorry." I ran my finger down Phaedra's cheek. A little shiver ran down her body, but she didn't seem distraught. I hadn't expected her to be. I knew I wasn't the love of her life either. We had known that about each other from the start.

"What do you think we should do? This isn't going anywhere," she asked, shrugging her shoulders.

"I don't know. Zaphire's still in the picture. I can't do anything, until they have properly finished and have closure. If that ever happens. They still love each other."

"Don't you think Eliza needs to know how you feel about her, so she can properly decide?"

"She knows how I feel about her," I said tersely.

"Does she though? Have you not told each other, and yourselves that your attraction is purely physical and the result of a chemical reaction between both your scents? You told her, you won't be second best, after Zaphire. But does she actually know you want to take care of her, love and protect her, share her life?" Phaedra asked. "Because that is what you want, isn't it?"

I didn't need to answer that. It was obvious I did want that. And Phaedra was right, Eliza and I had been lying to each other and I had been lying to myself too. I just nodded.

"We need to take a break from each other, Zack. It was good for the both of us while it lasted, but now is the time you step up. You need to let her know how you feel, before it's too late. You can't sacrifice your happiness for your sister. If

Eliza chooses Zaphire, with the full knowledge and extent of your feelings for her, and knowing you do want a relationship with her, then that'll be the time to move on. Not before."

Could I do this to my sister? No. Fuck it. Could I imagine a life without Eliza without even trying to make it happen, though? I tried to visualise it. Could I live with the 'what if' question forever haunting my life? I saw Phaedra wince in pain, I hadn't been cloaking and my pain was immense. And clearly difficult to shield against.

"Sorry, Phae. Now I've fucking hurt you twice," I whispered mournfully. "Can you stay the night? One last time? Don't hate me for asking," I pleaded. I really needed her to stay, I needed her comfort and I fucking needed her in bed. As soon as possible. I didn't care what anyone might think about my rather indecent proposal. I had to distract myself. I'd made up my mind about Eliza, but I didn't want to think about it. And Phaedra and I knew how to distract each other in many different ways. I hoped she agreed to stay. Although she rolled her eyes, my wish was granted. Phaedra's eyes changed instantly to seductive and full of lust. I think she needed it as much as I did.

***

'Lithium' by Nirvana woke me rudely from my slumber. I'd only recently changed it and it still did the job well. I always had to change the tunes, as my brain subconsciously would start ignoring the songs as a wake-up call, if I had them too long. I quickly checked my other phone to see if Rick had left me a message, but there was nothing. I grunted in frustration. A quick glance over to Phae lifted my mood instantly. Waking up next to Phaedra was always bliss. I thought about our decision to break up and doubt started to creep in. We were throwing away a good thing. Okay, we weren't each other's love of their life, but we gelled. We complimented each other so well. She could lift me out of my grumpy moods so easily, and I gave her confidence and made her feel looked after.

I think if our brains could decide everything in life, we would stay together. It made sense. But even for Dullards, it was often the heart that decided in matters of love, and with us Sensorians, it was almost impossible to deny our senses the thing, or person they craved. And I wanted Eliza. All of her. Her body, her face, her brain, her words, her moods, her stubborn streak, her giggly girly-ness. I wanted to tame her feisty attitude, but also be challenged by her. I wanted to possess her, make gentle love to her and have rampant sex all the time, make her mine, and protect her. Not very politically correct, but that's how I felt. And I couldn't deny myself the chance of making that happen. I was going to fight for her.

Phaedra's fingers gently trailed over my chest, down to my stomach and finally resting on my dick, which immediately responded. We were long past the point of caring, that someone was probably watching. In fact we cheekily quite enjoyed giving them a little performance on occasions.

"One last time?" she whispered, in a ragged breath. I grabbed her arm and rolled on top of her, pinning her hands above her head.

"You naughty girl," I rasped, my body and mind not willing to resist the temptation. I relished her satisfied grunt when I entered her.

CHAPTER 24

Eliza

Michael wanted me up and ready by 8am this morning. I'd had a rough night's sleep, dreaming of my mum and all the horrid scenarios playing through my head over and over again. I didn't know how long I could keep quiet about it. I wanted to scream at Markus to go and find her. Do something! It was excruciating, sitting here and not being able to express my frustration. But I had to. For now. It was my best chance of actually being able to help her sooner rather than later. Daniel's death played heavily on my mind too. The boy had been a pain, revealing our location, but he didn't deserve that. I remembered how gentle and caring Daniel had been. He'd tried to look out for me. He was just doing what he thought was right. There hadn't been a malicious bone in his body. I couldn't imagine the pain Daniel's family was going through. First his sister's ordeal, and now this. It was beyond awful. It was pretty clear that this upcoming mission was going to be dangerous, and more people might be killed. People I loved.

Michael had organised a session with Rob. I hadn't forgotten my absurd crush on him during isolation, and still felt a little tingle in my tummy thinking of him. He had to fit it in before the jobs he had to do today, hence the early start. Rob was always extremely punctual and knocked on my door at exactly the arranged time. I opened the door, and was a bit put out by the serious expression on Rob's face. He meant business.

"Right, we're gonna ramp up the skill level today. I want to test if you're ready for an advanced use of VH," he jumped straight in. No time for niceties apparently. Maybe he had noticed my little teacher's crush before and didn't want to encourage it.

"What did you have in mind?"

"You know where you normally have to be in line of sight of someone to establish a link? We're going to extend that ability. It's possible to establish a link and VH them without that. If you have recently seen someone, or have a strong connection with someone, it's possible to link to their eyes. It's all about your own visualisation skills and concentration. Really being able to tap into your subconscious and make use of the connections within your mind. It's difficult, but the most accessible ones are people you are close to; family, or anyone you have a bond with. Do you understand?"

"I guess so. I'll have to try. I don't really know where to start?"

"Choose someone."

"Okay, I'll choose Zaphire. I saw her yesterday, and it was intense."

"Perfect," Rob nodded. "That could work. Now concentrate on your connection. Feel her presence. Imagine what she might be doing, right now. Tap into your subconscious."

I tried. I thought about our love, and how she would just be waking up now, maybe having a shower. I tapped into our bond, what I felt like looking into her eyes, the feeling it would awake in my heart and stomach, the longing I felt for her. But nothing happened. Absolutely zilch. I looked up at Rob, feeling disappointed.

"I'll try someone else. Maybe Michael. I've been in close proximity with him a lot of the time. It may be easier," I said, trying to convince myself. I tried again. Tried hard. Nothing. Maybe I just couldn't do this yet. I connected to Rob's eyes, just to remind me of the feeling of VH. I quickly hopped out. Seeing my pathetic despondent self did nothing but diminish my confidence even further.

"Don't get angry, but maybe try Zack?" Rob suggested rather carefully.

"Zack?" I questioned reluctantly.

"You have a connection, that's for sure, and, uhm, you had a rather physical and emotionally charged encounter with him recently, so..."

"So?" I pressed, forcing him to say it.

"Well, so it's worth a try?" he said, still looking rather cautious, not knowing how I might react.

"I suppose so," I begrudgingly admitted, thinking it wouldn't work anyway since I'd failed with Zaphire already.

"Go back to the moment he barged into your room, how did you feel? Try and look him into the eyes and make a connection in your mind," Rob encouraged passionately.

"I felt...,"

"Don't tell me. Feel it. Visualise the moment. Hone into his eyes..." I heard Rob croon in the background whilst I went back to that moment, connected to his eyes and..., a flash shot into my brain. Phaedra's face, flushed, mouth slightly opened, eyes closed, head slightly back.

"Hell, no!" I screamed, feeling mortified once I realised what I'd stumbled into.

"What? Did it work? What did you see?" Rob asked excitedly.

"You don't wanna know," I squealed, slapping my hands in front of my eyes.

"Oh no, was he having..." realisation washing

over Rob's face.

"Yes," I squeaked, still feeling highly embarrassed, but couldn't help myself bursting out laughing.

Rob couldn't hide the smirk on his face either.

"But it worked! You did it!" Rob shouted, the happiest I'd seen him in ages. "I'm so proud of you!"

"Yeeaah, hmmm," I drawled, suddenly feeling rather sick. "You don't think he noticed, did you?" Nerves riddled through my body. "He'll be furious if he finds out I tried to hack into his vision without his knowledge!"

"Nah, he'll be none the wiser," he reassured me confidently. Another feeling took over. It took me a second to recognise it, but there it was; jealousy. Rob looked at me peculiarly, reminding me to cloak instantly, but it was too late.

"You don't still have feelings for the bloke, do you? The dickhead! Excuse my language, but he assaulted you!" Rob looked at me indignantly, not understanding why I should feel anything but

.186

contempt for Zack.

"I can't help feel what I feel, Rob. I hardly get it myself!" I bit back, feeling annoyed at him, but also at myself. Why did I keep feeling jealous, whenever Zack got involved with someone? I didn't want a relationship with him, so why begrudge him that. I'd chosen Zaphire, and I was happy with that, even though it wasn't quite working out at the moment. Anyhow, Zack had made it perfectly clear that he wouldn't be second best. So, that was that. And to be honest, even though in the past I'd wished I could have them both, I couldn't actually imagine a proper relationship with him. He'd be impossible to live with. Though, Phaedra seemed to be managing quite well. *Bloody hell. Stop this!* I needed to move on.

"Can you try Zaphire again? You've done it once, so it should be easier to achieve. Can you imagine the possibilities if you get this skill nailed?" Rob continued, way too enthusiastically.

"I'm tired. I don't want to fall into something I

don't want to see again. Can we practice with the person knowing I'm going to do it next time, please?" I asked, a little grumpily.

"Fine. I have to go to work now anyway," he agreed begrudgingly and got up to leave. "Be ready tomorrow morning, same time."

CHAPTER 25

Zaphire

I arranged for Sam, Ned and Brody to meet me in my room over lunch. I needed to talk to them without being watched or listened to, so both Zack and Eliza weren't invited. They wouldn't have been allowed anyway. I rushed back to my room after Saleem had finally given me the all clear to go. Sam was still in a practical, so she would join us a little later. We hadn't had a chance to talk among ourselves about the impending covert mission with Frank. I couldn't wait to see what the others thought. Brody and Ned were waiting by my door already.

"Hey, Miss Punctuality! What time do you call this?" Brody joked, as both boys mockingly checked their watches. I huffed as I let them in, not rising to their jibes.

"Just grab yourselves a drink and something to eat and sit your arses down. We gotta talk."

"Have you heard anything more?" Ned asked,

but not letting anyone answer before continuing. "I still can't quite get over Frank being involved in this. Does anyone else think it could be some sort of trap to test us all?"

"I did think that for a bit too," Brody said.

"Think what?" Sam waded in, as she stormed through the door.

"This. Being a trap. To test our trustworthiness?" Ned repeated for Sam's benefit. It had played through my mind as well, but I'd dismissed it as being unlikely.

"It's a bit elaborate, isn't it? Wouldn't Frank have anything better to do?" Sam answered, having mulled over the idea for just a second.

"Suppose so," Ned muttered, still a little unconvinced. "But we're done for, if it is," he sighed. "And what if Markus is right? That Rick has just made this whole thing up, just to focus our attention somewhere else, rather than dismantling his organisation. Like a decoy action. I dunno. I just don't trust the guy."

"You could pull out, Ned. You don't have to

commit to it," I fired at him a little too sharply, feeling somehow annoyed at Ned's doubtful attitude.

"I think Frank just wants to find out one way or the other, sooner rather than later. He doesn't trust Rick either, but we're not going in blind. We know there's a chance it's all bullshit," Brody offered and I agreed with him. Frank wasn't stupid. He just didn't agree with the 'no action' policy that Markus had adopted, since the last mission's debacle.

"It's so bloody difficult communicating with Zack and Eli with those damned anklets of theirs," I added, airing my own frustrations. "Frank better come up with something, or else I see little chance of succeeding."

"I know he's got some signal jammer device of some sort. Archie told me he'd requested it, not long ago," Sam chipped in.

"Yeah, but that doesn't get rid of the fucking cameras." Brody slapped the table in frustration.

"I hope Zack will hear from Rick soon. It's

soul destroying, just sitting here. Waiting for something to happen," I eye-rolled.

I couldn't wait to hear something, anything. I decided to text Zack, knowing it was pointless as he would let us know if there were any developments.

-*'Any news?'*- I thought it was vague enough to send to his normal number, not wanting to draw too much attention to Zack's burner phone. He didn't answer straight away, but after ten minutes I heard my phone ping. I rushed to see it.

-*'Broke up with Phaedra'*-

Hmm, not the news I was expecting.

"Guys, did you know Zack broke up with Phaedra?" I gossiped straight away. They all shook their heads.

"I'm not surprised. He really wasn't that much into her," Brody said, shrugging his shoulders. "They're more like friends."

"This might be Zack's first ex he actually stays friends with. So unlike him," Sam added.

"As I said, it's because he doesn't 'love' love her. The feelings aren't too deep for him to get all worked up over," Brody shrugged.

I remembered I'd better reply to Zack's revelation.

-*'Shit that sucks'*-

-*'Yh'*-

-*'Are you ok? xx'*-

-*'Yh'*-

Wow. Typical of my brother. Two letter responses. I promised myself to go over and see him a little later, after my afternoon shift. Their break-up worried me. I'd been happy he'd found someone, if anything to take his mind and focus away from Eli. So selfish of me, to immediately think of that. I groaned inwardly, not best pleased with my feelings.

"I gotta go," Sam announced. "See you after your shift?"

"Yep, sure. Text me."

We all had to get going, none of us totally

satisfied with the whole situation we'd found ourselves in. The waiting game continued. Maybe I shouldn't wish the time away. The next mission felt dangerous and could end up in heartbreak, but I couldn't help getting excited about it.

CHAPTER 26

Zack

I could feel the buzzer of the burner phone vibrate in my pocket. I fished it out quickly, as the feeling was disconcertingly close to giving me pleasure. It was sometimes an embarrassing side effect of having such heightened senses to everything, including being touched, especially when caught unexpectedly. It was Rick. I quickly glanced up at Vivian, to see if she'd noticed, but apart from a little twitch in her face, she seemed utterly absorbed in the work she was doing. I asked for a toilet break, which she granted with a slight wave of her hand. The toilets had become a sort of refuge for me, as unlike other places, they were fairly CCTV free.

-'*Meet at BF14 4SF 14 @ 10pm tonight. Both you and E must be present'*-

Fuck. That didn't give us long to organise something. I quickly acknowledged the text and forwarded the message to Frank before deleting it.

Just as well, as Vivian asked to check my phone straightaway when I emerged from the toilet. I feared she'd noticed the buzz earlier, reminding me I had to be careful around her. She was extremely difficult to read and as observant as a dog waiting for its dinner.

"Who was that? I thought I heard it go off?" She stared me down, studying my output. I had to cloak hard.

"I didn't hear anything?" I lied, looking as nonplussed as I could. She let it go, but I could tell she wasn't happy.

I hoped Frank could work his magic, because I couldn't see myself or Eliza secretly slipping out of the compound tonight. Of course Rick didn't know that Markus was unaware of our actions, so he wouldn't see a problem with the timing. For the time being, I had to sit tight and let Frank get on with it. It was so fucking hard not being able to fully throw myself into the mission. It felt like being benched in a football match, watching from the sidelines. So fucking frustrating.

The day dragged on. Vivian was still as narky as anything, and didn't even let me go and get my lunch today. She went herself though, and probably had a nice chat with her friends. At least she brought me back a cheese and ham baguette with a coffee.

I had gathered enough manipulation material to release six people from our cells, but I wished I could be the one forcing them to comply. I was good at that, and I craved it. She wouldn't let me do it though. I was to carry on sifting through the files. The small office we shared was getting to me. I wasn't claustrophobic, but I started to sympathise with people who were. I needed to get out and exercise. That would help. I tried to ask her several times, but she shushed me every time I opened my mouth, so I put in a request per email, which she ignored for about an hour. It was 4:30pm when she finally acknowledged it. I legged it to my room to get changed, hoping to hear some news from Frank. Maybe he would be in my room again? But when I opened the door, no one was there. How was this mission even going to work? We couldn't communicate with each other properly and to arrange a mission as complicated as this, that was essential!

The gym was full. Fuck it. Nothing was turning out great today. A feeling of weariness invaded me, leaving me lacking the energy I felt before. I sat down on the floor, head in my hands, resigned to the fact I had to wait for a space to become available. I felt a warm glow settling next to me. I didn't need to look up to realise who it was. Her gentle voice whispered in my ear.

"Hey."

"Hey, Phae," I said, not really knowing what else to say. I missed her already, and it had only been this morning we said our parting words, with promises of staying friends. I didn't quite know how to do that. I had no experience with staying friends with an ex. I feared if we saw each other, we would soon be having sex again. I hoped Phaedra was stronger than me. It would be nice to be able to stay friends, and I didn't want to mess it up.

"Look, there's a space on the weights. Do you want to take it?" she offered kindly. I nodded and smiled at her.

"Thanks," was all I could think to say, whilst getting up and claiming my place at the weights station. I was so fucking rubbish.

The gym emptied out somewhat after a while and I was free to do what I wanted. I chose to do a bit of rowing next. About twenty minutes in, Phae tapped my shoulder.

"Wanna do a bit of sparring in the ring?"

How could I refuse? I was in there like a shot. Boxing was my favourite, and though I knew I couldn't give it full blast, I knew I'd enjoy giving Phaedra a good work out. She was no natural, but fearless nonetheless, and therefore fun to spar with. She landed a couple of good blows too.

"So...hey...have you spoken to Eliza yet?" she panted.

"Still not fucking allowed," I growled, also panting quite hard. She did make me skip around a lot.

"Ask Markus for permission. Tell him you need to resolve it, before you can work with her on the next mission," she managed to squeak out between avoiding punches and throwing some.

"Good idea," I said with some admiration. Why on earth had I not thought of that angle? He wouldn't refuse me, even though he wouldn't know how soon that mission actually was! The only irritating thing about it was that either Michael or Vivian would have to sit in. Not much I could do about that. I couldn't really leave it till we saw each other later, as then we would have to concentrate on our mission, and would have no time to talk about emotions. I wanted Eli to know how I felt about her. My mind was made up. I finished the round with Phaedra, freshened up and made my way to Markus' office. Not an hour later I was on my way to Eliza's room. Michael was on his way there, so thankfully I didn't need Vivian to attend. All I had to do was wait until Michael was there. Markus had been quite practical about it; he didn't need a lot of convincing. As long as it was supervised, he allowed me to see her.

I stood by her door. No sign of Michael yet. I checked both my phones to see if there was any news. Nothing yet. It was nearly 7pm. Only three hours until the meet, and I was still none the wiser about the arrangements. I was getting nervous.

I picked up Zaphire's scent. *Fuck*. I realised she was in there with Eli. I concentrated my efforts on finding out what was going on behind that closed door. I wasn't sure if I really wanted to know, but I couldn't help myself. I could make out a rather tense atmosphere; unease and indecision are rather potent scents. But then it hit me, I detected lust and more worrying, love. I took a deep sniff. Yes. Unmistakingly the scent of love. Deep love. I should have left. There and then, but I found myself zero-ing in on the sounds inside. I heard whispers. I put my ear closer to the door.

They must have sensed my being there, surely. Unless they were too wrapped up in each other. Images started to fill my mind. They must have made up. Maybe I was too late with my revelations. My mouth went dry, my head started spinning slightly. Then I heard Zaphire whisper, clear as day; *I love you, I'll always love you...*

I didn't need to hear more. I turned around abruptly and sped off, nearly knocking into Michael, who swore, and called me back. I kept walking. I'd been too fucking late. I couldn't tell her. Not now they've made up. I marched on, back to my room. I needed to be away from people, but I heard Michael's footsteps catch up with me, so no such luck. I threw my door open, kicked the bin over with such force, it went flying across the room and slammed my fist on the kitchen counter. I regretted doing that immediately, with the pain of the impact travelling up my arm. I needed to get any hope of a relationship with Eliza out of my head. It was never going to happen. I needed to get over it, no point fucking wallowing in it. But as I was telling myself this, my heart grew heavy and a dark feeling took over my whole body. I wanted to crawl into a hole, bury myself under a pile of blankets and just disappear. What was the point of anything? The more I realised I couldn't have Eliza, the more I understood I needed her in my life. This was a fucking disaster.

"Zack?" Michael's voice brought me back from the spiral I was heading into. "Are you okay?" he asked much kinder than I could actually handle at that moment. I had to swallow a couple of times to make sure my voice didn't come out as a quivering mess.

"Yeah," I managed to say rather gruffly, already knowing Michael wouldn't believe me for a second.

"Right. You need to get this out of your system Zack, whatever it is. We need you being able to focus for the upcoming mission. So talk," Michael insisted. I knew he was right, and it was even more urgent than Michael thought. In fact I only had a couple of hours to get to grips with this.

I decided to open up and see what advice Michael had to offer.

CHAPTER 27

Eliza

"I love you. I'll always love you..." Zaphire whispered. A warmth started spreading through my body, rudely cut short by that word. That rotten little word. "But...," she sighed deeply. "I'm not sure if I can make a relationship with you work."

"We love each other. I can feel it. I can feel it in here," I clasped my chest with one hand and placed the other gently onto Zaphire's heart. "That must mean something. Love can overcome everything," I pleaded, but a foreboding feeling of loss settled in my stomach.

"I don't know...," she hesitated. "I just can't shake this feeling that it'll never work. Is it worth investing more time in?"

"Yes, yes it is!" I replied emphatically. "We only had such a short time together. I have so much more love to give," I started to sound a little whiney, but I couldn't help myself. I didn't want her to give up on us. Not without trying. I didn't want to admit defeat.

"Please, please don't decide now. Wait, at least 'till we've done our mission tonight." A deadly silence followed; the realisation of my slip up hit me right in the stomach. The silence didn't last long, Zaphy jumped right in it.

"Tonight?" she laughed out loud, trying to cover up my mistake. "Wishful thinking on your part. I reckon Markus won't be ready for any action for a while. He's still searching for more information to corroborate Rick's story."

"What's the story?" I asked, remembering I officially didn't even know my mum was missing, hoping no one was listening too closely to our conversation.

"You know we can't talk about this," she said decisively and got up.

"Please, don't go..." That whiney tone coming out of my mouth started to irritate me. "We haven't finished our talk," I said more assertively, trying to reach out for her face. She recoiled just a little, but enough for me to take the hint. Another stone hit the pit of my stomach. "Let's just spend some time together. Have some fun?" I tried once more.

"Okay, maybe," she finally gave in, but it didn't really feel like a win. But it was better than a flat out 'no'. I had to hold on to that. I had to fight for her.

Any ideas we had of having fun together were interrupted by Michael, who had chosen exactly that time to phone me. He told me to send Zaphire away, who complied with a roll of her eyes, giving me some hope that she actually had wanted to spend some more time with me.

"You need to get some exercise in today. Get changed," he ordered.

***

All freshened up and fed, I checked my phone for the time. It read 7:30pm. Still no news on tonight's mission. Had something gone wrong? I still couldn't see how the hell Zack and I would get out of the compound, unnoticed. Then I heard a soft knock on the door. I nonchalantly walked to the door, not to alert anyone who could be watching, of the surge of adrenaline the knock had caused. I must stay and look calm for the cameras. It was Ned's sister, Sofia. She quickly squished a note in my hand, whilst telling me Ned would like to come over soon, and whether that was okay. A typical thing Sensorians did; sending the kids out on rather unnecessary errands to make them comply with, and get used to orders. Nothing would seem out of the ordinary here.

I quickly went to the toilet to read the note. *Get dressed warm, but don't put a coat on. I have one for you. Make your way to reception. Make up an excuse, anything, if you're challenged. You must make sure you are there in 10 minutes.*

This was it. Our mission was live. My adrenaline fuelled body sprung into action, though still trying to make my movements look non-urgent. My phone went ping. It was Michael, wanting to know what Sofia'd wanted. I quickly texted back, reassuring him it was just a message from Ned, asking when he could come over. He seemed satisfied, as no further questions came. I wondered whether I should ask him if I could leave my room to stretch my legs a bit. It was a risk as he could say no, and if I went against his decision he would be on my case like a shot. I decided against it. He hadn't expressly ordered me to stay in my room, so if he challenged me, I could feign ignorance. I put on a thick dark blue hoody and slipped on my trainers and went for it. Out the door, towards reception. My heart beating fast like a runaway train, my mouth dry, my brain focussed.

Reception was empty, apart from Frank who was perched upon a stool at the counter, seemingly having a little chit chat with the woman behind it. We had receptionists on duty all day and night, like a hotel. They were a vital part of keeping the compound running smoothly. The new guards were not there. They must be patrolling somewhere else. Frank's eyes signalled me to slow down. I checked some leaflets in the stand, but kept my senses focussed on Frank. I suddenly felt urgency in the air, I checked Frank and he waved me towards the door with a flick of his fingers and a glance towards the exit. I paced towards it, hopped over the stiles, as I had no card to present. I heard Frank make his excuses and felt him follow me out. The cold air, saturated with snowflakes, hit my face and cut off my breath for just a second. A black van screeched to a halt right in front of us and its doors slid open. Frank and I jumped in and we sped off.

A hugely tense atmosphere hung in the van. It was filled with the stench of stress, the pungent smell of adrenaline and the sweet smell of excitement. I shielded immediately to protect myself from a melt-down situation, not quite able to process all these vibes and scents at once.

Zaphy sat in the corner, observing me a little wistfully. I wish we'd had the chance to hang out a bit more. I yearned to experience her fun side again, her gregariousness and ability to light up a room. I missed it so much.

Zack was leaning back in his seat. A hard, cold expression on his face, a mask. His piercing dark blue eyes, nearer to black. I recognised it from when he had to discipline me as my trainer. He shut off his feelings completely. I wondered why. I knew it was a serious mission and concentration and focus were a must, but Zack somehow took it to the next level. It gave me the shivers and a heavy sense of foreboding settled upon me.

CHAPTER 28

Zack

"How long do we have?" Earlier Frank had informed me that Archie had tampered with our surveillance system, so that all cameras were down and our anklets were off-line too. He would only be able to stall for so long, as Markus would be on his case to find out what the problem was, and to fix it. Also, Michael and Vivian would have gone to check our rooms instantly. That's why Archie only altered the system, just seconds before I left the building. There had been exactly thirty seconds between me and Eliza getting into the van. Brody and I'd left via the side entrance, carefully avoiding the patrolling guards. The others had been in the van already. So now the race against time was on.

"No idea," Frank barked. "But we have to move fast." He started handing out anklets, similar to the ones Eliza and I were wearing. "Put these on," he ordered Ned, Sam, Brody and Tristan. "Archie set them to the same frequency as theirs," flicking his head towards Eli and me. "They won't be able to separate who is who, without camera back up. They will be able to hear you, so don't give away clues, and whisper only, so they won't recognise your voice."

"What about me, Sir?" Zaphy piped up, eager to be involved. Frank's dark glance shut her up immediately. He was in full flow and did not want to be interrupted.

"You four will be our decoys. Ned pair up with Sam. Brody with Tristan. Both pairs will move in opposite directions, and away from Eliza and Zack. Hopefully this will stretch their resources to give Zack and Eliza enough time to meet Rick, where they will undoubtedly have a system in place to scramble the anklets." We all nodded, understanding our task. "When you get caught," addressing Ned, Sam, Brody and Tristan, "Which you will; you must say nothing. Endure your detainment and possible punishment. I will take full responsibility later and might at some point send Zaphire back to involve Markus, if we need to. He'll be angry, but he will come and help. I'll deal with the consequences later. But until then, they must know as little as possible. I don't want them barging in, just at the wrong moment. Zaphire and I will stay with Eliza and Zack for as long as possible. They may not accept our presence, but we'll deal with that if and when that happens." Frank looked us all over, one by one, making sure we were all focussed and on the ball. "Understood?"

"Yes, Sir," we all said in unison.

Frank signalled for Eliza to swap seats with Sam, so she sat across from me and next to Frank. His face was stern. I got the feeling neither I, nor Eliza were going to enjoy this conversation. I had listened carefully to Michael after I'd opened up about my feelings for Eliza, and the hopelessness of it all. I'd taken his advice on board. It had been harsh, but necessary. I didn't have time to ponder, Frank's voice demanding attention.

"I don't know what exactly is going on between you, but I can feel tension. Whatever it is, it has to be sealed away. For this to work, I need the utmost professionalism that I know you're both capable of. No teenage tantrums, especially you Eliza." She balked at this, nearly rolling her eyes, but managing to control herself. "You are not important in this mission. Whatever you feel or think or sense; it's nothing. The mission comes first. Do. You. Understand?" Emphasising the last three words forcefully.

"Yes Sir," both of us said a little more loudly than probably intended, to convince Frank. He wasn't finished yet.

"Zack, you'll be responsible for Eliza. You are far more experienced and therefore more able to judge the situation. But this will only work if you, Eliza, completely submit to Zack. I do not want to see any improvisation, or actions taken where you think you know better. It is vitally important. Do what Zack tells you to do, no deviations."

I answered again with a confident "Yes Sir," but I checked Eliza over. She was conflicted. It hadn't escaped Frank's notice either.

"You don't agree?" he asked menacingly. "Don't you trust Zack?"

"No..., no, it's not that. Of course I trust Zack. It's just, why don't you trust me? What if my instinct tells me something that Zack doesn't pick up? It's my mum, so I should be the one to decide," she challenged. She was so fucking brave and stupid at the same time.

"And that is exactly why you shouldn't be the one. You'll make irrational decisions, based on your connection with your mother," Frank insisted, not budging. "Do you understand? I need to know you're going to comply. I don't want to be responsible for loss of life because you can't do as you're told."

I needed to talk to Eliza myself. She won't listen to Frank, and if he wasn't convinced of her commitment, he might call the whole thing off. I glanced at Frank, who nodded, knowing what I intended to do and giving me permission.

"Eliza. Look at me. I will do everything in my power to find and rescue Alice. I would give my life, if that's what it takes. But you have to let *me* decide. You have to accept I have more experience in using my senses than you. I pick up things that you may miss. On the other hand, I will rely completely on your VH skills, if I need you to use them, and I will trust you." I could feel her resistance melt. She understood. Giving her the full responsibility over using her VH skills had won her over. Frank was satisfied. Just in time too. We were near the arranged address and it was 9:50pm. Frank's phone pinged. It was Archie letting us know the system was back on line, he couldn't eke it out any longer.

"Seems like we're on. Sam, Ned, Brodie and Tristan: Go now. Use buses, taxies, anything to get as much distance between you and us, as quickly as possible," Frank ordered. "Let us know if and when you get caught, if you can."

We hugged and said our good lucks and goodbyes as Frank ushered them out of the van. Tristan flicked the keys of the van into Frank's hands.

"You might need these."

Then they were off. My nerves went up a notch. Waiting was the worst. Eliza looked a little pale; tiny beads of sweat appeared on her forehead. Zaphire had been uncharacteristically quiet. In fact, I expected more closeness between Eliza and Zaphire, now they were seeing each other again. But, though I didn't feel any animosity between them, their connection wasn't as euphoric as I expected. *Fucking stop it!* I slapped myself mentally. Michael told me to stop analysing Eliza's private life. It was none of my business. I needed to get her out of my head. She was just a member of my team. Nothing more, nothing less. I might need to resort to the elastic band approach. Physically hurt myself every time I think of Eliza in any other way than purely professionally. Michael had said it helped him in the past.

"Let's go," Frank announced. "Your goal is to find out where Alice is, if she's not here. Let them lead, do what they say, no heroics. Leave the rest to us."

We had no idea what to expect or what we might find at the address that was provided to us. The house looked empty. The drab looking curtains were drawn, there were no lights inside, not that I could detect. I concentrated hard to hear any signs of life. I detected heartbeats. Two fairly slow ones, though still higher than at rest, and one even faster one. Probably one woman and two men, all were in a heightened state of alertness.

"Stop," a male voice whispered, but it sounded loud and clear to us. "Just Eliza," it commanded.

"Not gonna happen," I replied, equally in a whisper, but forceful nonetheless.

A tense few minutes elapsed. We just stood there, hoping they weren't scrambling our anklets' transmissions yet, as we were vulnerable for detection now. It would be more suspicious if they suddenly disappeared off the radar, attracting the attention of our pursuers.

"Just you and Eliza," the voice with the heavy French accent finally came back. I turned to Frank. This would be his call. He nodded. We would have to go into the lion's den alone. I checked Eliza over. She looked nervous but in control.

"You listen to me. Understood?" I felt compelled to ask once more.

"Yes, Sir," she answered determinedly. I was 95% convinced. But I knew not to underestimate Eliza's stubborn streak. I'd have to keep her on a short leash and observe her closely.

"Good. And let me do the talking. That's a fucking order." It came out much harsher than I intended, but with Eliza's past record that was probably a good thing.

CHAPTER 29

Eliza

I knew Zack didn't fully trust me to follow his command. It was obvious from the amount of venom in his voice. I couldn't blame him. To be honest, I didn't fully trust myself either, but I knew they were right. He is more experienced, and I should let him take control of the situation. I didn't want to mess this up. It was my mum's life at stake. If it had just been my father involved, I would be more optimistic, but Jean-Pierre was even more ruthless than Rick. And then there was the unknown factor of this organisation that Rick claimed was involved. They might not care about my mum's life at all when they got what they wanted. Despair started to settle in. What were we doing here, just the two of us? What chance did we even have?

"Keep it together, Mankuzay," Zack ordered, clearly picking up on my spiralling feelings of desperation. I spotted a tiny glimpse of reassurance and encouragement in his eyes, trying to peak through the mask he'd arranged his face in. More than I'd seen during this mission so far. I didn't like cold Zack.

We walked up to the door, which opened just before we got to it. Frank and Zaphire could do nothing but watch us walk into the unknown. The adrenaline in my body shot up even higher, if that was even possible. I couldn't see who'd opened the door. We knew there were three of them, but didn't know their whereabouts in the house. We stepped inside, trying to work out where everyone was. It was dark, so we totally relied on our other senses.

"This way," Zack said confidentially, moving as if he could see his surroundings clearly. I caught a scent too. Worryingly, I couldn't pick up my mum's at all. Rick was there all right, the familial scent exceptionally strong.

"She's not here."

"I know. I wasn't expecting it to be that easy," Zack sighed a little.

To be honest, I hadn't either. I'd just hoped. I

could make out that the three people were in a room, just a few meters away from us.

"Step inside," Rick ordered. Hearing his voice almost made me physically sick, but it also felt so very familiar and somehow safe. I stopped dwelling on my emotions. I had to. They didn't make sense anyway. We moved cautiously into the room. The three people present were standing by a table at the far end. A dim lamp lit up the room, enough for us to see everything bright as day, as our eyes only needed a little light to see well. Rick approached, but Zack stepped forward, holding his hand up, as if he was stopping the traffic. Jean-Pierre and Irena's face tightened, but Rick smiled a little. Zack pointed at his anklet. Rick nodded.

"All sorted," he replied to the implicit question. That meant we were now off-grid. I knew he would take the precaution, even though in his mind Markus was fully aware. He didn't know we arranged this meeting behind Markus' back. He wouldn't want anyone listening in, just in case.

"Where is she?" I spat at him. Zack almost

killed me with his cold stare. *Oops.* He was meant to do the talking. I nodded an apology.

"Hello Lizzy. I'm glad to see you're well," Rick said softly, ignoring my attack. *Ugh.* Why did his voice immediately touch my whole being? Hearing him calling me Lizzy made me feel warm and secure instantly. I fought the urge to run straight into his arms and sink into his embrace. I felt Zack scrutinizing my every move and sensory output. *Cloak, you stupid girl.* I really showed my inexperience.

"So, what's the deal Rick? Why are we here?" Zack stood firm. No one was going to move any closer.

"I'm so happy you managed to get Eliza here," Rick started.

"Cut the crap. Where's Alice? Where is this organisation you were talking about? What do we need to do?" Zack's tone was calm but urgent at the same time, demanding straight, no bull-shit answers. I saw Rick's face give away a tiny amount of stress. I could see he struggled with losing control of the conversation. He glanced at Jean-Pierre, who gave him the slightest of nods.

"About that. There may have been a slight misunderstanding there."

I noticed Zack stiffening. He had feared, but not expected this. He thought he'd read Rick correctly, but I knew you could never really read my father. He was an enigma, even to me. I bet Zack was giving himself a mental hammering.

"There was no misunderstanding. You lied," Zack shot back, his voice betraying his indignation.

"And you so easily believed it," Rick mocked, a cocky smile hovering on his face. "So eager to accept I'd seen the errors of my ways."

The dimly lit room felt ever so slightly more oppressive than just moments before, but Zack stood taller, ready to take control again.

"What. Is. The. Deal?" he growled.

"Alice is safe. For now. I want to start a new life in Canada. A chance to start over, pursuing my ambitions without being persecuted by Markus. I want Eliza to come with me. Once she's out of the clutches of you lot, she will learn that my way is her best option for a fulfilled and free life. Alice has agreed to come with us."

I didn't believe that for a moment. I wanted to speak up, but Zack beat me to it. Luckily, as I didn't want to suffer his death stare again.

"Agreed, did she? Don't make me laugh. She would never agree to that without being 'persuaded' in some way," Zack scathed.

"You may or may not be right, but it's inconsequential. She's coming with us. So Lizzy, what's it to be? Stay here, never see your mum again, or come with us and make a new life?" My father's eyes firmly stared into mine. My mind went blank. What exactly was he asking me to do? Leave everything behind and start a new life with him and mum, who didn't even want to be there at all? How did he think that was going to work? How did he think we were going to be happy like that? Why had he not just left on his own? I glanced up at Zack, expecting him to give me some guidance, some sign. What was I meant to say? I didn't want this. Zack stood firm. His face gave nothing away, but I knew he had something to say. I let him take charge of this one.

"Eliza's not going to make a decision on this preposterous proposal. We need to know all our options," he challenged.

Rick stepped forward, but Zack matched him, and Rick's posture immediately showed that he thought there was no point in starting a physical fight. Not at this moment. They would win, but nothing would be achieved.

"Let me put it this way; I have put Alice's fate in Jean-Pierre's hands. I know she's my weak spot and therefore makes me vulnerable."

Zack's face went dark as he seemed to understand exactly what that threat meant. My heart sank. If Zack thought that was bad news, it probably limited our options quite severely.

"What does that even mean?" I shouted, a bit too high and a bit too loudly, but I couldn't help myself; panic had started to eat away inside me.

"It means that Alice is not safe, unless you

comply," Zack said gravely. I don't think I've seen Zack this serious, ever. He was having difficulty cloaking his anxiety and stress, but mine just hit the roof. I lunged forward at my father and pelted his face with my fists, one after another, but for no longer than a few seconds. My arms were restrained, and I felt myself being pulled back roughly, into Zack's arms. His scent overwhelmed my already overloaded senses. It brought a strange sense of calm over me, totally at odds with the situation. How had he managed that?

"So what's your plan, from here Rick? How do you envisage this working exactly? You're just going to take Eliza and fly to Canada? She needs her passport for a start," Zack challenged again.

"Don't you worry about that. It's not your concern anymore. All is prepared. You need to leave and we'll take care of the rest."

"Over my dead body," Zack answered resolutely.

"Well, that can be arranged," Rick threatened, causing Jean-Pierre and Irena to snigger, but my anxiety and rage to rise again. "But I wouldn't want to anger the Sensorian community even more by taking out their golden boy," he sneered.

"The boy could come in useful," Jean-Pierre suggested carefully.

What the hell did that mean. Our situation looked pretty dire. We had no plan, other than Frank and Zaphire hopefully being able to follow us. However, I doubted Rick hadn't thought of that himself. We just had to go with the flow, and see what opportunities would be thrown up.

Jean-Pierre got his gun out, I suppose just in case we got any ideas of escaping. They didn't need to worry. We weren't going to try, as we needed to find out where my mum was held. We weren't going anywhere, except for following Rick. I hoped my VH would come in useful as Rick still wasn't aware I possessed that gift. However, it would be next to useless, if I had no way of communicating my findings to anyone. Suddenly, I felt utterly redundant. All I had done was bring our community trouble. Maybe I should just leave with my father and give up. Give in to the familial bond and thrive, as my father seems to think I would. Maybe I could persuade him to give up on his grand ideas and just live, somewhere remote. Just me, mum and him.

"Sit down," Irena ordered after patting us down and taking our phones. She made us sit opposite each other. "Wait there for further instructions."

We complied without protest. I glanced over at Zack. He was looking at me intently. He flicked his wrist sharply with his fingers and turned his face away from me. Something was up. I needed to find out what that something was. I observed him whilst he did his best not to turn his face around. I felt his struggle. My eyes settled on the back of his neck, where once my hands had caressed his defined muscles, and then desperately had tried to grab his short hair, whilst we kissed. The feelings of lust flooded back, but it wasn't just that. I remembered my admiration for him and my desire to be in his good books, so he would afford me a smile. I missed teasing and challenging him, which always made his jaw clench, itching to retaliate. I missed his friendship and fiercely protective streak. I even missed the pain he inflicted on my body with his hard training schedule. As I was thinking that, I knew I could never abandon him willingly, or any of the others for that matter. Everything I believed in and worked for would have been for nothing. It wouldn't make sense. And anyway, I loved Zack. It was so obvious. Right then, I knew it was true. It always had been. I had no idea what to do with those feelings, and I was glad I managed to cloak well. He was with Phaedra now. I needed to fix things with Zaphire.

CHAPTER 30
Zaphire

Frank and I waited outside the house. It was getting cold in the car, as we switched the heater off, not wanting to drain the battery. I wrapped my scarf a little tighter around my face to fend off the chill. We both fully expected the mission not to end here. It was almost guaranteed that they would take Zack and Eli someplace else. That's where Alice most likely would be too. We also knew it wasn't going to be easy to follow them. But Frank seemed to be confident. He told me Archie had been working on a way to override the scramblers, and when the moment was right, he hoped to bring them into play. It may or may not work, that's why he hadn't told Zack and Eli. They shouldn't rely on it. The side effect would be that Markus would know exactly where they were as well. We would need to act fast and bring Markus up to speed with our actions. He would be angry, but he would know to act first and leave the disciplining to later.

I hoped.

I sensed movement, my heart rate jumped up. Frank was on high alert too. The front door swung open with purpose. Jean- Pierre emerged, his gun pointed directly at us. *Christ!* We ducked down low into our car. My blood ran cold, thinking of what they did to Daniel. I was dead scared.

They moved swiftly into their vehicle, but not before Jean-Pierre released two shots and shredded our two front tyres. *Bloody hell!* The sound of the shots pierced my ears like two needles being jabbed in there simultaneously. It took us both a couple of seconds to recover. Why did their ruthlessness and readiness to use weapons always surprise us? It shouldn't. It made us look stupid.

We didn't have a back-up plan for this! We couldn't follow them by car anymore. Frank was frantically punching numbers into his phone to order a taxi. We wouldn't be able to use it to follow them. The scent would be too dispersed by the time it got here. But at least we would be mobile. I bloody well hoped Archie's IT skills

.233

would live up to its expectations. All we could do was sit there and watch their black BMW speed off.

"Text Archie he needs to unscramble their scramblers. And, uhm, has Tristan been in touch?" Frank's voice still sounded a little shaky.

I checked my phone, but there was nothing. Either they had been caught without being able to let us know, or they were busy trying to keep under the radar. I gave him a ring.

"Yes," a rather stressed sounding voice answered.

"Are you okay?"

"Yes," Tristan answered a little unconvincingly. "But I don't know for how long."

"Can you get your colleagues to keep a look out for a black BMW, number plate HK20FGS?"

"Copy that. Consider it done," he answered hurriedly. Tristan fully trusted the police force he worked for to come up with the goods. They always did. But it sounded like Tristan and Brody were in a bit of a tight spot and probably were on the verge of being apprehended. I wondered who had been sent out to hunt us all down. Markus won't know what to make of it all. This has been the most serious breach of protocol ever. Frank, a leadership member, explicitly going behind Markus' back? Unheard of. I didn't know if Markus would ever recover from this. It might lead to serious questions over his leadership. A spike of guilt ran through my body. Markus cared for me and Zack, had brought us up, given us all we needed. He loved us and we paid him back by seriously undermining him. Not once, but twice now.

"Snap out of it, Zaph," Frank snarled, showing his stress. "Taxi's here."

***

Frank walked up to the compound purposefully, I followed significantly less confidently. I clocked at least six guards gathering by the door. That was new. It wasn't going to be a warm welcome. I was shitting myself. Our community's new fear of the outside world had made the leadership step up security. Our stunt wouldn't have helped. It looked like the guards were not just there to patrol the compound and surrounding area now, but were sent to guard the reception hall in numbers. I hadn't really paid them any attention before, since there was no need to. They were just there, doing their job, and there hadn't been as many of them. The situation had changed for me now though, and I observed them with trepidation.

The moment Frank stepped foot inside the door, they swarmed him, and then me. Before I could even open my mouth, my arms were behind my back and in handcuffs. Frank suffered the same treatment. He didn't resist. He calmly let the guards do their job and I followed his example. I trusted he knew what he was doing. The guards marched us straight to Markus' office, one in front, one either side of us, and two bringing up the rear. It all felt totally surreal. Moments later we were escorted into the room and placed in front of

Markus, who was flanked by Laura, Michael and Vivian.

"No need for the cuffs," he quietly informed one of the guards, who promptly unshackled us. The office was full of questions. The air thick with scents, so intense we all had to shield to be able to even utter a word. I noticed Markus struggling to maintain his shield and cloak his feelings at the same time. If he failed, we would all feel the excruciating pain he was capable of emitting. I willed him to stay on top of it. I wasn't sure if my body and brain could cope with that onslaught, and I wanted to remain conscious and alert for this meeting.

"Frank, please explain yourself. What the hell is going on?" Markus started, sounding more confused and hurt, than angry. Frank drew a deep breath to steady himself. His pores were oozing sweat, so much so that even a non-Sensorian could work out the stress he was under. His hands showed a tiny tremor when he lifted them in a defensive manner in an attempt to appease everyone in the room. His eyes were twitching ever so slightly.

"I decided to start the mission to get Alice back, without your knowledge or permission. I felt it necessary as the leadership's indecision was putting her life in danger. We have no idea what organisation is involved, if any, and how patient they are. I felt the leadership had lost focus and dwelled on the failure of our last mission, clouding their judgement. No one was open to this discussion, so I took it upon myself to involve some members of our team to take the first step. It was always my intention to report back to you, hoping that by then, you would see sense and agree with my plan. I gambled, but I know and trust that, whatever your feelings are about the way this was done, you will fully support us and make this mission work. I will of course accept any repercussions and consequences of my behaviour after the mission is completed, if you feel it necessary to do so."

Frank made it sound so reasonable, even

though he was basically accusing the whole leadership of poor judgement.

Markus swallowed heavily, a couple of times. Sending and receiving subtle messages to his allies, using only their bodies. Even though we were in such a mess, it was quite amazing to see it at work. Frank's body was rigid, waiting anxiously for Markus' reply, telling me he wasn't all together sure about Markus' response. My stomach tightened even more. Bile started to rise. *Breathe.*

"Okay. Let's deal with the situation first. Give me an update and we'll decide how to proceed," Markus decided. A glimmer of resignation escaped his otherwise determined face. He'd decided to be practical about this. I let out a deep sigh, feeling a heavy weight had lifted, at least a little. Even Frank's body showed signs of relief. We had been given a chance to get this mission back on track to get Zack, Alice and Eliza back safely.

Moments later Sam and Ned joined us in the meeting room. They both looked a little worse for wear, which told me the guards hadn't been too friendly. I didn't like the militarisation of our community. It was meant to protect us from the outside world, but it was quickly being used to control us Sensorians too. Apparently Tristan and Brody were on their way back. They were picked up not long ago, so they might escape the rough treatment Sam and Ned had endured, now Markus knew about our plan.

Frank outlined what had happened so far. Markus lost it when he heard Zack and Eliza were captured. All colour drained out of his face. He slammed the table with his open hand. "This is *exactly* what I'd feared! How could you have been so damned irresponsible, Frank!" He took a moment to regain his composure, whilst Frank remained wisely silent. "We've got to get Zack back. And Eliza and Alice," he added as a bit of an afterthought. I knew where his priorities lay. At least Markus was on board with it now, and a flicker of hope ignited in the pit of my stomach. We might actually pull this off.

CHAPTER 31
Zack

Something was off. I couldn't put my finger on it exactly, but it was a vibe I picked up between Jean-Pierre and Irena. They knew something that Rick was unaware of. I wanted Eliza to keep her eye on Jean-Pierre. She needed to VH him and get a good connection. It might help us find out what was going on. I used my eyes to give her a silent command. She nodded, she understood. We worked so closely together before, I was glad our minds were still very much in sync. Even after having been apart for months.

We arrived at our destination after about an hours drive. I longed to stretch my legs, as we'd been awkwardly squashed in the back, with our arms tied behind our back. Something I had objected to, but had just got sneered at by Rick.

"Get a move on!" Jean-Pierre ordered. I tried to take as long as possible to do anything, to slow us down, to give Frank and Zaphy time, but he wasn't letting me get away with it. He pushed me forwards and I nearly stumbled. Keeping balance was quite difficult with your fucking arms tied behind your back. Eliza was getting the same treatment, with Irena actually pushing and dragging her along by her neck. The journey had been uncomfortable, and I didn't see an end to it yet.

"Take it easy on Eliza. Cut her cable ties. She's not a prisoner," Rick warned Irena. *There it was*. That miniscule glance she threw at Jean-Pierre, giving away some understanding between them, which Rick was not part of.

"Sure," Irena huffed. She cut Eliza's ties and loosened her grip, but still ushered Eliza forward. I wasn't afforded the same leniency by Rick. I guess he did see me as his fucking prisoner; a useful tool that could be used at some point to further his cause. Maybe he saw me as his way out. I tried not to think about it too much. An image of Ned forced its way into my brain, barely alive dumped on our doorstep. I shivered and shook my head to get rid of that disturbing picture. *Fuck*. I hoped

Frank was on top of it, and help was on its way.

Once inside, I knew Alice was there. I could smell her. It was a fresh scent. I was pushed in a different direction, away from Eliza. That fucking didn't bode well.

"I'm not going anywhere without him," Eliza hissed. Jean-Pierre didn't stop pushing me forward though.

"I mean it!" she shouted.

"Jean-Pierre, it would be easier to keep them together. Or at least near each other. We can keep an eye on both of them. Just make sure he's tied securely to a chair. I want Eliza to enjoy the reunion with her mother. After all, that's why we're here, isn't it?" Rick intervened.

Though on occasion there seemed to be a slight shift in power balance towards Jean-Pierre, Rick still held his own. Rick was clever, and Jean-Pierre knew that.

"Mon chéri, Rick is right. Relax. Zack can do no harm," a soft voice cut in. Angelique entered the hallway and strode up to her husband, threw her arms around his neck and gave him a passionate kiss. The burning desire was real and for all of us to feel. She wasn't embarrassed, just laughed a little cheekily.

"Listen to your wife for once. She might reward you later," Rick teased and the mood lifted somewhat between the two men, as they sniggered. I smiled to myself. Men are so basic. I included myself in that.

"He wishes," Angelique mumbled, not too pleased at being made fun of. "Let's go into the living room. I bet Alice can't wait to see her daughter. It took you a while to come. She was starting to wonder whether it was ever going to happen."

Eliza's face was thunderous, but her eyes lit up with excitement at the prospect of seeing her mum. There was no hiding that feeling. Angelique led the way, and as soon as Eliza stepped through the living room door she rushed forward and slammed into her mum with such force they nearly tumbled over. I loved feeling and experiencing her intense love for her mother, and the relief she felt was overpowering. It made me feel the same. Sometimes being able to share emotions was not a burden, but a gift. I felt elated, just like Eliza and her mum did. It didn't last long. The strong sense of worry and stress that they both started to emit spoilt the party. Then hatred, pure and unadulterated vengeance. I needed to shield, and quick. I also needed to keep my own feelings in check. I sensed someone observing us from a little way away, trying to keep out of the picture. I smelled the unmistakable scent of Jessica. Of course she had to be fucking involved in this as well.

CHAPTER 32
Eliza

Her warmth was electric. Her arms felt like a fluffy blanket enveloping me on a cold winter's night. Her smell, so reassuring and instantly making me feel safe and cared for. Loved, without conditions or expectations. How I missed her. How I needed her. But she needed me too. She needed me to be strong and get her out of here. I knew she didn't want to go with Rick to Canada and I resolved to do everything I could to stop that from happening. After the initial bliss I felt my mum's body tense up, a tear started to form in her eye. I hated Rick for having put her through this.

"I thought you loved her. I thought you'd do anything to protect her from having to go through this!" I shouted at Rick. I didn't cloak, I wanted him to feel the full force of my disgust and hatred. But I think the only person affected was Zack, by the look on his face. Rick just stared at me, shaking his head a little, a smile playing on his lips.

A smile! Bloody arsehole.

"Listen Lizzy. I do love your mum, and you. I hate the way you betrayed me, but our bond is too strong. That's why I know, that deep in your heart you love me too. It's too hard to fight against. As soon as we're in Canada, and away from all this, we will be able to restore our trust in each other and build on our love. I'm absolutely sure of it." Conviction shone through in all of his senses. I was convinced he did really believe it. I didn't share his conviction though. Not at all. But he wasn't going to believe me. It was fixed in his mind. I wasn't sure how to play this. I wanted to scream NEVER, but thought better of it. I kept schtum a little longer. Keep him guessing.

"For now, we need to relax a little. We travel tomorrow. First, we need to get rid of your anklets. The jamming will only be effective for so long. It can be over ridden. After that's sorted, we'll have some dinner."

"Sit still," Jean-Pierre warned sternly as he

wielded a bolt-cutter to attack my anklet. It didn't work, as it was too thick to get a good grip on both sides.

"A tin snipper might work. It's thinner. Bar that, we might have to chainsaw it off," Rick suggested a little cautiously.

"No way you're getting near me with a chainsaw!" I squealed a little more girly sounding than I wanted. Zack made a low growling sound. He'd been awfully quiet, but I think the chainsaw suggestion, just tipped him over the edge.

"Get your fucking hands off me. Just give me that tin snipper," he snarled when Irena approached him with said tool in hand. Irena looked over at Jean-Pierre who gave her a curt nod. He untied Zack's legs and arms, who immediately snatched the tool out of her hand, shoved it under the strap and started snapping away at it. It was tough, but started to give away. The muscles in his arm and hands strained from the effort. How I wanted those strong arms around me, and his hands. What I would give to have his hands on my

.248

body. With a grunt he managed to cut through the last bit of strap, threw the anklet aside and moved over to me. Irena's hand shot out onto his shoulder.

"Don't move without permission," she snarled. Rick stepped in.

"Let him cut Lizzy's anklet. Then tie him up again."

His fingers wrapped around my leg to steady it. His touch raised the goose bumps out of their slumber. A tantalising heat spread from his firm hold; my senses started to overreact. I needed to calm myself down. He wasn't mine to lust over. He was with Phaedra now. *Breathe. Sea. Waves. Waves lapping at the shore.* Zack avoided eye contact, fully concentrating on the tool in his hand. He gently slid the tip of the cutters under my anklet and started hacking away at it, until it snapped off eventually. It felt strange. Light. Empty. I'd grown used to the weight and push of the strap onto my skin. Now my leg felt naked. But nice. Free.

As soon as he was done, Irena tied his arms

and legs back onto the chair he was placed on.

"Irena, drive the anklets away from here and then disable the jammer. It should direct them away from us," Rick ordered and Irena agreed immediately, grabbing the anklets, leaving no time to waste. My heart sank. Our hopes of rescue were diminishing by the minute.

"Let's have some food. We had some pizzas delivered earlier. We've been keeping them warm in the oven, but they should still be good. Open a bottle of wine for us, Jean-Pierre. It's time to celebrate."

How could this man be so deluded? To think mum and I would be celebrating! I walked over to Zack to undo his bindings.

"Not him," Rick ordered abruptly. "We need him weak. I'll get him some water. Later."

"If he doesn't get any food, I won't have any either," I protested vehemently.

"Is that right?" Rick gestured to Jean-Pierre, who prowled over to Zack. Stood in front of him and punched him in the face. Zack just grunted, not wanting to show the pain he was in, but he couldn't stop the tears being forced out of his eyes. I felt it, as if it was my own face that was punched. Zack lifted his face in defiance, expecting another blow to land. The skin under his left eye had split and started oozing blood. With the lack of ice it was bound to swell up nastily. Jean-Pierre rubbed his fist, readying himself for another one.

"What's it to be, ma fille? Refuse to eat? Or be a good girl, and sit at the table with Rick?"

Grrrrr. I hated Jean-Pierre. I glanced over to mum, whose eyes were wide with shock. She shouldn't have to witness any of this. I threw a desperate look at Zack, who nodded. "Go," he mouthed. I couldn't really do much else. At least the table was just around the corner in the L-shaped dining room.

Rick made us all sit at the dinner table, whilst Jean-Pierre poured everyone a glass of red. A place was set for Irena, so I assumed she wouldn't be too long. I was surprised to see Jessica sitting quietly at the other end of the table, sipping her wine. In all the emotional turmoil, I had completely missed her scent. She emitted confusing signals. I couldn't quite make out whether she was happy to be here, or just content and grateful to be wherever Rick was.

I glanced over to mum. She looked defeated and disillusioned. She hadn't spoken much; very unusual for mum. She was never normally lost for words. I couldn't wait till we were able to talk freely. I needed to know how this had happened. Had Rick been charming the socks off her, before he forced her into this? Was her heart broken again? I felt Rick's piercing eyes sting all over me. He was observing me like a hawk. I tried to VH Irena to give me a little practise, but I didn't have a strong enough connection with her and she still wasn't back. I hopped into Jean-Pierre's eyes instead. That was easy enough. I couldn't do it for too long as Rick demanded my attention, and I didn't want to give him reason to be suspicious of me. He still didn't know I had this gift.

"If you could just accept your fate, Lizzy, life would be so much easier for you. We're bound together, forever. The sooner you realise that, the better for all of us."

I kept quiet. I didn't want to give any of my feelings away, so I concentrated hard on cloaking, just nodding my head a little as if I was considering it. He seemed satisfied that I didn't challenge him. The next few minutes were taken up with chewing and slurping noises, amplified by the stifling silence. It was awkward to say the least. Distant and hasty footsteps approached towards the front door. Irena; her scent revealing her imminent arrival.

"Mmmm. Pizza! I'm starving," she exclaimed on coming in, seemingly totally oblivious to the icy atmosphere. Angeligue pushed a few slices onto the spare plate and filled up a glass of wine. Irena shook her head slightly.

"No thanks. No wine for me. Someone needs to stay alert," she declined decisively. "You have to have your wits about you with this one around."

She threw me a vicious look, clearly remembering how I managed to surprise and overpower her, and stuff her into a cupboard when she last needed to guard me. Laughter escaped Rick's mouth.

"So true, Irena!" Then his face turned serious. "Did you manage to set a good false trail?"

Irena scoffed. "Of course. It will lead them far away from here. No worries."

It was as I expected, but couldn't help feeling even more hopeless. Rescue seemed extremely unlikely.

CHAPTER 33

Zaphire

"Archie! I frigging love you!" I exclaimed as I planted a kiss full on his lips. "You're a genius!" He wiped his mouth, a little colour rose to his cheeks.

"Yeah right," he huffed the compliment away quickly. "Look, at the moment they're travelling further north." His forehead furrowed as he scrutinised the data coming in. No sound could be heard apart from a loud humming. "It sounds like they're on a train..., but oddly no sound of other people talking or anything?"

"We need to check what train and where the next stop is, and send people to board the train there, if we can get there in time. Zaphy?" Frank directed urgently.

"On it, Sir."

"Tristan, is there any chance we can use the police?" Markus chipped in. Tristan looked doubtful. With the compound moving, he'd had to transfer to a different unit, which had been quite tricky, the police being none the wiser he was a Sensorian. He'd had to ask a lot of favours and manipulate his way into the force near us, and was reluctant to ask too many special requests. He had already got them to track the vehicle earlier, which had raised a few questions. Thanks to Tristan's colleagues we knew where they were headed, though.

"Only if we inform them fully and report them missing. I'm not sure if you want to go down that road?"

"I don't think so. It will raise too many questions," Markus decided without consulting the others. I suppose there was no time for lengthy discussions. Anyway, we couldn't really have police involved in anything we did. Most of our missions involved plenty of illegal action, let alone our latest coercion tactics and holding people in our cells illegally! If the police started to sniff around here, we would all end up in prison. Not to mention the hundreds or probably thousands of cases that would be thrown out of court, if it was discovered that the evidence used was gained by methods outside the boundaries of the law. It would be a disaster. We have always been able to clean up our own mess. I just hoped this time would be no different.

I located the station they would arrive at next. The train would be there in twenty five minutes. I informed Frank.

"We won't get there in time, but we can send people. Just in case they get off, or follow the progress of the train. No point hanging around here. Do you want to go, Zaphire?"

I contemplated it for a minute, but my gut feeling told me something was off. I wanted to see the history of the trackers, from the point Archie'd managed to override the scramblers. It was something Archie had said, about there being no voices, not even in the background. Just the constant thudding and buzzing of the train. It didn't feel right. I wanted to investigate it.

"No, maybe send Ned and Sam up with

Michael and some guards. I want to track it from here," I told him, not without eliciting an odd look from him. They left to organise the team to try and gain some ground on Zack and Eliza, whilst I lingered with Archie.

"Let's look at the tracker history then," Archie suggested, completely anticipating my request. Archie had managed to hack into the system when the anklets weren't on the move yet. There was no sound initially, as he managed to get the tracker to work first, but after about ten minutes the sound was live too. It wasn't very clear, but we heard a mumble of voices in the background, then some doors slamming, a car starting. Irena sang along to a Russian sounding pop song. No Eliza, no Zack. Were they even there? Were they dead? Was she moving their bodies? No. I dismissed that. She wouldn't be doing that on her own, surely?

"What's going on, Archie? Doesn't this sound strange? Why is Irena in the car, on her own, with Zack and Eliza? Why are they not making a sound?"

"They might be gagged?"

"But wouldn't we hear an occasional grunt, or a shuffle or anything? Something's wrong."

"Hmm, keep listening for a bit more. We may hear something," Archie suggested sensibly, even though I was itching to tell Markus. There was nothing but Irena's off-key singing. Then a strange click, as if something was turned on or off. Suddenly the sound was much clearer. There was a lot of clunking and clattering. Then a massive screech, a bit like a train braking. A couple more thuds, and then just a rhythmic clunking and buzzing sound. A picture formed in my mind.

"I know exactly what happened there!" I exclaimed excitedly, jumping onto my feet. The chair I sat on promptly crashed backwards with the speed of my move. "They must have removed the anklets, driven them to a train station, switched off the scrambler and thrown them onto a train. Might even be a frcight train, explaining the lack of the hubbub of voices. It's a distraction! A decoy! They are still where the recording started. We need to find that address immediately!" I shouted, already half way out the door.

I raced towards Markus' office, my heart pounding, hoping he was there. He was busily talking to Frank, annoyed at me bursting into the room. But he sensed it was important. In true Markus style he ordered me to calm down first, though. I had to take a couple of breaths to gather myself. I tried to talk slowly. I failed miserably.

"It's a ruse. They're not there! They're still at the house! Got to go there, not the train station!"

"Zaphire!" Markus called me to order again. "Start at the beginning. You're not making sense." I forced myself to be patient and told them what I'd discovered. I clocked Archie running towards us. He must have found the address. Perfect timing. I couldn't wait to be in that van, and on our way to get them back.

CHAPTER 34

Eliza

The atmosphere was excruciating. Mum kept sending Rick distraught looks, which visibly upset him. I believed he did love her. He did not want to cause this pain, but he had convinced himself we would be able to forgive him, in time. Jessica was quiet, but with way too smug a face. I couldn't stand looking at her. In the end Rick cracked and gave up on making conversation. He'd tried, but it was forced and nothing more than one-word answers left my and my mother's lips.

"See them to their rooms, Angelique. And make sure you lock their doors." He turned to face me. "You'll find some clothes and essentials packed in a suitcase for you. If there's anything else you need, let us know. We'll check on you in half an hour." I hated the prospect of being separated from my mum again. I felt her anguish too.

"I love you. Don't worry. We will sort this

out," I whispered in her ear when I hugged her goodnight. I knew everyone could hear, but I wanted it to be for us, just us, so I blocked out that knowledge and pretended it was a private moment.

"I love you too, sweetheart. Be strong. Don't worry about me."

Angelique tugged at our arms, and reluctantly we let go of each other. Mum sounded stronger than I thought she was. She hadn't given up hope yet. Maybe she acted so demurely to lure Rick into a false sense of security. I hoped so. At least I knew she was safe. No one was going to hurt her.

"What about Zack? Please don't be cruel. Let him come into my room, or at least give him a bed to sleep on," I pleaded.

"No, I want him broken and tired. I don't trust him not to try and fight tomorrow. Sorry Lizzy." Rick didn't sound that regretful to me. I think he rather enjoyed making Zack's life miserable. Jessica just snorted at my request, and gave me a haughty and condescending little smirk.

I should be tired. It must have been past midnight by now and on a normal night I would be ready for bed. My adrenaline overrode all feelings of exhaustion, though. I was wired for action. But I was stuck in my room. I decided to follow Jean-Pierre. I'd hacked his vision quite a few times this evening and I had a good connection. It was easy to do, even without him being in the same room. Nothing happened at his end. He swatted Angelique away a few times who wanted some attention; he clearly had other things on his mind. I got bored so I checked over my provisions. They all looked adequate. I didn't need anything else. Just before the half hour was up, I checked on Jean-Pierre again. He was on his phone typing a message. Unfortunately, I couldn't see who it was to.

-'The packages are ready for collection. We have one extra. Be careful. It's dangerous, though tightly wrapped'-

What the hell was this! It didn't take a genius to work out who he was talking about, clearly us, but who was he talking to? I needed to concentrate to get back into his eyes again.

-*'Can we leave the non-essential?'*-

-*'Negative. We need it to make the other ones work'*-

-*'OK. ETA 01:30'*-

But we weren't meant to go until the following day? This wasn't right. I needed to discuss this with Rick. Zack's mistrust of Jean-Pierre, which he'd tried to convey to me, was justified by the looks of it. I didn't have to wait too long until the knock on my door sounded to check whether I needed anything else for my travels tomorrow. It was Irena.

"Can I please talk to my father? I need to ask him something about tomorrow," I tried.

"You can ask me. Rick's busy," she answered sternly. I didn't know if I could trust her, so I pushed a bit harder.

"No, it needs to be him. I need to sense him, to trust his answer."

"Tough. I'm not falling for your tricks. Ask

me," she persisted.

"You need to ask him. It'll be better for all of us," I threatened.

"You have no power here, Eliza. Tell me what you need."

"I have power. My co-operation is important to my father. Ask him to come and see me. Let him decide if he thinks it's important enough. You wouldn't want me complaining about you to him, would you? He'll do anything to keep me happy, if he can help it."

I heard her grumble and walk off agitatedly. Hopefully to go and get Rick. I wasn't sure my threats had worked; she didn't seem as perturbed by them as she should have.

I waited anxiously. I tried to hack Irena's eyes to see if she was fetching Rick. I managed to stay with her for a bit and she did seem to be on her way to him. Then I lost her. She was more difficult to hack than Jean-Pierre. Maybe she was more guarded, closed off. I don't know. I hopped back to

Jean-Pierre to kill the time, and to see if there was anything else going on. He'd turned his attentions to Angelique. Something I didn't want to see, so I left them to it quickly. I tried to see where Irena was again, but nothing. Rick was closed to me too. I just had to wait. Minutes felt like hours. Time was moving ever so slowly. I was about to give up on ever getting to talk to him, when his scent announced his imminent arrival.

The door unlocked and he strode in, looking a tad annoyed at being summoned by me. But I was sure he would want to know this. I told him what I found out. About the strange messages Jean-Pierre had sent and received. His face was blank.

"How do you know this?" he hissed.

"I just know. Trust me," I tried to convince him without giving away my gift of VH.

"But I don't. It's all to your benefit if I go to Jean-Pierre, accusing him of all sorts. You want to sow distrust amongst us. It's not going to work Eliza. I know you're desperate to do something, but this is so obvious, it really wasn't worth your while." He turned around and was nearly out of my room already. I had to do something!

"I'm a Vision Hacker!" I blurted out. "I saw the text messages through his eyes! Believe me! It's true." He stopped in his tracks, swung round and stared at me with an expression of disbelief mixed with admiration and surprise. "I can prove it, if you let me?"

He turned around slowly, fishing something out of his pocket and staring at it.

"What am I looking at?" he asked, his voice gruff. Did I detect a tiny bit of emotion, I sensed sadness and joy. I needed to concentrate. I needed to succeed in hacking his vision. Nothing.

"What. Am. I. Looking. At?" he repeated tensely. I could sense his impatience rise to intolerable levels. I needed some more time.

"Wait. Let me concentrate. Give me that. At least," I pleaded. He nodded his head, once again studying something in his hands.

I got it. My body shivered and a little gasp escaped my mouth from what I saw.

"It's me. When I was a baby. And..., and mum and you," I whispered, trying to keep my voice steady. "You're looking at a photograph of us."

He turned around slowly.

"You bloody well are a VH! How did you manage to keep that from me!" he exclaimed with a mixture of annoyance and amazement.

"Do you believe me now? What I saw? Because if it's true, something is going on that you don't know about," I reminded him abruptly.

He looked at me darkly.

"We best be prepared." His voice matched his eyes; grim, dark and determined. The scent of fear of betrayal hung heavy in the air.

CHAPTER 35

Zack

The zip tie bindings cut into my flesh. They were done up too tightly. I had no room to wriggle and I could feel my hands and feet were slowly losing feeling. It was going to be a long night.

I sensed someone approaching and held out a little hope they had changed their minds and were bringing me some food and drink. My hope was dashed pretty quickly when I realised who the visitor was. Jessica. That didn't spell anything good. She sashayed past, revelling in the power she held over me. She teased the gag out of my mouth and tried to kiss me.

"What do you want, bitch?" I snarled at her, shaking my head vigorously so that her kiss smeared across my face. Vile.

"Ooo, feisty... Just came to see if you're still securely detained." She let out a little giggle. "See how the tables have turned." She stood in front of me, caressing my face tauntingly with her finger.

"What I could do to you now...," she teased maliciously as she trailed her finger down over my chest, and further down to my trousers. She pinged the edge and ran her finger inside it.

"Get your fucking hands off me! You pathetic little..."

"Jessica!" A stern voice sounded, interrupting the tirade I was about to burst into. "Get back upstairs. Now!" Rick shouted, making Jessica shrink and forget about her advances instantly. She hurried out of the room. Rick stuffed the gag back into my mouth, turned around and left me without saying a word. I was alone again, shuddering at the thought of Jessica's plan to assault me. *Evil bitch.*

No one came to give me water. I'd given up hope that it might suddenly materialise. I think they really wanted me without any strength left at all. I hoped they could see some use for me, or else they probably would leave me to die in the most excruciating way. I needed my brain to move away from all these doomsday scenarios. Frank will come through. I had to keep thinking that, but it was a challenge to stay positive. My eyes were getting heavy, but my dry mouth and throat kept me from falling asleep. I think it would be a fucking relief if I could just pass out, but it wasn't happening. My body stayed annoyingly alert.

My self-pity was interrupted by a noise outside. A car turned up, but it wasn't disguising the fact it arrived, so I doubted it was my lot. It sounded like a big van or minibus. Maybe it was there for tomorrow. Then I heard voices quietly talking, but they weren't speaking English. It sounded Eastern European or Russian. They approached the house and someone opened the door to let them in. Their scents started to penetrate the house. One smelt vaguely familiar. Yes. It was a relation of Irena. Had to be. Maybe a cousin, as the scent was similar, but too different for it to be a brother or sister. This was odd. Rick hadn't mentioned anything about other Sensorians joining them in Canada, but then he hadn't really divulged any of the plans. It was very well possible that more Sensorians were involved. The most predominant scent was that of Dullards though; sweaty and adrenaline filled.

It went quiet for a while, but then all hell broke loose. Everything happened at the same time. Shouting upstairs and in the room next to me, a door was forced open by the sound of splintering wood and the huge bang that preceded it. Footsteps running around. I could do nothing but sit tight. I couldn't even shout, as my mouth was still stuffed with a makeshift gag. A gun went off. *Fuck.* A screech and a howl rang through the whole house. It was Eli. I would recognise her scream out of thousands. Not knowing what had happened killed me. Was she hurt? Dead? Was someone she loved hurt? Alice? Fuck. I felt so useless. I tried wiggling the chair again, but nothing moved. It was too heavy and my arms and legs just wouldn't budge. Then my mood soared; I detected Frank's scent and, above all else, Zaphire's. They were here! Relief flooded over me. But then my door slammed open. It wasn't one of us. *Fuck it.* Two men, all dressed in military uniform with masks covering their faces, ran in. One sliced the zip ties off my legs, and he dragged me roughly from the chair, out the door. My legs were dead. They wouldn't move. It felt like they were someone else's legs. Then the feeling returned. A burning sensation, like a thousand lit matches licking, attacked my legs. I didn't have much time to focus on who was taking me, being forced to run with them. I willed my legs to work, to resist them. To make it hard for them to move me. I fought as best as I could, aiming kicks at their legs, making my body as stiff as I could. I didn't want to be dragged along the floor, but it would slow them down, so I made myself as heavy and awkward to move as I could muster. They were fucking strong though, and weren't pussy footing around.

"Chyort! Yobni ego!" Irena's 'cousin' shouted just before a fist cracked open the cut on my cheek. I smelled the blood before I could feel it running down my face. Kicks and fists to the rest of my body followed without a break. Pain coursed through my entire body. Burning, stabbing, throbbing pain. I felt my resistance slowly wane. They managed to drag me out of the front door and into the minibus. A pair of cuffs were hastily fastened around my ankles, but not before I kicked one of them right in the face, splitting his lip.

"Sukin syn!" the man cursed, spitting his blood in my face.

Another body was flung into the seat next to me. I knew instantly it was Eli. Thank fuck she was still alive, and I didn't smell any blood either. She wasn't wounded, at least not by the gunshot. She was restrained with cuffs too. Seconds later, Irena, Jean-Pierre and Angelique joined the masked men, five in total, and the bus sped off. I have to say I was fucking happy to see Jessica wasn't one of them.

CHAPTER 36
Zaphire

The house was dark, but we sensed movement. A minibus was parked on the drive. The driver just got out and walked to the bushes to take a piss. We parked our vans a little way away, not to alert them of our arrival. There were twelve of us. Frank and Vivian in overall charge, Rob and Brody second in command. Four guards bolstered our team. All of us were carrying. After the last mission Markus had made gun practise obligatory for everyone over eighteen, so we at least knew how to use them properly, though we were only given access on specific missions. Missions like these. A heavy warning came with carrying. Only use in case of self-defence. Misuse would lead to a lifetime ban.

We took advantage of the driver's toilet break and crept past the vehicle to the back of the house. Tristan attached a tracker under the wheel arch, whilst Ned stood watch. It literally took thirty seconds or so, and they both re-joined us quickly.

The driver was no Sensorian and was oblivious to our movements, so we easily entered the garden unnoticed. We had to work fast, but silently. If anyone was awake they would hear us, or our scents would alert them, even though we sprayed ourselves with the neutralising spray. The disguise wouldn't last long.

"They're not alone. There are more Dullards as well as an unknown Sensorian," Frank stated. We'd all picked up the scents already. "Rob, can you hack anyone inside?"

"The Sensorian is related to Irena," I informed everyone. I recognised their familial scent. Irena's imprinted on my memory thanks to the unpleasant encounter I'd had with her before, when she had captured me.

"Nope. Eliza is asleep, or has her eyes closed. I need a visual with the others to be able to hack into them," Rob updated. Frank swore under his breath. "I know, but I can hack into her eyes as soon as she opens them up," Rob added to try and keep positive.

Frank opened the patio door silently with his expert burglary skills, and we filed in one behind the other. I detected Alice's scent. She was definitely here. It was strong and fresh. I could smell Zack. I couldn't help but gasp as the distinct scent of his blood penetrated my nostrils. Brody glared at me. I needed to keep my emotion under control, not to give us away. But it was to no avail; the sudden noise and movement in the house indicated that they had discovered our presence already.

"I'm in. I can see Rick and Alice. They look alarmed. Bollocks. Two people in masks just entered their room. Go! Go!" Rob urged us on. We stormed forwards, drawing our guns, kicking the doors open. All cautiousness left behind. The scene that unravelled before our eyes in the next room was shocking. It all went so quick.

The two masked men hesitated for a second when they clocked us, assessing their next move. Eliza took that opportunity to lunge forward to attack them. She threw herself on one of them, but the other one aimed their gun at Alice, and shouted at Eliza to stop. Rick jumped up, screaming a loud 'no', causing the masked man to jerk his gun in Rick's direction and shoot. Eliza shrieked, causing all Sensorians to cringe for just a second, and giving the two attackers time to retreat with Eliza in their clutches. I ran forward towards Alice, the man aimed again, but they were surrounded by us and more focussed on getting out than harming Alice. He aimed his gun at Eliza's head instead.

"I will shoot girl," he growled with a heavy accent. It sounded Russian. I did not doubt his intentions one bit. We moved out of their way, our guns now fully trained on them. But we couldn't shoot, it was too dangerous. They hurried out, followed by our guards, Vivian and Brody. The rest made our room secure and started to check out the adjacent rooms. Rob found Jessica cowering in one of them. He detained her and shoved her in the room with us. I hurried over to Alice, who was white as snow and staring into space, probably suffering from shock, whilst Frank checked Rick over. It didn't look good, but I sensed he was still alive.

CHAPTER 37

Zack

I noticed Eli's tears, even though she wasn't making any sound. Her face was wet with them. My heart broke, seeing her in so much emotional agony.

"What did you do to him! Why did you have to shoot!" she suddenly screamed, her voice high pitched and cracking, trying to lash out with her bound arms. *Fuck.* The son of a bitch had shot Rick.

"Agh, he'll be fine. He only got the leg," Irena scoffed. "Don't be such a baby."

"I'm sure the others will look after him and Alice. You should be happy. At least she doesn't have to go to Canada now," Angelique chimed in, making the others snigger a little. "Now sit quietly. It will be all the more comfortable for you if you don't make a scene, ma chérie."

Eli was seething. She wasn't cloaking and her anger was felt by every Sensorian in the bus. It was too strong to completely shield. The Dullards were unaffected, of course. One of them moved over to sit next to me and pulled off his mask, revealing he was actually a she. Or, maybe not. Hard to say, but they had big soft brown eyes with a dainty nose, but heavy eyebrows and a square jaw line. They looked in their early twenties.

"How are you feeling? I get water for you," they said, rolling the 'r' with a heavy Russian accent. They rummaged around in a bag, fished out some bottled water, removed my blooded gag and held the bottle to my lips. I drank eagerly, although it made every inch of my face ache. The taste of blood in my mouth dissipated a little. They got a first aid kit out and started to tend to my cuts and bruises, though many were under my clothes.

"Good job, Ilia. We need to patch him up a bit. I don't want to present Colonel Turgenev with weak looking specimens. They are among the best and they need to look it. Give him some food too," Jean-Pierre ordered.

The Russian Sensorian, who I believed to be

Irena's relative, scoffed, but didn't overrule the order. I considered refusing, just to piss them off, but I gathered I could use the strength it would give me.

"Who the fuck is Turgenev?" I mumbled. It hurt to speak.

"Shhshhh. You find out information soon. Drink. Eat food," Ilia soothed quietly. He cut my arms free but only to move them to the front, then bound them again. My shoulders jarred with the movement. He handed me a sausage roll, which I eagerly ate. The scent of testosterone he emitted told me he was more male than female, but I was still guessing. I didn't know whether Ilia was a male or female name. I didn't care; he or she was looking after me. Their team consisted of Irena's cousin, who seemed to be in charge, and the only Sensorian besides Irena, Angelique and Jean-Pierre, plus Ilia, two men, one blond woman and a big burly driver. Jean-Pierre seemed to be regarded with some respect. Angelique was tolerated and Irena was treated like one of them.

"Eliza?" I called softly. She turned her face towards me. The pain, fear and anger in her eyes dug deep inside me. Despite the hurt, she looked so beautiful. Her dark messy bob perfectly framed her delicate face. I dug my nails into my leg. *Stop fucking thinking about her like that.* "Are you holding up?"

She nodded, a little hesitantly to start with, but her eyes started to convey determination.

"Mum's safe." Her body relaxed with relief. "That's all that matters. Frank and the others will look after her."

"Skazhi im, chtoby oni zatknulis! Skazhi im govorit' tol'ko togda, kogda k nim obrashchayutsya!" Irena's cousin bellowed.

"Shut the fuck up, you two. Dimitri doesn't want to hear your voices again, unless spoken to," Irena translated.

I hated being controlled like this, but I was used to it and did know when to follow orders. In this case there wasn't a lot of choice. Though Jean-Pierre wanted us to look presentable, I don't think the Russians cared too much. Certainly not the one I managed to kick in the face by the look of his furious expression.

CHAPTER 38

Zaphire

"He's been shot in the leg. Hc's passed out. Lost a lot of blood. We need to get him to the hospital," Frank ordered decisively.

"Why not let him die? Focus on helping Eliza and Zack instead? Markus is going to make sure he gets the death penalty anyway," I objected. Frank glowered, making me shrink away in pain.

"He tried to save Alice's and Eliza's lives. He deserves a chance. Don't you ever suggest playing judge and jury again," he threatened menacingly.

He was angry with me, and I sort of knew he was right. I saw Rick put his own life in danger to save theirs, but he was a traitor, and in our community that spelled certain death. Unless Frank knew something that I didn't? I felt a little unfairly judged by my comment. I tried to keep out of Frank's way, focussing once again on Alice. I tried to give her some water.

"They've got my girl," she wailed, suddenly sobbing uncontrollably.

Vivian and Brody came rushing back into the room.

"They're gone. They took Zack and Eliza. We need to use one van to follow. We'll stay far enough away so they don't notice us. We got the tracker on. Who do you want to go Frank?" Brody spoke rapidly, needing a decision straight away.

"You, Vivian, Tristan, Rob and the guards. Send Ned and Sam back. We'll sort Alice and Rick out. Go," Frank ordered, cool as a cucumber.

"I need to go!" I shouted, desperately. "You can't stop me! Zack's my brother. I have to help!" I jumped up and manoeuvred myself behind Brody. A flicker of doubt crossed Frank's face. There was no time to discuss this. He had to agree with me. He just had to!

"Fine. Go. But do not let me regret that decision. Keep your emotions in check!" he decided after a few seconds, his face stern and his voice strained. He glanced over to Brody, who nodded with a knowing look. A look that said; I'll watch her. *Ugh.* I wish they didn't do this. It made me feel like a little child. But as Frank had agreed to let me go, I decided not to challenge them.

CHAPTER 39

Eliza

His eyes scanned the room

Dark and threatening

They rested on me

His gun pointed past me

A shift in focus

I see mum

wide eyed, her mouth open

a silent scream

a movement, triggers the shot

Rick.

Blood...

Violently shaking, I let out a scream. The pain of watching my father get shot again, even in my dreams, was too much to bear. *Shit.* I must have dozed off. Russian voices shouting. I couldn't make out the words. Next, Irena's voice hot in my ear.

"Move. Quick, come," she urged. Did she

sound a little concerned for me? I didn't kid myself. Irena was ruthless. "Some advice; take it or leave it, but don't piss off Dimitri. If you pass, you can do well here, have a good life. There's no way out. Trust me. And I'm not saying this just for your benefit. It will reflect badly on me, if you turn out a waste. I recommended you."

I knew there would be something in it for her, but I decided to take heed of her warning. Dimitri looked dangerous. He was built like a brick house. His undeniable handsome face permanently contorted in a frown with a ruthless expression in his eyes. He was not to be messed with.

I decided to try and subtly stall them, give Frank time to come up with a plan. If we ended up dead, it would be of no use to anyone. I promised myself to play along the best I could. I climbed out of the car. I was confronted by the sight of a huge mansion house, surrounded by ornate but lethal looking fences. I looked back down the drive and spotted two ostentatious stone eagles sitting atop the pillars flanking the gate, giving the impression the owner of the house was somewhat of a poser.

Zack clearly wasn't on the same page as me. He gave his capturers as good as he got, but the end result was the same; us standing in front of the heavy-set front door waiting to be let in, Zack in considerably more pain than me.

The door was opened by a stoic looking man, ushering us in. Dimitri immediately started to shout what sounded like orders, and men and women walked off purposefully, presumably doing the tasks he gave them. He was clearly in charge. Irena stayed by my side, and Ilia with Zack, whilst a trunk-of-a man restrained him. Jean-Pierre and Angelique had followed the blonde woman down the corridor, lined with gold framed mirrors and paintings. Their footsteps silenced by the luxurious thick, red carpet. Jean-Pierre and his wife seemed familiar with the place. *What the hell did these Russians want from us?*

"Otvesti ikh v komnatu dlya doprosov. Derzhat' ikh vmeste," Dimitri barked.

"To the interrogation room," Irena whispered,

earning her a warning stare from Dimitri, which she promptly ignored as she carried on. "Keep calm, it'll be fine. You'll stay with Zack."

I tried to catch Zack's eye, but he was looking straight ahead. I could feel the effort it took him to cloak his physical pain. It took all his strength, but he succeeded. He didn't want to give Dimitri the satisfaction. Dimitri was right behind us, rattling in Russian to one of his team members. What I would give to understand what they were talking about.

We were led down to the cellar and came to a stop in front of a steel enforced door. Dimitri opened it and motioned for us to enter. The room was soundproofed, that much was clear. It wasn't as dark and dank as I'd expected. Instead it was bright, with harsh lights beaming down. White metal benches lined the walls, screwed down into the floor, I suspected so they couldn't be flung about. A chair stood proudly in the middle. It had restraints connected to the legs, arm rests and even a head piece. It looked frightening. My heart started to race and my throat went dry, as I realised

I was being led towards the chair by the firm hand that had wrapped itself around my arm. It wasn't Irena's. It was Dimitri's. I knew he could sense my fear, my rising rebellion. I had to quell it, disguise it. *Cloak, damn it.*

"Sit," he ordered. I obeyed. "Good girl," he said, nodding self-satisfied. *Condescending prick.* Irena fastened the restraints. This did not feel good. I felt extremely vulnerable. Everything was out of my control. I started to shake a little. I couldn't stop it.

Zack was placed on the bench on the wall to the side of me. I could just about see him, but I didn't need to. His divine scent was all over the room. Hard to ignore. He managed to cloak his distress well, leaving just his heady, musky scent. The two guards sat beside him gave him no room to manoeuvre.

"I explain why you here," Dimitri started in his broken English. "Colonel Oleg Turkenev work for FSB. He look for Sensorians to help with interrogation. Look to see if people tell truth. You

.292

are better, more efficient, than machine and torture. Understand?"

Both Zack and I nodded. We were up to our necks in this mess. The Russian secret police. *Christ*. How had this happened?

"Good. See? Not difficult to be good boy and girl," he sneered. He was only pushing thirty himself at the most, but treated us like little kids. Infuriating. "My job is make you comply. Lyubymi sposobami. Irina? Zastav' ikh ponyat." His voice sounded frustrated with his lack of English.

"Dimitri says he can use any means possible to make you comply." Irena translated. "I would take that threat seriously, if I were you," she added quietly.

"I go to find your weakness. I use. You will comply." Dimitri circled me, stopped when he faced me again. His finger traced my face softly and travelled slowly down my chin, onto my neck, and even lower, onto my breast, his other hand ripping my top to the side to expose my skin. My

.293

blood boiled. My breathing sped up with my anger, the humiliation.

"Keep your filthy hands off her, you fucking son of a bitch!" Zack roared from the side. My body cringed and warmed at the same time. His emotions hurting me, his intentions heartfelt. Dimitri laughed and swung round to face Zack.

"Eto ne zanyalo mnogo vremeni, glupyy idiot," he smirked, making the other Russians snigger loudly. "That took not long break you. You strong? You dumb?" His face nearly touched Zack's, and he took a deep sniff. I could tell Zack tried to head-butt Dimitri, but Ilia held his head tight. "Maybe you love girl? You cloak well. But fool. What is punishment for speaking?"

Oh no, for fuck's sake, not again. No more pain for Zack, *please.* I opened my mouth, but Irena gently nudged me and shook her head, a dark warning lurking in her eyes. That told me enough. I would not be spared, if I spoke out of turn. I couldn't stop the tears springing from my eyes, though. Snot slowly trickled from my nose. I didn't want Zack to suffer for my sake. Dimitri was wrong. He didn't love me. Not in that way. He had Phaedra. This was too much.

"Razdvinut' nogi," he ordered. The men responded by roughly ripping his legs apart. "You cloak pain. I not want to feel it. If I feel, I kick again." He glanced over to me for a moment, to gauge my reaction. I didn't leave much to guess how I felt. It was tearing me apart. I screamed like a banshee, but only inside my head. There was no doubt he sensed my pain. He smiled viciously at me, then his head snapped back to face Zack.

Bile rose up into my throat. The nutter was a sadist! I could feel Zack steel himself. His legs were in a vice like grip by both men beside him, he had nowhere to go. A sick grin spread over Dimitri's face right before his foot lashed out, kicking Zack right in his balls. I waited for Zack's pain to hit me. Nothing. Just a little grunt. His eyes watered, but I could not feel a thing. Bloody hell. How?

Dimitri's smile faded. But I felt a little

.295

admiration hiding among a whole host of feelings, most of them vile. I think Zack passed that test. I threw up. I couldn't keep it in. The sick splattered all over Dimitri's shoes and up his legs. It didn't even faze him. He hardly noticed.

"Moya rabota sdelena.Ya znayu, kak zastavit' vas oboikh podchinit'sya. Irina perevedi." He sounded and looked satisfied. I noticed he pronounced Irena's name differently from us.

"Da, Serzhant Asanov," Irena answered deferentially. "Dimitri says his job is done. He knows how to make both of you comply," Irena translated. "Let's get you cleaned up and ready to meet Colonel Turkenev in the morning." I realised we'd basically been up all night, and it didn't look like we were going to get much more sleep than the nap I had in the car. "Ilia, get some ice for Zack. He must be hurting." Irena added, more compassionately than I thought her capable of.

When Dimitri left, Zack let it out. He could cloak no more. Irena and I shielded, but his pain was too strong. It was not just his balls that hurt. It was his pride too.

CHAPTER 40

Zack

The ice, if anything, raised the heat in my groin to even more unbearable levels. I saw black, and throbbing stars bounced in front of my eyes. Before the ice started to work its numbing magic, I nearly passed out. I breathed through it as best I could. Ilia's cold hands felt nice on my forehead.

"Stay with us Zack. No good to pass out. I be punished for not looking after you good," he almost pleaded. "How I can patch you up to look good for Colonel Turkenev?" Sweat started to pour down his face. He was worried. I was worried too. I felt sick and unable to move. Maybe I should make life difficult for Ilia and the rest of them, and not be ready for the big meeting. But Dimitri would know if I hadn't tried and faked it. That would not be a good outcome. I had to try.

"How long do we have?" I managed to grunt.

"Hour and half," Ilia whispered rather despondently. My head fell back and I could only manage a groan. My senses suddenly stood on edge. I could feel Eli approaching. She kneeled next to me. I turned my head. I didn't want to look her in the eyes. She did not need to see me in this pathetic state. It killed her to see me in pain, her empathy soared. I wanted her pain to stop. I eventually turned and did look at her, in an attempt to reassure her. Those beautiful, inscrutable, grey eyes still took my breath away momentarily. I shook my head slightly to gather my thoughts.

"I'll be fine soon, Eli. Please don't worry. My nuts have had worse treatment, trust me," I forced a smile, but it was a lie and the words I uttered made my whole body ache, thanks to the previous beatings. She smiled back, but I knew I hadn't convinced her at all. Ilia shooed Eliza away.

"I make you warm bath and take these pills," Ilia fussed. "You feel better in hour. I checked Google." I looked at them a bit dubiously, but knowing it was in Ilia's interest to patch me up, I trusted the pills were fine to take. "After bath, ice back on."

After about half an hour I managed to get up and walk around a little, and Ilia escorted me to the bath. Eliza had been taken to another room, presumably to take a shower and put on some fresh clothes. I didn't like not being near her. I didn't trust Dimitri one fucking bit. Not that I was in any position to protect her, but not knowing was even worse.

I slowly but surely started to feel better. I wasn't sure what pills I'd been given, but I wanted a stash of them. They fucking worked wonders.

Eliza came back in accompanied by another subdued looking young Sensorian, and guarded by a blonde woman and the trunk of a man. The boy clearly wasn't here on his own volition either. I tried to place his scent, but drew a blank. The look on Eliza's face on clocking me was priceless. Her face broke out into a beautiful warming smile. I don't think she had expected me to have recovered so well. I hoped the pills lasted. It felt so good to make her happy. My heart swelled with joy. The curly haired boy held out his hand to make my acquaintance. I grabbed and shook it firmly.

"Rafferty Donahue. You must be Zack Mackenzie?" It was a question, but he knew the answer. Eliza's scent was all over him, instantly raising my heckles. She must have met him earlier. Why on earth did I feel protective and jealous straight away? Fucking idiot. I forced myself to nod and smile.

"Nice to meet you. Wish the circumstances were different. I take it you've been captured too?" I offered, trying to sound friendly, but the scowl on Eliza's face told me it wasn't working. The words came out fine, but I couldn't make it sound nice. Rafferty didn't seem fazed by it and just shook his head.

"Yeah. I've been here a few days and I can't say it's been fun. I come from a strict place, but this is next level. It's downright cruel," he said, looking indignant.

"Where are you from, mate?" I was curious to know. His name sounded Irish, but I knew the Irish clans and Donahue wasn't one of them.

"You won't have heard of us. My father wasn't very sociable after my mum died, but very dependable and loyal. Kept us hidden away from everyone most of the time. Then about a week ago, he answered an emergency call from a nearby family and took me with him for training purposes. Normal procedure. This time however, the clan we went to help was all but gone, and before I knew it I was captured, my father fought and got shot dead in the process. And here I am," he said, his face expressionless.

"Tikho! I mean, quiet! Dimitri comes," Ilia warned.

The fear in Rafferty's eyes was gut-wrenching. His friendly, confident manner shrunk away in seconds. It was heart breaking to witness. His shoulders hung and he shuffled backwards, trying to hide behind the two other Russians. My hatred for Dimitri sparked up a level again. God only knows what Rafferty had been subjected to in the past few days.

Dimitri entered. Everyone fell silent.

"Polkovnik Turgenev gotov ikh osmotret'." He looked at Irena to translate again. It seemed he really hated speaking English.

"Colonel Turkenev is ready to inspect you," Irena obliged. Dimitri rattled some more instructions to the Russians who all sprang into action. Irena stayed with Eliza, Ilia with me and Blondie with Rafferty. We were marched through several corridors in the mansion. I tried to make a mental map of the place as we walked. I noticed Eliza also spied the place, probably committing the route to memory, like I was.

Dimitri halted and turned around, staring us down for what seemed like minutes.

"Remember. Talk only when spoken to. Is important. You think you can do that?" His eyes rested firmly on me. I nodded, not daring to risk opening my mouth this time.

"Now, I need answer," he growled. *For fuck's sake. What a moron.*

"I'll do my best," I answered through gritted

teeth. I sounded like fucking Eliza when I was training her. I knew that answer wouldn't satisfy him by any stretch of the imagination.

"Yes, master, is the correct answer, Mackenzie," he drooled with his customary sick grin plastered all over his face. "You learn." I cringed inwardly, but knew I had to comply. "I Sensorian too. Don't forget. I feel you disgusted. Cloak better."

"Yes master," I said blankly, hoping to avoid more scrutinising.

"Good boy," he crooned. *What a fucking patronising git.* "Ya sobirayus' poveselit'sya s etim!" Dimitri snorted, and the other Russians laughed heartily. I didn't want to know what he said. Ilia nudged me when Dimitri's attention was averted.

"Don't make Dimitri angry. You will regret," he warned me. I think I got that message loud and clear earlier, but Dimitri was so incredibly infuriating!

The door to the room opened and we were led into the most opulent office I had ever seen. It was filled with ornate art, luxurious dark blue carpet lined the floor, and mirrors with big golden frames were placed in strategic places, making the light in the room bounce around like magic. A massive desk sat at the far end of the room, and behind it was a distinguished looking man of around fifty years old, with an unforgiving stare directed at us from underneath his bushy eyebrows.

"Welcome, new recruits." Turkenev's voice boomed through the room, the three words dripping with authority. "Sergeant Asanov, you failed to bring in Rick Mankuzay?"

Dimitri squirmed and nodded, mumbling something that sounded very submissive. Turkenev looked at him haughtily, without mercy.

"We'll talk consequences later. Now, introduce these specimens to me with your assessment of their attitude and abilities, and your management strategies for each of them." He spoke with a slight Russian accent, but his English was faultless.

"Konechno, Polkovnik, ser," Dimitri started.

"In English. I want them to understand." Turkenev interjected. Dimitri nodded, but I could feel his confidence falter just a little. He straightened his shoulders and took a deep breath.

"First one; Rafferty. Fast, strong, obedient. We have sister, Carol. She is thirteen and no Sensorian. No use for us but good method to keep Rafferty in check. He fucks up, she get punished, badly, as well as him. Works well. Rafferty complies. No problem."

No wonder Rafferty feared Dimitri and his cronies. Poor guy. His little sister's fate is literally in their hands. What a fucking nightmare.

"Eliza and Zack. Great assets. Eliza, good 'intuitsiya', clever, loyal. Zack, strong, strategic thinker, leader potential. Both stubborn as hell. I thought it be problem, but I found trigger so easy. I confident they comply."

I looked over to Eliza. She looked as fucking downhearted as I felt. We both knew our triggers, so Dimitri had basically won.

"Eliza in love with Zack. She does not want him in pain. She feels guilty. She rather it her that is hurt. Fool. So if Eliza steps out of line, I will beat him to inch of his life, if necessary. Simples."

She's in love with me? Love me as Zaphire's brother surely. Lust sure too, but not in love. She couldn't be. The horror in Eliza's eyes told me enough. She wasn't going to risk being trouble. That was her resistance crushed. I knew that, even if I told her that I would take a beating, if it meant she could make it out of here, she wouldn't risk it. But I did expect a few punches, as Eliza was known to speak before thinking, though I'd been the one to do just that, so far. She'd been unexpectedly in control of her mouth.

"Zack the same. He extremely protective. Loves her. If Zack make trouble, I rape her in front of his eyes."

Fury built inside me. My body trembled. I growled like a wolf protecting his mate. It took all my strength, not to jump at him, rip his head off with my bare hands. His vile face was right in front of me, smirking. I wanted to head-butt him. Kill him. Right now.

"I look forward to it too. I think it will happen soon," he taunted, showcasing a big grin. The atmosphere in the room was tense. His face turned grim looking again. "But, did I hear sound come from your mouth Zack? Open your legs," he ordered, kicking one of my legs to the side. "You know punishment for that," he sneered.

"Stop Serzhant," Turkenev intervened decisively. "I don't want to see you dishing out your punishments. And don't damage his manhood. He might be good for breeding. He looks a fine specimen."

Dimitri huffed. I scoffed internally. Breeding stock now too. Fucking hell. We were living a nightmare.

"Look. Recruits," Turkenev continued. "This all sounds particularly gruesome and cruel, but there are benefits for you too. If you embrace your situation, work hard and not give us trouble; you'll have a good life. You will work for the FSB as an interrogator and you can even become an advisor to the top brass. Jean-Pierre and Angelique are flying to Russia as we speak, and will be present at all the meetings the President attends, monitoring the intentions of the delegates he meets. You'll get a luxurious flat, food and all your needs will be met. Life is not going to be that bad, if you comply. And don't forget we are your masters, because your life and those you love are at our mercy."

"We'll be your slaves! Your dogs!" Eliza spat out, unable to keep it in. Her eyes immediately flicked to me, apologetic, already regretting her outburst, her hand clasping her mouth. Dimitri wagged his finger.

"Tut, tut Eliza. Big mistake," he said languidly. Shaking his head, he sauntered back to me.

My heart sank. Another beating on its way. I cloaked my fear. I didn't want her to feel even more guilty than she, undoubtedly, already felt. Dimitri's fist landed in my stomach. I doubled over, groaning, barely able to keep standing. The pain slowly spread around my gut.

"Take this outside. Seychas zhe!" Turkenev roared. I felt the hands of Ilia and Trunk Guy slip under my arms and was dragged out. The others followed right behind me. Once outside the room Dimitri finished off my punishment. I could feel his sadistic pleasure in doing so.

"Zastav' eye smotret' na eto," Dimitri snarled. One of the guards took Eliza's head and forced it in my direction. She was made to watch. My poor sweetheart. Searing pain everywhere. I lost count of the punches and kicks. I was vaguely aware of everyone's staring eyes and feelings of outrage and disgust, but in the end I blocked everything out. Internalising the pain, until the blows finally stopped. I was dragged along the floor, unable to walk by myself and placed on a bed. Ilia's hands worked his magic with ointments and he forced some pills down my throat too. Then the world just slowly disappeared. I fought my eyes closing, but it was impossible. Darkness enveloped me like a welcoming warm bath, and I succumbed to it.

CHAPTER 41

Zaphire

Their minibus drove through a set of gates with guards into a massive drive, leading to an impressive looking country house. We were a long way behind them and decided to stop. It was too suspicious to come past straight away, as it was only a small quiet country road. We knew where they were. It was time to retreat and make a plan. We needed to find out who lived there and what exactly we were dealing with.

"Rob, how near do you have to be to hack into Eliza's eyes?" Tristan asked.

"I need to sense her, so I would have to be much nearer than we are. The drive is quite long, so I would probably have to get within the fences. Brody and I will see if we can get in by foot. We should do it now, under the cover of darkness. It will start getting light in a few hours. We can try and find out as much as possible and feed it back to you."

"You should bring a guard for protection," I suggested. It seemed like the place was heavily guarded itself, and I had an unsettling feeling growing inside me. "Vivian?"

"The fewer people, the better. In case we have to hide," Brody dismissed my idea resolutely. Vivian agreed. I wasn't happy. My gut feeling told me the place was incredibly dangerous. But Rob could use anyone's eyes as look outs, so maybe they were right. I hadn't made my mind up whether to fight for someone else to join them or not. I didn't have much time as they were going to leave imminently. Tristan fitted them with ear pieces and they left the van.

"Give me a pair," I hissed at Tristan, who was too perplexed to react decisively, so I snatched some out of the tray and fitted them myself. "Can you cope with the communications?" He sent me such a dark look, it made me quiver slightly.

"Of course," he growled. "But, what are..."

I didn't let him finish. I jumped out of the van and ran to join Rob and Brody.

"You need an extra pair of hands. Trust me," I panted, after my short burst of activity. I ignored their scowls, but their emotions of anger and worry were a little harder to shield from. "I'm not going back. Just accept it. It's non-negotiable."

"You stubborn twat," Brody grumbled. "You're playing with fire. If we get caught..."

"Yeah, I get that. But we won't. We have to believe that," I bit back. They both sighed and shrugged their shoulders. I accepted that as a win.

We scouted around the perimeter of the property. Dogs were being patrolled around the fence, but there were gaps. We'd sprayed ourselves with neutralising spray. It should put the dogs off. Rob kept an eye on, quite literally, the guards, swapping between their sights, and we found the perfect spot to enter. We had to time it to perfection. We observed where and when the guards were patrolling. It turned out we only had forty five seconds to creep through and sprint to the bushes, just beyond the edge to give us some cover. The CCTV could possibly spot us, but

Tristan was working on interference. He wasn't as good as Archie, but with him on the other end of the phone giving instructions, it should work. We waited for Tristan's signal. All of us barcly breathing, to make as little sound as possible. There weren't any Sensorian guards. That made our lives a little easier.

Brody signalled we were good to go. We just had to wait for the right time. Brody signed again. I crawled through, with Brody right behind me. We sprinted to the agreed spot, which left eighteen seconds for Rob to complete the run too, which he managed easily. He gathered himself to concentrate on the guards eyes again. We just needed to get close enough so we could sense any of the Sensorians inside. Eliza would be the most preferable as Rob had the strongest link with her. A couple of cars were parked around the side of the building. That's where we had to go. It would give us some protection from prying eyes. Rob gave us the nod and we ran across the wide open lawn, hoping no one would spot us. Once we got to the cars, we dived in between and caught our breath. Rob took a moment to go to each guard's eyes, but none of them had spotted us. One of the dogs had pricked up its ears and sniffed the air, but after a few seconds it had lost interest. Rob exhaled with relief. It was our job now to keep an eye out around us, so Rob could concentrate on making a connection with Eliza. With every passing minute the tension mounted. I had to focus on my breathing to keep calm, and stop myself from asking if he'd managed to hack in yet.

Finally, Rob signalled he'd made contact. His face went blank and he was totally immersed in what he was seeing. He winced a few times. I didn't want to think about what he saw. I stopped looking at his face, and concentrated on my surroundings and any impending danger. It was just as well I'd come, as it proved difficult to keep an eye on all areas. Brody and I stationed ourselves at different angles from Rob, so we could see all around without having to move too much, minimising the danger of detection. I heard one of the guards and his dog walking along the perimeter. So far, they'd ignored the small car park where we were hiding. Tristan confirmed he was still managing to play havoc with their CCTV system, but suspicions could arise soon. He warned us not to be too long. After a good ten minutes, Brody tapped Rob on the shoulder and made the return to base signal; a quick spin of the finger. Rob nodded, though irritation was written all over his face. He probably was getting some good intel. He shook his head slightly and he was ready to return. I couldn't wait to hear what he'd found out.

We managed to slip back out fairly easily again and ran back to our van. We found Vivian and the team also eager to tell us what they'd found out, but they let Rob speak first, as it was all fresh in his head. He got out a piece of paper and drew out a room, placing people around it as he'd seen them. Zack and Eliza and one male stood next to each other in the middle of the room with another male near them. A man sat behind a desk at the far end of the room and Irena and two others stood on the side.

"I don't know what was going on, a lot of talking by a young man, like he was introducing them. By the end Zack suffered a severe beating, which Eliza was forced to watch. It was horrendous, and Zack was then dragged away. They were led away to somewhere else in the building, but then you tapped me on the shoulder, and I lost connection for a moment. I think I know where in relation to the other room they were, but that's about it."

"Useful info, Rob. Well done," Vivian complimented appreciatively. "We have some good intel too. The guy behind the desk is highly likely Oleg Turkenev, high up in the FSB." She showed Rob a picture, who nodded immediately.

"That's him."

"Markus assumes they are recruiting Sensorians as interrogators," Vivian continued. That made sense. No better interrogator than a Sensorian let loose on a Dullard. "Colonel Turkenev is known to be a strict chief who's not shy of using torture to get his ways. Unofficially of course. Though nowadays he doesn't get his hands dirty, one of his subordinates, rumoured to be a man called Dimitri Asanov, does that now. I have no pictures of him, but it sounds like he could be the one that did most of the talking. On a different note; did you see Jean-Pierre and Angelique anywhere?"

"No, they weren't in the room. None of us got their scent, so they might not even be in the building."

"There's no information on the building to be found. It's all blocked access. So all we have is Rob. You might have to go in again and see if you can get some more information about the layout of the place and how many of them there are," Tristan interjected.

"I could sense two other Sensorians, apart from Irena. I suspect one of them was captured like Zack and Eli, the one who stood next to them. The other's the arsehole who beat up Zack. The rest are all Dullards," Rob continued

"So this Dimitri Asanov, most likely a relative to Irena, is definitely a Sensorian? We need to go back in again. This guy is dangerous," I suggested urgently. "It's still dark."

"No, I can't hack into their CCTV again. At the moment it just looks like a random glitch, but it will look suspicious if I do it again so soon. It will trigger an investigation."

"Tristan is right. We'll have to wait until tonight. We'll find a place to stay, have some food and sleep. We'll return tomorrow early evening. It'll be dark by 5pm," Vivian decided. I knew she was right, but I was itching to go in. Every hour seemed crucial.

"What if they move them during the day? I think we need to have eyes on them. We can take shifts," I suggested. Vivian nodded approvingly.

"Good point Zaphire. We'll divide into teams. You and Brody can have first shift. We need to get an extra car first. I'll have one sent up to you. It won't be long, but wrap up warm."

Brody looked less than impressed.

"We've only just warmed up. Can't someone else take first shift?" he whined without much conviction. Vivian just looked at him, not even dignifying him with a response. Minutes later we stood outside, with promises of coffees and a car to arrive soon.

It turned out it took another hour before the promised articles arrived and in the meantime it had started to sleet. Our moods had taken a deep dive, silence hung between us, but we huddled together to try and keep warm. Finally, we were joined by Mark, one of the guards who'd driven the car down. He was a surly looking bloke, but actually had a great sense of humour, entertaining us with funny stories for the remainder of our shift. Nothing untoward happened and as such we had nothing to report to the incoming shift. Mark drove us back after we swapped over. I looked forward to a hot shower and bed in the motel Vivian had booked for all of us. I tried not to think what Eli and Zack had to endure the following day. I hoped they could stay out of trouble. As soon as we knew more about the layout and people at the place, we could go in and attempt to rescue them. I just hoped they would stay put and give us that chance.

The following evening Brody, Rob and I went back in, the same as the previous evening. It all went smoothly. Rob was able to hack into Irena's eyes for a bit, and learned more about the layout of the building, and in which rooms Zack and Eliza were held. Unfortunately, Tristan called us back after only about twenty minutes. Getting all the info we needed was going to be a slow process, if we could only go in for such short periods of time. But there was not much we could do about it. We didn't want to run the risk of being discovered. We didn't have enough intel yet to go in all guns blazing, so we had to keep on gathering it steadily throughout the night. It was a painfully slow operation. I just wanted Zack and Eliza out of there.

CHAPTER 42

Eliza

Dimitri had split us up. I was in a room with Irena and Natalya, the blonde girl. We spent some of the day sleeping, recovering from the long night. The rest of the day was pretty boring and was spent just lounging about, watching TV and eating. But at least we were left alone by Dimitri. I checked on Zack a couple of times during the day, but only by the end of the afternoon could I hack his vision, and even then, it wasn't particularly clear. He must have been heavily sedated. I couldn't see much, apart from the TV, and Ilia coming into his field of vision occasionally, looking concerned. It made my stomach turn. I would definitely do my best not to rile Dimitri again. I couldn't cope seeing Zack in so much pain. I could have hit myself when I challenged Colonel Turkenev, and I'd expected anger or some sort of accusing feelings from Zack flooding me. I wouldn't blame him if he had, but there wasn't anything. I could only sense a fear for what was to come and acceptance. No bad feelings toward me at all. It had surprised me. Maybe he did still have feelings for me. But he had Phaedra now; he was just doing his duty. However, the fact he had cloaked to spare me those accusatory feelings, even if he had felt any, made me love him even more.

I hoped Zack would be able to keep toeing the line, and not upset any of the Russians, better than I'd managed so far. My fate would be horrendous, if he didn't manage it. I pushed that consequence as far away in my mind as possible. I couldn't bear the thought. I couldn't help but shiver. If Zack did lose it, I vowed not to blame him for what Dimitri would do to me.

Irena and Natalya took it in turns to leave the room and do the tasks they were given, but they didn't stay away long. They clearly didn't trust me to be on my own with just one of them. I suppose my history with Irena didn't help, having tricked and overpowered her when Rick had me locked up in my room. This room was locked and guarded on the outside. The windows were the only way out, but when I had a peek, it was too big a drop, as we were two levels up plus there were steel spikes on the outside window sills. Irena scoffed when she noticed me scouting an escape.

"You may as well give up, Eliza. There is no way out of here. It's the same for me. I sometimes regret the decision I made, but I have to live with it," she confided in me, when Natalya went to the bathroom. My ears pricked up. Irena regretted something. That had to offer a way in somehow.

"What happened? How did you get involved in this?" I asked, though I suspected her cousin Dimitri had something to do with it.

"After the Sensorians were outed in the news by Daniel, Dimitri was found out to be one, as the Russians recognised some of his behaviour and put two and two together. He'd managed to keep his gift secret until that point, during the five years he'd worked for the FSB. They immediately recognised his huge potential, and made it his mission to seek out and persuade other Sensorians to join. Jean-Pierre and Angelique were on his radar and they managed to secure a good position, gaining Colonel Turkenev's trust quickly. Other Sensorians did not come forward voluntarily, but Dimitri managed to persuade me to join his team. I had no idea how this organisation worked, but to be honest, once my cousin had set his eyes on me, I had run out of choices anyway. This was going to be my future."

I heard the regret and resignation. Maybe I could persuade Irena to help us. I'd have to promise things I couldn't guarantee, but it was worth a shot.

"This isn't the life you signed up for when you joined Rick. You were all about living out in the open, not having to hide who we are, and reaching our full potential. This is the opposite of that; worse than all Sensorian communities, strict as they may be. We will be their workhorses; they own us because of what we can do for them. We're not their equals."

"Jean-Pierre and Angelique are. They managed to get into the high ranks pretty quickly. We can work towards that?" she suggested timidly.

"They do that on purpose. They give a few of us high status, to keep the rest in check. To give us hope that one day we can become like them. That will happen to very few of us. Also, I bet Jean-Pierre and Angelique are just their puppets. They can do their job, but they'll be under the full control of the FSB. They will have no freedom either." I countered. Irena kept quiet. I felt the turmoil in her head. I knew I only confirmed what she thought herself, but she had more or less convinced herself that this was how life would pan out for her. No way to escape it. I might trigger a little spark of defiance. I was going to try it. I was taking an enormous risk and it may backfire spectacularly, but I had to try. If it worked it would increase our chances of success manyfold.

"I'm putting our chance of escape in danger by telling you this. Do with it what you will, but consider it for a while at least, before you make your decision. I know that a team of Sensorians is nearby. They have tracked us down. They're planning to break us out. You can come with us, if you help us. If you contact them, we could coordinate the attempt. Insider knowledge and help would be crucial." I scrutinised every sense she put out. It was all over the place. I couldn't tell what she'd decide.

"Whatever they plan to do; it'll never work. The Russians are too organised, too brutal. They'll all end up in the same boat as you. The best message I can send is to give up. Leave and cut their losses."

"They'll never do that. We're a family and we fight for each other. Don't you want to be part of that?" I tempted.

"They'll never accept me. Markus will punish me. Maybe even execute me. I can't take that risk, Eliza." She sounded defeated. The life had definitely left her. Her hard front had melted away, she sounded nothing like the tough Irena I had met in Rick's compound. It was just a shell. "And how do you know they're even here?"

"I know Rob Vision Hacked me," I blurted out. "Yesterday, and briefly earlier this evening."

"That's impossible, you can't tell when someone hacks you..., unless..., you're a VH yourself!" she exclaimed, realisation showing fast on her face as she spoke. I nodded my head. I'd exposed all my cards. I desperately hoped it was going to pay off. "I don't know," she hesitated. "I don't think I can help you... I'm scared of Dimitri. He'd know something was up. He's incredibly intuitive plus he's one of the best trackers I've ever come across. Once he's got your scent, he won't let go, he won't lose you."

We couldn't discuss it anymore. Natalya sauntered back into the room. I had to wait and see what Irena was going to do with the information I'd given her. Knots tied in my tummy. I decided to take a shower and would try and grab another chance to speak to Irena when Natalya was asleep. I quickly tried to hack into Zack's eyes to find out how he was, but all was black. He clearly was out for the count, again. I felt awful. He has had to endure so much pain in the last two days. The more I thought about him, the more I realised how amazing he was. I know Zaphire had blown my mind, and had opened a whole new world of love, but the love I felt for Zack was different. What I thought was superficial lust, had turned slowly into a deep respect. I trusted him unquestionably, with my life. I knew his faults and shortcomings; his arrogance, his stupid male alpha-ness, his need to control, but none of those outweighed his loyalty, his sense of responsibility and fairness. I wished things could have been different.

I couldn't sleep. Adrenaline still drenched my system. There wasn't much I could do about it. I could hardly go for a run, so I tried my breathing exercises, over and over again. I kept an ear out for Natalya's breathing, to determine how fast asleep she was. When I noticed her breathing pattern and output of senses matching that of someone in deep sleep, I crept over to Irena. I needed to continue our conversation. Irena heard me coming, of course.

"What do you want?" she hissed, not all too friendly. Maybe I'd lost the opportunity. "I told you, I can't help you. I won't tell Dimitri what you've told me so far, but that's it."

"Please Irena, this may be your only chance to get out of this too. I promise Zack and I will fight your case in our community. They are a fair bunch. If we get out, we would owe you our lives. We might die trying, but we may as well, if we stay here. Is it not worth considering it a little longer?"

"I'll sleep on it. I'll let you know in the early morning. Please leave me alone now. I need to think." She resolutely turned around to block me out. I'd done all I could.

I slunk off back to bed. I hoped the seed I had planted would grow during the night. I kept everything crossed, that it would.

CHAPTER 43

Zack

Her beautiful face lit up when she saw me
I walked towards her, feeling a shadow approach
fast
I wanted to turn, but my neck was rigid
Zaphire
Swooping in, like a light summer's breeze
Eliza's face now in ecstasy
My feet rooted to the floor, heavy like cement.
Both faces turned dark
Clouds gathered
Dimitri

"No! Get away from them!" I heard myself roar, as if in a film. I slowly realised I was in bed. Soaked through and aching all over. Damn, all my insecurities were addressed in that dream. *Fucking great.*

"You okay?" Ilia grunted from underneath his quilt. "It's 4am. Go back to sleep."

"Can I have some more medicine, please?" I groaned, knowing I could never get back to sleep without it. I was too fucking achy, plus my head was pounding.

"No more sedative. But I give painkiller," Ilia sighed, heaving himself out of bed to grab a packet from the table. He tossed me a couple of pills, which I swallowed dry. He passed me a bottle of water. "Drink."

I nearly emptied it in one go. I didn't realise how thirsty I was.

I fidgeted and turned over and over, without ever really falling back to sleep, until the alarm went off at 7am. Rafferty yawned loudly, stretching his body, popping all his joints, going over them methodically one by one. When he started on his neck, I couldn't cope with it anymore. My body tensed up, tiny prickles running up and down my body with each and every click.

"Stop fucking doing that, Raff. Bloody hell man!"

"Ah, sorry, mate. I should know better," he

apologised sheepishly.

"Yes, you fucking well should," I grumped on, not feeling in a very forgiving mood.

"Stop silly argument," Ilia ordered. "You get ready now. We are going Russia today."

That was bad news. It was like being punched in the stomach all over again. If our team had come up empty, it would be the end of our lives as we knew it. It would be fucking impossible to escape once we were in Russia. I stomped on the rising feeling of panic and hopelessness. I needed to keep my head clear. We had to do something, but I couldn't come up with any viable plan. I could fight, but they would win. There were too many for me, even if Rafferty and Eliza joined. All the Russians were trained fighters too, plus they carried guns. It would never work, and worse, Dimitri would get his way with Eliza. That could not happen. I wasn't letting that happen. We had to trust that our fellow Sensorians would come up with a plan, even though it was cutting it fine.

Raff panicked. I could feel his inner turmoil

rising. Aggression being right at the top, fighting to be let out.

"Rafferty, focus. Think of your sister. Tell me her name," I tried to distract him from his spiralling emotions. He flicked his eyes over to me, struggling to keep it together.

"Carol," he grunted. "Fucking arseholes!" he shouted at no one in particular, but the Trunk came over, threatening to escalate the situation. I walked over, hands up, not wanting to draw the Trunk's annoyance to me. Ilia looked nervously on. I felt that if he hadn't been a FSB operative, he would have been a decent person.

"Raff, come on. Calm down. You don't want your little sis to suffer. Apologise to him." I said softly, but sternly. Defiance flared up in Rafferty's eyes, but one look at my face, my authoritative mask full on, made him come to his senses.

"Apologies, masters," Rafferty quickly mumbled, head bent down. Trunk smacked him one, but then snorted, and moved back to his position. Crisis averted, I hoped. It didn't look like

Trunk was going to report it. Rafferty looked like he was back in control of his emotions, sheepishly rubbing his cheek.

We went back to getting ready. We needed showers and food. They'd given us some plain black cargo pants and a T-shirt, with a black zip-up top. I noticed some suits hanging around as well. They were of exquisite quality made by Armani. Ilia spotted me checking them over.

"Suits for later," he volunteered the information.

Moving my body was still a chore. Everything ached, despite the pain killers. Ilia shot me a worried look, when he spied me wincing as I put my clothes on.

"I hope your girl behave today. Your body can't take much more punishment," Ilia warned unhelpfully.

"I'll be fine. Whatever she does," I growled, not willing to admit my doubts about my feisty Eliza's self-control. "As long as I don't lose it. I would never forgive myself. Ilia, if you can find it in your heart, please stop me, if it looks like I'm going to do something stupid. I need all the help I can get."

Ilia looked at me pensively, but nodded curtly. That's all I could ask for. "Dimitri do more testing before we go. Prepare."

"Thanks for the warning," I sighed, but appreciated the gesture.

Not long after, we were told to line up. Eliza joined us. I suspected testing time was coming up soon. Eliza threw me a funny look. I wished I could read her mind. She definitely tried to convey something. I used all my senses to try and glean the information out of her. I sensed excitement, adrenaline, fear. Only the last one I could definitely understand in our current situation. She must know something. Something positive, something that may help get us out of here. A little ember of hope ignited inside me. She smiled the tiniest bit. That confirmed it. Whatever it was, it seemed like we had a chance. I just hoped Irena and Dimitri wouldn't pick up on her senses. It would raise suspicions straight away. She should not feel excited. Adrenaline maybe, but not excitement. I quickly scanned over Irena, but she emitted nothing but a stoic look on her face. As if Eli noticed my concern, which she probably had, her senses shut off. She was cloaking now, so she'd wanted me to feel her emotions, warning me to be ready for action. We just had to get through this next test. Whatever Dimitri had dreamed up for us was guaranteed not to be fun or easy. But with the renewed hope I felt stronger already, both physically and mentally.

Dimitri strode in, pristine uniform, perfect hair, his punch-magnet face looking arrogantly down at us. He walked past us a few times, circling us one by one.

"I check to see you know who is master. You must follow my command. You submit. You do not question. Understood?" he faced all of us so we all replied with a dutiful 'yes master'. He stopped in front of Rafferty.

"Kiss my boot," Dimitri commanded. I

noticed Raff struggled to keep an eyeroll at bay, but he complied, just about quickly enough. Dimitri nodded and moved over to me.

"Kiss my ass," he grinned maliciously, whilst turning around. He knew exactly how to humiliate a man and to draw out any resistance. I put my pride aside, sank to my knees and planted my lips firmly on his arse cheek, pulled back and stood up. He turned around, put his face inches away from mine.

"Now, thank me." His spittle covered my face. *Fucking gross.* I sighed.

"Thank you very much, master," I complied, not quite managing to keep the sarcasm out of my voice. He stared at me a good while. I knew I hadn't convinced him of my submissiveness.

"What you thanking me for, svoloch'," Dimitri spat out. *I punched him, full in the face.* In my head, that was. I steadied myself somewhat before I answered the fucking twat.

"Thank you for allowing me to kiss your arse, master." I managed to somehow sound less sarcastic; my mind firmly on the possible escape Eliza had given me hope for. The dickhead could do or make me do whatever he liked. I might play broken, but I certainly wasn't. After fully scrutinising me again for minutes on end, he finally moved over to Eliza. I feared what he was going to make Eliza do.

"Kiss my dick," he sneered at my fiery sweetheart. I spotted Irena lifting her head. A flicker of emotion, maybe even defiance, flew across her face. Dimitri clocked it and stared her down with his ruthless eyes, daring her to say something. "Irina?" he goaded. Irena kept quiet and lowered her eyes and withdrew her challenge. I could feel Eliza's resistance and humiliation. She had every right to refuse. I quickly glanced over at her, trying to convey to her that it would be fine. I would cope with another beating. She hesitated but sank to her knees. I wanted her to stop. *Please, don't do it, my love.* I begged in my head. I couldn't do anything, the moment I'd open my mouth in defence of her, he'd probably make good on his threat and rape her. *Sick fuck.* Eliza lent forward and brushed her lips against his trousers. His face was victorious. He was convinced he'd broken us, enough to comply at least. Eli got to her feet quickly, not cloaking her feelings of pure disgust, fury and hate. It hurt like hell. I had to up my shield, but her emotions were raging and hard to defend against. I noticed Dimitri wince. He struck her right across the face.

"Cloak. Now," he bellowed. She complied, but a little satisfied smile played across her face, pleased she managed to hurt him, even though it was just a little. Rescuing a little bit of her pride. She was fucking strong. I was in awe. Her resilience had surpassed my expectations, which told me more about me than about her. I would never underestimate her again.

"When in Russia, we practise more. For now. It will do," Dimitri decided. "Ustroyte im horoshuyu vzbuchku," he ordered the other Russians in uniform. They sniggered. I'm sure that didn't spell any good. "Zatem podgotov' ikh k puteshestviyu. My vyezzhayem v tri chasa."

"We have to do beasting, then you get ready for travel. We leave at 3pm." Ilia translated matter of factly. Exercise I could do. It won't be fun with my bruised and battered body, but I would endure it. We had no choice.

CHAPTER 44

Zaphire

I got woken up by the buzzing of my phone. A text from an unknown number flashed up. My heart stuttered slightly, feeling suspicious straight away. I checked the time. It was 6:14 am. I sleepily read what it said. I instantly sat bolt upright. I felt the adrenaline pump through my body at lightning speed. I jumped out of bed, threw on my crumpled heap of clothes from yesterday and raced to find Vivian. I shook her roughly to wake her up, only to be met with a grumble of expletives.

"You've got to read this, Ma'am!" I shrieked way too high pitched, not improving Vivian's state of mind.

"Get your hands off me, and calm down," she snarled whilst slightly recoiling from my -far too close- face. But she took the phone off me, and immediately sprang into action after reading the text. "Who would have thought she would turn to

.343

us? But we need to be careful, it could be a trap."

"It could be, but they don't know we're here. We would've picked that up yesterday evening. I'm sure," I countered.

"Can never be too careful. We'll proceed with this as it's the best intel we have, but with caution. Text the others to meet asap. We'll discuss our options then," Vivian decided. "I need a quick shower to get my brain working properly," she mumbled a little distracted. She clearly wasn't a morning person. I myself could do with one too, my hair was literally a birds nest and I stank of musty sheets and morning breath. No wonder Vivian had kept her distance from me earlier!

Only ten minutes later we were all huddled over the text message trying to make sense of how it came to us, and how much we should trust it. It claimed to be from Irena. She told us they were going to move the four captives at 3pm, towards a local airport. She told us their exact number of operatives, of which only she and Dimitri were

Sensorians. In return for the intel, she asked to be included in the rescue mission. She wanted asylum and protection in our Sensorian community and a guarantee not to be harmed. Eliza would back her request. She ended with a 'please don't reply'.

"She must be pretty desperate to give us the information upfront, unless it's a trap of course. Or maybe the risk of contacting us is too great to try it multiple times," Brody speculated.

"The fact she asks us not to reply does indicate that," I pondered. "I don't know about you, but I have a good feeling about this. I think it's genuine."

"Who's the fourth captive? We only picked up one other Sensorian." Rob remarked astutely.

"Good point, but it doesn't make much difference knowing who it is. We just need to accommodate for the extra person, and possibly Irena, if Markus will agree to that. Is the general consensus we should act upon this intel?" Vivian asked, actually looking for our opinions. We all nodded. Risky as it was, it was worth a shot. It would be much easier targeting a vehicle rather than entering a building.

"I'll inform Markus and get him to send back-up. We could do with a few more vehicles too." Vivian decided.

We used our time to work out our strategy, talking through each and every scenario we could think of, including it being a trap or a hoax. We decided we needed Rob to go in once more to see what preparations they were making, and whether those tallied up with leaving at 3pm. It would be more dangerous as it was broad daylight, but we did know their security detail intimately. We were confident we could pull it off, without being detected.

"What's Markus and Laura's view on accepting Irena?" I asked with mixed feelings.

"They green-lighted the whole operation," Vivian confirmed. I wasn't sure how to feel. I hadn't forgiven Irena yet for having been on Rick's team. She'd been responsible for my kidnap and complicit in the ruthless treatment I received. She seemed anything but vulnerable then, so I didn't completely trust why she would want to be rescued. Unless the prospect of life with the Russians was so bad in her mind, that she was willing to risk being judged by us and our rules. I don't know what Eliza had promised her, but whatever it was; it must have been compelling enough. Unless Irena was playing us.

CHAPTER 45

Eliza

"Aaaaaargh," was the only thing I could exclaim when I collapsed on the ground. I welcomed the cold, almost frozen grass caressing my overheated and exhausted body. The relief wasn't to last long.

"Up! Now! Lazy piece of shit bitch!" Ilia screamed in my face, as he kicked my arse. This was a side I hadn't seen of him. His delicate, beautiful face at odds with the raw masculinity he was displaying. I'd taken him for a rather gentle soul, but that was clearly not all he was. He was enjoying this beasting session a little too much. Maybe it gave him a sense of power that normally eluded him in his normal role at the FSB. I struggled back up, on to my feet, ready for the next set of punishing exercises. In the meantime, he'd sent Rafferty and Zack to run up the hill and back again, and they just joined me, dripping with sweat and red faced. Raff deposited the contents of his stomach on the grass with a loud hurl.

"Fucking dirty pig! Run up hill again!" Ilia roared.

I thought Zack had put me through my paces before, but this was gruelling. Especially the shouting. Russian style beasting seemed to involve a lot of derogatory name calling, kicks and punches to keep us moving, and a lot, and I mean a lot, of shouting. With no energy left to shield, I almost got to the point where I would fall into a full melt down. Both men weren't far off either.

One of Ilia's colleagues came trotting over to us, just when Ilia was about to shout another set of punishing exercises. He stopped for a moment to listen to the guard and turned back to us.

"Shame. Session is over. Get lazy worthless asses over to clean up. Now!" he shouted once more and revelling in it. He laughed out loud. "That was fun." All he got from us was derisory looks and sighs. He didn't care. He just sniggered to himself once more.

All the beastings in the world could not put a downer on my real sense of excitement and positivity caused by Irena's decision to help us. I couldn't help feeling optimistic about our chance to escape. By now, our team would have called for back-up and will outnumber the Russians by quite a margin. However, when I got out of the rather uncomfortable shower and had tended to the cuts and bruises I sustained during the beasting, the look on Irena's face was one of extreme worry. She'd been fairly relaxed before, but the stress was pouring off her now. I needed to speak to her in private as soon as we could see an opportunity.

When Natalya went to the loo, I pounced on Irena.

"What is it?" I hissed urgently. Irena bit her lip and shook her head.

"Something's up. Dimitri's asked for more guards. Colonel Turkenev has sent for reinforcements. Dimitri must feel something. I told you he's incredibly intuitive," Irena answered in a slightly panicky tone.

"It doesn't mean he knows anything. He's just taking precautions. How many reinforcements can Turkenev get his hands on in such a short amount of time?"

"I don't know. They have sections everywhere. We'll have to wait and see," Irena answered cautiously. She grabbed her hair and smoothed it back nervously.

"Our team will notice them coming, they won't be taken by surprise by it." I tried to remain positive. I had to. It was our only hope. Natalya returned to the living room, observing us. She radiated suspicion.

"What you talk about?" the burly blond woman challenged.

"Eliza asked why she needed to wear the suit," Irena lied smoothly. "I explained she needs to look like a rich business woman, boarding a private plane. We best do something about that emerging bruise on her face. I thought Ilia was told to avoid the face in the beasting?"

"Dimitri did that one," I reminded Irena. "Ilia

only targeted the body, as he was told to. What's the story with him, anyway. He seemed less brutal and more caring than the others, but the beasting brought the animal out of him. He was relentless!"

"I don't know him very well, but I heard he got teased about his pretty looks and gentle nature by the others a lot. Then he got to beast them once, and it unleashed something feral inside him. It only comes out in those sessions though. After that, no one teased ever again." She shrugged her shoulders, as if that explained it all, and she didn't really care anyway. "Now, hurry up and get dressed."

But before I got a chance to start getting changed, I spotted a demure looking girl sitting across the room. That had got to be Carol, Rafferty's little sister. They sported the same bouncy curly hair and sparkly green eyes. The poor girl looked petrified. It broke my heart seeing her bruises. They hadn't spared her. The marks on her face looked to be a few days old, but there was no telling what her expensive looking clothes hid underneath. Bile rose into my throat. These people were vile. I was absolutely disgusted.

I walked over, and kneeled beside her.

"Hi, I'm Eliza. You must be Carol?" I asked gently. Her sorrowful eyes laden with anxiety looked at me. Her little hand touched my face.

"They hurt you too?" she whispered, glancing over to the Russian women.

"Did they do...?" I asked gently.

"No, not them. They just watched," she interrupted. I threw an angry look over at the two women, but it didn't take me long to work out that Irena, and even Natalya, felt ashamed and unhappy about Carol's treatment. I suppose they didn't have much choice about it.

"I'll look after you, sweetie. You'll be fine, I promise," I vowed, knowing I might not be able to keep that promise at all. I told myself it was for the best, to keep her calm and feeling safe.

"I know you want to, but these people are evil. I know you can't promise me anything," she whispered sadly. "My brother couldn't." She'd learned quickly. My heart ached for her and I wrapped her small fragile body into my arms, feeling her wince in the embrace. My blood started to boil again.

"Get up and get dressed. Now!" Irena shouted, roughly breaking up our hug. She needed to keep up the appearance of being cold and in control in front of Natalya. I understood that. I winked at Carol, who smiled back weakly, and made my way to the suit hanging ready for me. I picked it up and looked it over. A real Dolce & Gabbana, no expense spared apparently. It fitted perfectly and the material felt amazing. I fixed my hair and let Natalya fix my face. I stole a glance in the mirror and a professional looking woman stared back at me. Not a sign of the hardships my body had endured not long before. The anxious look in my eyes told a different story.

CHAPTER 46

Zack

I glanced over at Rafferty. He looked like a different man, looking like he was in his mid-twenties, rather than his seventeen tender years. His curly, normally unruly, brown hair was styled and slicked back. The dark blue suit with a crisp white shirt and stripy tie made him the picture of a rich businessman. I imagined myself looking similarly smart, with my grey suit, black shirt and tie.

I could hardly move, as every inch of my body ached, but I think I looked the part. Ilia sat me down on a chair. He was transformed back to his usual, more caring, self; offering ice, ointments and painkillers.

"I need to do make-up to cover bruise," he grumbled. Was that another one of his skills? Make-up? I wouldn't even know where to start, but he had a bottle of something called primer in his hands and started smoothing it over my face. "This colour matches good," he mumbled like an expert, whilst checking out a little bottle. The Trunk looked on with no expression on his face whatsoever, clearly used to witnessing Ilia working his make-up magic.

"You really are a Jack-of-all trades, aren't you? You seem both male and female, nurse, disciplinarian, and now a make-up artist too!" I joked, making Rafferty smile. It was met with a stoic stare by Ilia, and a quick prod on my bruised cheek.

"My name is not Jack," he muttered, making me snort a little. "It's not funny," he rebuked.

"Okay, 'kay. Sorry, master," I grovelled. Didn't want Ilia to get upset with me, but he just snorted, and carried on applying another layer of some other product to my face. It felt a little suffocating on my skin; I didn't like the feel of it at all. It didn't take Ilia long and he dismissed me from my chair with a swift nod.

"Check in mirror," he ordered, as if I would have an opinion on his handiwork. I couldn't give a

shit whether my bruise showed or not, but I
humoured him.

"Great work!" I faked an enthusiastic
sounding compliment. It did elicit a little smile,
which he quickly hid from my view. As if that
would hide it. I felt his glee bouncing off him.

"Uzhe pochti 2:30," the Trunk prompted Ilia.

"I know the time, Alexei," he answered
prickly, but shouted some instruction to the two
other operatives, who immediately sprung into
action. "Stand behind each other. Hands in front,"
he ordered Raff and me, whilst slapping handcuffs
on us. He marched us out of the room, down the
stairs and into the lobby. Dimitri stood waiting for
us, not in his customary uniform, but in a sharp
charcoal suit instead. Still looking intimidating as
hell.

My heart stilled for a moment when I caught
sight of Eliza. I stopped breathing. Her scent
warned me of her presence, but I wasn't prepared
for the beautiful vision that I laid eyes on. She
wore a tightly fitted light blue suit, showing off her

petite body and shapely legs. Her face, Instagram perfect, was clearly plastered with make-up to cover her bruises. I preferred her natural glow, but she did look incredibly professional, and sexy as fuck. I couldn't stop the heat rising to my face, and worse, my groin. The sneer on Dimitri's face told me my fluster hadn't escaped his attention, as he shook his head quietly chuckling to himself. *Dickhead.*

A little face, surrounded by dark blond curly locks, poked out from behind Eliza, trying to steal a peek at us. Her face lit up when she caught sight of Rafferty's smiling eyes, but the blonde guard pushed her roughly back in line. That had to be Carol. I sensed Rafferty's anger rising again, but so did Dimitri. He strode over to us and stood in front of Rafferty, eying him up and down, registering every little emotion Rafferty emitted, assessing the danger it may pose.

"Are you going to behave?" he barked at Raff, who immediately lowered his head and eyes.

"Yes, master," he answered loud and clear, but

submissive at the same time. He was well trained. Dimitri nodded, satisfied in the belief that Raff wouldn't let his anger dictate his actions. He felt sure Rafferty would comply.

Both girls' hands were also restrained. Nothing was left to chance, and they certainly didn't underestimate the danger the girls could pose, if left uncuffed. I could see Eliza tense up as the clock crept slowly towards three o'clock. I willed her to cloak as hard as she could, so she wouldn't alert Dimitri or Irena. I picked up a strange vibe between Irena and Eliza, but I couldn't make out what it meant. It could be nothing, but if it meant anything, I hoped they could contain it so Dimitri wouldn't feel it. If we were going to be helped to escape by our team, it was going to happen en route to the airport. It had to. I hoped I had interpreted Eliza's messages of hope correctly, otherwise we were just letting this happen to us, without any fight. It didn't feel good, but I knew fighting now would jeopardise any mission that I hoped was planned for our rescue. I had to suppress the rising tension and slight panic that was building up inside me. I had to stay positive and as relaxed as possible.

Dimitri shouted some instructions and we were pushed to march out. Three vehicles pulled up simultaneously outside, two of them filled with Russian operatives. *Fuck.* That would complicate matters. We were shepherded into the middle van. All of us captives, Dimitri, Ilia, Irena, Trunk and Blondie piled into the vehicle, where the Russians belted us up. Dimitri took his place next to the driver. Behind them, Carol and the Blonde, then Raff and the Trunk, Ilia and me, and in the back seats, Eliza and Irena. Once everyone was buckled up the three vehicles sped off, seemingly not bothered by the icy conditions.

CHAPTER 47

Zaphire

Rob had wanted to go in on his own, deeming it too much of a risk to have the three of us caught and depleting our numbers. I challenged his reasoning, because going it alone meant, whilst he was hacking, he couldn't keep an eye out for himself and so would put himself at more risk of discovery. In the end Vivian decided that one of the guards would accompany him, to be a set of extra eyes. It was better than nothing, but I still would have preferred to send two guards.

Brody, Tristan and I drove them up as far as we dared. Luckily the approach to the mansion was woody and if you stayed off the main road, it was easy to take cover. We parked our van in a little lay-by and waited for news from Rob. It was tense. None of us spoke. We just sat there, each of us battling our own nerves, trying not to emit too much stress. It was 1pm and the clock was ticking. We decided we needed as much up to date information as possible, but couldn't risk going in twice, so we'd opted to go in about two hours before the expected departure. We should catch any preparations being made or changes of plans.

"We're in," came a quiet message over the system. I could hardly breathe, sweat started to appear on my brow. It was harder sitting here, waiting, and not knowing what was happening, than being in the thick of it. I swallowed hard and took a deep breath, to release some of the tension. The others were doing the same. The time crept past at snail's pace. It was excruciating. Forty two minutes later, we got a text message. The ping was so loud it made us all jump.

"Damn it. Put it on silent!" I cursed, but couldn't wait to hear what it said. Tristan's face showed worry. "What is it? Tell us!" I urged impatiently.

"He wants to stay there for just a little longer, so he can give us the exact information on when they're leaving. He's managing to hack into Eliza and Irena at the moment, and wants to strengthen the link. He says we need to mobilise our troupes and get ready. It seems they are making preparations to get ready to go. One worrying fact is that they have called for back-up, and Rob has spotted two more vehicles filled with uniformed men and women. He could make out about twenty extra people."

"Fuck me. That's a lot! How many has Markus sent us for back-up?" Brody jumped in.

"I think Vivian said he would send 2 MPV's up, so that would be fourteen at the most."

"Shit. Are you sure that's it, Zaph? It'll mean we're in the minority. Bollocks. Tristan, inform Vivian. Markus might be able to send up some more, though it's cutting it fine."

This worried me. They may have found out about Irena's betrayal, which would ruin the whole element of surprise. Or they're just being cautious. We had to continue with our plan. We had no choice.

"Vivian says Rob is good to stay. She'll send someone to pick him up when he's done. We should go back and get ready," I decided.

Once back at the hotel we were greeted by Sam, Ned, Phaedra, Saleem, Archie and Claude. They all looked happy to see us, but felt immensely tense. Everyone was dressed in black combat gear, with full body protection, and noticeably, all carrying.

"How's Rick?" I asked, feeling a little pang of guilt by my earlier readiness to leave him to die.

"Still critical. He lost a lot of blood. He was barely alive when we finally got him medical help," Sam updated me. She looked impassionate. I don't think she carried a lot of love for Rick either. "I hope he'll make it. For Eliza's sake."

I nodded. Yes. I did too. At the very least it will give her a chance to say goodbye to him, before Markus will exact his punishment, if that still was to happen.

"Any idea on how Zack is?" a worried Phaedra asked. I gave her a hug, trying to put my own worries aside and make her feel as confident about Zack's well-being as I could.

"It's Zack. He knows how to endure and survive. He's a little worse for wear as far as Rob could tell, but they need them, so they're not going to seriously harm them. That's what you have to tell yourself. Soon, they'll be home and safe. We will succeed."

Her arms pressed a little tighter around me. I tightened my grip on her, losing my cool a little too.

"You're doing great, Zaph. Thank you," she whispered.

It was time to get ready and in position. Vivian divided us into four groups, spread over the four vehicles we had. Markus had sent another group of six guards, but they most likely wouldn't get here in time. It was up to us and the original reinforcements sent.

I didn't know how much training our guards had received. They were employed as building security really, and had only been on the job for several months. They were recruited from those who normally would have worked in admin, those that had opted out of working actively on missions, a couple of foreign Sensorians who offered their help, plus a few retired men and women. Not exactly elite operatives. I was worried. The FSB would be highly trained and would know how to defend against attack. They will shoot to kill, and though we were all dressed in Kevlar combat gear, Zack, Eliza and the other captives, wouldn't be. A sick feeling slowly took over my positivity. I shook my body violently to get rid of it. This mission will succeed. I had to remain convinced of that.

CHAPTER 48

Zack

I glanced over at Eliza. She was in a trance-
like state. I knew that look. She was definitely
hacking into someone's vision. Maybe Dimitri's. I
turned my attention to him. He got his phone out
and checked something. If she saw what he was
looking at, it could be useful, though how she was
going to get that information across, was a
different matter. I wondered if a double vision
hack was possible? Maybe that's what they were
doing? Could Rob use Eliza's VH to gain
information? I didn't know if it worked like that,
but if it did? That would be awesome.

The scent in the van altered abruptly. I felt a
change of mood in Dimitri. *Fuck.* Something was
up. I looked over at Irena. She'd sensed something
too, her eyes widened slightly and a tiny tremor
disturbed her lips, but Eliza was blissfully unaware,
still in a trance.

Dimitri rattled something to the driver, who

stopped the car. This is not what we needed. The other two vehicles stopped too. Dimitri turned around and glared at us.

"Who hijacked my eyes?" he growled menacingly. "Irina, who has that skill?"

"I don't know, Serzhant," she lied just a little too quickly, obvious to any Sensorian. I suspected she must have found out about Eliza's skill, but she tried to cover it up. *Why the fuck would she do that*? It clearly didn't fool Dimitri either. As soon as she noticed that, she added, "but I think it might be Eliza."

"Chyort! Chyort voz'mi!" Dimitri roared, definitely swearing his head off. He stopped to think for a moment and shouted another string of what sounded like commands. The next minute, all vehicles made a U-turn, I presumed, intending to go back to the mansion.

"We are compromised. Change of plan," Irena informed us, her eyes flicking restlessly from side to side. This wasn't going to plan.

"How did he know he was being vision

hacked? He's not a VH himself, is he?" I hissed to Ilia, Dimitri shouldn't have been able to pick up on that.

"I don't know what you talking about, but Dimitri know everything. Always. His intuition is impeccable," Ilia stated with conviction. His vocabulary was surprisingly good at times. Irena glanced over. At that point I knew she was on our side. I had no fucking idea why or how, but somehow Eliza must have persuaded her. Things were looking slightly up again, though the worry and fear in Irena's eyes was immense. She did not like the change of plan one fucking bit.

A couple of loud bangs reverberated in the air. The vehicle jolted and out of the corner of my eye I saw something approach in a blur. Our van got shunted or hit something, and careered out of control. We screeched to a halt, slightly spinning in the road. The force slammed us back into our seats and jolted us forwards and sideways, the seatbelts digging into our bodies. There was a second of silence, after which all hell broke loose! The front doors swung open, weapons were drawn, focussed faces all around us. As if in slow motion I witnessed Irena draw her weapon too, but she aimed at Eliza's hands, making sure she held them out. *No! Fuck!* Had I read her wrong? She shot through the cuffs. She stuffed a weapon in Eliza's, now free, hands. Thank fuck for that!

At the same time, I moved my body and before Ilia had even registered, I kicked him with both feet, square in his stomach. He doubled over, I grabbed his weapon and aimed at Dimitri, but he was in a fight and I couldn't get a clear shot at him, especially as my movement was restricted with my hands still cuffed. Rafferty was struggling with the Trunk and I clouted him with the back of my gun as hard as I could, trying to help Raff out, but not trusting myself to shoot at such close range. It didn't have much effect. The Trunk reared up, grabbed Raff by the throat and shook him violently, until the Blonde shrieked, painfully loudly.

"Stop! Sit down everyone!" She had little

Carol in a vice like grip and held her gun to the girl's head. We all froze. Rafferty was dumped to the floor. He grabbed his head and let out a petrified howl. Ilia had recovered and shoved me back in my chair, grabbing his weapon back. Irena looked mortified. The stench of panic filled the air. My stomach content wanted to make its way out.

Another loud crash sounded outside, and more gunshots. Ilia and the Blonde exchanged looks. In that split second the side door of the van opened and people dressed in black swarmed in, shouting and overpowering everyone in sight. I saw Ilia jump out and run off, ducking and diving as he was being shot at. Dimitri was nowhere to be seen. The Trunk was lying on the floor clasping his leg in agony. Two people overpowered the blonde operative and pushed Carol out of danger. The rest of us were dragged out and forced face down on the floor. For a moment, I had no idea whether this was good or bad, but then my senses kicked in, and I recognised the scents. Zaph, Ned, Brody, Sam, Phaedra, Saleem, all of them were there. I heard another car speed off, but not before they opened fire on us. Thank fuck we were partially covered by our own van, and the vehicles surrounding us.

"Get down! Eliza!" I shouted, noticing a gap in our 'defence', just where she was crouching down. I lunged towards her trying to protect her. But I heard a yelp of pain and a deep groan. Someone, or more were hit. The smell of blood filled my nostrils. The smell of Eliza's blood. My body went cold. I felt sick. A crushing feeling of horror filled my senses. I sat up, only to be pushed back down again.

"Stay down! It's not safe!" Brody barked. "You're not wearing any protective clothing!"

"It's Eliza! She's hurt!" I shouted, fear making me break out into a clammy sweat. I tuned into Eliza's vital signs, they were hard to detect. "Fucking do something!" I screamed at no one in particular. A guard's knee still prevented me from moving. It killed me not knowing what had happened to Eli, and how she was doing. After a few terrifyingly, agonizing moments I heard someone move behind me.

"All clear!" Vivian shouted. "Let's get out of here!"

I gathered all my strength and threw the guard off me impatiently, and hurried over to Eliza. Her stomach and back were covered in blood. It looked like a bullet had gone straight through. Sam sat next to her, arms covered in blood too, trying to stem the bleeding. Eliza was unconscious. I kneeled next to her and grabbed her face with both hands, getting increasingly frustrated with my limited movement thanks to the fucking cuffs.

"Stay with us, Eli! Please, please, please, don't.... Please, listen to me. We'll get you to a hospital, we will get you through this," I stammered hurriedly. "Please, Eliza. You can't leave me. You can't! I love you...Please, I love you." Tears fell freely from my eyes, as Eliza's vital signs became weaker and weaker. I was spiralling, it was like a plug had been removed and all my emotions flooded me. "I can't lose you," I whispered again and again, cradling her face. I smelt and tasted the salty tears, trickling down into my mouth. It had been a long time since I'd experienced that.

"We've got to move, brother. Let us move her into the car," Zaphy urged as she pushed me gently but resolutely aside. Everything was a daze. I couldn't think clearly. I was stuck, I couldn't move. Zaph took over. She shoved me next to Eliza, then grabbed my face and made me look into her eyes.

"Be strong Zack. Be strong for her," she urged. She was right. *Fuck it.* I needed to stop plummeting and wallowing. I gave myself a mental slap and concentrated on supporting her, shoving my own feelings aside. One thing puzzled me. Why did she let me sit next to Eliza? Why not sit there herself? She was Eliza's girlfriend after all. Why? I put it to the back of my mind as I tried to keep the hastily put together bandage from the first aid kit in place. It was drenched with blood. I tried to stem the bleeding, holding the bandage firmly in place on both her stomach and back.

"How long?" I barked

"About forty five minutes. They're getting all set up for her. The fact she's still alive is good news. Keep applying pressure. The bleeding is slowing down by the looks of it," Zaph spoke reassuringly. I wasn't so sure. I felt Eliza's weak pulse, still ebbing away. She briefly opened her eyes, only for them to roll around, not focussing. She wasn't there.

"Hurry the fuck up! We're losing her!" I shouted again, my voice filled with fear and panic. "Stay with me, baby. Don't you dare give up, tiger." I kissed her gently on her head, her lips, her eyes, keeping my hands firmly on her wounds. "I love you, Eliza."

I felt Zaphire's eyes literally burn a hole in my back. But at that moment, I couldn't care less.

CHAPTER 49

Zaphire

Thank goodness we had Rob. Without his eyes we would never have picked up the change of plan. As they were doing their U-turn we sped forwards and gained momentum, enabling us to catch up before they reached their full speed. Our plan of trying to separate the cars and isolating the van that carried Dimitri and the captives fell apart and we had to improvise. Our team was designated to target the main van, whilst the others were tasked to distract the people in the other vehicles. We shot at their tyres, and shunted it, to add more chaos. Whilst they tried to regain control of the van, we jumped out of ours, ready to force entry. Ned and Brody charged at the driver and Dimitri, whilst Saleem, Claude, Sam and myself focussed on releasing the captives. We jumped in horror when we heard the gunshot in the back of the van, and the subsequent struggle. We regrouped to work out what had happened. I could see one of the

Russians holding a gun to a little girl's head. We needed to be fast and precise. All of us knew exactly what to do and we burst open the side door of the van. The stench of fear and stress nearly knocked us back, but we were prepared. One of them kicked his way out, wielding his gun, but not actually shooting, more concerned with getting the fuck out of there. Claude and Saleem overpowered the blonde operative within seconds. She had no time to react. Thank God.

The little girl collapsed on the floor, her face absolutely petrified. It didn't take us long to gain complete control. Some of our guards came to help too. It was all a done deal within minutes.

Dimitri had somehow managed to escape into one of their other cars, which screeched off, but the loud crack of a gunshot, and the subsequent yelp and groan told us the worst had happened. One of us got shot. Eliza. We couldn't move. Guns were still being fired, so we had to stay down and make sure Zack and the others stayed put too. Brody had a hard time keeping Zack down and urged for a guard to help him. I could feel Zack's anguish cutting through me. I had to focus on the little girl. I needed to keep her safe. I wanted to be with Eliza but Sam was closest to her and checked her over. I could feel it was bad, but I was even more concerned with the state of my brother. He looked in shock, his face ashen grey, his eyes wide in horror. All I wanted to do was embrace Zack, but all he was focussed on was Eliza. Once the threat had lifted, we bundled both of them in the car and sped off to get medical help.

Well, I had my brother back. Looking at him tending to Eliza, distraught and desperate to get her to hospital, I felt..., well I don't know how I felt. Elated and relieved to see him alive, of course. But confused over his emotional state. I had never seen him showing his feelings that openly. I felt jealous over their seemingly strong bond. Angry too. But mostly confused over my own feelings for Eliza. I loved her. I wanted to be with her, to be the one taking care of her, but my feelings didn't seem as intense as Zack's. My first thought had been with my brother, not Eliza. What was wrong with me? Maybe I had psychologically distanced myself too much from her already. After all, it had been me, not her, who didn't want to rekindle our relationship. But I needed her to live. I needed to see her sparkly eyes and her always ever so slightly defiant expression again. I needed to feel the love she felt for me. I was being selfish.

"We're here." Brody turned around to check on Eliza. "How's she doing?"

"Barely alive," Zack grunted. "But her heart is still beating. Hurry the fuck up!"

Hospital staff came running, trolley at the ready. It was the same hospital we always used. No questions asked. They whisked her away, and prevented us from following in after her. Instead a member of staff directed us to a seating area with a coffee bar. It was rather luxurious, almost like we were in a hotel. It felt bizarre. We sat in stunned silence, not knowing what to do or what to say.

It was just our van that had gone to the hospital. Vivian and the others were on their way back to the compound, ready to update Markus and deal with the Russians. They'd also taken Irena, Rafferty and Carol. The poor little girl was in complete shock when we left them, white as a sheet and trembling all over. Rafferty didn't look much better. His agony and worry for his little sister nearly incapacitated us, as he was in no state to cloak any of his emotions. We didn't blame him, but everyone was absolutely exhausted and drained.

We all desperately needed sleep, to recharge, but none of us could even contemplate closing our eyes for any amount of time. So Claude, Brody, and Ned, were huddled around a little table, drinking coffee. Zack slouched, zoned out, in a big leather chair, not wanting to communicate with any of us. All of us had tried, but he had rebuked our attentions with a gruff 'leave me alone'. Brody had managed to remove his restraints, to which he nodded a 'thank you', but retreated back behind the wall he'd erected straightaway.

Once Eliza had been taken away to the operating theatre, Zack had plummeted into his private despair. He didn't want to talk about it, not even to me. It made me feel so alone, as I did want to talk. In the past, he'd always been there for me. Sam came and sat with me, and gave me a warm, consoling hug. I hadn't realised how much I needed that.

"Maybe we should send for Phaedra? She seems to be able to get through to Zack much better than any of us can," I suggested.

"I think he needs you, Zaphy," Sam pondered.

"But he knows I'm here for him. And I need him too, but he's too withdrawn to notice at the moment. He just won't open up to me. Especially not where Eli is concerned."

"It's worth a try. I don't like seeing him like this. You drink your coffee. I'll get on to it." She turned her attention to her phone and started messaging Phaedra. Hopefully with some success.

It had been an hour now, and still no news. Eliza was being operated on, and we'd been reassured that if there was anything to report, they would let us know straight away. All we could do was wait, excruciating as that was.

CHAPTER 50

Zack

Two hours. Two fucking hours, and still no news. I got up, stormed up to one of the nurses and grabbed her arm. Her heart jumped in fright. I must have looked quite scary and intimidating; blood smeared all over my shirt and a manic expression on my face, but I didn't care about the poor woman's feelings. I felt Zaph right behind me, but I ignored her.

"Find out what's going on with Eliza. Now!" I barked rudely at the nurse. I didn't care about the looks I received from the people around. Someone must fucking know something! Two security guards stepped towards me, but I felt a soft hand on my arm and a familiar scent entered my nostrils. *Phaedra.*

Out of the corner of my eye I saw Zaph dealing with the security guards, and Phaedra smooth- talked the nurse, apologising on my behalf for frightening her and being rude. I wanted to defend myself and shout at them all to leave me alone. I needed to find out what the fuck was going on with Eliza, but Phaedra's gentle touch and soothing vibes brought me down a little from my heightened state of agitation. It was enough to stop me from pursuing the nurse, and not to shout at Zaph and Phae.

A senior looking nurse walked resolutely up to us.

"We don't appreciate you frightening the staff, son. If it happens again we'll have you escorted off the premises," she declared with authority. I snorted, but Phaedra nudged me viciously in my side. Normally it wouldn't have hurt as much, but my body was still covered in bruises from the beatings. I winced. Phae wasn't empathetic.

"Apologise, you dimwit," she hissed in my ear. Bloody hell. I'd better comply. Phaedra squeezed my arm again, making me feel like a naughty child.

"Sorry, nurse. It won't happen again," I muttered under the woman's icy stare. She shook her head, but left us to it. Still no news about Eliza.

"Now, listen, you grumpy arse," Phaedra started. "I know you're suffering, but so are all of us here. Look at your sister. She needs you too. She's been nothing but a rock, and you've been self-pitying. Snap out of it, man."

She actually sounded annoyed. Pretty pissed off even. Couldn't she see how much I was hurting? Eliza was the one for me. I realised that now, more than ever. Whether she would choose me or not, I was bound to her. I would be anything she needed me to be. But now, she might never know. I might never get to tell her whilst she's actually conscious. I needed her to live. Desperately. Or else, what was the point of it all. I might as well...

"Snap out of it, dammit!" Phaedra growled again. "I can feel what you're going through. You're not exactly cloaking very well! Stop spiralling. Think positive."

She grabbed my face and forced me to look at Zaphy. She looked broken, lost. Equally as distraught as me. A feeling of shame crept in. I hadn't even checked if she was okay. Everyone had made an effort with me, but I'd rebuffed all of them. And I had totally neglected the feelings of my own sister. *Fucking selfish arse.* I nodded.

"You're right. As usual," I admitted begrudgingly. I made my way over to Zaph, who looked up as I approached. Tears filled her eyes. She ran over to me and hugged me tightly. I held her for ages, just letting her sob, my shirt getting soaked with her tears. I sensed Phaedra approach and another scent hit me. *Alice.* Her hurried footsteps echoed along the sterile corridor.

"How is she?" she yelled, her voice shrill from worry. Her anxiety was through the roof, but being confronted with the sorry look of the two of us shaking our heads brought the mum out of her.

"Hey, come here you two," she beckoned softly as she pulled us into a tender hug.

Both Zaphire and I threw our arms around her and smothered her in between us.

"How are you holding up?" I managed to ask, sounding almost in control of my emotions.

"Barely. I'm an absolute wreck!" Her eyes were red rimmed and it looked like she hadn't slept in weeks. Her skin, ashen with dark circles plastered under her eyes.

"Still no news?" she asked, with a tiny little bit of hope buried under the knowledge the answer was most likely going to be 'no'. Both Zaphy and I shook our heads, not managing to look at all hopeful.

Fast footsteps approached. I whipped round and saw a surgeon pacing towards us. My stomach lurched. This was it. I tuned into his feelings. They were muddled, stressed, worried but I detected relief too. His face looked serious though. Too serious for my liking. I needed to hear the words.

"Are you Eliza's next of kin?" he enquired. Alice nodded frantically.

"The operation was successful. She's still very fragile and the next forty eight hours will be crucial. She's a fighter, though. We nearly lost her a couple of times, but she pulled through. I think we can be cautiously optimistic that she will make a full recovery."

The relief in the room was overwhelming. I felt like I could finally breathe again. She was alive! I picked Zaph up and swirled her around, kissing her forehead, before putting her down. My body hurt like hell. Alice fell into my arms, the strain finally too much, she sobbed and sobbed.

"Can we see her?" I asked the surgeon, desperate to see her as soon as I could.

"Only next of kin at the moment, I'm afraid," he answered resolutely. I feared that was the case. I would just have to wait a little longer. Alice straightened herself out, wiped her tears and took my hands in hers.

"I'll tell her you're all here for her. As soon as it's allowed, you and Zaphy can visit her." She turned around and sped after the surgeon, desperate to see her daughter.

I still couldn't quite believe Eliza was going to be fine. I didn't dare to believe it, until I could hear and feel her vital signs. I wanted to be with her to make sure. I didn't trust the machines to check her vitals as well as I was able to. I needed to sense them for myself.

"Coffee?" Phaedra offered. I accepted gratefully. I hadn't drunk or eaten anything yet, but felt I could do with some now. The mood was almost euphoric, even though we knew she wasn't out of the woods yet.

"I thought we lost you to your demons, mate. Glad to have you back!" Brody laughed way too exuberantly, the tension definitely defusing.

"Yes, well. Women will do that to you. Reducing even the strongest of men to go weak at the knees," I retorted, to be met by a chorus of snorts, derisory laughs and taunts by Sam, Phaedra and Zaphy. I sniggered at their indignant faces and at Ned and Brody's fake shocked expressions.

"As I said, glad you're back," he chortled.

A bit later Alice returned; her face worried but relieved.

"How is she?" I fired at her.

"She's not woken up yet, but they said she's

doing great under the circumstances. We need to send for some of her clothes. Maybe you should all go to the compound, get some sleep and freshen up at the same time."

"No fucking way, Alice. Excuse my language, but I'm staying here. I'll ask for some clothes to be sent for me too." I wasn't going anywhere. I wanted to sneak into Eliza's room and keep an eye on her vitals. I didn't tell anyone though. I planned to slip in later, after I received some fresh clothes. I would find a way in. Alice nodded, she understood. I had to talk to Zaphire. I needed to understand what was going on in her head. She had said very little and didn't seem too perturbed with me telling Eliza I loved her. I moved closer to Zaphy and touched her gently on the arm.

"Come and talk?"

She came along, but reluctantly.

"What about?" she asked, but she knew exactly what about. She was deliberately being obtuse, so I ignored her question.

"What's going on between you and Eliza?"

"What's it to you?" she answered rather aggressively. I stopped walking and turned to face her.

"Stop being a brat, little sis," I growled at her sternly. "You know exactly what I mean. I declared my love for Eliza in front of you, and you don't seem to give a shit? Previously I only had to look at her a bit wistfully, and you would have killed me. I know you went through a rough patch, but I heard you two. In your room. You made up, you told her you loved her," I rattled out, hardly pausing to take a breath.

"Whoa, whoa, whoa. You listened in on us?"

"That's not the fucking issue right now, is it?"

"It bloody well is! The stupid thing is, you clearly didn't spy on us long enough!" she spat.

"I didn't spy! I happened to hear..., that's all. What the fuck do you mean?"

"I told her I didn't think our relationship would work. I don't trust her enough. I would always be suspicious. It wouldn't work for me." Her voice hitched in her throat at the end. "We practically broke up. Or, at least, I think we did. Eliza still wanted to try..."

I didn't know what to say, so I opened my arms and folded her into my chest. All this time I'd believed they were back together, very much in love again. I'd been wrong. It explained a lot. Zaphy exhaled long and deep, letting her body melt into mine.

"Why didn't you come and talk to me? You used to tell me everything." I felt incredibly sad. Something had come between us. And I knew it wasn't something, but someone.

"I didn't think you'd be too sympathetic, always waiting in the wings for an opportunity. I wasn't ready to lose her to you that quickly." She looked up at me barely managing to keep the accusation out of her eyes.

"Oh Zaphy. I'm so sorry. I'll back off, if you want me to. I don't want to hurt you. I can wait. When you're ready, we can talk. You two need to sort out what you really want. Then Eliza can make her decision."

Waiting was definitely not what I wanted, but I'd do it for Zaphy. Anything to help her through this. It was anything but guaranteed that I'd come out on top. I knew Eli loved Zaphire, and if Zaphy would give her a chance she would jump at it. I knew that for sure. However, I didn't know for sure what Eliza felt for me. I didn't even think she knew herself.

"No. It's not fair on you. You need to tell her how you feel. I can't make you wait. Eliza would want to know," Zaphy said after a while. I could tell her head was ruling her heart, as her emotional distress was there to be felt. I wasn't sure if I could really believe her words.

CHAPTER 51
Eliza

Beeping. Annoying beeps. I shuddered slightly. My body didn't feel like my own. Was I still asleep? Why was I asleep? Did the Russians drug me? Was I dreaming? Where were they all? I was aware of another human near me. I focussed on my senses and worked out pretty quickly it was Zack. Where was I? My brain was both racing and sluggish, like attempting to run through mud. I slowly realised my eyes were still closed. My eyelids felt heavy and sticky but I forced myself to open them, and tried to work out my surroundings. It clearly was a hospital. Machines were attached to me, and I, myself, was the cause of the beeping sounds that annoyed me so much. What on earth happened to me? I remember being in the van, and then, nothing. Absolutely zilch. Zack moved over to me. I could hear his breath quickening and his heart rate rising.

"Eli, can you hear me?" His voice soft and

eager. I wanted to answer but my mouth wasn't up to speed with what I wanted. "Can you hear me, tiger?" Worry lines etched across his forehead. A tense muscle twitched around his mouth.

"Yeah," I finally managed to groan, to Zack's obvious relief.

"Listen, I'm gonna wake up your mum, and leave you both for a bit. I'm not supposed to be here. I just needed to make sure you were okay. I'll see you when I can." He gave me a kiss on my forehead and went over to mum. I was so confused, but I couldn't make my mouth talk and ask questions. So frustrating. Mum startled on Zack's touch. Zack put a finger to his mouth. That didn't stop mum.

"What are you doing here, Zack!" she exclaimed, surprised and accusingly.

"Sshh, Alice, please. Eliza's awake. Let the doctors know. I'm going. See you later." With that, he snuck out of the room. Mum literally jumped out of her bed and was at my side with two gigantic strides. She pressed the button for assistance. Nurses and doctors came rushing in. I wasn't sure if I could cope with all this mayhem. I closed my eyes and wanted to sink back into the dark, but mum wouldn't let me.

"Stay with us, darling. Just for a bit. Let the doctors do their thing," she urged. I conceded so I fought to stay awake and endure the doctors' investigations.

I blinked. That went better than before. I must have passed out again as there were no doctors nor nurses, and the room was bright and sunny.

"Mum?" I whispered, but it wasn't mum who sped to my side. It was Zack again.

"Where's mum?" a tiny hurt look crossed his face, but disappeared as quickly as it came. Maybe I imagined it.

"She's just getting some lunch. She'll be back in a minute. You look a bit better. How are you feeling?"

"Bit better. My mouth works. Drink?" I waved my hand about a bit to receive a glass. He didn't pass it, but held it and put the straw in my mouth. Bloody hell, the water on my tongue and throat felt good.

"Is Zaphy here?" I croaked, spotting another flicker of what looked like an expression of pain on Zack's face. He swallowed before answering, not looking me in the eyes.

"She, er, she'll see you when it's allowed. I'm still breaking the rules at the moment."

"Why you?" I wondered out loud. He didn't answer straight away. Just looked at me.

"Because I had to," he lied. I might be recovering from something bad, but my senses worked perfectly fine. I didn't pursue it. I would get to the bottom of it eventually. My mind wandered to the pain in my stomach.

"What the hell happened?" I managed to groan.

"What do you remember?"

"We were in the van. Oh, it got rammed or something, we skidded. Irena shot through my cuffs...," I had to think for a moment, but my mind was blank. "Nothing after that." I felt dejected.

"Okay, I'll fill you in. The blonde held a gun to Carol's head, we had to surrender, but then our people burst into the van and managed to overpower Blondie. They dragged us out to safety, or so they thought. Ilia and Dimitri escaped. They shot at us when they departed and you happened to be in their way. You went unconscious pretty much immediately."

"Shit," I sighed. "How's poor Carol?"

He smiled and shook his head.

"You're amazing, you know that? Trust you to think of others before considering your own pain. But yeah, she was in complete shock, understandably. But she's getting the right support and she's safe now, with her big brother at her side."

"And dad?

"Alive."

"He saved mum."

"Yes, he did." Zack nodded. "He did indeed." He hesitated for a second, but carried on talking. "He's staying here, in the same hospital, but in a different wing."

"Can I see him?"

"Soon."

A searing pain shot through my tummy and I let out a gasp of pain. My heart started racing. Zack pressed the button for me and hastily hid in the bathroom, just before the nurse came running in.

"You need a top up of your painkillers, my luv." She glanced over at my heart monitor. You seem a bit agitated. Are you okay?" she asked as she fiddled with the drip that administered the morphine.

"Yeah. Just in pain," I replied weakly, trying to get rid of her as soon as possible.

"You get some more rest, luv. The top up should help," she fussed, straightening my bedding and fluffing the cushions a bit. She left pretty much immediately after that, leaving me to rest.

Zack poked his head around the corner and slipped back into the room. I felt the morphine taking effect, and the world became a little out of kilter. Zack must have noticed my increasing loss of alertness, and didn't try to talk to me. He sat by my side, until I heard my mum entering and sending him away. He exuded resistance and annoyance, but I felt him slowly get up and leave. But not after he examined me thoroughly with his senses. I could practically feel him going over all my vital signs. When he was satisfied, he left us to it. I felt myself drift away into what I hoped to be a peaceful sleep.

CHAPTER 52

Zaphire

I was sick of waiting and hanging around. I decided I was going to go back to the compound with Sam for a bit, and let Zack do his thing. He would let me know as soon as I could go and see her. I needed to keep busy, before my head and body exploded with nerves and worry. Brody and the others had gone back to the compound, apart from Ned who had decided to stay and hang around for Zack. I wasn't sure whether Sam came for her own sake, or whether she wanted to keep an eye on me, but whatever her motivation, I was glad of her company. It suddenly dawned on me I had to face Markus!

I hadn't heard anything from Brody or Frank. I wondered how their reception back at the compound had gone.

"Have you heard from anyone who's gone back?" I asked Sam whilst we were on our way to the taxi waiting to take us home.

"Yeah. It's all incredibly tense. Phaedra texted and said Markus looked like he could explode any minute. Frank has kept to himself, or is made to keep to himself, but no official consequences or punishments have been ordered. There's a rumour Markus is arranging to call us all back at some point for a big meeting. If he doesn't summon you, it's probably best to keep out of his way.

"Damn. What a mess. All of it," I sighed, not just lamenting my relationship with Markus, but also the whole me, Zack and Eliza triangle thing. I decided to confide in Sam. "What the hell is wrong with me? I feel like I'm part of some dumbass chick flick! I love Eliza but can't see a future with her, but then again, maybe I can? Zack loves Eliza too, and has declared that for everyone to hear, apart from Eliza, and Eliza wants the both of us. I just can't work out who she loves more. She told me before it was me, but who knows? That could've been on impulse. And are we right for each other? She clearly trusts Zack more than me, with everything that has gone on in her life. Was I just her one lesbian fling? Was any of it even of any importance?" I paused my rant for a moment to gauge Sam's reaction, but she was cautious, cloaking somewhat, and definitely shielding from my outpour of emotions. "Sorry Sam, I'm rambling."

"No, keep going. It's good to talk it all through. But the most important thing is to work out what you want, regardless of what Eliza and Zack want. Then you go from there."

"But, I dunno what I want," I whined. Hearing myself made me feel disgusted. Previously, if anyone had come to me with this pathetic story, I would have kicked them up the arse, and told them to sort themselves out. Maybe I had been heartless before. Or maybe I had to kick myself up the arse.

The taxi arrived and both of us plugged our headphones into my phone and chilled to Catfish and the Bottlemen for a while, staring at the landscape shooting by. I didn't want to talk anymore. Sam grabbed my hand and squeezed it in support. She didn't let go. It was nice not to have to think for a while. Enjoying the quiet before the inevitable storm.

Our compound loomed. We were rudely drawn back to reality after having fooled our minds with relaxing tunes. My nerves built exponentially. Sam paid the taxi driver by card and then we stood in front of the building. Guards moved in our direction, having noticed us. They opened the doors, and waved us through. I noticed the receptionist making a quick phone call. I hoped not to Markus. I didn't have to worry, as seconds later I saw Laura striding towards us, a deep worry line prominent between her brows.

"I'm so glad you're back," she gushed, whilst taking me in her arms. "In one piece." She looked me over, and nodded, satisfied I was fine. She gave Sam a hug too. "I'm here to warn you. Markus is on the war path. He's happy everyone is back and that it looks like Eliza will be fine, but his resolve to deal with everyone who ignored his orders hasn't abated. It's gone up tenfold. Something bad is brewing, but he's not talked about it with me, which is doubly worrying. I get the feeling he's purposely leaving me in the dark as he knows I probably won't agree with him. He suspects I'm going to go berserk if I hear his ideas. It worries me."

"That does sound bad. So, what do we do?" I asked, wondering if there was anything we actually could do.

"For now; keep out of his way and keep out of trouble. He's not challenged anyone yet, but he has put Frank under house arrest. The cells are full, so there are guards by his door 24/7. He's not even letting anyone from the leadership talk to him. Frank hasn't got his phone or computer, so there's no way of communicating with him. Brody was initially also locked in his room, but he's been allowed out now."

"I don't like the sound of this at all." Sam shook her head. "We need to find out what Markus is planning, to have at least some way of preparing for it."

"I agree. Laura, please keep trying to find out what's going on in his head. I'm scared. Markus can be ruthless, if he thinks it's the best way to protect our community."

Bloody hell. What if Markus was going to use our most extreme measures to control and quell the insubordinate actions of Frank and anyone else that worked with him. It didn't bear thinking about. Surely Markus wouldn't go that far. I had to believe that. Whatever Markus was, he wasn't stupid or crazy. I had to hold on to that.

Laura left us to it, after making sure we got to our rooms, without being swamped with people wanting to talk to us about our rogue mission.

"Just keep a bit of a low-profile, my sweet. Don't go out to the cafe, stay in your rooms as much as possible," Laura warned. I knew it was for our own good, but it sucked. Sam went to freshen up with the promise to return to me afterwards. I took that time to do the same and felt a hundred percent better for it. I texted Zack with an update on the Markus situation. His answer came back quickly, with his trademark use of the F-word dominating the reply. It made me giggle a little, despite the seriousness of the situation. Zack really had a foul mouth, and it wasn't getting any better lately. He urged me to go and try and speak to Frank, but I couldn't see the use in that. Frank wouldn't know anything, and my priority was finding out what Markus was planning and how worried we should be.

Sam was back and I resigned myself to a fairly quiet evening. However, Sam had pursued other plans and she was followed in by Brody, Phaedra and Tristan, all carrying plenty of beers and wine. It looked like we were going to try and put the world to rights, fuelled by lots of alcohol!

CHAPTER 53
Zack

I sat sulking on a chair in the corridor, positioned in such a way I could see Eliza's door. I was waiting for Alice to leave, as I wanted to sneak back in. Anyone who wasn't next of kin still wasn't allowed to see her, and the doctors had told us that we, most likely, would have to wait till tomorrow. Ned sauntered over to me, his movement casual, but with a determined look in his eyes. He dragged me out of the chair, and pushed me towards the canteen.

"You need to eat, mate."

"I'm not hungry. A coffee will do," I answered grumpily.

"Not taking no for an answer, dude," he replied, equally as grouchy, but with a slight nervous edge in his tone. He knew pushing me could be a dangerous thing to do, but it never stopped him from speaking his mind.

Soon we were sitting behind a steaming plate

of spaghetti carbonara, with a fresh salad on the side. I couldn't lie, it did smell delicious, and I tucked in ravenously. As much as I hated being pushed about by my friends, I was glad they did on occasion. But I wasn't going to let them know that. Had a reputation to uphold.

"What Zaph said about Markus sounds bad. I'm worried, mate. I know he's like a father to you, but it sounds like he's rattled. You could be in serious shit."

"I'm more worried for Frank. I'm doomed to go back into fucking isolation. I've sort of resigned myself to that. But Frank? Markus has never had to deal with insubordination from his own leadership team. It could go two ways; he takes a long hard look at his management style and reforms, or he's going to go extremely hard on Frank to scare people so much that no one will ever do that again. I think the first reaction is extremely unlikely, so I fucking fear for Frank."

I respected Markus. He's a formidable and clever leader, who would do anything to protect our community, but he's also inflexible and hates challenges to his authority. I didn't want to fear the worst for Frank, but I was truly worried. He could face a long prison term. His wife, Clare, would be distraught. She was ten years younger than him, and it was no secret they were trying for kids. This could turn out to be a disaster for them.

Ned attempted to distract me from my pessimistic musings with talk about football transfers and epic boxing matches I missed during my time in isolation. He showed me funny YouTube videos and talked excitedly about this immersive game called No Man's Sky, made even better with a VR option. He was doing a good job, as I did temporarily get swept away in his enthusiasm.

Unfortunately, I had no opportunity to slip into Eliza's room again for the rest of the day. Whenever Alice took a break, doctors were with her and they were resolute in denying me entry. I did try several times, but they started to become a little pissed off with me. I stopped badgering them when they threatened me, once again, with being removed from the hospital.

Ned went back to the compound at about 9pm, but I decided to stay and try again later. At about 11pm I ventured over, listened by her door, and could only hear the rhythmic breathing of both Eliza and Alice. I slipped in, to find them both fast asleep. Eliza's vitals sounded strong and her scent was clean, apart from the morphine and antibiotics. I didn't detect infections or any suspicious scents at all. That was promising. I sank down into a chair and tried to get comfortable, to at least attempt having a bit of a nap.

"Zack?" Eliza croaked softly. She gestured for me to come over and patted her hand on the bed, whilst she shuffled aside slightly. "Come, lie here," she whispered. I obeyed, happily. I placed myself on my side next to her, carefully avoiding the tubes. She grabbed my hand and closed her eyes. She was back asleep within minutes. This felt so fucking good, I didn't even want to go to sleep

.411

anymore. I grabbed the chance to savour the smell of her hair and the warmth of her body. I traced the soft skin of her face with my fingers and imprinted it into my memory. I was exhausted though, and the world slowly became distorted. I fought hard to keep awake, but I must have fallen into a deep sleep eventually, as I was startled awake by firm hands shaking my body. I opened my eyes. A bright light hurt my sensitive retinas. I had to close them for a moment to give them time to adjust. It was a young night nurse, shining a bright light into my eyes.

"Sir, you really have overstepped the boundary now. I've called security, and they'll escort you off the premises immediately," she whispered sternly. "Don't resist. You should be happy I didn't phone the police. Come on now; up you get."

Damn. I really have blown it now. They might not let me back in. *Fuck it.* I got up and mumbled an apology, hoping to sound suitably contrite. I tried to gain her sympathy by telling her the depth of my worry. I put on my most charming smile and pleaded mercilessly. Her expression was strict, but I felt a little spark of sympathy. I might be lucky and get away with showing my face again. True to her word two security men came up. She quickly explained the situation and they walked me out, with one of them holding onto my arm. My initial reaction was to shake him off, but soon thought better of it when his grip tightened. I didn't want to provoke them. They made sure I ordered a taxi to leave, and stayed by my side until I had actually stepped inside the car. They really didn't trust me.

It was 4am by the time I reached our compound. All was dark but for the light shining in reception. A couple of guards rushed to the door to check me out when I tried to push it open. One of them recognised me and clicked the button to open up, another new safety addition. It was all starting to feel a little too much like a fucking fortress for my liking.

"Stand over there, Sir. We've been ordered to

put a new tag on you as soon as you enter the building. Please don't resist," the guard requested forcefully. I shrugged my shoulders at them and ambled over to the place they wanted me to stand. The anklet felt rather familiar almost instantly. "We will escort you to your room, where you will have to remain until further notice."

"I'm going back to the hospital tomorrow," I said, put out by this turn of events. Zaphire hadn't mentioned anything about her having been put under house arrest. I should have known. Markus probably suspects I helped Frank organise it, whereas he'll see Zaphire as just participating. Such an assumption. Zaphire will be offended when she finds out.

"You'll have to ask permission tomorrow," guard number one answered rather harshly.

"I'll stand guard," number two offered. "You return to the reception, okay?" Number one agreed quite quickly. I got the feeling he didn't like me much. Before I closed the door on the guard he stuck his foot in and leant forward. "For what it's worth, I thought what Frank and you lot did, was right. Markus was dithering."

I nodded in thanks, but aware of my anklet. I put my finger to my lips and pointed at it, warning him not to say anything else incriminating. His eyes went wide with fear. He had stone cold forgotten the electronic tag that guard number one had put on my ankle just moments before. Clearly, not the brightest spark in the pack. I went into my room and couldn't wait to crawl into bed. I was fucking exhausted. I had only just pulled the cover over myself when I heard the guard outside being reprimanded and sent away. He hadn't gotten away with it. He'll probably be transferred to a different job. Markus wouldn't stand for guards who questioned his decision making.

They were already listening into my conversations. Bloody hell man, that hadn't taken long. I gave in to my exhaustion and snuggled up into my duvet. The world slipped away from my consciousness pretty rapidly.

CHAPTER 54

Zaphire

"Let me see my brother!" I shouted at the stubborn guard stood by Zack's door. He didn't relent to my demands. In fact after the third time of asking, he didn't even respond anymore. Just stared straight ahead, completely ignoring my presence. That's when I started shouting.

I could easily take him. He looked strong, but that meant nothing, if you didn't know how to use it. The new guards relied heavily on the fact that no one from our community would dare challenge them, as challenging them would mean defying Markus' orders. I contemplated for about half a second to barge past him, but thought better of it. I turned on the balls of my feet and dramatically flounced off.

I messaged Ned, Brody and Sam to meet for an emergency meeting. However, in the mean time I received a text from Alice, saying we were now allowed to see Eliza. She asked if I could let Zack know, as she couldn't get in touch with him. Eliza had asked for the both of us. I somehow had to persuade Markus to let him go and see her. It wouldn't do her recovery any good, if she was worried about Zack. But..., I really did not want to go and see Markus. I didn't think I could cope with his judgement. I'd have to ask Laura.

My friends had already gathered by my door to discuss Zack's fate. Rafferty was there too. He was a cutie, young but rather hot. A little fiery with a hint of rebellion hidden within, but he was a good'un. He'd been quickly adopted into our group, and his sister Carol had made friends with Ned's sister. They seemed happy to be included into our community. I could only imagine what it must have felt like being ripped away from their own family after they'd died, and we all did our best to make them feel wanted from the moment they arrived in our compound.

I told them I had to get to Laura, and was trying not to bump into Markus. I didn't want to use my phone, just in case it was monitored somehow. I didn't trust we had complete privacy anymore. I didn't want Markus to intercept this conversation.

"Easy," Sam said with a wink. "I'll just go and get her. No problem."

True to her word she returned ten minutes later, with Laura in tow.

"What's the matter, love?" She looked and sounded worried, a slight edge to her voice.

"Eliza can have visitors," I smiled shyly.

"Well, that's good news, isn't it?" she asked with questioning eyes.

"Yeah. But er...,she wants to see Zack too?"

"Ah. Yes. I imagine she does. But that can't happen I'm afraid. Markus has been quite clear about that. Zack's not to leave his room or have contact with anyone." It didn't look like Laura would be receptive to my pleas and reasoning, but I tried anyway. I had to, for Eliza's sake.

"Could you possibly have a word with Markus? Please? I think Eliza needs to see Zack. She'll worry and that won't help her recovery. Please Laura? For me?" I put my biggest puppy eyes on, but Laura's demeanour was rigid. She didn't even have to answer, I knew I hadn't succeeded.

"I'm not going against Markus' decision. Zack knew the consequences of his actions. He'll just have to endure them. And I'm sure Eliza will be fine. Just don't do anything stupid? Please?" she urged. I could see in her eyes that she had sensed my rebellion already, even though I mumbled a reluctant 'of course not'. I needed to get Zack out of that room somehow, with or without the help of Laura. It seemed without.

***

"The tag is going to be the main problem. If we're gonna do it, the guards are the least of our problems," Sam snorted, after I explained the situation to them.

"We need to ask Archie to disable it, at least for a while. If he's able to, we can get Zack out and to the hospital, before they notice. He'll have to face the consequences though afterwards, and so do we. Is it worth it? Will Zack want to sacrifice even more of his freedom? He's a hundred percent sure to go into isolation, if he does this." Ned questioned. "In fact, do we want to sacrifice our freedom by helping?"

"Fair point. I'm prepared to do it, but I totally understand if you don't. I just feel I need to do this for Eliza. She'll worry if he's not there, and that's not going to help her recovery. She's still incredibly fragile. Mentally too." I looked each and everyone in the eyes, so they could feel and see my sincerity.

"I'm out. I'm sorry. I have tested this community so often, I'm lucky Markus allows me to be part of it still," Ned confessed with a sigh. I nodded encouragingly, giving him a hug. I could see Sam was wavering too.

"Look, Sam you really don't need to be part of it. I won't hold it against you. I understand. Honestly."

"I'm so sorry, but I really want to keep my punishment to the minimum. I was just about to get back into my course. If you really need me, I'll do it. But if you can avoid it, then I'd rather pass."

"I'm in. I want to help. I think Eliza needs the both of you there. And I think Zack will give his right hand to go and be with her."

"Thanks Brody." I smiled at him. I knew he would. "There's another obstacle; I'm not sure how Archie feels about it all. It's a bit different from helping with the mission to rescue Alice. I'll go up and see where he stands. I don't think he'll rat us out, even if he doesn't agree to do it."

Archie saw me coming a mile off. His face betrayed a slight fear of what I was about to ask him to do next. I explained what we needed doing and why, and I'm afraid to say I shamelessly flirted him into reluctantly agreeing. He'd been lucky that his tampering hadn't been detected yet. Markus wasn't great with technology, and so far Archie had been able to do lots under the radar, blaming technical difficulties for his failures. However, this time it would be too much of a coincidence to blame glitches. He said he would do it, if I or Brody would take the rap. He gave me a little gadget that he could activate to cause a disturbance, so the anklet's info would be unreliable. We would have to confess to have stolen the gadget and hacked access to it. The list of offences was growing by the minute, but I didn't care anymore. He'd also check who was on observation duty and send someone to distract him or her briefly, to avoid us being seen on camera. It would be super time sensitive and we needed a huge dose of luck to pull this one off. We had tested our luck several times already, and I wasn't sure if this was just one step too far. It wasn't a very tight plan.

CHAPTER 55

Zack

The sound of my sister's voice outside my door woke me from my slumber. I was bored out of my brain with no access to my phone nor computer, and I wasn't allowed to see anyone either. I couldn't be arsed to watch any more series or films on Netflix, so I'd given in, and closed my eyes for a bit. My senses were still alert enough to work out something was up outside, and I got up ready for whatever was going down. I sensed Zaph and Brody were involved, so I was prepared for anything.

My door swung open and Zaphy burst in, immediately followed by Brody who carried in a restrained guard. The man groaned, but couldn't make too much noise due to the cloth stuffed inside his mouth. Brody swung the guard onto a chair and bound him to it, and put him back outside the door, away from the cameras.

"We need to be super quick. Do you want to

see Eliza, even though you'll be caught pretty soon, and go in isolation when they do?" she asked me in a hurry. My heart leapt. I fucking loved my sis!

"The fuck I do! How?" I responded, equally fast.

"Take these; put them on in the corridor. We literally have minutes in here before the camera is monitored again." She handed me a bundle of clothes. We paced out of my room. I put on the long overcoat, normally worn with a suit, and wrapped the scarf around my neck and face. Zaphy shoved a woolly hat on my head and handed me her pass.

"Use this to get out. A taxi is waiting for you right outside the building. They'll take you to the hospital. I'll follow you there in a minute. Hurry. Good luck! This plan isn't foolproof!" she warned, and pushed me to start walking. The guard watched us with red hot glaring eyes. He couldn't believe what just happened on his watch.

"Thanks Zaph and Brodes! See you there," I whispered slightly out of breath as I paced away.

My heart pounded furiously, but I had to keep an air of calm over me when I walked into the reception. I cloaked as hard as I could to cover my tell-tale signs, but anyone close up wouldn't fail to see the perspiration on my forehead. So, I kept my face down and held my card out confidently to the reader. The guard on duty looked over, but as the gate opened without a problem, his attention was taken by someone entering the building. Luck was with me. For now.

I scanned the road and saw the taxi, waiting for me. I hopped in and she moved off straight away. She knew where she was going, it seemed. Good. I tore off the scarf and hat, wiped my face dry and took a deep breath. I didn't imagine I had long, but it was such a good feeling, knowing I could see Eliza and sense how she was doing, in person. I knew I was going to be locked away again, whether I did this or not, and would've hated not seeing her one last time. I needed her to know I was there for her, no matter what.

The moment I stepped into the hospital my heart jolted. *Fuck! No!* I fucking well picked up a sliver of Dimitri's scent. And when I sniffed again, Ilia's scent was prominent too. I scanned the area, but I couldn't see them. The scent was fresh, they couldn't be far. But it was just me here, and Zaph had not given me a phone, so I couldn't contact her. *Fuck it.* I ran into the corridor, the scent getting stronger with each stride. They would have no problem locating Eliza. Her scent permeated the air too. I struggled to maintain my calm, but I needed to stay focussed, if I had any chance at all to be of any use. I walked purposefully to Eliza's room, trying not to look lost, and avoid being challenged by anyone. I put my scarf and hat back on, to minimise the chance of any of the nurses or security recognising me, and barring my entry. It worked. I got to Eliza's door unnoticed. I threw the door open, hoping to see her safe and well.

No such luck. Alice sat in a chair and smiled, happy to see me. She'd moved on from her distrust of me, and fully accepted I had Eliza's and her best interests at heart. She was none the wiser of the danger Eliza might be in. *Fuck.* Her whole bed had disappeared.

"Where's Eliza?" I asked, hoping against hope she was just in the toilet and that they were replacing her bed or something. I knew that wasn't the case. I could smell Dimitri and Ilia all over the room.

"Oh, don't worry. Some doctors took her for a scan. You just missed her," she answered, totally at ease, not picking up on my concern at all. I swore under my breath.

"Two men? Russian accent?"

"Yes, they were lovely. So polite and professional! One even changed her drip bag, without waking her up," she cooed in admiration.

I was out of that door within seconds, no time to explain to Alice, who looked a bit perplexed at my terseness. It was easy to follow their trail, but I had no clue what to do when I'd tracked them down. Eliza would be out for the count. No guesses what was in that drip. So it was just me against them. They would have picked up on my scent by now, so I couldn't surprise them. They'd be carrying weapons, as they would have expected some resistance if any of us Sensorians had been in her room. It was a fucking nightmare. One I didn't quite know how to make end well.

I kept following their scent. It was heading downstairs. I guessed they were going to wheel her out of the hospital, pretending she had to be transferred. All I could do was stall the procedure, draw attention to them, and hope the pursuers that Markus surely had sent on their way to retrieve me, would be here soon. Zaph wouldn't be too far behind either. She was meant to join me soon after, at the hospital.

I saw them, literally about ten meters away from me, pushing the trolley bed up the ramp of what looked like a private ambulance. They were on high alert, their eyes darting all over the place. They must have sensed me, and knew I was near. The only thing I could think of was to put in my feeble plan, and draw attention to them.

"Hey there! Where are you going with that patient?" I shouted with as much authority as I could. Several of the personnel looked over. "I didn't think she was meant to be moved," still talking much louder than needed. Dimitri and Ilia shot each other confused glances, uncertain as to how to react. There were too many people there to start something radical. I gambled on the belief they wanted to get out unnoticed, with as little fuss as possible.

"She's being transferred," Ilia said, confidently pushing the trolley in further. Dimitri climbed into the driver's seat. They weren't going to stop. *Fuck!* I had to do something. I couldn't just let them drive off with her. I sprinted up to the ambulance. Ilia slammed the door shut, and ran around to the front and hopped into the cab. I raced forward, whilst they started moving off, grabbed hold of the door, which, luckily for me, opened. It took all my strength to swing myself up into the back of the ambulance, but I managed, hurting every single aching part of my body. I didn't fucking care. I was in. I checked Eliza over. She seemed fine but completely out of it. I quickly disconnected the bag from her cannula. The effects of the drug should wear off fairly soon.

I wasn't sure if Dimitri and Ilia knew I was in the back, or whether they even cared. I supposed, if they did know, they might think they're lucky to have caught the both of us, not perceiving me to be much of a threat on my own.

My tracker should be working and, for once, I kept my fingers crossed that Markus' crew would catch me. I peeked out the window and saw several people with their phones out, filming the action and our fast disappearing vehicle. I'd created enough of a kerfuffle to catch people's attention. I fucking well hoped it would help Markus find us.

CHAPTER 56

Zaphire

"No, no, no! Bloody hell. Alice! Where are they? Where did they go?"

Alice's face was a little nonplussed. She clearly had no idea something was seriously wrong.

"Well, Zack rushed out when I told him Eliza had been collected by some doctors. He was a bit rude actually. Left without saying a word." Alice's face showed a slight irritation, but now worry crept in too. "Is something wrong?"

I didn't answer either, as I was already out the door before she finished her question. I smelled Zack and possibly two more Sensorians. I recognised the scents from our encounter with the Russians. I followed the scent through the corridors, impatiently pushing past people, earning lots of tutting and foul stares. This was not good. I needed to phone Markus. I couldn't avoid speaking to him any longer.

Markus picked up after just one ring. "What

the hell have you done?" His threatening growl made my blood run cold for a second. I shook it off and ignored his question.

"Are you tracking Zack?"

"The hell I am. Tell me what's going on. Now!"

I removed the phone from my ear slightly as Markus' angry, booming voice was almost too much to bear.

"The Russians kidnapped Eliza from the hospital and I think either Zack is in pursuit or he's with her. Don't lose them!" I spoke so fast, I hoped I made sense. But, by the barrage of expletives on the other end of the phone, I gathered Markus had understood me all too well. "I'm following their scent. It's still quite fresh."

The scent took me to the ambulance parking basement. I could sense adrenaline and confusion oozing from the people who were there. Excited chatter reverberated through the enclosed space. I tuned into some of the conversation and located one of interest. I paced up to them.

"What happened? What did you see?" I shouted at no one in particular.

One of the bystanders got her phone out. "Look, I filmed it." She shoved the phone right in front of my face. I had to take a little step back to focus, but I could see Zack jumping into the back of the ambulance. I got my phone out and asked the girl to airdrop it to me, which she happily did, revelling in the attention she got. I sent the footage to Markus. You could clearly see the number plate too. Markus sent me a message telling me he'd asked the hospital not to inform the police just yet, and give us some time to track them down ourselves. He sounded quite confident we would. He also told me that Michael would pick me up in about five minutes. They were tracking Zack, and Markus had a plan to shepherd the ambulance to a place where we could surround it, out of the way of prying eyes.

The crowd started to disperse as nothing else seemed to be happening and I walked off to find a good place for the car to pick me up. Slightly away from the stubborn few that still hung about.

A scent crept into my nose and my senses went on high alert. Rick. *Bloody hell.* My neck cricked with the speed I looked around. Sure enough, Rick came hobbling towards me accompanied by two guards, who both looked apologetically at me. I'm sure, bar from shooting him, there wasn't much they could have done to stop him. Rick's face was determined and grim.

"What the hell, Rick?" I shouted, confused by his presence.

His face contorted with a mixture of worry, anger and pain.

"I sensed the Russians. I had to find out if Eliza was okay? What the hell happened?"

"Eliza was taken by the Russians and Zack jumped in the back, so he's with her too," I hastily explained to an astounded looking Rick.

"Why on earth were there no bloody guards protecting her?" he shouted.

I shrugged my shoulders. It hadn't occurred to us they might try again, in such a public place at that. They must have been desperate to come back with something. We grossly underestimated their fear of repercussions. As it was just the two of them, I doubted Colonel Turkenev was involved in this latest attempt to recapture Eliza. It would have been far better organised. No, this was an attempt to make up for losing their prisoners.

He shook his head in disgust. "Do we know where she is?"

"Markus is tracking them. Zack's wearing his anklet. I'm waiting to be picked up. We're going to surround them. There are many more of us as it was only the two of them. You best go back to your bed. You look terrible."

"No fucking way. I'm coming."

I tried dissuading him some more, but a car swept into the underground ambulance bay, and Michael waved me inside. Rick followed in my footsteps, and climbed in the car too. It left the guards unsure as to what to do. They didn't have a choice, as we drove off immediately, but not without Michael losing his rag for a moment about

Rick's appearance, slamming the steering wheel hard with both hands.

"What the hell do you think you're doing! For fuck's sake, Rick! I haven't got time to deal with this. Belt up and keep your mouth shut. We'll deal with you later."

Michael knew exactly where to go. He drove in silence, concentrating on his earpiece telling him the directions. After a few minutes I dared to open my mouth.

"I know I'm in trouble for releasing Zack, but at least we know the Russians got Eliza and where they are..." I tried talking myself out of the sticky situation I had created for myself.

Michael glanced over, sighed and shrugged his shoulders. "Save your excuses and justifications for Markus." His eyes returned to the road, ignoring my sulk.

I focussed my attentions on my phone and messaged Sam, Brody and Ned, telling them all about Rick's unexpected appearance. You had to admire this man. I mean, he could hardly walk, but he still managed to persuade his guards somehow to obey his demand to help him find Eliza. He was just so charismatic. How he thought he'd be able to help, I had no idea. But then, Rick was always full of surprises.

CHAPTER 57
Zack

Eliza opened her eyes as she started to regain consciousness. They darted around like a frightened animal, but once she locked onto mine, they came to rest. The steely grey of her irises was a little less bright than normal, but they managed to draw me in nonetheless. *God, she's so beautiful.*

I leaned into her a little. "Hey, tiger. You're back."

She whimpered and brought her hand to her throat, making a little rasping sound.

"Do you need water?" I looked around and my eye fell on some water bottles stuffed away under the seat. I quickly unscrewed the top and brought it to her lips, lifting her head with my free hand.

"Thanks," she said, barely audible. "What happened?"

I was just about to explain, but the ambulance slowed down and came to a stop. I heard Dimitri and Ilia's raised voices, speaking urgently in

Russian. It required my full attention to decipher their sensory output. I put a finger on Eliza's mouth. "Quiet." A foreboding feeling flooded my senses.

The back door opened and both Dimitri and Ilia barged in, weapons drawn. *Fuck it.* Dimitri checked on Eliza, grumbling angrily when he noticed the drugs disconnected from her cannula. The scent of Michael, Brody, Zaphire and several other Sensorians wafted in, but also the distinctive smell of a Mankuzay. And it wasn't Eliza. *What the fuck was he doing here!*

"Let's talk. We have you surrounded. Put down your weapons," Michael said. He sounded calm and in control.

"I rather die than go back to Turkenev empty handed," Dimitri shouted with his heavy Russian accent. "So, you shoot? We shoot. Or let us leave."

"No one needs to shoot anyone. We can't let you leave with Zack and Eliza. Eliza needs to go back to hospital. She's not safe here. What do you want?" Michael answered.

.439

"I need you to move. Let us go. Or both will be shot."

This wasn't going anywhere. We were all going to die at this rate. Both Dimitri and Ilia showed no sign of capitulating. The muzzle of Ilia's gun was pressed hard against the side of my head. My stomach complained, bile rising up.

"You can have me instead!" Rick shouted. "Let them go. I'll come. Willingly. That must be better than two reluctant youngsters that will only give you trouble?"

I felt Dimitri waver. He was considering the proposition at least.

"No! I can't let him do that!" Eliza sobbed, getting very agitated.

"Eliza, shut up! You stay the fuck out of this," I growled. "I order you to." I hoped my stern stare would jolt her into obedience. The last thing we needed was an emotional stubborn Eliza stirring up trouble.

"But, he'll hate it there...," she started up again. Fucking not listening to me. We'll have to have words about that, if we survive this.

"Listen Lizzy. You're right. I'll hate it there. It's worse than being part of the Sensorian community. But think about it. I'll get to live. And with Markus on the war path, I'm not so sure I will escape his harshest punishment, and even if I did, my life would be over. At least I can still work for the Russians. Give some meaning to my life. It'll be better. I'll be okay. Trust me." Rick wiped his forehead, sweat flinging off to the side. He didn't look at all well, but he carried on. "If they'll have me instead of the both of you, then, at least I can make up for what I have done to you. And your mum."

"Please Zack, don't let him do this." Her eyes looked up at me in despair. "Please do something. He saved mum. Markus won't execute him. He'll give him a chance," she said so quietly, I could barely hear it. But her desperation was clear.

"It's our only way out Eli. We have to let him do this." I answered resolutely. I wasn't going to let those Russians capture her again, and Rick was our ticket out. If they accepted the proposition.

The look on her face was one I would not forget easily. Utter desolation. Her anguish and soft pleas ripped through my heart. But I could see no other way out, even if it meant she might hate me forever.

"We need two Sensorians. We'll have Rick and swap him for Eliza," Dimitri decided. "Get in the van, hands out."

"What about Zack?" Zaphire squeaked from the back.

"He come with us," Dimitri answered. "No negotiations."

Michael's face dropped but nodded. My heart sank. This was it. I was going to be a bloody Russian slave. Fucking interrogating people for the rest of my life. Never, ever see Eliza again. I wouldn't even get the chance to make up with her. Nor see her beautiful smile. Never hear her naughty giggle ringing in my ears again. Never be outraged again by her blatantly defiant looks and eye-rolls. I will never get to feel her soft lips caressing mine again, let alone explore her body. A feeling of darkness engulfed my whole being. The world started to swim in front of my eyes. In a daze, I saw them wheeling Eliza out, only slightly aware of her whimpering calls for me and her dad. At the same time, Rick entered the van and offered his hands to be restrained by some cable-ties Ilia fished out of his pocket.

It was as if I wasn't there. My body was someone else's. This couldn't be the fucking end of it? But one look at Michael's defeated face and Zaphy's horrified expression told me enough. Ilia still had his gun pressed against my face, not taking any chances. *Fuck.* I heard Eliza's faint voice sobbing my name again. It was gut-wrenching, like someone got a knife, stabbed me in the stomach and twisted the blade over and over again. It completely paralysed me. For a second, I couldn't think or move.

Then, something snapped inside me. My instinct took over. I was not going to let this happen to me without a fight. Dimitri had gone back into the driver's seat. Ilia was just a Dullard, and didn't notice my sudden rise of adrenaline. He leant over to shut the door, and in that moment of inattention to his gun, I launched myself at him, tried to grab the gun but narrowly missed it. *Fuck!* I just about managed to knock it out of his hand, when he turned around and tried to punch me. I saw it coming and dived under his arm towards the door. I tumbled out and hit the ground hard. Michael, Brody, Zaph and the others immediately jumped forward and surrounded me in a protective circle, all with their weapons pointing at Ilia. Dimitri took one look in his mirror and decided to drive off, fast, making Ilia scramble to the door to close it. My head pounded, my heart raced. I couldn't believe I fucking pulled it off. I was out.

"Zack! You friggin' idiot! You could have gotten yourself killed!" Zaphire pounded and slapped my body, tears streaking down her face. Her eyes shone with happy anger and next I was smothered by her arms and body in a hug so tight, it hurt.

"Zaphy, please. Let me breathe," I managed to grunt.

Michael barged in to break up our reunion. "We need to go. Eliza is bleeding. Hurry and get in the van." Eliza had already been taken from her bed and placed carefully in the front seat. We piled in the back and drove back to the hospital, breaking all the speed limits.

The energy drained from my body and I collapsed into my seat. I ached everywhere, but I didn't care. Eliza was safe.

CHAPTER 58

Eliza

Dark corridors, rows of doors
One after another, after another, after another
I 'm running, fast
Opening each and every door
Turning corner after corner
Never ending
My heart's pounding
I need to find them

I woke up with a jolt. I was in a bed. Back at the hospital. The last thing I remembered was my father and Zack in the ambulance, about to drive off. The Russians traded me for my dad, but they wouldn't release Zack. Then I must have passed out. I couldn't believe I'd lost both my father and Zack in one go. I felt so drained, devoid of emotion. I couldn't comprehend it. How could I live with this? I had to find them. I could not leave them as slaves to the Russians. Their spirits will be utterly broken. And it was all my fault. Everything. None of this would have happened, if I hadn't gotten myself shot.

The door of my sterile looking room opened. Mum carefully peeked around it, not wanting to disturb me. Her eyes brightened when she realised I was awake, but that was immediately replaced by worry. She hurried over and gave me a hug. Her arms gently wrapped around me, making sure she wasn't hurting me. It made me feel instantly secure and loved. My body actually felt quite good and I was able to sit up, as long as I didn't make my tummy muscles strain too much.

"What are we going to do? Rick and Zack? We can't just leave them there!"

A confused look covered my mum's face, but then realisation dawned.

"Oh, sweetheart. You need to know that Zack is safe. It was a close call, but he managed to get himself out of that ambulance. He's fine."

Relief flooded over me. *Zack was safe?* My emotions started to return like an avalanche, nearly suffocating me. Happy at first, but then anger welled up. It took me by surprise, but I couldn't help it. I felt furious.

"Why did he not try and stop them taking dad? He could have tried!" I couldn't stop the tears that had been building up behind my eyes. Now it was like the dam was broken, I had no control left. My body shook with the outpour. Mum held me, carefully but tightly, until I stopped shaking and there were no more tears left. She made me take a few deep breaths, and wiped my eyes and the snot from my nose. I felt calmer.

"Don't blame Zack. You were his main priority. Always have been and always will be." Mum surprised me with her support for Zack. I knew she had started to trust his intentions, but I didn't think she was one of his staunchest supporters yet. But here she was, defending him. "Rick wanted to do this for you. To give you your freedom. Trust me. For all his strange ideas, and outlandish world visions, he did love you. And me, for that matter. And I think he realised that more and more. I know he hasn't gone about showing it in the right way, but I think deep down he knew that too. The sacrifice he made, will give him the hope that you can see him in a different light. Not as a selfish, delusional megalomaniac, but as a father, capable of atonement. Let him have that."

I let her words sink in. I could see she was probably right. But, I wasn't quite ready to forgive Zack. He knew Rick had thrown himself in front of Alice to save her. That should have been enough to at least consider helping Rick, rather than encouraging him to save our backsides. He could have tried to talk Rick out of it. But instead he told me to shut up, and let my father surrender himself to the Russians. I wanted to shout at Zack. I needed someone to blame.

"Where's Zack? Can I see him?"

"I think you need to rest. Zaphy will come and see you later, if Markus lets her." She clearly evaded my question. She always forgot I could feel all her emotions.

"Are they in trouble?" My voice sounded

oddly high in my ears.

"Don't worry about that for now. Just get some sleep. Your eyes are nearly closing by themselves," mum smiled, waving away my concerns. I wanted to know, but mum was right; I was struggling to keep awake. She gently stroked my face and circled my eyes, then leaving her fingers pressed against the sides of my head. It felt so good. So relaxing...I gave in, and let myself drift away.

***

Over the next week, neither Zack nor Zaphire came to see me. And neither did Brody. Sam popped in every day, and Ned came and cheered me up endlessly with his stories. Michael came to check up on me, and Rob gave me some exercises to do, honing my VH skills. Michael had my anklet put back on, which the doctors had reluctantly agreed to. It reminded me I was still not a free woman. Even Markus and Laura came by.

But everyone avoided my questions about what was going on with the others. If I persisted too long, they would sigh and leave. It was so bloody frustrating.

My plea with Markus about trying to get my father back fell completely on deaf ears. He told me, in no uncertain terms, that there was not even the tiniest chance he'd consider a rescue mission. In his opinion, Rick had made his bed and now he had to lie in it. He had made it possible for Daniel to out us to the world, and Markus felt he must pay the price for that. I had cried, begged, promised the world, threatened all sorts, but Markus was unwavering in his decision. And though my friends sympathised with me, no one seemed to support my idea to challenge the Russians into releasing him. They all tried to convince me this way was for the best. Even mum told me I should come to terms with it. That it had been the best possible outcome for all. Rick was hardly an angel, and he knew he had to bear the consequences of his decisions. Maybe they were right. If only I could talk to him once more, maybe then I could find my peace with it.

I was getting better. Each day I felt my strength build up and my wound was healing well. The doctors were pleased with my progress. Mentally I was still a mess, but though I couldn't fool my fellow Sensorians, the doctors were none the wiser, as I knew exactly what to say to avoid their concern.

"Miss Mankuzay, as you're healing well and able to move around independently, we've decided that if you're happy with it, you can go home today. We can sign your discharge papers and someone will talk you through your after care," Dr Crane said, with a big encouraging smile on his face.

"Yes please," I squealed in delight, throwing my mum the biggest grin. She still looked concerned, but that was her job. She took Dr Crane aside and grilled him about the safety of their decision. But the doctor was used to dealing with over protective family members and skilfully managed to convince her that it was the best thing to do, and that it would actually help me in my recovery. It was a done deal. I was on my way home. A tiny little worry crept in as to what was waiting for me back at the compound. Being injured was not going to help me avoid the consequences of breaking the rules and going against Markus' decisions. I was aching to find out how Zack and Zaphire were too. I missed them, and I was worried about them. But that worry couldn't stop me feeling happy about being able to return home. Come what may.

CHAPTER 59

Zack

Today was the day we would find out what Markus had in store for us. I hadn't seen anyone since my return to the compound, as I was put into isolation straight away. I didn't even get to see Laura or Markus. I'm not ashamed to admit that this last week had been the lowest point of my life so far. I felt that Markus and Laura, who I considered to be my parents, had fucking abandoned me. I felt utterly alone.

I knew I had let Markus down and he'd probably lost all his faith in me. I could imagine he was wondering why he'd even bothered taking me and Zaphire in, all those years ago. All we had done was disappoint him in the last year. I searched my soul to see what I could have done differently, but no matter how I turned it, or tried to see it from Markus' point of view, I always came to the same conclusion; I would have done exactly the same. This made it kinda hard. Did I not trust Markus' decisions anymore? Not even a year ago, I would never have doubted Markus. I'd broken some rules, had been fucking annoyed with him and maybe even argued with him a few times, but I always believed he knew best. What the fuck had happened? I needed to talk about these feelings with someone, but I was denied access to anyone. I just had to wait. Fucking frustrating.

I heard someone approach my cell. It was Vivian. She was still my handler, as Markus called it. She smelt focussed and full of anticipation. She carried a nervous energy with her when she entered. I stood aside, my legs slightly apart, hands behind my back and head bowed. The standard pose expected from a prisoner. As that's all I was, and probably would be for the foreseeable future. What a fucking waste of my life. And what for? For doing what I thought was best.

"I need to cuff you. Turn around," Vivian ordered. That was new. I couldn't help but look up and when I caught her eye, I could feel her reluctance. She desperately tried to cloak it.

Interesting. She didn't like the way she was meant to treat me. I sighed and did what she told me to do. It was pointless questioning or arguing over it. She placed the cuffs on my wrists. I heard a tiny intake of breath, as if she wanted to say something to me, but thought better of it. Nothing would be private. I was still wearing my anklet.

"Come." She held me by the arm and guided me along the corridors to the big hall; the only place in the compound that could hold all the Sensorians. It looked like Markus had made it a public trial. A feeling of impending doom settled in my stomach. What the fuck was all this?

Just before she opened the door I saw Frank, also handcuffed and accompanied by Michael. I could swear Frank had aged at least fifteen years. He looked a lot greyer and he'd lost weight, making the lines on his face stand out more, worry etched on his face. However, when he spotted me he smiled and nodded encouragingly.

"Don't worry Zack. We will be treated fairly. You have to put your trust in that," Frank said, trying to reassure me.

Michael stepped in front of Frank, who immediately lowered his eyes and head. "No more talking."

I looked around for Eliza, Zaphire and Brody, but couldn't see them coming. Maybe they were already inside. I hoped they would treat Eliza carefully. She can't be fully recovered yet. I hoped she was being truthful about how she was feeling and not putting on a brave face, and having to pay for it later. I knew Eliza too well to know she could fool almost everyone, including herself into thinking she was fine.

When we stepped inside, however, I could only see Lois and Jessica flanked by guards. My eyes roamed around as I sensed all my friends were here, but they just weren't where I expected them to be. Eliza was sat beside her mum. Brody was beside his parents. Zaphire, Sam, Rafferty and Ned were all sat together. But significantly, they were all sat in the audience seats, none of them were in the accused section. It was confusing, but I was pleased. It meant they somehow had got away without charges? It didn't feel right though. What the fuck was Markus up to? I was worried. Something big was about to happen. I could feel it in every fibre of my body. The looks on my friends' faces weren't promising or reassuring either. On top of that, I could sense Frank's unease about the whole set up too.

We were guided to our places. The four of us were stood up, whilst everyone else stayed seated. Two guards took over from Michael and Vivian, who made their way to their seats. Laura was already at the leadership table. Markus was yet to enter. A nervous vibe bounced around the hall. Anticipation was at an all-time high, and a buzz of voices reverberated through the place. Markus entered and commanded silence, just by his presence. His eye caught mine for just a second. The steely determination I found in them chilled me to my core. *Fuck*. The man meant business. I felt scared shitless. Suddenly I wasn't so sure about Frank's reassuring words. Markus was out to make a point. Reassert his leadership. This wasn't going to be easy, by any means. I didn't want to waste my life locked up for years, but I had no control over the outcome of this. All I could do was hope for the best. That wasn't fucking much to hold on to.

"Welcome everybody to this difficult but necessary occasion," Markus started in his usual authoritative and calm voice. "I fear this is going to be, by far, the most difficult trial I have ever had to preside over. In an effort to make it as fair as possible, I have decided to make it an open trial. I have come to some decisions, and I'm willing for them to be scrutinised by all of you. It is a little unorthodox, I realise that, but considering this trial is about insubordination at the highest level, I thought it fair to do it this way. After this trial, we will be clear, once and for all where our community is heading, and how it wants to be governed." He looked around the hall, to be met with a mixture of understanding and worry. No one seemed to know where this was going. Least of all, me.

"This is how it will work: I will tell you the conclusions I have come to for each of the accused. If anyone feels they strongly disagree, they can challenge the outcome. The challenger needs two people to support their challenge. However, to prevent everyone just challenging for the sake of it, there is a condition attached. If you lose the challenge, you will be facing the same consequences as the accused or equivalent, at the discretion of the leadership. The two people supporting the challenge will also be facing consequences." Markus paused with the obvious intent to add gravitas.

"I have randomly selected eleven people from a group of Sensorians who have positions of responsibility. They will have received an app, which will anonymously record their vote to either accept or reject the challenge. I won't be voting. It will be a majority verdict, no one can abstain. Is that all clear?"

The room reverberated with a resounding, but also slightly confused, 'Yes Sir'. I didn't know what to think of it all. It sounded like something bad was coming. I couldn't shake the feeling of unease and doom bubbling up inside me. Fucking marvellous.

CHAPTER 60

Zaphire

My brother seemed calm and collected. He stood in his designated area, head held high, observing the room and Markus. He was putting on a brave face, but I could tell that, underneath the shield he'd drawn up around himself, he was nervous and confused by the situation he was confronted with. He was trying to assess what was going on. But like most of us, wasn't able to read Markus very well. He, too, was cloaking his feelings and intentions. Eliza's emotions, on the other hand, were out there for all to feel. That girl really needed to learn to cloak at the appropriate times. Her anguish, guilt, and annoyingly, love for my brother was painful to experience. It threatened to smother my own state of mind, and I quickly had to shield better, to stop her emotions from taking over my own. I really didn't want to feel her love for my brother. I wanted to feel her love for me.

Markus prepared to announce his verdicts. The whole room fell into a hushed silence. Nothing could be heard apart from beating hearts, breathing and the occasional growling of stomachs.

"I'll start with Lois Langford. After a lengthy discussion with the other members of the leadership, I have decided to give her the benefit of the doubt. She never answered the invitation to join Rick's gathering. She may have been tempted, but she never acted on it. However, as it will be difficult to trust her fully again, she will be removed from the leadership and will never hold a position of any responsibility again. She has served her time in isolation and will be released today under the guidance of Michael. Anyone who wants to challenge, make yourselves known."

No one answered, unsurprisingly. Lois looked immensely relieved.

"Thank you, Sir," she answered softly.

I was surprised. This was not the harsh decision I'd expected, and clearly Lois neither. I looked over at Brody. He looked concerned. What was behind this? I just couldn't help thinking something was off. Something was brewing that I knew I wouldn't like. Markus had not gathered us here to just let everyone off with a light sentence.

Next up was Jessica. She looked scared, nothing left of her cocky attitude. But I knew beyond a shadow of a doubt, if she had the chance, she would instantly return to her, less than charming, self.

I once felt sorry for her, when she was still dating my brother. She'd been in love with him, but he ended up using her for his own pleasure, when he'd realised he didn't want to be with her anymore. He let it go on for far too long, and it had made Jessica resent him, and rightly so. Zack could be such a dick. I turned my attention back to Markus, who was about to speak.

"I considered Miss Summer for the ultimate punishment for her betrayal and despicable actions; death." Markus paused for a moment to let the seriousness of his statement sink in. It was met with a collective intake of breath by everyone there, but most notably, by Jessica. "But, Miss Summer, as you're under the age of twenty one, we decided to uphold the restriction on that penalty. Instead, you will be held in isolation indefinitely, retrain, and if and when deemed suitable, released with an electronic tag for life. You will never be eligible for a position with responsibility."

Jessica looked a little shell-shocked. Her eyes fixed at something in the distance, her face drained of colour.

"Does anyone want to challenge this verdict?" Markus asked out of obligation. I didn't think anyone was going to stick their neck out for Jessica. She came off lightly, really. She could live her life and with good behaviour be part of our community again, albeit in a menial job and tagged for life. She could still make her life worth living. It was in her own hands now. The punishments seemed perfectly reasonable so far.

It was Zack's turn. My stomach somersaulted

and I broke out in a cold sweat, I was so nervous. My brother straightened his shoulders, ready to receive his verdict.

"The leadership has decided that for the latest offences and blatant disregard for orders from superiors, we hold two people responsible. We decided to overlook anyone else involved in those actions, including Eliza, Brody and Zaphire who were released today, and will instead make an example of those ultimately responsible. We agreed that without Zack Mackenzie and Frank van der Veldt, none of it would have occurred and hence they will be the ones facing the consequences of their insubordination. Let their verdicts be a lesson to you all."

Bloody hell. This did not sound promising. Markus looked grim and determined. Zack and Frank both looked stoic. Resigned to their fate. Frank's wife, Clare, looked terrified. Her sister sat by her side, holding her hand for support.

"Zack. You have shown us that you didn't learn a thing from your time in isolation. Instead you went willingly and knowingly against the leadership for a second time. By doing so, you and Eliza got captured by the Russians, and consequently, put our people into danger in the ensuing rescue mission. However, you wouldn't have been able to act out your plan without the help of Frank, so I hold him ultimately responsible for your actions. You may have had intentions, but I doubt you would have been able to successfully break out and act upon them without Frank. You are still young, and your intentions have always been honourable, so I have not given up on you yet. However, your punishment must be severe and lasting. This will be your last chance to prove that you can work within our Sensorian community and not be a threat to our safety. Once you reach the age of twenty one, any, and I really do mean *any,* form of insubordination, will be punished by death."

What the hell! Holy shit!

Zack's lowered eyelids flicked up, and for the first time he showed his emotions. He was shocked and infuriated. He quickly cloaked again, but Markus had felt his anger. "It seems that any other threat or punishment makes no impact on you. You will be placed in isolation until your twenty first birthday, and you will be fitted with an electronic tag upon release. I will be your handler and will have ultimate control over all your actions, until you prove we can fully trust you."

The hall was silent. The verdict left me reeling. I didn't understand. This was a new rule. Up until now, only betrayal could lead to punishment by death. Never insubordination. It was extreme. Everyone realised what had just happened. If this could happen to Zack, it could happen to anyone. A feeling of unease penetrated the hall. The stench of tension, stress and adrenaline heavy in the air. Windows were being opened. It was getting a little too much to bear for everyone.

"Does anyone want to challenge this verdict?" Markus asked, scanning the room to sense people's feelings. A lot of muttering broke out in the hall. I could sense people felt the same as I did. I wanted to challenge it, for Zack's sake. But I was scared. I didn't want to lose the challenge and end up with the same fate. I could see Eliza was on the verge of speaking up. I caught her eye and in that moment her voice rang through the hall, loud and clear.

"I want to challenge it!" Eliza looked defiant and determined, but anxious as hell. God, the girl was brave! Impulsive maybe, but damned brave.

My heart thumped so hard it felt like it was going to break my ribs. The murmurs increased in volume and became ridiculously loud. Markus called us to silence.

"You need two people to second you," Markus reminded her.

She looked over at Brody, Ned, Sam, Phaedra, but they all shook their head, hardly daring to return her gaze. I understood their reluctance. Her eyes landed on me.

"I support Eliza's challenge." It was out of my mouth before I realised it and as I said it, my body shook. I knew I had to do this for my brother, and for Eliza, but I was scared shitless. We needed one more. My eyes pleaded with everyone who dared to look me in the eyes. Murmurs started to rise again. People discussing what to do and think.

"No." Zack's voice boomed. "Please, no one else support her challenge. I can deal with this verdict. I promise. It's too much of a cost for you to challenge it." He looked around the room, his natural authority radiating off him. Everyone fell silent immediately. No one else spoke up. His eyes fixed on Eliza, and he nodded encouragingly. She looked distraught. I was too, but I also felt relieved. *Does that make me a bad person?*

"Then the challenge can't be accepted. Let's move on now," Markus decided without hesitation.

CHAPTER 61

Zack

What the fuck just happened? Markus had managed to make insubordination punishable by death! And the only one that dared to challenge, was my fearless tiger, Eliza. My admiration and love for the girl was immeasurable. But I'll have to keep her out of my mind for nearly another year. I would be going nowhere until my twenty first birthday. Fucking hell man. I shook my head, as if I could shake my worries away. I needed to concentrate on what Markus was saying now. By the looks on people's faces and the increase in rankness in the room, it didn't promise much good. *Fuck!* What did I miss?

"...and therefore, in an unprecedented decision, and one that I had to make with a heavy heart, I have decided that Frank van der Veldt, will be sentenced to death by lethal injection..."

Deathly silence.

Clare gasped, shrieked, jumped up and

promptly collapsed. Frank looked like he's just seen a fucking ghost, utterly distraught and confused. I felt numb. This was fucking crazy. Markus had fucking lost his marbles. Though, as always, so bloody clever too. Letting everyone else off and making Jessica's and Lois' punishment as reasonable as can be, and then slamming us with this. Fucking genius. Maximum impact achieved.

Markus lent forward, his hands resting on the wooden bar he stood behind, scanning the room once more. "I know this punishment may seem harsh to some of you. But we are under threat at the moment. We're far from safe with the Russians' knowledge of our existence and soon other countries' intelligence agencies will be onto us too. We cannot have people who'll go off on their own missions with blatant disregard for our community's safety. Our community will descend into chaos, and ultimately its demise will follow. No one will be safe. We have no room for mutiny. It has to be dealt with severely. I need to be able to trust my leadership team. We have no choice."

Fuck me. I looked around the room and, to my disgust and surprise, noticed some people nodding their heads. Quite a few, in fact. They were in support of this abhorrent spectacle.

Clare was sobbing in the background. Everyone felt her pain and distress, stabbing, piercing through our brain and body. Frank managed to shield his emotions better, now he had slightly recovered from the initial shock. My brain worked slowly, hampered by all the emotions in the room, but an overwhelming feeling of injustice engulfed me. This could not go ahead. The fuck it couldn't.

"I challenge the verdict!"

The words hung in the air like a dense fog. The room shuddered again. The outpour of emotions on top of what had happened before was getting unbearable. I saw a few people doubling over, holding their heads. More windows were thrown open. I wanted to sit down, bury my head. But I stood up tall, staring Markus straight into the eyes. A flutter of shock and concern shone through for just a second, but then they turned cold as ice. He lent back, and placed his arms behind his back. He shifted his body posture a few times. He was stalling. He hadn't expected anyone to challenge, least of all me, his son for all intents and purposes.

"You understand that if you lose the challenge, you will almost certainly suffer the same consequence? Your age will not protect you." Markus' voice trembled slightly, his face grave. Laura had turned white. Frank looked at me incredulously, not quite believing what I had just done.

"Yes, Sir. I understand." *Bloody hell. What the fuck had I done?* I knew I had to. There was no way I was letting this injustice happen without a fucking fight.

"You need two people to support you."

I could tell Markus felt fairly sure no one would, and therefore the threat to his authority would be over. Then a change in his posture told me he'd also noticed the feeling rising up in the room that I felt right that moment: Resolve.

"I will support Zack."

Eliza's soft voice broke the silence. My heart jumped with joy, but equally, my stomach churned, threatening to empty itself, with worry and fear for the consequences to her.

"And me." Clare immediately followed, her voice hoarse from crying.

Markus' face dropped. He hadn't counted on the wife and would be girlfriend to support their loved ones. Or on anyone to challenge his verdict with the threat of death hanging over them. He had underestimated their resolve. His shoulders slumped a little, before straightening himself up again and stepping up to the challenge.

"So be it," he sighed. "Make your case to the eleven chosen ones. They know who they are, but their identity is to remain secret, to give them the security that they can vote anonymously and without retribution."

Laura stood beside Markus, but her eyes were on me, wet with tears, silently begging me to withdraw my challenge. That was never going to happen. I had to concentrate on formulating my challenge. I had to fucking come up with something to convince the eleven of all the wrongs that were about to be committed. My brain was dead though, I had no fucking words. In desperation, I looked over at Eliza. Her beautiful steely grey eyes bored into mine, centring me. Her pupils were dilated, signalling she still felt attracted to me. I sensed my own pupils responding. An image of her, nearly naked, from when I burst into her room and forced her into the shower to deliver a message, flashed before my eyes. *Focus, you dickhead!* I berated myself. She beamed an encouraging smile, as if I was just about to do a little drama performance or something. An inner peace settled over me. This was it. Frank, Eliza and Clare were relying on me to pull this off. It was now, or fucking never.

CHAPTER 62

Eliza

I saw his eyes looking for me. He was faltering. I was surprised he wasn't looking for Phaedra. She was his girlfriend and rock, but he only had eyes for me. I needed to be strong for him, to give him the confidence to do this. Frank's life, and his own, depended on it. Clare and I would be punished too, if it all went wrong. It was vital he performed at his best. Authoritative, clear, passionate and convincing. I knew he could do it. The mood in the room was fluid, it could go either way. I smiled at him and immediately I could feel his body relax. He straightened his shoulders and took a deep breath. He was about to begin his challenge.

"Honourable members of the chosen eleven, and all fellow Sensorians, let me begin by explaining why I felt I had to challenge this verdict, with the risk to my own life. It's not just about saving Frank's life. And it certainly is not, that I don't agree with Markus. Our community is in danger and we have many challenges ahead. But this verdict will be a turning point we would never be able to come back from. It is of utmost importance to think long and hard about this decision." He paused for a moment. Steadying himself again.

"Sentencing an outstanding member of our community to death, purely because he took matters into his own hands, is not the way forward. He felt the life of Eliza's mother was in danger by Markus' inaction, and wanted to respond. It will not make our community stronger to have such a high penalty on initiative. In fact it will make it weaker. Without Frank's insubordination, we would have been responsible for the death of Alice. In my mind there's absolutely no doubt the Russians would have lost patience with Jean-Pierre and Angelique's plan, and would have taken control. For them, Alice was a burden, and therefore wholly expendable, and er..." He stopped, gathering his thoughts. He seemed to be annoyed at himself for hesitating.

"So in the future, if anything like this happens again, but no one dares to speak up because of the fear of death, what would happen? We cannot have a community where the leadership can decide everything, unchecked, without being challenged, by anyone. If insubordination from members of the leadership becomes punishable by death, our community will come dangerously close to an autocratic society, and that surely is not what people want?" He looked people in the eye, forcing them to confront their own beliefs.

"I agree, we have to have rules and people have to abide by them. Orders need to be followed. But the punishment for failure to do so must be reasonable, and fit the crime. The circumstances that caused someone to break those rules, and the frequency it occurs, must be taken into consideration." *Come on Zack. Keep going!* I mentally encouraged him, wishing I could shout it out.

"Frank van der Veldt has always been

regarded as the voice of reason within the leadership. He has always toed the line. It had to be an exceptional circumstance for him to disobey Markus' orders. We must believe he would never have done it, if he hadn't been absolutely sure that there was no other way." He looked over to Frank who still looked in a state of shock, but nodded in a sign of acknowledgement.

"Please, let moderation prevail over extremist actions. We need to stop the radicalisation of our community, which is born out of fear. We've seen it everywhere now; increased security and the numbers of guards on the rise, increased surveillance and more control over our movements, and now these extreme punishments. This is not the life I want for our children. We need to control the threat in a way that does not impact on our freedoms even more than we already have to endure. There has to be a balance." He was so right. I just hoped others would see it this way too.

"I beg you all; look deep inside your hearts and decide whether you feel this is the right way forward. Do you really believe that Frank needs to, and deserves to die, to protect our society? If you have any doubts at all, even the tiniest bit, please support my challenge. Thank you for listening."

He scanned the room for a second, eyes shining with emotion and conviction, but then stood back. He lowered his head and closed himself off to everyone. Cloaking and shielding. He looked exhausted and you could see by the slight tremble in his body that the wall he built around himself was hard to maintain, requiring all of his energy. I could not reach him. I desperately tried to catch his eyes, but he only looked at the floor. I think he didn't want to feel the mood of the room, too scared to be confronted with possible failure.

I tried to tune into everyone's feelings around me, but it was hard. There was a lot of confusion, anxiety, hope, anger, and indecision in the air. There was no telling what the chosen eleven would decide. As we didn't know who they were, it was impossible to zero in on them to get a more accurate reading. All we could do was wait. My mum grabbed my hand in support. I knew she felt incredibly guilty for having been captured, and she felt responsible for the whole situation we were in. I tried to reassure her and convince her she was not to blame, but she wouldn't listen. She was distraught. But she still had the strength to be there for me. I had no idea what would happen to me, if the challenge failed. I didn't even want to think about it. I blocked that possibility out. It was too overwhelming and too hard to deal with.

Zaph came over to me, surreptitiously, as we weren't meant to move around the room. Her face showed pain and worry, but a glimmer of anticipation and hope broke through too.

"The tension is excruciating," she groaned. "I don't know how much longer I can cope with this." She glanced over to Zack. "Or him." He was still stood like a statue, exuding nothing but a little tremor in the muscles of his face. "Can you VH the room? Find out who's voting and what they've decided?"

"I can try?" I hadn't even thought of that. The least it would do is keep me occupied, driving my brain away from the possibility of Zack's death, or my own. I wasn't even sure if I wanted to live without him. I emptied my brain of any thoughts and opened up my mind. I scanned the room for Sensorians who were in a position of responsibility. I started with the top ones. One of them must have been randomly selected. I looked at Laura, Vivian and Rob. None of them looked like they were casting a vote. They were observing the room, much the same way as I was. I wondered if Rob was doing the same as me. I locked on to Michael. He was checking his phone. I jumped into his eyes; a connection easily made, as he had been my handler over the last few weeks. He was typing. 'Reject'. *Shit. No!* The bloody bastard had voted against Zack. My mouth went dry, I must have given away my despair as Zaphy grabbed my arm hard, and shook me out of his eyes.

"What did he vote?" she asked quietly, but

.483

desperately. I saw she knew the answer already. I shook my head gently. I wanted to move on. Find another of the eleven. I clocked Claude on his phone, hacked him, but he was just looking at his Insta account. I swiftly moved on.

"See if you can see anyone on a phone and tell me," I whispered to Zaphy. She immediately tugged my arm and nodded in the direction of Bryan Ellis, the head of archiving. He looked nervous. I quickly connected to him. I just caught his message before he pressed send. Another reject. My body started to feel heavy. My stomach a jumbled-up mess and my chest tightened.

I frantically searched the room for anyone else that could be casting a vote. Tristan. He was staring down at something. I quickly checked what. It was the voting app. I felt relieved. Surely he would be backing Zack. He started typing. 'Reject'. *No!* This couldn't be happening. His finger hovered over the send button. I stopped breathing. That would be three out of the eleven. Only three more and it would be over. Frank, and most likely

Zack, would be killed. I concentrated on Tristan again. He hadn't sent it yet. He looked at Zack, I didn't want to be in his eyes checking Zack over, the man he would be sentencing to death. Hatred grew inside me like a wildfire. *Fuck you, Tristan.*

Tristan looked back at his phone again. This was it. He was going to press that button. But then he started to delete his answer. My heart warmed and I could breathe a little easier. He typed in 'Accept' and hit the send button straight away. Thank God for that. That was one in our favour. We needed five more.

I was about to find another voter, when Zaphire clasped my hand. She nodded over to Markus. He moved over to the podium, seemingly ready to make an announcement.

"They can't all have voted yet!" Zaph's voice unnaturally high, filled with panic.

"Looks like they have. Markus looks grim. What's he feeling, Zaph? Focus on him," I urged her desperately, knowing she would be best placed to tune into his emotions, having been close to him most of her life.

"Fuck it! I can't work him out!" Zaphire squeaked, exuding desperation.

The tension was too much. I couldn't cope. I turned to my mum and lent into her. Her arms formed a protective barrier, but even they wouldn't be able to stop what was coming. Markus prepared to inform us of the outcome, but I couldn't watch. I didn't even want to listen. Zaphy forced herself next to me and mum embraced her too, so we formed a tight huddle, but none of us felt ready to face the verdict.

An adrenaline filled, nervous energy grabbed hold of the place. People shuffled anxiously about and the hushed atmosphere rose to a crescendo of chattering voices. I wanted to block everything out, but my shielding ability failed me. It was forcing itself into my consciousness and I burrowed a little deeper into my mum's arms, to no avail. I just had to face up to it. Let it wash over me.

CHAPTER 63

Zack

Markus' eyes met mine, briefly, as I looked up when the commotion around me forced me out of my self-imposed withdrawal. What I saw did not fill me with confidence. His eyes showed a mixture of regret, determination and resolve. All of which could be interpreted as good or bad news for me. Not long to wait now. I would know my, and Frank's, fate in a few minutes. I felt like I was staring over the edge of a cliff, waiting for the wind to either push me over, or away from the abyss. There was no way of telling how it would end. I dared to glance over at Eliza.

Her, Zaphy and Alice were all huddled together, none of them looking either at me or Markus. I tuned into Eliza, but immediately wished I hadn't. Her agony pierced straight through my heart. What the fuck had I done? Thinking I could change everything by challenging Markus? What a fucking idiot. I hated myself for putting Eliza and my sister through this. But a little voice in the back of my head kept telling me, it had been the right thing to do. I wouldn't have been able to live with myself, if I hadn't challenged Frank's verdict. It had been my duty and moral obligation. But now it was time to face the consequences of that decision. Markus lifted his arm, and everyone fell immediately silent. This was it. Will I live or die?

"Fellow Sensorians, the randomly chosen eleven have all voted to either accept or reject Zack's challenge. I shall open the app, and it will tell me the result. Once we know the outcome, we will discuss how to proceed."

I studied his face and body intently, totally focussed on his output of signals. His face dropped, his mouth quivered a little. Still, it didn't tell me fucking anything. But then, he was a master at cloaking. *Just tell us the bloody outcome!*

Markus leaned forward a little and looked me directly in the eyes. "Zack, are you ready to accept the outcome of the vote?"

"Yes, Sir. Ready as I could ever be." I managed to keep my voice steady. I think. It felt like it was just me and him in the hall, everyone else had disappeared from my awareness. I could hear my own heartbeat galloping in my chest. My throat felt tight. I had no saliva in my mouth. I breathed in, but was unable to let it leave my lungs.

"Your challenge has been accepted. Eight Accepts to three Rejects."

Oh my fucking God. And breathe! I couldn't help break out in a massive smile and instinctively tried punching the air, but instead yanked my arm as they were still in cuffs. I checked Frank. He still looked shell shocked, but his wife Clare was weeping happy tears and signalled her thanks to me with her hands clasped over her heart. I searched for my Eli. Where was she? I wanted to see and sense the relief she undoubtedly felt. I found her eyes staring at me. They were wet with tears. I could feel them stinging behind my own eyes too, until they started to free flow down my cheeks. I remembered Phaedra's words. There was nothing wrong with letting it all out sometimes. However, I wiped them away with my shoulders, as well as I could. Too late though, Eliza had already noticed them, and a smile broke through on her own tear-streaked face. She wasn't going to let me forget that. Ever. Little minx. But I didn't care. I wanted her to know how much it all meant to me.

"This outcome has presented me with a problem," Markus resumed, snapping me out of my euphoria. He looked rather grave. "As relieved as I feel not to have to condemn my own protégé to the death penalty, it shows the support for my leadership and my decisions are in the minority. By a big margin too." He exhaled loudly and paused, shifting his weight from one side to the other. Was he nervous? Undecided? It was odd to see him unsure of what to do next. I got the feeling something fucking huge was about to happen. "Before the outcome was known, I promised myself to do something, if the result went against my decision. Now it actually has happened, it proves to be rather difficult to do," he confessed. "However, it has to happen. I have decided to step down as your leader."

Gasps of shock and surprise echoed through the room. *Did that just happen? Did Markus resign? What the actual fuck?* Markus looked dejected but resolute. He'd made up his mind.

"First of all, we need to deal with the four accused and exact their verdicts. Frank's has been annulled, so we have to call another meeting for that, but that will be up to the new leader. He or she will be appointed by a panel consisting of the current leadership and other senior members of our community. In the meantime I will pass the leadership over to Michael, my second in command, who will be our interim leader."

Michael looked as bewildered as everyone else. He had certainly not been made party to this decision beforehand. Markus hadn't quite finished yet.

"It has been an amazing, but demanding and certainly stressful job, and I thank you all for your support over the years. It's been an honour serving you, but it seems my time is now up. I wish the new leader the best of luck and I will support and help, whoever it may be, to the best of my ability, if they wish me to. I will always be at your service."

I didn't know what to think, or how to feel. This was fucking out of the blue. And sensing the room, everybody shared my shock. It was only Laura whose face didn't show surprise. She knew exactly what Markus had planned. There wasn't much they didn't discuss.

Michael stepped up, rather reluctantly. He was the most loyal supporter of Markus, but I also knew he never fancied himself a true leader, and it showed on his face. However, as he's been tasked with the interim role, he would do it to the best of his ability. That was the kind of guy he was. He'd never shirk away from any responsibility given to him.

"With this rather unexpected turn of events, I suggest we adjourn any decision making on what happens next with Frank's punishment, like Markus proposed. So, Frank will have to go back into his room, with house arrest, and wait for a further decision on that. Lois, you will come with me and we'll talk through your release. Jessica and Zack will start their term of isolation with immediate effect."

Oh fuck it. In my celebration of winning the challenge I completely forgot my punishment hadn't changed. I had to go into isolation until my twenty first birthday, which wasn't until about eight months later. Then I'd be on a lifetime threat of death for any insubordination. My heart sank. Any hope of me starting some sort of relationship with Eliza was dashed again. By the time I'd come out she would have moved on, for sure. We were not allowed any contact. Not fucking ideal, as I hadn't even told her how I really felt about her! Not whilst she was conscious, anyway.

"Michael, I mean, Sir? Please may I have

permission to speak?"

"Go ahead. Make it brief."

"Sir, may I please talk to Eliza, before I go into my isolation cell?"

"Request denied. You are not to speak to anyone," he answered coldly. Then signalled to the guards to take me and Jessica away.

"Laura, please?" I begged my carer, when she caught my eye. The one who would always try and fix things for Zaphy and me. The one I was sure, loved me. Her eyes portrayed pain and I knew she wanted to help, but she shook her head in defeat. She couldn't do anything for me.

It was like a bomb blasted in my brain. I couldn't fucking do zilch. Completely powerless. My last hope squashed, I turned to Eliza, caught her eye and put my hand on my heart and blew her a kiss. I hoped she understood how much she meant to me. How much I loved her. If only we'd had a chance to explore it. Her face showed so many emotions, the poor girl was clearly heading towards a sensory overload. When I glanced over my shoulder, just before leaving the hall, she had collapsed to the floor, sitting down, head buried under her arms, knees drawn up. My heart broke.

CHAPTER 64

Zaphire

Zack and Eliza's emotional exchange told me everything I needed to know. They loved each other. Deeply. I knew she also loved me. Still loves me. But I also knew their connection was so much more than that. I was always going to be fighting a losing battle. However, eight months was a very long time...but first, I had to deal with Michael.

"Alice, are you okay taking Eliza somewhere quiet? Sam, can you help? I have to see Michael." Both of them nodded their head.

"Yes, we got this," Sam confirmed. "Don't do anything stupid!"

I raced after Michael. I was fuming. I quickly caught up. I yanked his arm to turn him around.

"You voted reject! You could have condemned my brother to death!"

"How do you...., oh wait. Of course. Eliza."

"It doesn't fucking well matter how I knew!

How could you do this to him? How could you!"
Anger tears started to prick behind my eyes.

"Okay. Calm down. Let's talk after I've dealt
with Lois. Come and see me in an hour. You'll do
well to remember your place in the meantime.
Treat me with respect, when I next see you. Go."

He walked resolutely on. There was no chance
I would get to speak to him right now. I had to
wait. I followed them to his office and parked
myself outside, sat down and leant against the wall.
I wasn't going anywhere. The moment he finished
with Lois, I'd be there.

After about half an hour, Brody turned up.
Probably checking on my state of mind, and
making sure I wouldn't do anything stupid. It
might not be a bad thing. My mood was not
exactly very rational at the moment. Michael was
the interim leader now. I needed to remember that
when I went in there.

"Come and get a coffee, Zaphy. Talk over
what you want to say to him."

"No, I wanna stay here. I'm going in there as

soon as Lois leaves. I don't need to talk it over."

"Don't be so damn stubborn. Come." He tried to pull me up, but I wasn't having any of it. I was staying. Brody admitted defeat, sinking to the ground, next to me. Head leaning back against the wall.

"The caf is so much more comfortable," he grumbled, but with a little glint in his eye. We just sat there, in silence. We didn't need to talk. I was glad for his calming influence. By the time the door opened and Lois was escorted out, presumably to her room, my breathing had returned to something resembling a normal rate, and the tears had stopped teasing behind my eyes. I was ready to confront Michael in a more rational way. A way in which I might not be reprimanded. He called me in.

"Can Brody please come in too?" I asked, hoping he would be allowed. Michael nodded his consent. I wasn't convinced Brody was particularly enthralled with the idea, but he wouldn't refuse. He had my back.

An awkward silence hung around the room as I was looking for the right words to say and Michael was just sat there staring me down. Brody stood bolt upright, waiting patiently for me to start.

"Well, Zaphire. What is it you'd like to know?" Michael tried to get the ball rolling.

"Sir, I'm sorry for my earlier outburst," I started but paused. "Actually, I'm sorry for addressing you like that in public, but what the hell did you vote reject for?"

Michael sat up a bit straighter, his eyes not leaving mine. He coughed a little, to clear his throat.

"Zaphire, listen. I know you feel hurt, but I felt I had no choice but to vote reject. I'm loyal to Markus and, even if I didn't agree with his verdict, I would never vote against him. Though, I would have tried my damn hardest to make sure Zack wouldn't have been given the death penalty. He doesn't deserve that. Trust me in that."

Too right he didn't deserve that. He only tried

to save Alice's life! I wanted to shout at Michael. But, in my heart of hearts I knew that his motives came from a place of integrity. A deep-seated sense of loyalty to Markus was at the heart of it. Michael was not evil. And I knew Markus wasn't either. But I needed to vent, to blame, to scream at someone. Brody looked at me with a warning glare. He felt I was about to burst, but it wasn't the right time or the right person to lose my shit with.

"Zaphy, take a deep breath. You said your piece. Leave Michael to arrange the election of our new leader," Brody tried to reason with me. His words made their way through the red mist. I knew I had to listen to him. Still in a daze, I turned around and walked out, Brody right behind me. There was nothing left to say. I was about to leave, when Markus arrived. I couldn't cope with him. He was wise enough not to stand in my way, when I turned and paced out of the room. I could hear another set of feet following us. It wasn't the men. It was Laura. She caught up with me within moments.

"Zaphire, please. Let's talk."

"Not here."

"Come to our place. Markus will be out for the rest of the afternoon." She looked at me with big, beseeching eyes. I couldn't refuse. I didn't want to refuse. Brody nodded encouragingly and I turned to face her. I didn't say anything, but she knew I would come. She gave me a quick hug, took me by the hand and I followed willingly.

"You have to put yourself into Markus' shoes. He was pushed into a corner with no satisfactory outcome feasible, without some drastic decisions being made..."

"But sentencing Frank to death! And then letting Zack challenge it! How am I going to forgive him for that?" I cut in, exasperated.

"But he's stepped aside now. He realised he didn't make the right decision. You must give him some credit for that," Laura argued back, hoping it would mellow my stance.

"I don't know Laura. I need time to process all

of this."

"Of course, Zaphy. Take all the time you need. I hope we can resolve this. We both love you very much."

I nodded. I knew they did. But I didn't know if I could forgive Markus. Time would tell.

Later that evening, I was back in my room, trying to relax. I had sent everyone away. I needed to be on my own. A little knock sounded on my door. *Great*. I knew who it was. Did I have the energy to deal with her? No. I was exhausted after talking to Laura, and dealing with the whole trial. But I called her in anyway. She stood by the door for a second, looking bashful. It reminded me of the first time I met her. Zack had opened the door to introduce me, but she lost it completely. My scent overwhelmed her so much, she wasn't able to control her urges. I think I fell in love with her right that moment. Her eyes had been bashful then, too, albeit a bit frantic from the overwhelming sensations she experienced for the first time. It felt like a lifetime ago.

"Merry Christmas?" She held out her hands with a tiny wrapped present in them. I totally forgot it was Christmas day tomorrow. I really didn't feel like celebrating.

"Aw, sweet," I managed to say, only just convincing enough to give her the encouragement to enter my room fully.

"It's only little..."

"It's more than what I got you," I cut in, perhaps a little too sharply. I could feel her growing sense of unease. Suddenly the strain and heartache she'd gone through earlier today was obvious to see. Her eyes were red rimmed, and big blue shadows showed prominently below them. It made her look extremely vulnerable.

"I er..., I meant to give it to you before. But you know, isolation got in the way. It was for your birthday..." She held the present out again, and I finally took it out of her hands. I tried to carefully peel the tape off the delicate purple paper it was wrapped in. Eliza had used way too much tape, so

I ended up ripping it all too pieces. It made her smile. A black leather string bracelet fell out, but I caught it before it hit the floor. A little silver heart dangled from it. It was gorgeous. Just how I like my jewellery; not too delicate, but pretty nonetheless. A warm feeling engulfed me, but it wasn't just mine. Eliza positively glowed when she sensed my appreciation of her gift.

"Even if we don't end up together, you will always be in my heart. I love you, Zaphire."

She helped me put the bracelet on my wrist.

"I'll never take it off," I said, fearing it was more of a break up present, than a declaration of commitment. "But you love Zack more." It wasn't a question, and I knew the answer. She bit her lip, and couldn't look me in the eye.

"It's complicated," she paused, clearly contemplating if she would elaborate on the cliché. I kept quiet. I wasn't even sure if I wanted to know about her feelings for my brother. "Maybe it's not that I love him more, I just feel more connected to him. Or something." She threw her hands in the air and turned around. "Ugh. I don't know." She concluded unhelpfully.

She turned back to face me and finally looked me in the eye. She couldn't hide her desire for me, as her pupils dilated and her breath shallowed. If only I could forget about her lack of trust in me when she first cut me out of her undercover mission with Zack. Blank out the betrayal I had felt, and the awkwardness of her love for my twin. Could I ignore the underlying emotions Eliza was feeling? I sensed she wasn't here to make up. She was here to break up. She just didn't know it herself.

"We were so good together, Zaphy. It was so easy and care-free. We fit together like hand and glove. Should we try again? Maybe it could work?" she pleaded with so much feeling. "And Zack's with Phaedra," she sighed.

Should we? I wanted to be reckless, and forget the stress of the last few weeks and just grab her. Kiss her all over and make passionate love to her. There was a time where I would have just done that. But too much had happened. It was complicated. I stepped away from her, in an attempt to regain full control over my urges. If I acted on them, we would end up together again, until Zack was released. Then we would have to go through an even more painful break up. I was absolutely sure she would choose Zack. But that wasn't the only issue. Something broke in me when I realised Eliza didn't trust me as much as Zack. I would always be second guessing her actions.

It suddenly dawned on me what Eliza had sighed about. She still thought Zack and Phaedra were together, and she wasn't happy about it. He hadn't been able to talk to Eliza at all. It strengthened my resolve.

"I think you should leave." I heard my own voice say, as if someone else was speaking for me. It trembled and was full of repressed lust, pain, and utter despair. She needed to go. And quick. Before I changed my mind. "And just so you know, Zack and Phaedra broke up." I closed my eyes for a moment and I felt her presence disappear. I thumped myself several times on the head. It hurt. Did I regret my, far too sensible, decision? Maybe. Hope was very hard to kill. I felt empty. Tears started to drip down my face. Everything was so fucked up.

CHAPTER 65
Eliza

I ran back to my room. Too fast, so I didn't see the kids playing in the corridor, and consequently bumped into one and nearly pushed her over. I mumbled a quick apology, but I hurried on as I didn't want them to see the tears that were undoubtedly coming. They just stared at me scurrying off, too scared to say anything.

What just happened? I felt sick. Lost. I'd gone to see Zaphire with the intention of talking about us. To see if we could give ourselves a chance to blossom. At least, I think I had that intention. She picked up a different vibe all together. She felt I was there to officially break up with her. Maybe I was. Had I lied to myself about wanting to give our relationship another chance? Maybe I only wanted it because I thought Zack was taken. Perhaps Zaphire had sensed my emotions better than I had myself, and now I had to deal with that. What exactly did I want? And Zack breaking up with Phaedra? That explained why he wasn't looking for her, but sought *me* out during the trial. Did he really love me after all? Had Dimitri been right? The thought of that vile man made me feel sick to the stomach. Hammers drummed in my head. I wanted to scream.

My mum found me, curled up on the sofa, face wet from tears. She came over and gave me a hug. One that only mums can give. I felt like a little girl for a moment, freed from all the complications I had to deal with.

"Hey, my sweet. Do you want to talk about it?" she asked, looking concerned. I shook my head. I needed to sort my head and heart out first.

"Just say if you do. Give yourself time. You've been through a hell of a lot." She continued stroking my head for a while. It really calmed me down. Mum was right. I didn't need to solve everything straight away. I needed time to heal.

"I have some good news," she said, after a while. "Michael has given me a permanent apartment to live in."

"That's fantastic! Wow! I can't believe he agreed to your terms!"

"It took a lot of persuasion, trust me. I had to compromise a little, so even though I won't have to answer to any of the Sensorians, and no one is my superior, I do need to log my comings and goings. I can't leave without someone knowing." The look on her face told me she wasn't completely happy with it, but that had clearly been a hard boundary for Michael. Mum hated the strict controls in our Sensorian community, but when Michael proposed for her to stay with us due to concerns for her safety, she accepted the offer. However, she didn't agree with the strings attached to the deal, and they'd been at loggerheads over it. He ended up withdrawing the offer, but apparently changed his mind. I was over the moon. It would be nice to have a little safe haven, away from the invasive rules and codes of conduct of the Sensorian lifestyle. Though at the moment, I was never totally free from observation, thanks to my anklet.

The news lifted my mood and I pushed thoughts of Zaphire and Zack away. I buried them. For now.

**

Life started to return to some sort of semblance of normality after about three months. Everyone was back to working on cases, almost like nothing ever happened. However, none of my mates were working in the field at the moment. We were all still juniors, mainly under Saleem's supervision. The atmosphere in our compound was still a little edgy, and we had to report anything that looked or felt remotely suspicious.

Sam, Ned, Brody, Zaph, Rafferty and I had gathered in Sam's room after work and permitted ourselves a few drinks and pizza. Zaphy and I had been avoiding each other for weeks, but after a while neither of us wanted to miss out on the get-togethers with our friends. It was awkward, but as long as we weren't alone in each other's company, it was bearable.

"Don't you think it's weird that British or American intelligence haven't been on to us? Surely they must at least have found the need to investigate us?" Zaph said. Ned jumped on that.

"Yeah. Doesn't exactly fill me with confidence they'll be able to uncover major threats to our country. I mean, we have moved and kept a low profile, but really?" We all nodded in agreement. It was definitely strange.

Rafferty burped loudly and snorted. "They'd be lost without us keeping an eye on everything!" he laughed. Zaphire laughed with him. Possibly a little too loudly. Rafferty blushed. The girl was incorrigible. She flirted with everyone at the moment. I thought she had gotten close to Samira, Saleem's sister, but clearly that didn't stop her from teasing Rafferty. Raff surreptitiously glanced over to me, but when I caught his eye, he turned an even brighter red. I raised my eyebrows slightly, but he looked away quickly.

"Brodes, when will Eve be here?" I changed the subject. Brody and Eve had been getting close, but he still was a bit reluctant to bring her into our group. It wasn't different tonight.

"I'll be seeing her in a bit."

"Bloody hell man, what are you waiting for?" Ned said, throwing a cushion at him good naturedly.

"Just don't want to scare her off!" Brody laughed, but signalled that was the end of it. He would bring her along when they're ready I suppose.

Slowly but surely the Sensorian story had disappeared from the news, and still no apparent approach had been made by any intelligence agencies. Daniel had definitely been the driving force behind our exposure. Thinking of Daniel made me go cold all over. He hadn't deserved his brutal execution. It was outrageous that it would go unpunished, but Jean-Pierre's associates, or maybe the Russians had made it look like he crashed a car into a tree, which subsequently caught fire. There wasn't much of him left to investigate, and it didn't look suspicious, so it was tentatively declared an accident pretty soon after his body was found. When I read the article I broke down crying at the injustice of it all, and for his poor family, who were none the wiser about the real reason their son had met his untimely death.

I felt Ned's hand on my back, rubbing it gently.

"Are you okay? You seem a bit lost?" he asked gently. I nodded and shook the depressing thoughts off me, offering everyone another drink. I didn't want to talk about it.

"Has anyone heard what happened to Irena?" I changed the subject.

"She's being held in a room under house arrest. I think they're waiting for the new leader to be chosen to make any more decisions," Brody said. "But I hope they're going to try and integrate her into our community. She took a hell of a risk going against the Russians."

"Even if she did it just to escape a lifetime of oppression," I added. I knew she wasn't a fan of our lifestyle, but she would have found having

Dimitri as her boss worse. I think she realised that, just in time to help us.

"When the hell are they going to make a decision on the leader? It's been three fucking months! It doesn't feel right having no one taking control," Ned grumbled.

"I overheard Markus and Laura this morning. I think there will be an announcement tomorrow," Zaph piped up.

"When were you going to let us know, man!" Sam shrieked. "Trust you to sit on that news!" Zaphire went red, realising she should have told us this as soon as she found out. Brody and Ned shook their heads in dismay. I tried to avoid looking at her to stave off confrontation. I couldn't believe she kept that quiet. Having a new leader, would mean we could rally to get Zack's verdict overturned, or at least shorten his stay in isolation. I had to hope this was a possibility. Not seeing him and resolving our feelings for each other was driving me insane.

"I dunno," she mumbled meekly. "But I've

told you now." She looked up, ready for anyone to challenge her, but no one did. That was more like Zaphy.

Zaphire had been right. A little later we had all been given a notification to gather at 10am the following day in the Great Hall of Doom, as we'd come to call it. The whole community was buzzing. This decision would show us what kind of future was in store for us. Just more of the same, or maybe a change in direction? We would find out soon enough.

***

Inside the hall, the tension was building. It was oppressive and difficult to cope with. I didn't think I would ever get used to dealing with big events like this. The emotions of others were starting to overwhelm me. Then out of nowhere, I felt someone squeeze my hand for support. I'd recognise that hand out of a million. Zaphire.

When it really mattered, she was there. She caught my eye and gave me an encouraging smile, before she let go of my hand, and mum took over. I started visualising the sea and waves to calm myself down and replenish my energy to deal with the upcoming revelations. I was vaguely aware Michael had taken centre stage to make the announcement.

"Fellow Sensorians, the team that was tasked to elect our new leader has finally come to a decision. The reason we took our time is that we had to discuss in detail our views of the future of our community, and what we would like to see happen. It took a while to convince some of the members to agree to a rather controversial proposal, but in the end everyone concluded it was the best option for us." He paused for a moment to acknowledge the team he referred to. They all nodded their heads. Some more enthusiastically than others, but they exuded unity. They were all behind the decision they had agreed on. My stomach churned. Why was it controversial? That usually didn't bode well.

Michael drew a deep breath before he carried on. "I think our decision does need some explaining, so before I tell you who's going to be our leader, let me tell you about how we came to this conclusion. You all know there was tension within the leadership as to how Markus had dealt with the threats to our society. He focussed on making the rules more strict and increasing security. His reluctance to start the mission to save Alice, in his mind to keep us safe, was not unanimously supported. Some of us questioned his approach, others even acted against it, with enormous repercussions to their own lives. We questioned whether this was the direction we wanted our community to go in. Withdrawing more, with less freedom and harsher punishments? We came to the conclusion that we did not want this. So the question became, who can be that person to lead us? Someone strong enough to keep control and discipline over our community, but also progressive and brave enough to make, at times, controversial decisions. Someone with natural authority and who has earned respect by having made decisions for the greater good, sometimes even jeopardising their own life. We need fresh blood. It would have been easy to promote either me, Laura, or Vivian, but we wouldn't be able to give our community what it most needs now: courage, energy, discipline, but at the same time safeguard our freedoms and quality of life."

The room had fallen quiet. My mind was racing. I knew who'd fit the bill, but that wouldn't be possible? Surely not? It couldn't be. I glanced over to Zaphire and Brody. They looked equally perplexed. Did they think the same thing? It would certainly be a bizarre turn of events and I couldn't help but let out a little giggle. Brody threw me a stern stare. I stifled another nervous snigger. The silence seemed to go on forever. Michael stood dead still, but finally his body language gave him away. He was about to put us out of our misery.

"We decided that there is only one person who can step up to fulfil all the criteria, and that is Zack Mackenzie."

Oh my friggin' God! They had actually done it! *What the hell!* How on earth had that come about! No wonder it took three months to sort out. This was insane! The hall exploded with excited chatter with a slightly rebellious feel to it. A quick scan around the hall confirmed that most of the young people were super excited, whilst the older generation exuded confusion and some reluctance. Overall it felt positive though.

Another thing dawned on me. Zack would be coming out of isolation. I would get to see him soon. I could feel a huge smile break through on my face and I hugged my mum so hard, she made a little grunt in protest. I hadn't felt this happy for a long time.

Michael waited for the energy to calm down a little before he motioned for silence.

"We realise Zack is very young to take on this

huge responsibility, and it took him a while to accept that this was his fate. He will, of course, have guidance from all of the leadership, which will be expanded with three new members; Rob, Saleem and Phaedra. We have reformed some of the rules so we will be able to challenge a leader. We can challenge if we have a majority with a margin of three, which Zack agreed to. We have to avoid insubordination caused by rules that are too rigid from now on. There should be an opportunity to object or block a decision by a leader, but only in extreme circumstances. Finally, we have also decided to release Frank with immediate effect, bearing in mind that with the new rules, he would have been able to gather support for his actions, and would have been able to do it legally. There wouldn't have been a case of gross insubordination. We will formalise everything over the coming weeks. Zack will acclimatise in that time and, when he's ready, will formally address you all. I realise this is a lot to take in, and questions can be directed to the leadership by email or appointment.

For now, you're all dismissed." Michael turned abruptly around and tried to leave the hall in a hurry. He clearly did not want to deal with any queries for the moment. I didn't blame him. The room was full of questions. Bloody hell. Talk about landing a bombshell! Most of us were still reeling, trying to make sense of the complete U-turn. It was mind-boggling to say the least.

CHAPTER 66
Zack

Fuck me. I didn't have many other words to express my feelings about what had happened in the last few weeks. It was absolutely the last thing I would have predicted. When Michael came to my cell and proposed their idea, I was dumbstruck. I thought it was a cruel joke, designed to mind-fuck me. I didn't understand why they would do that to me, but it was so left field, I couldn't take it seriously. It took some serious convincing from all the leadership, but it was Phaedra who finally managed to persuade me it was real. She was going to be inaugurated into the leadership too, together with Saleem and Rob.

Fucking leader of the Sensorian Community. Me? Now? I still couldn't wrap my head around it. I wasn't sure I'd made the right decision to accept. The responsibility was going to be crushing. What if I made the wrong decisions? It could spell the end of our community, our safety net. I will be responsible for everyone's lives. I didn't think I was ready for it, but the whole leadership was behind it, and assured me they would be there to guide and support me. They explained they would put a failsafe in place to help prevent dangerous or erratic one-man decisions.

Their conclusion was announced today and I was waiting for them to report back as to how it had gone down. Earlier today, I had been transferred from my cell to one of the desirable apartments on the top floor, which would be my new place to live. They had taken my anklet off, and had reassured me there was no CCTV in my new home. It was almost too good to be true. If I hadn't been reading everyone's output non-stop, paying attention to the tiny tells people tended to have, even when trying to cloak, I would still think it was all an elaborate hoax. But I'd found nothing, not even a hint of cloaking. It all seemed genuine.

Michael burst into my room, momentarily forgetting he was now supposed to knock. I didn't remind him. He had a few weeks grace, as it wasn't formalised yet. It would take some getting used to. Me, being everyone's superior. I couldn't help smiling a little to myself. The fucking irony of it all. Markus apparently was digesting the whole situation and I was told he 'needed some time'. It was going to be bloody awkward. Laura had already come to see me last week. She just hugged me. We didn't talk an awful lot. I just savoured being held by her and feeling loved.

"Zack? Sir?"

My head snapped up. I'd forgotten to acknowledge Michael. This time, he'd remembered the appropriate address.

"How did it go?" I asked. But looking at him already told me it went as well as could be expected.

"No one saw it coming, so understandably there was some confusion. Overall, a positive response. You'll be fine, Sir."

"I know I will. I'll have to be. What's next?"

"You need to use the next few weeks to

acclimatise and sort out your personal life. You've been more or less in isolation for three months so you need to give your senses time, but your head needs to be clear and focussed. Whatever is going on between you, Eliza and Zaphire needs to be resolved, and the sooner the better." Michael never beat about the bush. I knew he was right.

"Am I free to go where I want now?" I asked, as I still wasn't quite clear about the proceedings.

"Technically you are, but I'd leave it a few days."

I heeded his advice. I needed to think things over.

***

I smelled her delicious flowery scent with a hint of vanilla way before she knocked on my door, exactly a week after I was made leader. I could sense her nerves, excitement and, *fuck,* even arousal. She was an open book to me, and it was immediately confirmed by the look she gave me when she entered my apartment. Her eyes wide open, pupils dilated, flicking her hair. I took a deep breath through my nose to really savour her, and to steady my own nerves.

I slowly let the air leave my body, whilst I worked hard to contain the urges I felt. Because they were raging through my, deprived of sex for months, body. We must talk first. I promised Michael. I promised myself. She wasn't going to like some of the things I had to tell her. Especially the situation of her anklet. It had to stay on. She was going to hate me, but I would explain. She would understand. Eventually.

She sashayed over. *Bloody hell.* Did she do that on purpose? *I must turn down the heating.* I felt way too hot. Only, I knew the temperature in my flat was barely eighteen degrees Celsius.

"Hi," she said. "Do I need to call you 'Sir'?" Her voice a little fragile, a little unsure, but she was teasing me. Challenging me. Did she really roll her eyes? She smiled a cocky smile. If she was truly mine, I would know how to deal with that.

She would be bare of clothes and on my bed. I would make her beg and definitely make her call me 'Sir'. The little minx. But she wasn't mine. Not yet.

"No, not in private," I said instead, ignoring her flirty, fluttering eyelashes. *Fuck. What was she trying to do?* We stood awkwardly in the middle of the room. Eliza waited for my invitation for her to sit down, but I had forgotten all social conventions for a minute. I couldn't help myself staring at her; my beautiful, brave Eliza. The image of her body, the one that had plagued my dreams for months, where she was wet from the shower, flashed before my eyes. So fucking sexy. My dick reacted instantly. *God give me strength.* I drew another deep breath.

The pink of her cheeks confirmed all the other signs she emitted. Her urges were getting the better of her. I needed to put some water on the fire.

"We need to talk," I said, gesturing for her to sit on the sofa. I placed myself next to her, but with enough distance between us, so our skin wouldn't touch by accident. I couldn't be sure if I could curb my desire, once that happened. She nodded. She knew it was the sensible thing to do.

I passed her a glass of red wine. I didn't know she even liked it, but the advantage of being a Sensorian is that I could tell instantly she loved red wine, by the feelings of her delight filling the room. When she took it, her fingers grazed mine. It felt like electricity shooting through our fingers, which caused her to jerk back and drop the glass. The wine splattered all over the sofa and floor.

"Shit! I'm so sorry!" She jumped up, raced towards the kitchen and got a towel to mop up. I was right behind her, grabbing the salt. I poured it all over the stains, emptying the pot. Eliza burst out with nervous laughter. I joined her.

"Your face! The shock!" she giggled.

Somehow she'd managed to get a little splotch of wine on her cheek. I wiped it off. The world stood still. My eyes sank into the deep grey of hers. My hand stayed on her cheek; it started to stroke it gently. It had a mind of its own. I couldn't withdraw it from her face. She didn't complain. My other hand joined and I felt myself cradle her face and lift it up slightly. My eyes hadn't left hers and my face moved closer to hers. *Fuck talking.* I pressed my lips against hers. They parted willingly, her tongue forced itself into my mouth. I wasn't the only one that had lost control of their urges. I deepened my kiss. I needed her so much. I needed this. Her lips felt so soft, and her mouth was like a warm bath. She tasted of chocolate and vanilla with a hint of spice. *Heaven.*

Her hands started to wander over my shirt, pulling it out of my trousers and giving her hands free rein on my back. Her nails dug in, slightly scratching my skin. It drove me wild. All my senses stood on edge. The feeling was exquisite, hot burning pleasure pain, making currents of pure desire run across my body. My dick strained against my jeans. It wanted out. It wanted in.

"Are you sure about this?" I breathed heavily in her ear. She nodded frantically. "But your anklet?"

"I don't care," she panted. That was it. All constraints were gone. I lifted her up and threw her on my bed. This was going to happen. There was no stopping us. One of my hands rummaged through the drawer of my bed side table, as if it had a mind of its own, and grabbed a condom. It was on before I knew it.

CHAPTER 67
Eliza

Oh. My. God!

I snuggled into Zack's body, admiring his hard muscles and toned shape. Bloody hell. Gorgeous was an understatement. His pheromones still drove me mad. How did anybody actually stop making love? There were no words to describe how he'd driven me to the edge over and over again, until my body finally relented, and I experienced the most earth-shattering feeling, like a million stars exploding all at once. Hot, cold, stabbing, excruciating, titillating and delectable waves of thrilling pleasure attacked my body. My whole being diminished into that little place between my legs. I wanted to feel like that again. Now.

Zack was drenched in sweat, and I ran my tongue over his chest down to his groin, savouring the exquisite saltiness, trying to tempt him into more action. He stroked my back gently, desire oozing from his body. He pulled me on top of him, his eyes dark and seductive.

"You are mine now," he grunted, sounding all satisfied.

"And you, mine." I whispered provocatively.

It didn't take much. I got my wish. I saw his hand feeling through the bedside table drawer again and he found what he needed.

"When can we get rid of this damn thing?" I asked, pointing at my anklet. We finally managed to drag ourselves off the bed and took a shower together.

"Shall we order take-away?" Zack replied. He clearly tried to avoid the subject of my tracker.

"Yeah fine. Indian?" I decided to leave the subject alone for a few more minutes. By the way Zack clamped up, I expected to hear bad news. I just wanted to prolong our bliss for a little while longer. Now the sexual tension was somewhat diluted I started to think about how our relationship, if that's what we just started, was going to work out. I didn't expect it to be easy.

Zack was waiting for me, all dressed in his black combat trousers and white shirt, and I could hardly stop myself from jumping him again. In fact, I didn't stop myself. I found myself pawing at his shirt again. He smiled and his eyes went dark for a second, but then he grabbed my hands and drew them to his mouth to kiss them.

"Steady, tiger. Let's eat first. We have to talk."

"I don't wanna talk, and all I want to eat is you," I answered rather petulantly. He just looked at me, let go of my hands and folded his arms. I had no chance of persuading him into more naughty things.

"Sit," he ordered in a rather business-like voice. This didn't bode well. He took his place on the other side, elbows on the table, his face resting on his hands for a moment. His eyes bored into mine. "I'm going to be totally honest with you as we're committing to each other; it will be the only way forward. I love you and I want our relationship to work. I consider you mine now. No more Zaphire. How do you feel about that? And how do you feel about us?"

How many questions? How *did* I feel about us? And about his rather dominant assertions over me? It was Zack to a tee. That's how he operated. He would have to temper that. I was only going to be his, if he was truly mine too. And that meant, trusting me.

This was worse than a cold shower. I knew how I felt about him. Once I knew he wasn't with Phae anymore I had allowed my feelings free rein. I was totally in love, butterflies and all, and I lusted after him. I wanted his body, his face, his eyes, his hands, everything about him. Could I cope with his arrogant, dickish behaviour at times? I don't know, but I wanted to. We simply needed to make 'us' work. I couldn't see a future without him. I gulped a big swig of wine, thinking it may help me find the right words to say.

"I think you know how I feel about you. There's no disguising it. I'm in love with you. I want to be part of your life and I want to be your everything." His eyes lit up. Even though he could sense my feelings for him, he still wanted to hear me say it. "But wait: Zaphy will always be special to me. I'll always love her, but I want to commit to you. I have realised we belong together." I sensed him tense up when I talked about Zaphire, but he let it go. It made me breathe a little easier. "But I don't know how our feelings for each other will translate into a relationship. You're going to be our leader. I'm nothing but a junior, and one that's not trusted, still wearing an anklet. How is that going to work?"

"Markus and Laura made it work?"

"They were equals." I reminded him.

"In our private life, you are my equal. I promise. That doesn't mean I won't feel protective over you. I will protect you, even if it's from yourself. But that's what I would do, leader or not. That's just me."

"As long as you'll let me protect you too," I said softly.

"I'll let you. Whether I'll listen is a different matter," he laughed. Then his face turned serious.

"So," he hesitated for a second. I could see he was conjuring up the courage to say whatever he had to say next. It made me hold my breath. "About protecting you..."

"Yes? Spit it out, man." I laughed nervously. He lifted his eyebrows at my irreverence, but shrugged it off.

"I have decided to keep the anklet on you. I was going to..."

"What?" I interrupted. "You decided? Could you have made the decision to have it taken off?" Anger built up inside me. *Why the hell would he do that?*

"Hear me out, please, Eli." He'd picked up on my agitation. "I've thought about it, long and hard. I even talked to the leadership. I could, in theory, use my power to release you from your anklet. I won't lie about it. But with the Russians and Rick still an unknown factor and possible threat, I don't think it's safe for you. The anklet will be for your safety, not your punishment."

I couldn't believe what I was hearing. It felt

like little ants of frustration started crawling under my skin. My face started to burn.

"So this is what your little speech was about, was it? Protecting me? Keeping me safe?" I sneered. His eyes steeled.

"I will do *everything* in my power to keep you safe. I do not ever want Dimitri or any other Russian, or anyone that could harm you, ever to get their hands on you again. I'm sorry, but my decision is final." He stood up, towering over me, emphasising his full authority. Sexy as hell, but so bloody annoying. I knew I'd have to put up with it for now, but I was going to make a point anyway.

"If this is how our relationship will go, I'm not so sure I want one. I'm going to my room. Don't follow me out," I hissed. I got up, and walked out of his room, not even waiting for dinner to arrive. I heard him sigh, but he let me go. No footsteps running after me. At least he obeyed my request. A tear ran down my cheek, but I wiped it away, angry at myself for getting emotional.

The first hurdle and I'd run off. *God!* Why did it have to be so difficult? But then I remembered a relationship with Zack was always going to be tricky and if I wanted one with him, I had to compromise. But so should he. I decided to let him sweat it out a bit. I was furious with him for not giving me my freedom back, but I could work on it. He wasn't going to be able to track me forever, and he would realise that at some point.

Instead of going to my room, I decided to go and see my friends for a bit and have an early night. My phone pinged. I glanced at it and caught Zack's name. I switched it off and put it back in my pocket, shoving him out of my mind.

***

Sam fixed me a chicken and lettuce wrap, which I ate eagerly. Brody and Zaphy came over too. Even Zaph was in a good mood and they managed to draw me away from my issues with Zack. They all knew I'd been to see him. They could most likely sense we made out, but my sensory output had warned them it wasn't all rosy, and that I'd come to take my mind off him. However, Brody and Sam couldn't help but make suggestive comments all evening anyway. I laughed them off. It was just what I needed.

At around 10pm, I sauntered back to my room, casually checking my phone. When I switched it on, there were numerous messages. I didn't need to read them to know what they were all about. When I got to my room, my heart missed a beat. It was Zack. He stood leaning against my door, legs crossed and arms folded. He was not a happy bunny. My whole body started to heat up and my stomach somersaulted, out of nervousness, but also because he was just so bloody hot.

"Hey," I said, trying to sound up beat. I didn't even know why.

"You ignored my texts?" His voice sounded hurt, rather than angry.

"I didn't want to deal with you," I answered a little prickly.

"Is that's how it's going to be? Things get a little tricky and you bail?"

Oh hell. He was right. That's exactly what happened. I knew he could feel my acknowledgement, but I still challenged him. I couldn't help myself.

"A little tricky? You want to control me! Keep tabs on me!"

"Can you blame me? It's for your own fucking safety!"

"Aaagh! This isn't going anywhere, Zack. Go back to your apartment. We'll talk tomorrow." I tried to be sensible.

"No. We'll talk now. I'm not going to let it fester overnight." Zack was adamant. He put himself behind me and leant both his arms against the door frame, trapping me. He wasn't going to leave.

"Move," I ordered, pointedly looking at his arms that formed my prison. He lowered his arms immediately, realising the effect it had on me. I opened the door and let him in. He waltzed in, still agitated.

"Look at your messages," he growled.

I fished my phone out of my pocket and opened his first message. The heat rose to my cheeks.

-'*Please don't be too cross. We'll find a solution. I love you xxx'*- A couple of minutes later he'd sent another text.

-'*Can you just text me so I know u r ok? Safe?xxx'*- And then another question mark.

-'*Ok. I know ur at Sam's. I had to check. I'm sorry. We need to talk. Please text me. Love you xxx'*-

-'*Eliza please?'*-

"Have I lost you already, Eli?" The pain he exuded was crippling. He was completely over-reacting. I had to put a stop to this.

"No, Zack. That's not it. You know I love you. We just need some time to figure out how our relationship is going to work. You can't think you've lost me after every single argument we have! I know I shouldn't have run off, but sometimes it's better to have some space and time to reflect, rather than going head first into a heated argument."

"But do you understand where I'm coming from? I never, ever, again want to feel like I did when I thought I'd lost you. You nearly died! It was the darkest moment in my entire life." His hands rubbed through his hair and his face contorted in pain. I could feel the angst, fear and dark feelings he was working through. It was horrible.

"I do get that, Zack. But there has to be another way. You can't tether and track me forever."

"Technically I could." His face was stubborn. "But I get it. If I were you, I probably wouldn't want to be with me either. I'm a pain in the arse." His demeanour changed from defiant to defeated.

"But so am I, Zack. We deserve each other." I smiled and moved over to him. I could sense his arousal as soon as my face got close to his. Our lips touched. Pure, unadulterated, scintillating ecstasy flooded my senses, and in that moment, I forgot about our quarrel.

Fine, our relationship wasn't going to be without its fair share of bumps along the way, but Zack and I were connected. From the moment I laid eyes on him in the cafe where it all started, we were bound. It had taken a while for us to both realise it, but we were meant for each other. Always have been. Always will be.

Six Months Later

Zaphire

It felt so good being back working undercover in the field. Not only was it my passion, it also gave me a chance to avoid the daily confrontation with Zack and Eliza's complicated but sickeningly blissful relationship. I knew I shouldn't feel the aching stabs of jealousy. It was irrational. I didn't want a relationship with Eliza and it felt good to see my brother so happy. But... *That annoying little word.* I couldn't help what I felt, and I took every chance to occupy myself otherwise.

Ned and I were sent on a mission to find out the truth behind the rumours about a militant faction in the climate change protest scene, who were plotting some serious disturbance. Chatter on social media had led us to a small trendy pub in an up-and-coming area of the capital. It was light and airy, not at all a likely place for a brewing uprising. We went with it any way. Couldn't hurt checking the place out. Some members were meant to meet here if our intel was correct.

The first thing I noticed was a girl about my age, maybe a little older, sitting alone at the bar. She looked slightly out of place. I focused on the beautiful tattoos adorning her neck, back and arms. They were all black, and looked like an entanglement of plants, flowers and animals. Her hair was short and dyed in a kaleidoscope of colours, in sharp contrast to the simple black vest and skinny jeans she wore. The girl must have felt my intense stare, as she turned around and caught my eye. Electricity shot across the room. My body jolted. The hefty scent of pheromones hard to ignore. It was instant attraction. I glanced at Ned. Had he noticed? A little smile played around his lips. I guess he had.

I contemplated going over to suss her out. Surely she must know something about this climate protest group. She totally looked the type. I hesitated a moment too long, and a business-like blonde lady, who looked in her early thirties, approached her decisively. They had a short talk and then joined an older man in jogging bottoms. An odd trio, to say the least. They exuded purpose and determination, with a whiff of excitement and stress. My interest was spiked. We needed to find out more about these characters. My instinct told me they were up to something.

"Stay close," I whispered to Ned. He smirked. I knew what he was thinking, but it wasn't my attraction to the girl that sparked this interest, though a little ember started burning in my stomach just thinking of her. Who knew what our encounter might lead to, but if she was involved in something shady, then the mission had to come first. If the rumours were true, these individuals could be planning a serious climate terrorist attack on an oil refinery in the country. We had our work cut out for the coming weeks.

***

Zack

"Sir, there are two detectives to see you," Brody announced, sounding rather worried. My head snapped up. *Fuck*. Detectives? That didn't sound good.

"Tristan doesn't know them. They're not people he has liaised with in the past," Brody added.

"Thanks, Brody."

I called Frank, who must have heard the stress in my voice, as he hurried over. "Can you be with me whilst I meet the detectives? I may need some help."

We hadn't had any trouble recently, and the only thing I could think that would bring detectives over, must be connected to the Alice kidnapping and everything that happened after. I sincerely hoped that wasn't the case. We had only just started to relax a little. We'd heard nothing more from the Russians, and no other agency had come knocking on our door. Irena had been keeping her ear to the ground for any hints of Russian activity.

She was keen to show she could be trusted, after I released her.

We had several missions running in the field, including Ned and Zaphy's climate terror cell investigation. They had travelled to the South of the country to get to the bottom of it. So things were more or less back to normal. Fuck it. I'd even considered taking Eliza's anklet off. It wasn't fun living with my girl who was intent on never letting that subject go. I'd put my foot down so far. I'd do fucking anything to keep her safe, even putting up with her constant threats and whines to leave me, or not to have sex with me until it's off. Fucking healthy relationship we have... Not. Definitely lots to work on still.

A knock on my door shook me out of my pondering. Brody let the two detectives in. One man in his fifties, dressed immaculately, the other, a woman, in her early thirties wearing tight black jeans and a T-shirt with an image of Elf on it, even though it was late summer. I can only imagine the annoyance this caused to her colleague. Especially, since the younger woman seemed to be taking the lead. She extended her hand to me and introduced herself and her colleague.

"Detective Inspector Riddell, and this is my colleague, Detective Hunt. Are you the CEO of this company?" She briefly looked over at Frank, and I felt her confusion. "You look very young to be heading up this company." I could literally feel her eyes roaming my body and the feelings of lust that it invoked. She suppressed them quickly and hid it well. She was professional.

"Looks like we have something in common," I countered, flicking my eyes deliberately at Hunt. He wasn't impressed. "And, it's not really a company, more like a trust." I let that hang for a second. "What can I do for you?"

"We're making some enquiries into the movements of Mr Daniel Robertson." She paused and looked me over. "Does that name ring a bell?" *Fucking Daniel. Coming to haunt us, even after his death.* I sensed she bloody well knew that we did know him. Why would they otherwise be here? I had to be honest.

"Yes. I do know him. He brought our organisation into disrepute and we had to move location to be able to carry on our work, out of the limelight." Hunt was scribbling down notes into his old- fashioned notebook. Riddell's eyes flashed. I could feel her excitement at my statement.

"So, does that mean you didn't like the man?" she asked, almost innocently.

"On the contrary. We met with him, as I'm sure you know, and came to an agreeable solution. We've not heard from him since."

"Did you not hear of his untimely death? His 'accident'? It was all over the papers," Hunt interjected, clearly not believing that to be the case. Frank jumped in before I could answer.

"We've been extremely busy, but I do recollect reading something about it. However, he was not of our concern anymore, so it didn't really make that much of an impact." Frank got me out of a tight spot.

"In fact, his death occurred on the night that

you and a colleague of yours went to see him," Riddell threw into the ring.

"Well, he was very much alive when we left him. I'm sorry I can't help you with this. Where did the accident happen?" I asked, trying to seem as natural as possible.

"We now believe it may not have been an accident. Some inconsistencies were found. He was found on the A68 in a burnt-out vehicle, seemingly having careered off the road, hitting a tree before the vehicle caught fire."

"Mr Mackenzie and his colleague were not near that location on that night. He was wearing an anklet tracker at that time. We can give you the data for you to check." Frank said, causing Riddell's eyebrows to shoot up.

"A tracker? And what was the reason for that?"

My heart rate surged. Just as well they weren't Sensorians. It would have raised their suspicion instantly. I steadied my breathing and my heartbeat slowed.

"Oh, it was just a precaution. We didn't quite know what we were dealing with. Standard procedure in our organisation," I said, trying to sound as nonchalant and dismissive about it as possible. Thank goodness that the data was still there, even though the device had been scrambled. It had still recorded my location. "Is there anything else I can help you with?"

"No, that should be all. We'll need the data and any other evidence that you can think of that confirms your whereabouts on that evening, please. We also need to talk to your colleague that accompanied you on that trip."

"Of course. Frank can you make sure Brody reports to my office?"

"Yes, Sir. Right away."

After their interview with Brody, who confirmed what I'd told them, I sensed they were satisfied with the information we'd provided them with. At least Hunt was. I was fairly confident they were just stabbing in the dark, and that there was no evidence to link us to Daniel's death. I did notice something odd about DI Riddell. It was as if she wanted to address something else. And I wasn't surprised at all that, after Hunt and Frank had left the room, she briefly stepped back into the office. I held back, anticipating her move.

"I don't only work for the police." She flashed another I.D. stating her employment by MI5. *Fucking hell.* I glanced out of the door, but Frank and Detective Hunt were gone. "Don't worry. Discretion and secrecy *is* our middle name," she smiled encouragingly, but a little smugly. I sensed sincerity, though. "We have a proposition. We know about your people's heightened senses and we'd like to make use of that incredible gift. We're not here to disrupt your lifestyle or force you into anything you don't want to do. We would see our working relationship as a mutually beneficial one. You get our protection and help, we get access to your intelligence and use your people for our missions. The fact that we have confirmed knowledge of your existence, means other agencies from different countries will find out too. We can protect, deflect and help rumours disappear. The link to Daniel will vanish. Think about it." She pushed a card, with her phone number on it, into my hand.

In the meantime, Hunt had returned to see why his DI was taking so long, but she nodded at him to wait a second. She shook my hand, said her goodbyes and walked out to follow Frank and Hunt.

Fuck me. It seemed like a good deal. The Daniel reference worried me slightly, as it could be used to our detriment as well. There was a threat hidden in the proposal. However, it could mean a new direction for us. One that could be more fulfilling but out of the limelight, away from the media's eye and protected from other threats to our well-being.

Markus would never have agreed to this. He would see it as a slippery slope, and would have denied any 'special gifts' attributed to us. He would have ridiculed Riddell for MI5's gullibility. It may have worked for a while, but I believed Riddell. Other agencies would come knocking, and the Russians would definitely try again to 'persuade' us to work for them. This way was the way forward. Now all there was to do was convince the rest of the leadership. I felt confident they would agree. It really was the only sensible option, and it had the potential to make our community thrive.

There was a reason they had chosen me as their leader. They knew I wasn't one for shying away from taking risks. And this was a risk that was going to pay off for us. It fucking well better do.

***

I decided to leave it until the following day to tell the leadership. I called a meeting of high importance at 10am, and left it at that. It was good to let the whole thing settle in my brain and not make any hasty decisions, but I knew I had made the right one.

I got back to my tasks for the rest of the day. There was always some dispute to sort out, or a problem with a mission cropped up that needed my immediate attention. I understood so much better why Markus used to always be snowed under with other people's business. The last month or so he looked much better and felt less stressful to be around. He'd found his niche in training the youngsters. He still felt if he could instil loyalty and discipline at an early age, they'd be more prepared for their working life later on. However, I'd noticed his methods had changed slightly. No more traumatic incidences in the Dark Room. He was much more encouraging and understanding.

He had shown me the required respect, and occasionally I felt actual pride radiating from him, but he hadn't voiced that to me yet. I suppose he knew I felt it anyway.

I was super grateful to Laura, who had taken over the finance of the community, as unlike Markus, I was dreadful with numbers and paperwork. Laura excelled in it. She loved her new found talent for investments and made our returns grow by the month. We even had all been given a rise in our allowance. It was a far cry from how our community used to be financed, with winnings from card games at casinos.

I was done for today. I walked back to my apartment and texted my friends. I invited them over for a quick drink. It was hard stepping out of our roles and we were still finding our feet as to how to relate to each other in private. I made my place a 'no work' zone. So all formalities were dropped once anyone stepped inside.

Rafferty was already by my door waiting for me.

"Sir," he greeted with apparent deference. I never knew if he was taking the piss or not. His Irish lilt somehow made him sound like he was never fully serious. He had proven to be a bit of a loose cannon. Good at heart, but struggling with impulsivity and his emotions. Not surprising after what he went through. Brody was his trainer and had a few struggles with him, occasionally airing his frustrations to me.

Sam came running up with Brody, Eve, Phae and Tristan not far behind. They all nearly bundled into me with exuberance. I opened the door to be met with two warm arms around my neck, which pulled me in under a barrage of kisses. Eli, looked up, suddenly realising everyone was there enjoying the show. She burnt bright red, burying her face in my chest. I shepherded her over to the kitchen, fully returning her hot kisses, whilst waving the others into the living room. I wasn't going to miss out!

"Let go of your missus and come and join us!" Brody jeered. Everyone joined in, sticking their fingers in their throats and making retching noises.

"Hey, Eli! Let Zack go! You two are like bloody Velcro!" Sam shouted.

I chuckled and let go of her, peeling her arms off me.

"Save it for later, yeah?" She nodded,

throwing me the most luscious seductive look. I nearly sent everyone away.

We ordered pizzas and watched *Tenet*. Yes, again! Still trying to work out the timeline in that film and whether there were mistakes, or whether our brains just couldn't follow it. Sam and Brody got into quite a heated discussion, which made the rest of us laugh. Then I noticed Rafferty staring at Eliza. He'd had a bit too much to drink and I could feel him getting agitated over something. Eli picked up on it too. She glanced up at me to check if I'd noticed. It was quite obvious he had developed a crush on her over the last few months, but he had never expressed it verbally. He just wasn't very good at cloaking it. Both Eliza and I had ignored it, though several times I really wanted to fucking punch him for the lustful feelings he emitted. His hormones were running a bit wild on occasion. Obviously, I didn't ever carry out my desire to hurt him. I was a changed man, wasn't I? I tried to be, anyway.

"When are you letting your girl off the leash, Zack?" he challenged. He had balls, I had to give him that; he hadn't even turned eighteen yet. But he was acting like a love-sick puppy. An annoying one, at that.

"I think that's none of your business, Raff. Just watch the film," I grinned, trying to make light of it. But he wouldn't have it.

"No, but seriously, man. You're abusing your power. It's just not on. She should be free to go where she wants, without you always knowing where she is!" he said, raising his voice. He looked around for support, but even though my mates probably agreed with him, they wouldn't back him up, not in my room.

"I'm not gonna fucking discuss this now. You can come to my office tomorrow and share your grievances," I spoke sternly.

"Yeah, you'd like tha', because you can bust my fuckin' arse then. I'm free to sjay what I wan' here." He started to slur his words slightly. Eliza's eyes widened, warning me to keep my cool. I sensed she totally agreed with Raff, but she kept quiet, not wanting to undermine me. But Raff felt it too, and he looked at me in defiance.

"Mate, you need to leave now. You're taking advantage of that privilege. Don't fuck with Zack. You'll regret it," Brody said, whilst getting up to 'help' him on his way. I stepped in. I didn't need Brody to rescue me.

"It's alright, Brodes. I got this." The room had now gone deadly quiet, everyone waiting to see what I'd do. I was used to this by now. I wasn't having some ratty seventeen-year-old get the better of me.

"You. Get your fucking arse off that sofa and get out. Now," I said calmly but firmly. "Sleep it off. I'll see you tomorrow at 9am in my office." I grabbed him by the arm and marched him to the door. "Have your apology ready and we'll forget about the whole thing. Do. Not. Be. Late. There will be consequences," I warned with menace to get the message across.

He looked around once more for back up, but

when he found only disapproving glances, he took his bat and ball home and stormed out, leaving the door open, not quite daring to slam it.

"The dickend will come to his senses," I sniggered, shaking my head. The others laughed. We chatted for a while longer, but then I kicked everyone out, as I had to be fresh for tomorrow. Just Eliza stayed. She practically lived with me.

"Babe?" Her dreamy eyes bore into mine. She'd clearly forgotten about the 'no sex till the anklet is off' rule she'd imposed yesterday, because as soon as the others had left, she practically jumped on me and we made love ferociously. She was now resting her head on my chest and looked up into my eyes. She was so beautiful, so alluring, cute, cheeky and sexy. Fuck, I loved her so much.

"Did you tell the leadership?" she asked with great big eyes.

"Tell'm what?" She looked a little guilty. "You didn't VH me today, did you?" I asked, trying to keep the annoyance out of my voice. It hadn't worked. I felt her shrink away slightly.

"Sorry," she squeaked.

"You have to stop doing that, Eliza. You can't be looking into everything I do." She eye-rolled at that, and I knew exactly why: I'd been doing the exact same thing to her! I ignored it. "And how do you know what she said anyway?"

"My lip reading's coming on well." She sounded a little too smug for my liking and not contrite enough. Fuck. I wish I could punish her. But I promised to keep work, my position as leader and our private life apart. It was going to be pretty damned hard if she kept pulling stunts like this. She knew I was angry though, which she hated. She mounted her defence.

"I just wanted to know what the detectives were here for, and then when she stayed back, I couldn't stop myself from carrying on hacking your vision." She tried to use her big eyes on me to soften me up. She knew exactly what she was doing, the little minx. But, okay. She did look a bit sorry too. I just sighed.

"You know we can't talk about things like that. Espccially as you still have your anklet on. Everything is recorded. Do you understand, Eli?" I couldn't quite keep the sternness out of my voice.

"Yes, but only Michael has access to it, hasn't he? And he doesn't listen all day, every day. He barely does nowadays."

"True, which reminds me..." Now was just as good a time as any other. Raff was right, and I knew for a fact that Eliza wholeheartedly agreed with him. I had made my decision. No more procrastinating. I hopped out of bed and shoved some joggers on. I knew she loved watching my body, so I left my top off. I also knew how to soften her up. "I have something for you. But you have to promise me one thing?"

I caught her curiosity.

"Okay?" she looked at me, all confused. Bless her. I got the bracelet I'd had especially made for her out of its box. I knew she hated the feel of hard or scratchy material on her skin so it had a smooth platinum strap, with seven rubies delicately laid into the shape of a heart. It was engraved with *Forever Yours. Forever Mine.*

"That's...it's beautiful," she gasped

"Now, don't get angry. It does have a tracker built in, but no recording equipment. You don't have to wear it in the compound, but I respectfully ask that you will promise to wear it, when you leave the compound?" I fastened the bracelet around her left wrist. It really suited her. She smiled enigmatically, not giving me an answer straightaway. "Then we can take your anklet off." I was serious as hell. It was only a small step, but a huge compromise on my part. It had taken me a long time to feel confident enough about her safety to give it to her, and release her from the anklet. I knew it was morally wrong to want to track her, but this was as far as I was willing to go, at this point. I hope she accepted it. I tried desperately to read her feelings, but I didn't need to. She jumped up and hugged me tightly.

"Oh Zack. I'll always wear it! We'll talk again

about the tracker," she warned. "But I'll take this. For now. I love you so much."

I huge relief washed over me. I leaned into her, and kissed her gently.

"Forever yours. Forever mine."

ACKNOWLEDGEMENTS

I think you know who you are by now, but I will still mention you all as I could not have completed the third instalment of The Sensorians Trilogy without you. Clare, a diamond. Having read all my first drafts and even reading through them again after many changes were applied, she has definitely had the rough end of the deal here! Carol, my very enthusiastic, second proof reader also indispensable, always finding other things to improve! Annemarie, who cast her professional editorial eye on it, equally magnificent. Her input actually made the ending of Zaphire's story a little more interesting! Margot's advice on aspects of description adding to the feel of the story, and detection of overuse of certain words, also immensely appreciated. The members (and fellow authors) of the Sconnie readers group who ARC read my work, in particular Amy Johnson and Elena Dumitrache Saygo, who gave me advice and pointers; thank you so much! Clare, Amy and

Annemarie also greatly helped with the blurb, my nemesis.

A special mention for this book goes to Alexandra Kazanenkova who has kindly checked the Russian language for me. Thank you so much. It can't have been pleasant, as the language wasn't very nice!

The cover of Resolve, once again designed by Miquel Gonzalez, is secretly my absolute favourite. Thank you so much once again for freely offering your time and amazingly creative mind! You can admire more of Miquel's work on his Insta account: luismiquelgonzalez or website: lumigo-film.com

Last but not least I must thank my family; Steve, Nienke, Bentley and Hanneke for their support and patience! I knew who to ask for help with my Insta account (thank you H and N!) and Steve, of course, with the inevitable computer support. Hanneke, the only one that has actually read all three, and helped point out some awkward sentences, loves the books. I'm still waiting for the rest of my family's verdict... ☺

AUTHOR'S PAGE

Thank you so much for reading the final instalment of The Sensorians Trilogy. I hope you enjoyed it and that the ending was satisfying, whether you were in the Zaphy's or Zack's camp, or a neutral!

It seems there may be another story in store for Zaphire so keep your eyes peeled!

I would be super grateful and honoured if you were able to take the time and leave me a review on Amazon and/or Goodreads. Us Indie writers are relying on you!

You can keep up to date with my exploits on my:
Insta Account: brigitte__books
Facebook Page: brigittewritesbooks

Printed in Great Britain
by Amazon

66321920R00338